BLUE SHADOWS FALL

PRAISE FOR BLUE SHADOWS FALL

"Small town secrets, Southern gothic atmosphere, and a certain pair of eyes that see disturbing things create a spellbinding read."

~Autumn Krause, author of *A Dress For The Wicked*

"This book is a completely original mashup: dystopian, dark fantasy, fairy tale, folklore."

~Sarah Goethem, author of *Wind Song*

"Come for the post-apocalyptic society and enhanced abilities, stay for the family secrets, political plots, and first love."

~Alison Kimble, author of *Strange Gods*

"With a lightning fast plot and a well-paced reveal of the town's secrets, this incredibly polished young adult gem is lacking nothing."

~Indies Today Editorial

"A spellbinding post-apocalyptic young adult fantasy set in a world that has survived the worst hardships and disasters."

~Readers Favorite Editorial Review

"Lenore has created a detailed world where the threat of dark elves is ever in the shadows."

~Rebecca J., Goodreads Review

"Throw in the excitement of Sarah J. Mass, mix in a slew of nerd fandom references like LOTR and HP, a give it a sprinkle of Southern flavor, and you've got this truly satisfying story."

~Amy Michelle Carpenter, author of *Becoming Human*

"Stutznegger creates an idyllic spot amid a frightening unknown outside world in Haven, one of those rare post-apocalypse communities you'd really want to live in."

~J. Trevor Robinson, author of *The Mummy of Monte Cristo*

"I've always told my son that being on the spectrum made him unique, and was like having superpowers. So I can't tell you just how happy it made me to read a book where this is exactly the case!"

~Samantha J. Rose, author of *The Very Real World of Amy Adams*

"We couldn't help but adore our sassy protagonist, Blue, with her funny expressions, quick wit, and bravery."

~Pages and Beyond Review

"By the end...I was just like...SO MANY PLOT TWISTS. And I didn't see any of them coming."

~Haley Kilgour, author of *Nanagin*

Immortal Works LLC
1505 Glenrose Drive
Salt Lake City, Utah 84104
Tel: (385) 202-0116

© 2021 Lenore Stutznegger
www.lenorestutz.com

Cover Art by Lenore Stutznegger

ISBN 978-1-953491-28-2 (Paperback)
ASIN B09J3FL9KK (Kindle Edition)

To my rock, my love, and eternal sunshine, Dave. You always chase the shadows away.

BLUE SHADOWS FALL

LENORE STUTZNEGGER

IMMORTAL WORKS

Salt Lake City

CHAPTER 1

The Raven

BLUE

Blink, count to five, then blink again.

I shook my head. No one but my brother was around for miles. Up here in the mountains, I didn't have to remember to blink. I pulled in a long, cleansing breath of fresh morning air as puffy clouds drifted across the purple sky. The sun rose behind the blue mountains, beaming ribbons of fuchsia.

Pitiful. Already sunrise and we'd only caught a few measly salamanders.

I scanned the woods as my twin brother snored beside me—his heavy breathing scaring every living creature away. Hawk lay nestled in the tall weeds, looking every bit like the lanky teenage warrior he was. Red clay and grass clung to his bare feet like well-loved socks. His camouflage t-shirt had holes the size of June bugs, and his mohawk had dented in the grassy mud. But his face, lax with sleep, radiated an innocence as false as that turkey decoy propped out in the open field. I wanted to smack him awake.

My bow rested in my arms, arrow nocked but slack.

Five robin eggs lay in a nest two miles away.

One peregrine falcon with a thirty-nine-inch wingspan soared twenty miles out.

A spider spun its silky web, the strands glistening with dew.

Six squirrels cavorting.

Four-hundred-eighty-eight trees in a blink.

Great, now I was counting trees.

I closed my eyes, allowing the momentary dark and lilting buzz of insects to clear my mind. The colors and light spun, mixing and glowing. Sometimes my sight was so distracting.

Seven turkeys hobbled into view, taking the bait. I elbowed Hawk's big ol' head, probably getting slobber all over my arm. He sat up.

Steady. Nice and steady. Breathe in, breathe out. I aimed my arrow at the left eye of one of the fat turkeys, careful to avoid the male.

Eighteen large quill feathers, twenty-eight yards away. Easy.

Breathe out and—

A loud burp split open the sky.

My arrow flew wide.

Turkeys scattered in every direction, feathers flapping, as Hawk fell back onto the tall grass, whooping with laughter. A cloud of pollen exploded into the air. I shut my eyes at the flying yellow spores.

"Hawk!" I smacked him on the shoulder with my bow.

Tears trailed down his pink-flushed cheeks. "Oh, *so* close!" Hawk howled. "You should've seen your face, Blue."

The rising sun crested the blue mountains, illuminating Hawk's perfectly ordinary hazel eyes. Out of the six of us siblings, Hawk and I looked the most alike and not just because we were twins. We shared the same sun-kissed skin, smattering of freckles, and fluffy curls. But, I didn't have a ridiculously showy mohawk. I preferred my brown curls untamed, flying wildly in the warm summer wind.

The only difference between us that actually mattered was my eyes. I often wondered what my life would've been like if my eyes were just plain, ordinary "Haven hazel" like Hawk's and everyone else in my family. But, they were blue. Bright blue, almost translucent. Different than anyone had ever seen before.

I smacked Hawk again as he rolled out of the way. "Hawk! We've been out here forever, elf-brain! I'm done." I shoved the hatchet and dagger in my pack, but couldn't help smiling. "That's the third kill you lost me this week."

"What?" Hawk teased. "Rackin' up kills like you're some kinda warrior? That's my job."

"Oh, right," I shot back. "I forgot, *oh mighty warrior*; what is it you do again? When was the last time you killed a Shadow Elf? Like...never?"

"You never know, could be something really scary out there like an angry boot or evil soup can." Hawk's eyes flicked over to mine. "But seriously, you've never seen anything out there, right?" Hawk cleared his throat and wouldn't meet my eyes.

My heart dropped, but as soon as the fear speared in, I squashed it with my go-to: obstinance. I'd been worrying about him for weeks, and *now* he started acting all vulnerable? Heck no. Not when he was about to go out past the wall and I'd have to stay behind.

If anyone knew what was out there, it'd be me. I'd run up here to Grandfather Rock every second I could spare to keep an eye out on the horizon. I'd hunt and clear my head, but mostly check for any stray movement. And now, Hawk was about to cross the wall for the first time, and I'd be turned if I missed something. Might as well put my sight to some use.

I'd always been able to *see* better than any normal human. Mama and Dad called it my "gift"; I called it my "annoying sometimes helpful pain in the butt thing I can do that I can't tell anyone about because it could get me killed."

My ASHPITBTICDTICTAABICGMK, for short.

Already, others eyed me suspiciously. The Haven girl with the unnaturally bright blue eyes. The one my family constantly fussed over—and not in a fun way. In the inexcusable way Mama kept *me* from the warrior trials but let Hawk train even though she knew it was all I ever wanted. This was the last year I could try for the trials. Dad taught me how to wield a sword, rifle, hatchet, and dagger. I was every bit as capable as Hawk, but they'd never once let me use my skills in public.

It was all for love, they said. Protection. They didn't want me to get caught staring too long and get pegged as some scary plague freak.

Enhanced senses were always the first sign of turning, but the Shadow War had been over for a hundred years. Everyone just needed to get over it.

Hawk practically pulsed with vulnerability like a lost pup.

My breath *whooshed* out in defeat. "I have never, in my life, seen any living thing outside our walls—except for a bunch of animals— but no humans, no elves. Nothing dangerous."

Our warriors patrolled the perimeter wall and journeyed out several times a year to reassess threats and collect supplies, but I still felt as if I was the only one with eyes on the horizon. Most in the village were happy to sit on the front porches of their comfortable homesteads, rubbing their plump bellies, red-faced from moonshine and happy in their belief we were alone in the world.

Our silos were stocked with enough grain to last through another apocalypse.

"Then I should have no problem getting you that new book...or do you want an old record instead?" Hawk knew my weaknesses.

"Both. You owe me."

"At least we ended up with some food after your ridiculous embarrassment back there." Hawk eyed the pile of feathers and seeds littering the grass. He swung the sack of live salamanders we'd trapped earlier toward our horses. "Too bad you missed."

"I *missed*?"

"Yeah, someone with your kinda skills?" He shook his head. "I'm just as surprised as you."

My face burned. "No album is worth this."

"Okay, so if I find that legendary Blue Weezer, I should just walk on by?"

"I hate you," I said as my heart squeezed.

Our horses grazed on the grass by the banks of Raleigh's Sorrow. The large waterfall kicked out plumes of wispy mist into the sunrise. My beautiful chestnut gelding, Pepper, nudged my shoulder as I rubbed his soft cheeks.

As Hawk knelt by the lake to drink, I memorized him. This was it, my last morning hunt with my twin. Today at noon, Hawk and Pretty-Boy Joe would go on their solo journeys of discovery, self-mastery, and whatnot.

Tomorrow, I had a dumb graduation of my own.

How long would it be until we'd have another morning like this? Just the two of us on the mountain, hunting, talking, the comfortable silence filling my soul like nothing else could. I'd have to stock up on Mama Darla's collection of pre-war books and comics to get through this next week, even though I'd already memorized every one of them.

And I needed peach cobbler. Lots of peach cobbler.

We'd stood at this spot by the waterfall more times than I could count. Trees and cottony cattails bristled in the humid summer breeze. Ants scrambled along the bank in search of crumbs. I used to spend hours staring at the ants here, the way their funny bodies twitched. I named them. Loved them.

In a blink, a memory flashed before my eyes. The one from that picnic when I was four.

Ants crawled in and out of the weeds. They took the strawberry from my small, chubby hand and tore it apart bit by bit. Their tiny pincers moved, juice coating their antennae. Black ants, coffee colored, six legs each, 978 of them but not all the same. They crawled in lines from my strawberry to the anthill with large hunks of berry in their pincers. Perfectly in sync.

This was the moment I learned I was different. Frightening. Strange. Someone that needed to be hidden away.

One little guy moved with a strange limp. The end of his antennae was bent, about to break. I dropped a fingernail-full of the strawberry over to my buddy, Anty. (I was very creative with my nicknames then.) He looked hungry. Probably couldn't smell right, either.

"Blue!" Mama shouted franticly. Mama smacked furiously all over my body. "You're crawling with ants! Bearon!"

Dad ran from the lake. I shook my head and pulled my focus out.

Ants clambered all over my favorite purple dress, covering my arms, up my neck—hundreds of them. I hadn't realized. I didn't know...

The bright scene from thirteen years ago faded, then vanished in a blur.

"What are you looking at now?" Hawk's head drooped. "I was telling you something amazing and you missed it."

I joined Hawk by the edge of the lake, tall grass itching my bare legs. My five siblings weren't exactly supportive of my sight. They hated it most when I'd get lost staring off into the distance and miss their incredibly earth-shattering insight.

"The day of the picnic," I answered. "Y'know, with the ants."

"Oh, that. You almost died, Blue. You were swollen for weeks." Hawk shook his head. "Y'know, I'll never understand how you didn't notice you were getting *eaten* by ants, literally."

"I know, I know."

"Seriously, Blue," Hawk continued, "You gotta be more careful, even up here. Someone might see you staring off or making some ridiculous shot, and I won't be around to protect you."

"As if I ever needed your protection." I scoffed. "Come to think of it, what would they even do? Turn me into some Enforcer? Have you ever even *seen* an Enforcer? I'm pretty sure Mama made 'em up to scare us or they're long forgotten, just like y'all warriors will be a hundred years from now. You're practically obsolete."

"You're just jealous."

"Psh, whatever."

But I was jealous. It burned within me stronger as this day approached. Hawk got to be the great warrior show-off, and I got to be the quiet, weird girl who stared too much and hardly ever left the house. But I was every bit as capable as him. Maybe that's why I loved the mountains so much. At least here I didn't need a chaperone.

My bare toes squished into the cool mud of the lake.

Fifty-seven tadpoles wiggled in the shallow water.

The humming of cicadas and crickets filled my ears, the

soundtrack of my life. I smacked a water bug cozying up to my ankle and sighed. I was so stupid. I'd put off looking for work all year on a ghost of hope, and my fate remained the same. Hawk and I were finally graduating that sorry-excuse-for-a-school, and I had nothing to show for it.

I couldn't formally take the warrior trials without my mama beating the ever-living life out of me, but I'd hoped for a fool's miracle. If I could've caught a captain's eye, then maybe they would have taken me on. Then Mama couldn't have argued. But while I waited, all the other opportunities at good work passed me by. So now I was stuck with the last available job in town.

I'd be scooping poop with Dingle-Berry Gerry at Jim's dairy farm forever and ever, amen.

My future was *the worst*.

Hawk stood with a loud stretch, his massive feet covered in a new layer of mud. "Time to get back home. Can't miss my ceremony."

"Yeah, yeah," I grumbled. Founder's Week. One-hundred-eleven years since our forefathers laid their weapons down after the wandering and killing was done.

Hawk's large head blocked the sun from my face. When had he gotten so huge? My nose wrinkled as the wind shifted. Or stinky? Man, his stench could burn the nose hairs off the devil himself. "Put those arms down, Hawk! You stink!"

Hawk's dimples deepened as his smile grew. His dangerous smile. "You mean, don't do this?" He raised his enormous arms behind his head and moved to smack me in the face with his sweaty pits.

"Gross, Hawk!" I threw handfuls of grass at him and ran from the slippery bank. Hawk chased me around the rocks and trees. That's it —he was begging to get dropped in the lake. I turned back toward the water's edge as Hawk tore through the trees like The Incredible Hulk. Right where I wanted him.

I moved to hip-check him into the water when a raven caught my eye, spinning lazily through the air.

Thirty miles away.

Black as night feathers, wedge-shaped tail.

Forty-five-point-seven inch wingspan.

I stopped dead still.

Hawk spun. "Too slow!" He reached for me, but I was gone.

Red crusted on the raven's claw. *Blood.* Just a drop or two, but a peal of alarm pounded through my head like the screech of a tea kettle.

"Blue?" Hawk called from miles away.

My sight fell dark. Black. Nothing. As if the earth swallowed me whole. I ripped the knife from my back pocket and rolled my eyes left and right. Nothing. Black as pitch. What was happening?

The raven cawed, a haunting refrain. Everything fell silent, still. My legs stayed firmly planted. *Muscle memory.* But my heart thumped in my chest like a jackrabbit's. I prayed for light as I gasped for breath.

Nothing.

Darkness.

A black pit all around me. I gripped my knife tighter, trying to stay grounded.

A faint, fuzzy glow emerged around the edges of my vision, spreading inward. Then a flash of light. I winced, my hand automatically shielding my face. *Wisps of gray smoke gathered like rolling thunderheads.*

Large, ancient buildings as tall as the sky replaced the smoke-filled blackness. Cracked brick buildings overgrown with thick weeds. Silver glass. Gray streets as far as the eye could see.

I lapped up the vision like a thirsty dog, reveling in the unfamiliar sight. *A city, a place I'd only seen in old books—where they'd all settled, the Shadow Elves, back in the days of the Shadow War. Now, they'd all died out, shriveled up, and blown away like dry husks in the wind for lack of human flesh.*

I turned in a slow circle, taking it all in. *A boy stood alone. His eyes darted about, then landed on me. He smiled. Straight teeth, left tooth chipped, barely. His face struck me with his unfamiliar beauty. A dimple on each cheek. Big, round, trusting green eyes. He laughed and reached for my hand as soft, chocolate hair fell into his eyes.*

A dark silhouette crept up behind him. The shape I'd been taught to fear above all others. Sharp, pointy ears. Knotted hair as white as a dove's feather. Large, depthless black eyes. A bolt of white-hot horror speared through my chest.

All fell to darkness again, and my legs gave out.

Strong arms held me. Hawk. My eyesight returned in a blink, but my head spun as if I'd been yanked out of water. The raven cawed as he flew into the pink horizon. The waterfall roared back into focus.

"Whoa! Whoa!" Hawk shouted. He held onto my wrist like a vise. I clutched my knife, ready to rip into his throat. I sputtered, my chest heaving, and dropped it in the clay.

Hawk helped me to the bank of the lake and sat across from me, staring into my eyes as if he could see what I'd just seen. "Where'd you go? I couldn't snap you out of it, Blue. It was like you were in another world."

I shook my head. "I *was* in another world."

One that no longer existed.

What happened? I'd only ever had visions of my own past memories, replaying over my eyes like an old moving photograph. But this? This was something new.

I'd made a catalog of every one of New Haven's 1,555 citizens in my mind through the years. Every unique face was seared into my vision forever—the last living humans in the world. But that boy's face? He was new, handsome, mysterious. I'd never laid eyes on him before.

One of my favorite pre-war books, *The Lord of the Rings*, flashed, unbidden into my mind. Not for the first time, I thought of the hobbits—comfortable, fat, and happy. They'd secured themselves a perfect place in the Shire, completely unaware of the dangerous powers growing around them.

But, what did it mean? That vision—hallucination?—it couldn't have been real.

A shiver snaked up my spine. That handsome stranger wasn't the only thing I'd seen in that decimated city. I'd seen one of *them*. A Shadow Elf. It seemed to be some unholy mix between an ethereal, flowing-haired elven prince straight out of a fairytale, and a deadly vampire.

A chill spiraled down my spine despite the humid heat of summer. It had to be some crazy new quirk. It had to be. Because if that green-eyed stranger was real and out there somewhere, it meant the elves were too.

CHAPTER 2

Goodbye, Bro

BLUE

Purple clouds rolled across the blue mountains as I followed my family to the warpath celebration. We didn't ride our horses today, but walked across the village, meeting neighbors and friends along the way.

Crisp ochre morning light reflected from the water tanks and solar panels dotting the roofs of each brick home we passed. Blue irises and pink azaleas bloomed from tidy planter boxes under windows. Horses munched barley from wooden buckets, as happy dogs bounded at their owner's heels. Goats roamed free, taming the foliage naturally. Kudzu vines covered almost every inch of the neat brick buildings as we entered the square. The old helicopter water fountain bubbled cheerily. Electric lights glinted within storefronts as busy shopkeepers set up for the celebrations that would last all week.

A tuft of brown and gray beard popped out from the chin of a snoring man laid out on a park bench. My best friend's dad must've had another one of his episodes. They'd become more frequent. Cerulean puffs of a breeze tousled his gnarly beard. Bluegrass and dandelions burst through the cracks beneath the wooden bench. The same weeds that'd grown through the fissures of concrete in the city I'd somehow seen this morning. I tried not to think about that stranger boy with the trusting green eyes.

But, his face flitted before me all the same. *His smile, his hand held out to me. Something about those dimples, the curve of his lips.*

Hawk demanded I tell Mama this morning when we got home.

No thank you. She'd never let me leave the house if she knew I'd lost control of my sight, even for a second.

The boy's face danced in front of me. Who was he? Was he even real or did it all just happen in my head?

Words from *Harry Potter* scrolled bright gold before my eyes. At this point, I could practically hear Dumbledore say that just because the boy and elf were in my head, didn't mean they *weren't* real.

That was not the answer I wanted.

And what was with the raven? I'd once read ravens were a bridge between the spirit world and ours, but that was just an Ancient American tale.

Was the stranger boy a spirit? Supposedly angels walked among us, invisible to our mortal eyes. At least that's what the preacher taught us on Sundays. Guardian angels were scattered across our town; stone and wood monuments of our loved and fallen dotted the land, from the tops of the mountains through the wide streets of the square. Maybe my enhanced eyes could see their spirits? But I never had before. My visions were strictly memories, flashbacks.

And I'd always been the one in control.

A sharp jab to my ribs broke me from my thoughts. "You're staring again," Lily whispered.

Right. *Blink. Count to five, then blink again.*

My best friend had taken over my mama's job of jabbing me back into reality, getting me to blink and act like I didn't see a million colors and shapes and patterns that apparently no one else could.

I steered her away from the sight of her pop laid out on the park bench. She didn't need to start her morning heavy with the shame of having the village crazy for a dad. I draped my arm across her shoulder and pulled her in. He'd wake up eventually and shuffle on home.

Neighbor greeted neighbor for the first time in weeks, catching up on the most recent gossip. Everyone buzzed, excited to leave their isolated homesteads in the hills, quit their farming for the week, and enjoy the excess. That's what Founder's Week was all about, really—

moonshine, cornhole, no work, and a lot of craziness we'd all just forget about later.

In a blink, *the stranger boy's face, his kind smile and charming green eyes, popped into my sight again. His eyes seared into my soul.*

I shook my head to clear away the image.

A wicked smile spread across Lily's face. "Why're you smiling? Excited to see you-know-who at the warpath?"

Heat rushed into my cheeks.

Lily giggled.

"You have no idea," I said. "Something really weird happened this morning."

Lily pulled her blonde hair back from her shoulder and leaned in, taking my arm. "Did he finally acknowledge your existence? You know you're worth more than just pining after some guy who doesn't even—"

"No, nothing like that."

"Good."

"I blacked out. I think."

"Oh." Lily reeled. "This is taking a bit of a turn. Continue."

"Then I saw this really hot guy, like tortured-prince-hot, in my head."

Lily inhaled sharply and squealed. "That's better! Like a hot guy was in your dreams when you blacked out? Who? My turn to blackout next."

"He was a stranger, Lil. Someone I'd never seen before. There was a raven and blood and stuff. I'll tell you and Griff later."

Lily and Griffin were the only others, besides my family, who knew about my sight. I hadn't been too great at hiding it during my first few years of school. Thank the angels Lily and Griff noticed and covered for me.

"Blood? Girl! I can't wait till later. Who cares about dumb ol' Griff!"

Mama shushed us right up as we neared the first of the ancient willow trees at the Sacred Wood.

We entered the grove of weeping willows, stone angels with veiled faces, and the slowly gathering crowd—637 people so far. The Ritual of the Warpath was the kick-off ceremony to Founder's Week. Tears of gratitude filled the eyes of those who passed through the wood as they offered white daisies to their loved and fallen.

Laurel's Angel statue loomed over the gathering crowd. Different from all of the other stone monuments sprinkled about town, she was a larger-than-life angel that commanded respect. She'd been carved over months and months by her grief-stricken husband, my great-great-grandfather Raleigh. A stunning sculpture of a beautiful young woman, with her face raised to the heavens in triumph, her strong feathered wings outstretched, and a sawed-off shotgun strapped to her back. One hand held her mighty sword, Elf-Wrender, a replica of the sword my dad now wielded, passed down through generations, and the other delicate hand stretched toward heaven, beseeching God for help against the horde.

Sometimes I wondered if her hand wasn't reaching toward God in challenge.

My great-great grandmother Laurel was the first Guardian Angel of New Haven.

The words carved beneath her statue called out from the grave:

"Build a home for me and bury me there. I promise with all the fierce love of a mother to guard it along with all of the hosts of heaven. But, as soon as you have to sell your soul to the devil and fight like hell—I'll be there, holding the brandy and a rifle."

Pride rose in me. I was Blue Laurel Haven, named after my unconquerable great-great-grandma. I hoped to meet her someday in the heavens, or hell, wherever I was destined to go after I laid down to eternal rest.

"C'mon, Blue." Lily pulled me through the Sacred Wood. I followed her along the path, her blonde hair swaying like a cotton bedsheet in the breeze.

My family continued behind, eager to claim a good spot to see the Warpath ceremony. Mama's hazel eyes already glistened with tears as my dad's large arms wrapped around her shoulders. Steadying her. Hawk already said his goodbyes back home this morning. Now he knelt at the feet of Laurel's Angel, his back curved in deference. The rest of my siblings—Cora, Fox, Kyra, and baby Shenandoah—picked wild daisies beneath the rows of willows to lay at the markers of our loved and fallen. The Sacred Wood held the scattered ashes of our dead.

People drifted past like ghosts. Some hummed quietly to themselves, some brought mementos or flowers to place at the crosses of their lost loves.

A purple wind wound through the trees.

Sixty-five trees.

Seven-hundred-sixty-four people.

No. No counting.

I blinked and kept my eyes moving, glancing around to see if anyone had noticed. But no one ever did.

As we neared the center of the wood, a stone of lead settled in my gut. Hawk and Pretty-Boy Joe, the pride of New Haven, dressed head to toe in camo, knelt before Laurel's Angel. The corners of my eyes stung. I focused instead on the cottony willow fluff dancing on the air currents.

"Hey." Lily nudged me with her elbow.

I jabbed her back and offered a queasy smile. She wrinkled her nose, not fooled for a second.

"Look. There's something to be said about knowing," Lily said as we found the cool shadow of a willow near the front. "I mean, you spent your entire senior year looking over your shoulder for a captain to notice you. For your shot. But now that it's over and done, at least you won't keep on worrying about it, right?"

I growled. If Mama would just stop treating me like an imbecile— I could've actually done something with my life. It was a miracle I was even allowed in town at all. My parents picked up the same argument every few years, the question of if I should even be going to school. Would it be better to keep me home and cause half the town to be suspicious, or let me go to school and draw unwanted attention from the other half?

I pushed the blooming negative feelings away. "I know. It's just, being here in this wood, it feels like I failed, and I didn't even get a chance to prove myself."

Lil wrapped her pale arm around my shoulder. I leaned my head against hers, careful not to get my wild, brown curls tangled in her face.

A collective intake of breath and silence fell over the wood as the rest of our town's warrior teams filed in around Laurel's Angel. The Falcons, Talons, Wings, and Fangs.

Heat rose in my cheeks as I concentrated on *not* looking at my brother's best friend as he strode in, tall and proud and *directly* in my view.

My eyes betrayed me anyway, drawn to him like an idiot hungry kitten to cream.

Kaleo was the new captain for the Falcons, even though he was just one year older than me—the youngest captain in decades. I'd been in love with Kaleo as long as I could remember. I don't think I impressed him much when I was a kid—with my gymnastics moves, acne, and incessant giggling. I did *not* want to re-see those memories. Ever. I think I would actually die.

He was just so...beautiful. His Hawaiian heritage was evident in his lustrous long, raven black hair. It was pulled back into braided pigtails today, emphasizing his sharp jaw and cheekbones. As if his immaculate face had been carved by the Gods of Handsomeness and Manliness. He wore the color of his warrior team, the Falcons—a green camouflage t-shirt with a large black falcon emblazoned on his chest. Leather belts strapped his body, housing his many weapons.

Brown arms the size of tree trunks? Check. More gorgeous than ever? Affirmative.

Another jab from Lil and I pulled my eyes away, warmth rising up through my neck. *Ugh. So awkward.* But Kaleo stayed in my eyes for a moment after I closed them, like a beautiful echo.

Six-foot-four.

Leather boots, size fourteen, with laces crisscrossing twelve times.

Lips 4.7 inches wide.

Three-hundred-seventy-seven thick eyelashes.

The sheer will of *not* looking at Kaleo about killed me, though he'd never even think to glance my way. The only way I knew he knew I was alive was by the number of times he and Hawk had covered my bed with crickets or thrown bones in my hair to see if the dogs would chase me. But he hadn't been around the farm much since his mama died a couple years ago. I was sure my whole body would explode if his eyes ever reached mine.

I stared, instead, at Pretty-Boy Joe's left eye as he knelt beside Hawk. Green flecks mingled with blue and gold in his iris like a warm summer's day.

A steady pounding of drums began, sounding deep in my bones. President Zhao strode before the crowd. *Good. Somewhere else for me to look.* She was a small woman with black hair chopped in a blunt angle to her chin. A long, gnarly scar that stretched from her left eye to the full pink of her cheek only improved her beauty. Word was, she got that from wrestling a bear to submission, but she'd never really shared the story. She knew how to fight. She knew how to survive. She was the first warrior in fifty years to be elected president.

Zhao raised a hand and the drums stopped. "Thank you my fellow New Haveners. Today's a day that we cherish above all others. It is a day we celebrate the warriors who founded our safe home"— Cheers erupted through the wood as she motioned toward Laurel's stone angel—"as well as our new warriors who seek to keep it that way. We come from a long line of strong, courageous fighters. Survivors. The strongest of the strong. We are proud to see this noble tradition continue."

Applause sounded through the wood. General Rose stood beside Zhao, directly beneath Laurel's Angel, ceremonial eagle feathers strung through his right ear—the large game kill from his own warpath many years before. He raised up both arms. The Ritual of the Warpath had now begun. "Today marks one-hundred-eleven years since our brave Founder, Raleigh Haven, and his two-hundred-thirteen Blessed, quit their twenty years of pain and travails of wandering these dreary lands."

Every New Havener leaned in. We loved to hear the story, even if we knew it by heart, and General Rose always threw in a bit of flare.

"Raleigh stood firmly over his newly buried bride, right here at this very tomb"—he gestured to Laurel's Angel—"and cried out the words we hold so dear. No more wandering. No more fighting. No more traveling this land, looking for salvation. Our salvation is right here in these blue mountains. This is it. We've trudged through the worst of humanity for far too long."

"We must be more," the crowd murmured in unison. "We must be good. We must be angels." Some chanted the words, some nodded along, but we all had them memorized. The words that created our home 111 years ago.

The general nodded. "They knew the world was at an end. Most souls had gone up to Jesus. All that was left in God's green land was them and those evil elves that constantly tried to eat them. They knew they must make a stand! But it had to be done in secret. In hiding. So they quietly repaired this old, worn wall. Covered our buildings with kudzu, allowed the foliage to grow natural and untamed—all to blend in. Raleigh and his Blessed did everything they could to stay away from the unwanted attention of human and elf alike. For when anyone had supplies, food, shelter, water, fire...*death* was soon to follow!"

General Rose lapped up the silence that followed. He loved the rush of an audience hanging on every word. I smiled to myself. That was something his son had not inherited. Griffin hated the heavy intensity of his father. More than once, we'd been stuck at his dinner table during one of his father's long-winded speeches about the ever-dwindling interest in our village's security.

"For there had been a plague, y'see! A *terrible* plague killed over half the population of the world. The sickness first killed the righteous, sent them right up to the angels, nice and gentle-like. Then left the wicked to be *burned* with a terrible, terrible punishment."

Here he goes.

"The sickness could no longer kill those wicked left alive. Their souls were too *filthy* to be treated so delicately. So, the illness grew stronger, smarter. It *metamorphosized* neighbor into nightmare, friend into foe, sister into stalker, mother into murderer, and father into—"

"Farter!" Dingle-Berry Gerry called out.

A few idiots chuckled, their laughter dying off into sputters. I sunk into the moss at the roots of the willow. That was my future work partner right there. Tooth decay, spittle, and a hankering for pork rinds at all times of the day. *Heaven save me.*

General Rose shot him a look that would've cowed an elf into submission. "From human to a predator that'd rip that shriveled heart out of your chest and eat it before you even had the chance to fill your filthy drawers." General Rose's wicked smile spread as he ran a hand through his silver hair.

Gerry swallowed hard, looking like he just might crap his pants right there.

General Rose's heavy-lidded eyes gleamed.

"Their human eyes, that once held the love of a mother for her child, clouded to blackness. Their beloved souls sucked from their bodies, leaving a husk of a shell now void of all feeling. All they craved was blood and flesh. Transformed! Changed into creatures of nightmare and death. The Shadow Elves. Their venomous bite would transform you, if they didn't devour you first!"

Everyone stood up with hoots and hollers, but Dingle-Berry Gerry's eyes narrowed at me. As if I would suddenly jump up and rip into someone's chest like a feral Shadow Elf. His sneer morphed into a suggestive wink. *Ew.*

This was where the story usually ended. Our heroic leader fights through hordes of elves, kills them all, then finds us a perfect, safe home. Done. The end.

By the way General Rose's eyes gleamed, he'd just gotten started. *Here we go.*

"We're sorry to see less and less of our town's graduates able to pass the warrior trials." General Rose's jaw clenched. "For the world out there is large and mostly unexplored. We are the true descendants of the two-hundred-thirteen Blessed that Raleigh and Laurel rescued and gathered in their twenty wandering years. Our people hail from exotic lands like my own from Korea. Georgia, Hawaii, New Zealand, Canada, Mexico, New York, California, Alabama, Virginia. We are black, white, and brown—but warriors all the same. We must do all we can to protect our own. You never know if any of *them* have survived the ravages of time."

My dad nodded in agreement. *Whatever, Dad, you didn't even let me try.* But, most New Haveners just shook their heads and rolled their eyes. Any mention of *them* made the town very uncomfortable. In a thriving town like New Haven, who needed warriors? The last action our wall saw was Ol' Man Amos getting heckled by that angry beaver while he tended to his moonshine five years ago.

But my dad often said, "We got our safety blanket wrapped around us so tight, it's strangling the good sense right out of us."

A flash of black hair and Griffin finally showed up. He sat between Lils and me in the cool blue grass.

"So, what's my dad done now?" Griff nodded toward General Rose. "I heard a ripple of annoyance."

"Ooh!" I teased. "That's your new nickname: Ripple of Annoyance. I'll call you ROA for short."

Griff stared at me, eyes wide, mouth agape—trying his best to look offended.

"Now let us begin!" the general continued, as if he hadn't just soured the mood. He signaled for the painting to begin.

The two warriors stood, towering and strong, their hair shaved in tight mohawks. A few warriors dipped their hands in the red clay of the earth and proceeded to cover Hawk and Joe's bodies head to toe. Once Joe's blond and Hawk's brown mohawks were covered in the rusty earth, they became nearly identical, though Joe's long blond hair started to fall over with the weight of the clay.

Envy tightened an ugly fist around my heart. *I should be up there with them.*

This painting of their bodies mirrored the camouflaging our ancestors did to survive in the Shadow War wilds. The mud helped protect them from the other-worldly senses of the elf mutations. Once the ritual began, the privates could not speak. They must show complete self-mastery until they received their new warrior names five days from now at the Naming Ceremony, the closing of Founder's Week.

Hawk had never known a quiet moment in his life. He'd toss out a pun or smart-aleck remark like hot pretzels whether you wanted one or not. But as I studied him now—hazel eyes straight ahead, subdued, mouth straight, shoulders back—he seemed...somber.

Hawk caught my eye and nodded, then looked away. We'd played this game since we were kids, and even though I was mad at him for something he had no control over, I watched. His lips moved almost imperceptibly, except to me, as he mouthed, *"Keep an eye on the horizon, Blue. Just in case."*

Okay, Hawk. I'll keep an eye out. His eyes shifted to me and I nodded. Message received. His shoulders relaxed, just a fraction. So did mine.

Once the cleansing was completed, General Rose raised his weapon-worn hands and offered his last words. "New Haveners, look upon your warriors new, just as our warriors of old." He turned to the warriors. "These next few days, you will have only your bodies, cleansed and consecrated to this earth, to depend upon. Keep 'em clean. This is a solitary journey, but you will not be alone. You each have a chosen animal to be your companion."

Hawk's dog, Ranger, licked at his knuckles.

General Rose called each private up and handed them their single weapon of choice, then spoke to them of their individual journeys.

They may not speak until their rite is completed.

They are to return in five days.

They must bring back their first large-game kill for the Naming Ceremony on Friday.

They must not be seen.

This was perhaps the biggest worry; the warriors could inadvertently lead outsiders back to our safe, hidden home. Not that we'd seen or heard of anyone for over a hundred years. Our warriors patrolled outside the walls regularly, but this was a solitary journey. There'd be no one to watch their backs.

Each private carried a cyanide pill, just in case. I'd never given it a second thought until my brother was handed that sickening oval pill. The thought of him having to use it made my stomach turn.

"Remember the Code of the Warrior," General Rose commanded. "We swear to demonstrate honor, love, reverence, generosity, courage, and mercy forever. We vow to fight and protect home and family above self. Protection. Safety. Life."

"Protection! Safety! Life!"

The surrounding warriors chanted so loud the hairs on my arms stood at attention.

Hawk and Joe stood strong and intimidating, covered head to toe in dark clay. Their bodies seemed to vibrate. I couldn't look away. I couldn't blink. The mud on the boys stretched out and grabbed me. My head swayed. My stomach dropped to my knees. It was that same dizzying sensation from earlier on the mountain. My eyes blurred and smeared. *Not again.*

In a blink, that strange tug pulled me under.

"Are you mute? You look as if you aren't capable of much more than a caveman covered in mud."

A group of men blurred before me in a yellow field. Ten?

Menacing. Outsiders. This was not in New Haven. Wild cotton stalks lay smashed beneath their boots.

"...or an ass." They laughed at that, sneering.

"What is this?" A man stretched out his sword toward my legs. *No. Not my legs. Not my eyes. These eyes were dim. Muddy. Hard to see through.*

"Is there anything down there? I mean, you are a man, right? Or are you some sort of minuscule—"

"Yeh," they all jeered. "Cock-a-doodle-do!"

The men guffawed. Humiliation. Anger swelled within me. Not my emotions. I was going to be sick.

"Habla Ingles? Españole? Francais?" A brown-haired man called out in a strange accent, "Oye, caveman. I would be very careful whom you choose to ignore, my friend."

Defiance flared within my chest. My eyes narrowed, but it was like looking through hand-blown glass. The shapes and images blurred, twisted—swimming in and out of focus.

The outsider drew his sword and stomped toward me. Long, ratty brown curls covered his head. Tattoos peeked from the collar of his navy-blue shirt. A gold cross flickered at his throat. A pang of recognition—his face. His green eyes. Not the caring smile he'd flashed me in my first vision with the raven. These lips twisted in a snarl.

Could it be the same stranger?

The green-eyed outsider pressed his sword against my throat. Fear clawed up my neck.

"I said, be careful." His words simmered dangerously. "There are ten of us and only one of you. Now, tell me what I want to know."

He pressed the sword harder into my throat as another outsider laid a hand on his shoulder. Another mop of brown curls and brilliant green eyes. His brother? They appeared identical through these muddy eyes. "Sir, please. Let us spare—"

The outsider with the sword snarled.

Pain lanced through my throat, stealing my breath—

The vision blurred like smoke. Gone in a wisp.

I fell to the ground, gasping. My lungs spasmed. I struggled to suck in enough air.

The chorus of the New Haven church choir rushed into my ears. I couldn't breathe. Couldn't—

"Blue?" Lily asked. "Blue?"

I rolled my eyes, but the vision had vanished. Tall weeping willows surrounded me again. Mama Darla led the church choir in a traditional New Haven song. Her round arms moved melodically to the music as everyone stood, arm in arm, hand in hand. They created circle after circle around the warriors.

"Blue?" Griffin offered me a hand and a calm smile. "Did you trip?"

He and Lily shared a pointed glance. Griff pulled me up as, hand to my throat, I swallowed over and over, gulping down breaths.

Tears streamed down my face as my chin trembled. My whole body shook with a new terror.

What had I just seen? I blinked again, straightening as I searched Hawk's hazel eyes, then Joe's. What were we sending them out to? My heart slammed against my ribcage, but I couldn't get Hawk's attention. And what would I do anyway? I didn't know if that vision meant anything at all.

But it'd felt so...real.

To my left, my sisters, Cora and Kyra, sang, puffy eyed. To my right, my parents, Baby Shenandoah, and Fox stood with arms linked as the singing took them over. Lily and Griff joined in as nonchalantly as they could with a squeeze to my hand.

The air shifted, blurring from buttery yellow ribbons of sunlight into the dark blues and purples of many heavy hearts weaving throughout the wood in song.

Fear gripped me, unwilling to loosen its hold on my heart. On my lungs.

A heavy weight of eyes pressed in on me from ahead. Kaleo.

Kaleo's nostrils flared. Jaw tight, eyebrows knit in alarm. Eyes like flint.

He'd missed nothing of what happened.

I pulled in a shaky breath and met his dark gaze, too overwhelmed to hide what was written all over my face. Everyone around me blurred, my only focus on Kaleo's thick black eyebrows furrowed over his dark eyes. His lip curled. The connection lasted for hours, minutes, seconds. Forever, or no time at all.

I narrowed my eyes, my blood pounding in my ears. *Go ahead and stare.* I was used to being stared at.

His eyes widened, just a fraction, then he leaned over to Jax, his first-in-command. I read his lips as he said, *"Something's out there. Wait for orders."*

Something was happening. Something dangerous. I knew it—felt it in my trembling muscles and itchy eyes. Did my visions have anything to do with it?

Kaleo's eyes flicked over to mine once more. In a blink, he spun and slipped behind the crowd.

Alarm pounded through my head. Without a second thought, I turned and ran from the ceremony, Kaleo's long, black braids my only lead.

CHAPTER 3

A Smack in the Face and a Bloody Nose

BLUE

I ran past everyone singing and holding hands among the guardian angels of the wood. I wasn't sure why, but after two separate visions of some handsome, evil strangers—then Kaleo's wild eyes and nostril flares—I had to find out.

"Something's out there. Wait for orders."

Daddy always said to trust that feeling, that little voice in my head that says, *"This is important. Listen to your heart and damn the consequences."*

Luckily, I wore my usual white tank and cut-off jeans. My trusty dagger slapped comfortingly against my thigh. Bare feet. Tight bra. The stars were aligned. I ran the way my dad taught me, careful to avoid loud sticks and dry leaves. Silent as a salamander. Mama always said I lived more like a fairy with hobbit's feet than a human child. The bottoms of my feet were practically leather at this point.

Kaleo's raven hair slipped from view behind the hillside as he ran full-speed like a mindless soldier. The entire south side of the village rolled out like a family of sleeping gray squirrels. Kaleo ran straight through several dogwood trees, sending a burst of pollen soaring. I flew down the hillside, confident that if I kept my distance, I could use my sight to my advantage. I already had his path all mapped out from my quick glance above. I followed the invisible pull of my eyes while I flew into the cover of thick trees.

Rocks, branches, weeds, and logs opened up to a wide horse trail. Dogwood flower petals, broken branches, and fresh footprints littered the dirt path past town. He was no longer in my sight, but I followed the signs. I ran past the fields of solar panels toward the south wood. Nothing much out there except a farm or two.

He was fast, but so was I.

I ran after him, but before long, I was choking on my lungs. Bending at the waist as I gasped and sputtered, hands on my knees.

Kaleo's trail had gone cold. *Stupid Soldier Boy.*

This was an old trail; animals ran this line all night long. Too many broken branches and crushed leaves lay scattered about out here for me to pick up on anything. Trees towered over me like sleeping giants. Blue birds and sparrows twittered, probably laughing at my stupidity.

I pulled in a tight breath, trying to catch it, then dropped onto a fallen log. What was I even doing out here? Why had I left Hawk? He'd been working toward becoming a warrior for so long, and I missed it. I wouldn't see him again until he came home.

I'm an idiot. Tears stung the corners of my eyes. What was happening to me? These strange visions had me feeling like I was losing control.

I released a breath as something caught my eye.

Bare traces of dogwood flower pollen were brushed up on the bark of a tree in front of me. I perked up, wiping my nose. Kaleo was covered in that same yellow dust.

A vision memory of Kaleo running out here flew before my eyes.

Kaleo burst through a field of dogwood trees, sending branches, leaves and flowers scattering. Yellow pollen clung to the back of his shirt and butt. Strong shoulders, muscles bulging beneath his thin shirt—

Ahem. So, the pollen, yes, it didn't get brushed up on that tree with the wind or rain. If I could just follow his trail of pollen, I might be able to find where he'd gone.

Dad always told me to use my gift and see how far it could take me. Experiment, as long as no one else was around.

I closed my eyes and pulled in a deep breath, willing all of the visual stimulation out. I opened my eyes, focusing on the yellow pollen. I tracked it from the bark to another tree. The golden spores flared brightly on a leaf.

I scanned ahead for the dogwood pollen's particular bright yellow color—the spherical shape I knew from endless childhood exploring. Slowly, as if water were being poured over a painting, all other colors blurred out of focus, fading into the background.

But the brilliant gold? It sharpened, focused.

I stifled a squee and took off.

Why hadn't I ever used my sight like this before? I followed my first instinct and ran towards the pollen. The yellow glowed like a beacon before me, as if someone had run over the trees with a lemon-dusted paint brush. The marks were few and far between, but I followed them with ease.

The path of pollen opened up before my eyes like a geometric puzzle piecing together. But just as quickly, my stomach clenched reflexively. This was when I usually stopped myself. I'd become wary, afraid of my eyes and what they could do. That feeling, like taking a bad step off the stairs, meant I was different. Scary. Someone to be feared.

Kaleo's path led straight toward the old gristmill, caverns, and wastelands. What was he doing all the way out here?

Curiosity got the better of me, and I pushed through the tall pines. The outer wall cut through the hill below like a moss-covered frown. Our warriors guarded that fifteen-foot tall, four-foot-wide behemoth night and day. It circled the entire village. Raleigh and his Blessed spent years fixing up this old structure, expanding and strengthening it. Kudzu vines and weeds grew through the red and brown brick, camouflaging it from non-existent outsiders. I hadn't realized I'd gone out so far.

The birds and insects had gone quiet. Silence pricked my ears like an alarm. My adrenaline spiked. I shouldn't be out here.

But there he was.

Kaleo crouched by something at the foot of the wall, some kind of lumpy burlap sack covered in drying mud.

Thirty-five-point-eight inches long.

Blue daisies lay strewn about the sack's opening, but it was impossible to see inside.

A branch snapped under my foot. *Crap.*

Kaleo's head shot up, a wildness in his eyes, the color drained from his face. A sneer formed on his lips. Alarm and adrenaline peeled through me.

I saw nothing of the playful guy I'd grown up with—the one who'd laugh until he cried, stuffed twelve of Mama's potato donuts in his mouth, and sang "Take Me Home Country Roads" horrifically. No. Pure malice shot out from his eyes. I stood as still as Laurel's Angel, holding my breath. No one else could see from this distance, right?

But his eyes, they clamped down on mine with a deadlock.

Impossible.

In a flash, he snarled and sprinted toward me faster than a diving falcon, his face twisted in an unrecognizable rage.

Angel, save me.

He was going to kill me. Breaking into a sprint, I stumbled over logs and past trees, but the pounding of his boots grew ever louder.

"Blue! Stop!"

Not on your life. I jumped and sprinted, but my legs burned. He'd catch up; he'd always beat me in a dead sprint.

He ran in from the side, cutting off my path. "Stop!" he growled.

"*You* stop!" I yelled.

"Now."

My breath hitched and sputtered. "No." I made a try for the left, but he was faster.

Kaleo flew at me like a hawk going in for the kill.

Holy angel of death.

He landed on top of me, slamming my back against the unforgiving ground, knocking the wind from me. My chest spasmed.

I coughed and hitched, trying to get air into my lungs. Faster than I could scream, he'd snatched both of my hands up by my head and his knees clamped down in a vice grip around my legs. We both sputtered and cursed, tall grass flying around in circles. An explosion of pollen soared around us.

I choked, pulling in gulps of air. "Get off me, you psycho idiot! What the hell?"

"Why'd you follow me? What're you doing out here?" He scanned around us, pupils dilated wildly, nostrils flaring.

A rapid heart rate of 167 bpm pounded in his neck.

All the while he held me flat and helpless on the ground. My arms and legs prickled with numbness. Useless. His stupid perfect face hovered inches from mine. Something I'd always dreamt of, but not in this nightmare.

"Never let them see you struggle." Dad's words from training rang through my head. I pulled in a sharp breath.

I was not going down like this.

First, misdirect.

I smiled up at Kaleo sweetly. "Anyone ever told you your breath smells like nachos? *Stinky* nachos?"

His eyes flew wide.

Got him. My mouth split open into a mad grin.

Second, go for the kill.

I brought my forehead up to meet with his perfect nose. *Crack!*

Hot blood sprayed down on my face as he jumped up, sense and reason instantly smashed into his impeccable face. Blood dripped from his shirt onto the weeds below. He cradled his face and swore. *Good.* I kept my eyes on him while I scrambled behind a large oak tree.

He scanned the clearing, his pupils shrinking smaller. His face transformed from wild anger to something I couldn't place.

It'd better be regret.

Silence stretched out between us like Grandpappy Winter's waistline. Both of our breaths surged in gasps. Fear hid behind his eyes, something I hadn't seen there since that summer before his mama passed.

"Go home, Blue," he growled, wiping the blood from his face.

"I *was* going home, until I saw you acting all suspicious."

"Oh, so your house is out here in the south wood now, is it?" he snarled. "Get on home. Now. This is no place for you."

"You're not my daddy."

"I can still teach you a lesson."

"You can't teach me nothin'," I snapped. "What's that burlap sack down there by the wall?"

Kaleo closed his eyes as if I were some tedious child. "You're still up to your old tricks—following me and Hawk around. When will you learn that this is not a game?"

I swallowed back the lump in my throat, eager to prove my worth. "So, the words 'something's out there. Wait for orders' were just nothing?"

Kaleo's cheeks flushed again. "How could you have heard me from across the clearing in that crowd? In fact, how could you possibly see anything all the way down there, Blue?"

I froze. I'd gone too far. I couldn't reveal just how good I was at reading lips and seeing far distances, though my pride burned to *tell him. Impress him. Make him notice.* I clamped my lips shut.

"I don't have time for this." He huffed.

I was so, so stupid. Why was I out here, following him along like some love sick puppy? I attempted to reclaim a tiny fraction of dignity as my face burned. "I just, it seemed like something dangerous was going on and I wanted to help—"

"You didn't help. You broke my nose." Crimson blood oozed between the fingers he held up to his face.

"Good. Hope I knocked some sense into you." Sometimes I just couldn't stop myself.

A chorus of insects filled the silence. Kaleo's eyes watered and he turned away.

Was he crying? I grimaced. "Listen, I'm sorry—"

"Enough, Blue. This is warrior business and you're nothing but a useless cow farmer. Right?"

The words landed like a blow. Kaleo knew I wanted to be a warrior more than anything.

"Tell me I'm wrong," Kaleo spat.

My heart dropped. "You know I can be more."

"You ain't nothing. Know nothing. Saw nothing. Got it?" Kaleo trained the full force of his disgust straight on me. "It's just some stupid bag of flowers. Now get on home. You're not wanted here."

Tears pricked my eyes and my chin trembled. Humiliation burned into my face. "What happened to you, Kaleo?"

"Go home."

With a gasp, I spun back toward home, my eyes blurry with shame.

CHAPTER 4

Sickly, Sweet Decay

KALEO

Blood oozed from my face and my nose pulsed with pain. I blinked over and over, dazed as I sat, practically laid out in the clearing.

What—just—happened.

I shook my head, trying to clear it, delivering a new level of agony. At least my nose had stopped spewing blood. My eyes watered with more than just pain. That smell. But—*ow*—it was definitely broken.

She broke my nose.

Blue. Blue Haven. Hawk's twin sister. Freckles. She—broke it.

And I hadn't even seen it coming. I barely had time to register the change in her scent. I knew she'd been following me. But I barely noticed her smell in the overwhelming storm of sickly-sweet decay that surrounded me. It suffocated me. The metallic sting of blood and wrongness—New, alluring, drawing me in, yet dripping in disease.

My body had moved of its own accord. I had her on the ground before I'd even registered what I'd done. I'd completely lost control. I was nothing more than a wild, savage beast. How had I blanked out so completely?

For a moment there, I wanted to hurt her. I *would* have hurt her.

I hauled off my shirt and mopped the blood from my face. My shirt was trashed. *I* was trashed. As soon as Blue broke my nose, though—she'd saved me. Her scent had shot straight through me. It infused with the rusty iron of my own blood, coursing through my veins. I could taste her on my tongue. She filled my every sense. She blasted through that sickly-sweet scent with a flamethrower.

I grabbed the sac of coffee beans I kept tied around my neck and pulled in a deep breath, nice and slow, before my nose swelled. Nothing. Even these stupid beans couldn't cleanse my nose of her. She was in my every breath. I couldn't shake her.

As if in answer, that other stench wormed its way in—the one that brought me out here in the first place. My eyes burned. Sharp, metallic, a newborn puppy, fresh-cut grass, but all of it *wrong*. I gagged again. My tongue was coated in the scent.

Everything I'd ever known was a complete lie. With this new revelation—nothing made sense. Nothing. My head swayed, my nose throbbed, but it was nothing to the sick pit in my stomach.

Get up.

I pulled my sorry butt off the forest floor and trudged back down to that sack by the wall. A violet cloud of sweetness surrounded it like a filthy tangle of cotton candy, dry leaves, and moss. But with every step, my nose clotted and swelled—just as useless as everyone else's in the village. *Good.*

My heart thundered against my ribcage. The sack, overflowing with blue daisies, was bigger than I thought it'd be. How had it gotten here? I searched the surrounding area. No one was around for miles, except Blue. I didn't have to smell her to know she absolutely loathed me now. The hurt in those brilliant blue eyes of hers—I pushed the guilt away and forced myself closer to the sack.

Dread curled in my gut. *Do it.*

I swallowed, steeling myself, as I put my hand on the sack's opening and peered inside.

CHAPTER 5

An Indecent Amount of Whoopie Pies

BLUE

I stumbled back through the square, grateful for the empty streets. The whole town was still up at the ceremony. Hot tears and snot streamed from my chin. I trembled past my old schoolhouse. The words of The Edict painted on the large wood doors, yellowed and cracked with age, jumped out and smacked me in the eyes. The ancient words screamed out from a more barbaric time. Words that haunted my daily existence.

THE EDICT - POSTED

1. Persons possessing enhanced abilities or behaviors similar to those of the S.E. including, but not exclusively:

Enhanced feeling, eyesight, hearing, taste, smell.

OR physical signs of a bite, contact with S.E., or contact with persons outside of the wall.

MUST be subject to search and quarantine until infection and transformation are deemed impossible. Failure to do so will result in death.

2. Any persons with knowledge of such an individual will be held equally responsible.

3. All who die from any means natural or inflicted must be burned with fire and consecrated to Heaven's Holy Angels to prevent any spreading of the demon's plague.

The words had always filled me with dread, but now they thundered through me with fresh accusations. Had Kaleo just insinuated that I had some sort of enhancement? Had he been threatening me?

In a blink, I peered through my five-year-old eyes as I took in these words for the first time. It was my first day of school. I hadn't been to the square more than a few times and that was before I could read. Even as a five-year old, I knew what S.E. meant. It meant them, the Shadow Elves.

A vision memory pulled me in.

"Blue!" Mama's call echoed through the empty school hallway. My mama, younger by twelve years, ran toward me out of the corner of my vision memory. Her brown curls bounced along with her round pregnant belly, her ivory face smoothed by her youth. "I thought you'd followed me to class, honey."

My eyes stuck to those red letters like thick tar. They seemed to reach out and grasp at me, tugging on my perfect pigtails—tearing at my clean blue dress.

Mama met me outside of the schoolhouse door and busied herself with tightening my braids.

I turned and looked up into her round face. "Am I a elf, Mama?"

Her eyes flew wide, her skin drained of its pink flush. With one quick glance around the empty square, she knelt down. "Well, do you have pointy ears?"

I felt my ears, but I already knew the answer. "No, silly Mama."

"And your eyes?" Mama asked. "Are they big, black, and scary?"

"No." I laughed.

She wrinkled her nose. "And when was the last time you ate somebody?"

"Mama! I ain't never ate nobody. Well, 'cept I did bite Hawk once, but he deserved it."

"Always remember that, honey. People just can't get over their old suspicions. Just remember: Blend in. Count to five. And blink."

I shook my head as the vision memory vanished in a wisp of

smoke. At just five years old, I hadn't noticed how my mama's eyes had misted over. How she'd looked as if she might cry. Or how Daddy stood over the two of us, inspecting every corner of the square, a hand on Elf Wrender's hilt. Ready. Waiting.

"You ain't nothing. Know nothing. Saw nothing. Got it?"

A sob burst through my tight chest.

I couldn't be down here when the ceremony ended. I didn't want anyone to see me like this. The three miles home barely registered as I ran. Through my pooling tears, the woods pulsed with an eerie glow —all blacks and blues and purples. I had to see Hawk. Make sure he was okay. I made a promise.

"Keep an eye on the horizon, Blue. Just in case."

My brick home sat at the foot of Grandfather Rock. A new crop of thyme and rosemary popped up from the green roof of Raleigh House, glinting in the golden glow of the afternoon sun. Peach and apple trees hung heavy with fruit. Our barns out back had aged to a cool, dry blue. Pepper huffed from inside as if he knew I needed him.

I grabbed my gelding from the barn, and he carried me up the mountain to my spot atop Grandfather Rock. There I sat, alone, crying, praying, angry, tired. While everyone else back in town commenced the festivities by getting drunk on Old Man Amos's moonshine, I sat on the mountain.

Within the hour, Hawk and Pretty-Boy Joe emerged from a secret tunnel under the wall with their animals. They hugged, pressed foreheads together for a long moment, then went their separate ways.

Hawk hiked down with Ranger at his heels as my anxiety spiked higher still. He drank from a nearby creek, kneeling longer than needed. Probably praying for courage. He looked back, just once, and smiled toward Grandfather Rock—as if he knew I'd be here.

My stomach pummeled. Had I been wrong not to warn him about my newest vision? Should I run out to him now? Call him back? Alert the warriors on patrol that a madman with a sword may or may not threaten to kill one of our own at some point in the past or future?

I'd never seen the future. Not once. I'd only ever seen my *own* past memories, through my *own* eyes. These strange visions were just that. Strange. Frightening. New.

I couldn't do anything for Hawk or Joe. There would be too many questions. As much as I liked to pretend the Enforcers were history, I still felt the fear that'd been drilled into me since I could spit. So, I just sat and watched the sun set gold, orange, and pink—as Hawk slipped out of sight through the branches of the tall pines.

At some point, Griff and Lily joined me up on the rock with drinks and vittles in hand.

"Hey, Blue." Griff's hands pressed into my shoulders. "We knew you'd be up here."

"You okay?" Lil asked.

But, I just sat and stared off into the golden orange of the sunset. Lil and Griff were used to my silence by now. My moods. Sometimes it was all just too much and all I could do was stare, allowing my eyes to blur and escape all the orbiting lights and shapes.

Lily passed out an indecent amount of whoopie pies. Griff brought raspberry licorice. We drank warm root beer and took a few sips of the moonshine Griffin nicked from the adult table. The soggy-bread-on-fire smell should've tipped me off. As soon as it touched my tongue, I spit it all over poor Griff's face. If our daddies could see us now, they'd kill us.

After my thoughts calmed, I told them about my two visions, and why I'd fallen to the ground earlier, gasping for breath.

"So, you were staring at some mud on your brother, then saw ten outsiders?" Griffin asked.

"Yeah, it was strange, like looking through a dusty old window." I said. "And no matter how hard I try, I can't see it again. I'd seen one of the men before, this morning, after a raven flew above me."

"Woah woah woah." Griffin leaned back. "So, both the raven and mud vision were murky?"

Griffin was not being pushy, he was trying to piece this puzzle together. So far, it wasn't making any sense.

"No, the raven vision was clear, bright. Through my own eyes," I answered. "So, that *has* to be the future, right? And this new one with the mud was foggy, dark, through the eyes and emotions of someone else, somehow."

Lily's bottom lip jutted out and she twisted her non-curly hair around her finger. "You're getting stronger."

Griffin's mouth turned down. "Or more out-of-control."

I'd never been great controlling my "gift" even worse at hiding it. Sometimes I wondered how good I'd be at controlling my sight if I wasn't always so focused on pretending it didn't exist. If Hawk was in danger, if those people were out there, I had to know. The worry chewed me up from the inside.

"Dad just led a huge patrol out last week, farther than usual," Griff assured me. "If there was anything out of the ordinary, they would've seen it."

Everything was safe out there—had been for 111 years now.

So why did I feel a cold claw of a shadow scrape down my spine?

I didn't tell them about running after Kaleo, the way he tackled me in the woods, and called me *nothing*. The wounds were still too fresh.

So, we ate and cried and laughed about the good ol' days. We knew once our graduation was over tomorrow, we could never go back to the simplicity of childhood.

The boredom of adulthood awaited.

CHAPTER 6

Bleeding Eyes

KALEO

Clumps of dirt kicked up from President Zhao's stallion as I followed on horseback through the south wood. The moonlight flickered between the branches above, casting a silvery strobe light on Zhao's black hair.

"How much farther?" Sweat dripped down my back. I struggled with every breath.

"Another two miles," she answered.

I couldn't stand another second of this. The burlap sack I'd found earlier today was now strapped to the back of my horse. My body repulsed at the close proximity. Adrenaline coursed through me. What were we doing? This was wrong. My nose burned as hot tears trailed from my eyes. Breathing through my mouth was just as bad. The metallic sting wormed through my lips and coated my throat. I gagged.

I hadn't wretched this much since I was a small boy, before I'd learned to dampen the daily smells that inundated me from every direction. My angel mama tried her best. She placed pots of fresh mint and lavender around my bedroom. She stuffed blankets into the cracks of my door and windows to give me the best chance of a restful sleep—one that wasn't full of the pungent reek of goat droppings. We were the main goat farm in New Haven, but we never kept any male goats on our property in the summer. Once those beasts went to rut, they'd spray their own piss all over themselves to attract the females. Mama said I used to wail all night long.

I might just take a tribe of male goats covered in piss over this misery.

The Havens took our male goats to their back forty for those four months out of the year, in exchange, I helped with chores around the farm. Virginia, who'd never let me work more than an hour, would send Hawk, Blue, and me away to cool off in the creek with warm caramel cakes and sweet tea in hand. In a matter of months, the deck-sanding morphed into strengthening exercises. Soldering pipes became sharpening swords. Mending fences were replaced by bow and arrow. Shooting the rats in the barn became target practice. It wasn't long before Bearon was training me right alongside his kids after school every day.

My ability strengthened along with my muscles.

Blue was always the first to try a new skill, usually the first to fail, too. But, the most determined of any of us, like she had something to prove the world.

But, that'd all come to a swift end almost two years ago. Since then, I'd been on my own.

I pulled another quick breath in through the tears. *Thank you, Blue.* My broken nose was a gift. The clotted blood in my sinuses helped to squelch the sour stench just a fraction. For the moment, I was still in control.

"Pull over there past the rock," Zhao commanded.

How could I trust her? She never prepared me, never prepared *our people* for this new reality. It was wrong. Heat flushed in my neck and anger surged, but I swallowed it down. I turned my mare toward the old, twisted rock Zhao indicated. In the dark evening light, the rock seemed to jump out from the ground, trying to escape Hell's fire below. An ancient loamy scent wafted from the damp earth. The ground felt a bit different here beneath Hekili's hooves. Softer.

The impossible bundle jostled as we rode. Too close to me. I wanted to smash it with my hatchet, then toss it into Hayden Lake and watch it sink to the bottom. But, President Zhao had other plans.

I tried to lean into the trust I'd built with her over the years. We had a chain of command for a reason. We had to obey orders. Trust in the wisdom of our leaders. She was methodical, calculating. She never acted until she'd thought through every consequence.

So why did I chafe at her command in this? Question her every motive?

This disgusting bundle shattered my sense of safety so thoroughly. We had no peace. No control. It'd all been a carefully crafted ruse. We were no safer than an exposed baby bird—vulnerable and flightless.

Nothing in my training truly prepared me for this.

Another breath through my mouth and my gut spasmed. Nausea roiled like a whirlpool.

I hopped from Hekili's back and spat onto the ground.

"I've got something to show you, Kaleo." President Zhao stood by the twisted rock. "But this is classified information that's been passed down from one president to the next. It's been forgotten by the civilians with time, and needs to stay that way."

Zhao's eyes rimmed with tired lines, lending her a look of someone twice her age. She nodded, knowing she'd never have to threaten me. She knew I would do whatever she asked without question. I never had to question before now.

"What do you want me to do with it?" I choked back the burning in my throat.

"You brought it here." Zhao's eyes flashed, shutting down any retort on my tongue.

Heat blazed through me. *I* didn't bring it here. Something else had.

"So now you take care of it." Zhao signaled to the bundle tied up to Hekili's hindquarters.

I fought through every instinct that told me to *run* with each step toward it. I mastered my rage, then followed Zhao's every order, hating every miserable second.

CHAPTER 7

Words from the Grave

BLUE

I woke with a pounding headache, eyes blurred, and my mouth gummy like I'd been chewing on sheep butt all night. I'd only had a few sips of moonshine, but apparently the stuff was very potent. My body screamed in protest as I sat up. Everything hurt.

If my stomach hadn't been growling so incessantly, I'd gladly have rolled back over in bed and whimpered pitifully, but starvation won out. Chickens squawked obnoxiously outside. The goats and pigs joined in the morning cacophony. The salamanders and possums didn't make much noise, but I could've sworn they moaned along with me as I braved the wooden stairs. With every step, a new pitiful sound escaped my lips. Kaleo had knocked the air out of me when he tackled me to the ground. My back and neck felt strained. *Punk.*

"Fox! Can you seriously stop chewing so gross for once? It's disgusting!" Kyra's voice screeched up the stairwell.

Fox huffed then proceeded to lap up his oatmeal like a noisy dog. If it hadn't been so hard to get down here, I would've run back up the stairs and crawled back into bed. I'd rather face an army of rabid Shadow Elves than my little sister in the morning.

You never knew which Kyra you were going to get, the sweet little ten-year-old who cuddled her kitten or the angry Kyra who wanted to crack your skull in.

Looked like it was angry Kyra yet again.

I shook my head and the room spun. *Bad idea.* My twelve-year-old brother's sloshy eating led to hunks of oatmeal dripping from the baby hairs on his prepubescent chin. I was starting to get where Kyra was coming from.

"Fox, stop teasing your sister. Kyra, you really just need to get over this food thing, honey. People are gonna be eating around you for the rest of your life," Mama was already exasperated.

Kyra growled.

"And no cats on the table." Mama went to swipe Tiger off the table, but Kyra snatched him out of harm's way. Mom wiped her soap covered hands down her apron then plucked my two-year-old baby sister, Shenandoah, up with a kiss and thigh squeeze.

Moms are so weird.

Pink and ochre ribbons of sunlight speared through the large windows in back, bathing the wooden table and porcelain plates in a fluorescent glow.

"Ah, look who's up from the dead," Mama said.

"I don't wanna talk about it," I grumbled through a mouthful of beautiful, warm sustenance.

Cora, my older sister by thirteen months, smiled a little too prettily at me. "I heard you crying all night. You missed the whole party." A conspiratorial smile lit up her face. "Come to think of it, Kaleo wasn't there either."

"Shut up, Cora." I was not in the mood.

"Maybe you two had your own party." Cora winked. Rose tinged her fawn skin, making her even more disgustingly beautiful. She'd dated Kaleo for a long summer a few years ago. The worst summer of my life, except that he'd been over every day. But back then I was in peak preteen show-off form. Memories of cringey dance moves, zits, and untamed frizz shuffled through my eyes. Not a pretty picture.

"Hey, you okay?" Cora must've noticed my tortured expression. Daddy always said I wore my heart in my eyes for the world to see.

Mama tried not to act too interested, but she'd scrubbed that same pan three times.

"I just thought I saw something, so I ran after it." I shrugged. "Turned out to be nothing."

"Blue, honey." Mama found her chance to strike. "Don't go running off without telling us where you're going. You left Hawk, left the whole family."

"I know. I'm sorry, okay? You'll be happy to know I'm never leaving the house again. Ever."

Mama abandoned the sink full of dishes and pulled a kitchen chair up in front of me. "You know that's not what I want for you, honey. I want you to be safe, but I know how you are. You gotta have your toes in the creek and your eyes trained on trouble." She paused. "I told you that story about when I was a young girl, right? You remember?"

"You've only told me a million times."

"And it matters more now than ever," Mama said. "That woman was torn from her children, killed, and burned on the outlook, just because she was strange. Too still, yet too fast. Too quiet. All us kids called her 'Scary Sally' until the rumors got to be too much. Enforcers hauled her off, and she was gone."

I sighed. "That was, like, thirty years ago, Mom. Things change. The Enforcers are gone, and no one hardly pays me any attention."

"How can you be so flippant about all of this?" Pink tinged Mama's fair skin as her temper flared. "You better believe there are people watching. Mama Darla remembers the early years. She remembers hiding in her cellar in terror. She remembers her Grandpa Raleigh as a nervous and tortured man. They lived through things you and I can't ever come close to understanding."

"That's right. I can't. It's done. Over. We are the last. All the elves and humans are gone. This is it." My stomach twisted on the lie. All except for that green-eyed stranger from my vision. No way I was telling Mom about him, though.

"Look." Mama leaned in. "I know you had your heart set on the warrior trials. I just pray you'll understand why I had to hold you back. Someday."

Not likely.

A thundering crash barreled up the back steps of the house, like the hooves of a thousand horses. Dad burst into the room with his massive smile and smashed me within his huge, sweaty biceps.

"Dad!" I groaned. *Gross.*

"How's my lil' Blue? Feeling any better?" He released his hold. "You came in like the dead last night."

"I'm fine."

"Better rest up, honey, this is your big day."

Not like I'd ever forget. Tonight, I'd stand up in front of the entire village and announce my stupid future, all the while dying inside. I could just see Dingle-Berry Gerry wagging his eyebrows and leering at me every second of the night.

Dad turned his attention to Fox. "Time to head back out and finish your chores, buddy."

Fox groaned. At least I had one thing going for me; it was the boys' week to do the morning chores, and Dad already smelled like wet possum hair. He dripped sweat. Our afternoon training session was going to be a nightmare.

School stopped teaching weapon training back in my parents' day, so my dad took it on himself to keep up the rigorous exercise schedule.

"Always be prepared! On alert! In control!" Dad would belt out. "This generation of kids is growing soft!"

He'd never continued on as a warrior himself but taught us that in this world we inherited, we needed to be able to fight and defend ourselves. Running, drills, lifting weights, sword wielding, and rifle shooting were just a few of the exciting activities on the list. Though I had to admit, the training did come in handy yesterday, with Kaleo acting all psycho.

"From what?" I'd once asked. "A zombie squirrel?"

The kitchen floor groaned as Dad sauntered over to Mama, stole a kiss, and grabbed some oatmeal. Kyra growled at the noise. Dad smiled with his dark dimples on full display. I swear you could fit a pecan pie in each cheek.

Mama held Baby Shenandoah on her hip and said, "Alright, Blue, time to stop moping and get outside. Mind taking a basket up to Mama Darla?"

I groaned as she placed a large wicker basket full of bread, eggs, and preserves on the table. She and I were the same height now. We had the same long, brown, curly hair, except I had a lot more of it. My hair had a mind of its own.

"Blue." Mama's voice took on a sharp edge. "You need some fresh air."

Baby Shenandoah's sticky fingers grabbed at my curls to bounce them.

"Well, excuse me if I'm having a hard time coming to grips with my sucky future that *you* are forcing me to live!" I grabbed the basket, then pulled Baby Shenandoah's tacky fingers from my hair. I swear her fat fist took about half my hairs with it.

Cora croaked, "You had seventeen years to get something better. Way to make 'em count, genius."

"*You're* a genius," I grumbled.

Cora beamed.

"A *dumb* genius." Man, I was the worst with comebacks.

I'd had enough of this house. It didn't help that I felt a pang of guilt every time I looked at Hawk's empty chair. Gripping the basket for Mama Darla, I ran out the back door.

Fresh air blew through my hair—instant relief from the stifling kitchen. My bare feet skipped along the smooth blue path leading out the door. Dad and I laid this path of flat rocks together when I was little.

A vision memory flitted before my eyes, washing over the blue stoned pathway.

"Daddy, why'd you name me Blue?"

He smiled, showing off both of his dark dimples and his bright white teeth. The wrinkles around his eyes were softer here. Younger. "Mama and I named you Blue 'cause you remind us of home. When we looked into your beautiful blue eyes on the day you were born, we knew you were special. Something about you reminds us of our little place nestled here in the Blue Ridge Mountains. It's like our own little piece of heaven on earth and it wasn't complete without you, Baby Blue."

I trod along the twigs and underbrush through the dark mist of the morning. It rained last night, just a little, and the air carried along a just-been-washed smell. Water particles kissed my corneas with a familiar pop of light as I walked along. I tried not to focus on it. Instead, I turned my attention to the cool, dewy grass beneath my bare feet.

Angel wings peeked over the top of the tree line, the tip of Lily's mama's stone angel statue. It sat on the roof of the rundown mansion Lily shared with her pop. Weeds and old rust-buckets lay strewn about their neglected farm like a hurricane dropped them off. Her mama's angel held a little baby in her arms. They'd both gone up to Jesus ten years ago now. Lily resembled her mama more and more the older she got. I wondered if that was what haunted her pop's eyes—made him so wild and frightening. Drove him to drinking all times of the day.

I pulled in a breath of fresh mountain air as I finished my trek through the valley and up to Mama Darla's. Maybe a new book or two would be just what I needed.

Dawn settled around Mama Darla's humble wooden cottage like an old friend. Dew glistened on every leaf and blade of grass framing the home. Wood logs lay in neat stacks next to the little brick chimney in even rows. Large planter boxes spilled with basil, cilantro, tomatoes, and okra. Peonies, roses, and daisies wound around fence posts on either side of her round front door—shaped as I imagined a hobbit door would be.

Mama Darla was basically my grammy. She'd raised my dad since the day "he'd come screamin' into God's green pavilion." Her twin sister, Catherine, died in childbirth, so my dad was left to Mama Darla's care.

She'd always known about my sight. She had a way of understanding people in a way no one else did. I needed to ask her about these new developments—the weird visions or whatever they were called.

No vapor rose from Mama Darla's cottage. Odd. She woke up long before the sun. A tug of worry gnawed at the edges of my thoughts as I reached the cracked cream paint of her front door and knocked. Mama Darla was old and had lived alone since my dad had grown. She might just box my ears for implying that she was helpless just by checking on her.

No answer at the front door, so I let myself in through the side, to the familiar sounds of wind chimes. My eyes adjusted to the dark of the kitchen in a blink as the sting of buttermilk and mildew filled my nose.

"Hello?" I called. "It's me, Blue. Brought you some bread."

The house held onto the chill of the night. Her kitchen was cozy, full of old wood cabinets and crocheted tablecloths. Dust motes danced in the sliver of morning light streaming through the windows. I didn't want to focus too close on those particles of dust we unwittingly breathed in all day. I made that mistake once and never wanted to think about it ever again.

The floors creaked and groaned, sounding every bit like their two hundred years. I peered into the living room. Mama Darla slept sprawled out on her recliner in front of the fireplace. She'd tucked a wool blanket over her lap. Books spread around her feet. Her rifle leaned against her armrest.

She'd just fallen asleep reading. Typical. The rifle? Not so much. *Why did she dig that old fossil out?*

Mama Darla was the Keeper of the Books and the storyteller of New Haven. There was no better library anywhere and no one who knew as much about the outside world than that snoring lady there. I smiled and reached over to tuck the blanket about her shoulders, jostling a book on her lap.

Like a fat lady to a flaky biscuit, my eyes snagged on the unfamiliar leather-bound journal laying open on her lap. An intricate sketch scratched into the paper. The masculine, sloped signature at the base of the page read *Raleigh Haven*.

The artwork drew me in like a demon to hellfire. Raleigh's full-scale drawing of a Shadow Elf jumped out of the page dealing a death blow. A sketch in motion, as though he'd scratched this image in a fever dream. Most of the paper had been etched to blackness with ink. Through the unmarked paper popped out sharp talon-like fingernails, slender and delicate, but poised to attack. Rags hung from its muscular form, a remnant of the human it'd once been. Elegant ears protruded through silky white hair. Its eyes were black, yet sparkled like stars. Unearthly. The teeth were not visible, but its face, mostly in shadow, was—beautiful?

A beautiful death.

Just like my vision with the green-eyed stranger boy. The creature behind him had been strangely alluring.

So, this was what they turned into. I'd never in my wildest dreams imagined they were so...pretty. The legends, the whispers—I'd heard the story of the elves my whole life, but I'd never seen any actual images from true eye witnesses. The survivors had seen enough. They'd wanted to forget.

So they filled our home with angels instead.

The Shadow Elves were beautiful, elegant, ethereal. The name had started long ago as a joke that went along with the virus's name, SE-23, but now that I'd seen a true sketch—the name Shadow Elves made sense.

"What're you doing reading over my shoulder?" Mama Darla's hand clamped down on my forearm. I squealed and she shut the journal with a quick snap. "Didn't your mama teach you any manners?"

My heart leapt into my throat. I shook my head, trying to clear away the image of that Shadow Elf from my eyes, but it was stuck like honey.

"Ha, that's what you get for waking an old woman." Mama Darla squeezed my cheek and smiled, still dizzy from sleep.

BLUE SHADOWS FALL | 55

A chill ran through me. Since she hadn't gotten her fire going, I busied myself with the kindling. I could do this with my eyes closed, though that elf was about sketched on the inside of my eyelids.

"You know I can do that myself." She stretched out, bending over to the side. Pops and creaks I didn't think were humanly possible sounded from her direction. But still, she made no move to get up and help with the firewood after all her fussing.

Mama Darla was all fuss and no fight.

"So, Miss Blue, why're you snooping around my house without so much as a good morning?" Mama Darla fanned herself in faux outrage. She'd tucked the journal down between her hip and the arm of the chair.

Interesting. She heaved her voluminous body out of her rocking chair, and I caught a flash of the journal behind her. Why was she keeping that book from me? She'd never withheld anything in her collection before.

"I'll go and put some eggs and tea on for us." She waddled into the kitchen. Black and silver curls bounced atop her head.

"I already ate," I said. "I'm just delivering a basket and hoping for a new book."

"Alright, darlin'." Mama Darla hummed an old gospel song I'd heard a thousand times as butter hit the frying pan with a sizzle. "You know you read through every comic and novel in my collection years ago!" She laughed to herself, but as she studied my face, her features softened. She could always read me. "Now you set yourself down and tell your Mama Darla everything."

So, we sat on the overstuffed couch and I gushed. I told her about my visions, the one with the raven and the one at the ceremony. She held my hand as I bumbled through the whole Kaleo burlap sack disaster when I got my heart broken. Tears streamed down my face as I complained about what my future held. My hopes for the warrior life were gone forever. I would be a farmhand at Jim's Dairy. Maybe I'd work my way up to milker or mechanic, but that was it—forever and ever, amen.

Through all of my crying and complaining, Mama Darla listened. Her beautiful, full face held only love. Mama Darla was always old, but never seemed to age. Though, her eyes—they darted over to her rifle and journal more than once.

"Listen, darlin', you are unique. One of a kind. So special, honey. More than I can say. I know it can feel lonesome to be the only one, but baby, it's just the way God made you. He made you *more*. And He put more in there for a *reason*. You just can't see it yet." As she spoke, her strong, full hands enveloped mine.

Guilt circled down into my stomach for sneaking a peak over her shoulder, but I pushed it away.

"You know what? I think I have just the book, honey. Come on back and let's have a look." Mama Darla heaved off the couch with a grunt.

I followed her through the living room and into my second favorite place in the world. Mama Darla's cottage was sweet and delightful on the outside—not much to see. It was meant to be a decoy for what lay in secret beneath.

The whole side of the mountain contained a large cavern carved out by time, water, and weather for millions of years. This humble cottage covered the entrance to the cavern flawlessly and unassumingly, protecting a priceless labyrinth of human knowledge in the sprawling caverns below. Everyone in New Haven had access to the materials kept here, but only Mama Darla and our family could go down into the caverns. We were bound to keep our knowledge protected in case of an unlikely invasion. Another relic of the old times.

I followed Mama Darla into the above-ground library, breathing deeply the hint of the heavy earth. Ancient shelves stretched floor to ceiling, covered in countless books, articles, and ladders that rolled along the walls. If you were looking for a library, this room would satisfy.

Mama Darla pulled down on the unremarkable book levers staggered about the room and an entire bookshelf groaned open. Blue electric lights buzzed above us as we descended the stairs into the cavern below.

I'd spent countless hours down in these tunnels, my eyes soaking up the art and books greedily. Useless DVD's lay beside priceless paintings, comics, vinyl records, and sculptures collected through the century after the Shadow War. This wealth of human knowledge could never be destroyed, but didn't have anywhere else to go. A catalog filled my eyes with every Star Wars, Marvel, DC comic, and Harry Potter reference, along with the movie covers I'd stared at for hours—especially Jurassic Park—imagining I could watch. We had power, but no functioning televisions. Tragedy at its core.

Mama Darla led us through a dusty old wing and lifted another faux shelf, revealing a worn pile of leather journals.

"This is one of a kind, now darlin'." Mama Darla caught my hands in hers. "This is the only one of its existence. It's about time you read your history. But I give you a piece of me when I hand you this book, and I'll be getting no rest until it's back in my wrinkled old hands."

Mama Darla handed over an old leatherbound journal, not quite as worn as the one I'd spied on her lap earlier.

"Thank you, Mama Darla! See you tonight."

She enveloped me in a warm hug, then I hopped out of the cavern and started down the worn mountain trail.

Halfway home, a faded yellow paper fell from between the journal's pages and fluttered into a blackberry thicket. I fished out the curious notebook paper and carefully unfolded it.

The writing was messy and stilted. Long-dried ink drops and tears littered the page.

I gasped, frozen in my steps. A voice cried from the grave.

It was written in Laurel Haven's own hand.

To My Children,
   We were animals.
   We are still. We are wild, feral things now. Even this pen, it feels

so strange in my hand. It's been too long. Usually when everything is quiet, the screaming begins. This quiet is different. It's the quiet before my death. I only have an hour, minute, maybe moments.

I don't fear death. Truly, I think heaven would scare me now more than hell. If I were to see the devil now, I'd laugh in his face, stab him through the heart, then we'd share a brandy.

Hardly anyone wrote down anything all these years. Years! A lifetime. And now I feel this urgency...as if the truths will be lost to time like sand between our fingers, slipping like my own life.

I couldn't believe I held Laurel Haven's hand-written note in my dirty hands. This was too precious to be shoved inside some old journal by accident. Had Mama Darla meant for me to find it?

Nineteen years? Twenty years now? I lost track, but someone will sort it out with the stars and get back to you. I was only 22 when the world ended. Happy. Unbroken. If I saw that girl now, I would weep. I mourn her easy smile and bubbling giggle. This war has raged a hole. Burned through my heart and changed me so thoroughly that all I can do is fight. Protect. Fear.

The only thing that gets me through is hope. In wrecking my life and soul, maybe you can have a real chance at living. At a future.

People got sick with the SE-23, so we built shelters, cared for the afflicted. The world pulled together. Then almost everyone died and everything went dark. Chaos reigned. The devil came out to play.

A few of us started to rebuild. We thought it was over. The plague was done! Ha. God mocked us, then left us to fend for ourselves. I still think aliens took over the bodies of the fallen. That's what the elves truly are—ha ha. Just another one of my hundreds of theories. But Raleigh thinks I just watched too many sci-fi movies. I don't care. I'll come back as an angel and prove him wrong.

I miss the movies. I miss popcorn. I miss butter the most.

But, life isn't what you think it'll be, is it? I always thought I'd be a dolphin trainer or an archeologist. Instead, I became a master in the art of killing. Bow, arrow, rifle, broken glass, sledgehammer, axe, screwdriver. Hell, I even killed a man using my bare hands and a rusty nail. He deserved what he got and worse. Elf-Wrender became my second arm.

I couldn't imagine this level of savagery.

The SE-23 mutated over time, getting stronger. Once infected, if the host didn't die, they'd start to change. Transform into these elf-like predators. Not quite vampires, not quite aliens. Beautiful. Lovely. No longer human, with a new intelligence. A new language and loyalty to their own.

We called them Nightstalkers.

Some called them Shadow Elves—that's the truer name. They wear the faces of your loved ones, but are more beautiful than you could ever imagine. Lovely things shouldn't draw you in and kill you. You almost want them to. They look like gods.

Raleigh's sketch dripped before my sight. They were lovely. Beautiful. Incredible.

We humans were already out of communication with each other. We were living in bunkers and makeshift camps, had no electricity, running water, hardly a scrap of food to speak of—then that mutation somehow took them over. We didn't stand a chance.

I couldn't imagine the shock when their loved fallen transformed into those beasts.

Chaos reigned, then we learned a trick or two. With the smoke, we started to fight back. We pushed them back to the cities. They can be killed by the sword or rifle if you're fast enough, but the smoke, that was the game changer. Your daddy knows. He'll write it down. And when he does, guard it with your life.

I hate the elves—but people? I almost wonder if humans are the worst of the evil in this world. The farther we traveled from the elf cities, the more communities of people we found were...wrong. Bad. Evil festering. We went in and cleansed them. The hurt and afflicted looked to us. We saved them from bad men who would take advantage of the weak. Of women in need. Of children.

The evil we saw...I wished for death more times than I can count.

My children. My beautiful and strong Kacey and Meredith. My loves, when I'm gone, remember why we killed all of those elves, but remember too why we killed all of those <u>people</u>. To save the poor and oppressed. Some, well, we can never know for sure.

Better to ask forgiveness than to be dead.

Find safety somewhere out there and take care of your poor daddy.

Love forever,

Your Mama

The buzz of the insects overwhelmed my senses as I stood on the side of the mountain. The words of my great-great-grandmother, Laurel Haven, filled my eyes as the ground seemed to dissolve beneath me, Mama Darla's book forgotten in the basket hanging at my side.

CHAPTER 8

Mildred Knows Best

KALEO

I smashed another nail into the fence with my hammer, whacking my thumb. Again. I growled and stuck my thumb in my mouth. First my nose, now my hand. I was losing it. How many nails had I hammered in my lifetime?

I'd been awakened this morning from my horrible nightmares by the clanking of pots. I cleared the stairs in one swift jump, hatchet in hand, to find two nanny goats waddling through my kitchen like they owned the place. And that smell far in the distance—always that metallic sting—was ever-present.

"You got lucky this time," I said to Lucy, my black goat. She stuck a tongue out toward my hatchet. I yanked it away and set it on the countertop. "That is *not* for eating."

Now I knelt by the fence behind my house. I'd been meaning to get around to this side of the farm all week, but things had come up. Bad things that threatened to tear into my dreams and rip out my soul with them. Mildred, my white spotted goat, pushed into my butt as I swore, thumb throbbing, then started my hammering again. Mildred laid her head on my knee.

"Thank you, Mildred," I said, "but I'm alright."

Why am I lying to a goat? I breathed in the sweet scent of alfalfa hay and freshly cut grass, chasing away the nightmares for now. A simple pleasure filled me. I enjoyed the work, getting my hands dirty in the damp earth. In the months that followed my mother's death, it'd been the farm, the animals, and land I'd worked that'd been my family. It was all I had.

Right after her death, two years ago, I'd shut up all the windows of our farmhouse. She was in every breath and thought. I'd held onto them like a greedy, selfish child, afraid the slightest wind would blow my mama's last scents from my memory forever.

Even from here I could pick out the musty burnt scorch mark on the oak table through the open window. It brought a flash of a smoking chicken roast. Mama had been too caught up in painting and the entire kitchen almost went up in flames. I'd shot a stream of well water from the hose and hit her square in the chest accidentally. She screamed in surprise, then let out a roaring laugh. We ended up sliding around on the kitchen floor, tossing the lesser-burnt morsels to each other across the kitchen island. The sharp scent of turpentine, sunflower oil, mud, and plants made up her mixed paint concoctions lining every available wall space. That was her. The scents practically radiated her contentment still.

In the months that followed my mother's death. I'd not only shut up the farmhouse, I shut myself off from everything and everyone. My senses dulled, my emotions along with them. Hawk and his father helped work my land. Jax, Dallas, and Brock's family pulled weeds and fed the goats, but I barely registered their appearances. I remained alone in my tomb of a house.

President Zhao, my mother's old friend, showed up on my doorstep. She brought baskets full of food and a no-guff attitude. She moved right in without a word. Mama gave me a safe place to survive my gift. But Zhao taught me how to hone it—sharpen it, forge it into a blade.

I've been working on opening the windows ever since to let the fresh air in, taking the scents of my mother with them, but never the memories.

"I'll be fine," I said to Mildred. "I just have to figure out what I'm gonna do." Another push from my goat's large head. "And, no, I don't have any more apples." I pulled my pockets inside out to emphasize the point.

My faith in our little village was collapsing, but I'd promised Zhao that I wouldn't go fishing for more information. She said she had it covered. The less I knew the better. Everything was fine.

But everything wasn't fine. The carefully built lies I'd been fed my entire life had crumpled—exposed as a façade.

Mildred picked up several nails with her tongue and sucked them in.

"No, girl!" I commanded, "Spit those out right now."

"Dang, Sniffles," Dallas crooned from across the field. "Talkin' to your goats again? What have we said about this?"

"Goats are *not* people," Jax recited next to him. "*People* are."

Both Dallas and Jax dismounted their horses and made their way through the field of circling goats to where I knelt surrounded by nails and broken fencing.

"Thank you for your words of wisdom," I said, unsurprised to see them. "Helpful as always." They probably thought they'd find me laid out dead in the field this morning. I hadn't missed a day of training since I'd been promoted to captain. The title still didn't fit right.

"Hey, we do what we can for your sorry butt." Dallas smacked me on the shoulder.

"What happened to your eye?" Jax wiped the sweat from his forehead, then tucked his brown hair under his baseball cap.

"Oooh, that looks bad!" Dallas shook his head, blond ponytail shooting a waft of his fresh tobacco-field scent. "One of these devil goats do that to you?"

My hands automatically went up to the bruises lining my eyes. "They only do that with you, Tex." My nose still throbbed. "They feed off your stupidity."

"Where were you this morning, Cap?" Jax asked. "I put the team through the drills, no problem, but it's not like you to just not show up."

Jax's agate blue eyes pierced through me like they always did. He had a depth—a substance to him—like a thick, unmoving boulder.

"Yeah, I was lookin' forward to kickin' your ass again." Dallas laughed. If Jax was a boulder, Dallas was a spazzy little tuft of goat fur, floating about wherever the wind would take him.

Dread pooled in my gut. These were my best friends. They'd fight off a gang of rabid buffalo for me, but I couldn't tell them a thing. My allegiance to New Haven and President Zhao came first. Again, I chafed against my orders. It was wrong.

Jax picked up my hammer and got to work on the last few boards without a word.

"I've just been a bit off," I answered truthfully.

"Well, we're about to change all that. C'mon." Dallas grinned and motioned with his head to follow. "Work's done for the day. Time to play."

I rubbed my sweaty hands down my shorts. "Alright, just got one more board."

Jax handed me the hammer. "Done. Let's go."

I went to grab my vintage Jurassic Park shirt hanging on the fence. It was utterly unwearable now, full of holes and grease stains, but it was comfortable.

"You don't need that," Jax said. "We're headed to the holler."

Dallas was a little less subtle. He wrenched the t-shirt from my grasp, tearing it further, then tossed it to the goats. Thinking it was food, they tore into it like a pack of rabid Shadow Elves.

"You can try, Sniffles, but no matter how big them muscles get"—Dallas punched me full on the chest—"You ain't ever gonna beat me for style. That shirt just needed to die."

I huffed out a laugh, but my thoughts landed unexpectedly on Blue. She'd read every single Jurassic Park novel and obsessed over the useless DVD's she'd never get to see. As if in answer, her scent floated toward me on a breeze. She had to be miles away. I breathed her in. Rich hazelnut and something sweet—poppies. She was across the river. I pulled in another breath, then another, trying to catch her. She was at Raleigh House, probably still sleeping.

"Hey, Sniffs." Dallas's eyebrow raised in question. "That apple pie comin' along alright?"

I startled, then shook my head. *What's my deal right now?* "Sure is. But your mom already asked me to dinner."

I punched Dallas with my middle knuckle protruding for maximum pain, then bolted to Hekili. Dallas roared after me. We climbed onto our horses and rode past the starchy corn fields and sweet soybeans, past the windmills and solar panels, to the bend of river we called the holler.

Glittering clouds of dragonflies surrounded the fish-tainted pool of water that slowed here, then jerked back into a swift flow carrying on toward Hayden Lake. The mossy stink of algae swirled, puffy white cattails floating in the warm breeze. Great blue herons dipped their beaks in the river searching after tiny minnows. I foraged some wild blackberries and green onions, reveling in the sweet and savory.

Jax and Dallas crashed into the water, sending the birds flapping. If this watering hole could talk, it'd tell a lifetime of stupid. Especially when Hawk was with us. There really was no limit to the amount of idiocy that boy could dream up.

He'd only been gone two days. He'd never believe what I'd been through back here in dear-old-sheltered New Haven. Maybe he'd know what to do about all this. He'd definitely hit me with some bad ideas.

Dallas climbed to the top of the waterfall and jumped like a flying squirrel off the top. Jax hooted, and I joined in. I needed this. I kicked off my boots and strode into the murky river. Maybe I'd just let myself float along for a while. I jumped the rest of the way in, reveling in the cool rush of water.

Dallas bobbed up from the water and spit out a mouthful. "There's a whole new brood of catfish upriver."

I recoiled. Dallas was the only other New Havener I knew with enhanced abilities, though I had a few suspicions about some others.

We'd known about each other's gifts since we were kids. Dallas and I were the only two who chose to eat lunch outside the school every day, even when rain fell in a deluge. The concentration of kid's lunches—the thick smell of cheese and certain meats almost always made me lose it. Dallas, on the other hand, couldn't handle all the tastes floating on the air. The information in the floating molecules of dry cornbread, honey ham, and baked beans overwhelmed him.

Our gifts were pretty similar, smell and taste. Connected, yet worlds different. Dallas could lick a boot and tell you who wore it and where they'd been. He was also a strict vegetarian. Too many memories and feelings remained locked in any meat he'd consume.

A wave of water hit me, and Dallas burst from the river, choking. Gasping for breath. "Somethin's wrong!"

Alarm peeled through me as his fear smashed into me like a tidal wave. Jax pushed his way out to him.

"I can taste it." Dallas's mouth twisted in disgust. "Somethin's not right."

He gagged and spit over and over. "Somethin's rotten. It's in the water."

CHAPTER 9

Daisies of Destiny

BLUE

I'd never worn a dress, not even to church on Sundays. Not many of us had skirts or dresses; they weren't very practical. But as I spun around in my bedroom, the light blue fabric of my dress hugged my waist and flowed out like a waterfall. Mama Darla did a good job stitching this one together. I bobbed along like a floating cloud in front of the mirror admiring the intricate belt of braided leather, beads, and golden threads cinched about my high waist. I was happy to see my curves filling out a bit.

But just as that little squeak of happiness poked in—worry for Hawk slapped it away. It felt stupid to be putting on a dress and celebrating, especially for an adulthood I dreaded. He was outside the wall right at this very minute. Had he run into any frightening outsiders? Or feral Shadow Elves craving the flesh of humans? Laurel's letter mentioned both humans and elves had survived out there for years. Why couldn't they be out there still?

These new visions troubled me.

The handsome green-eyed stranger smiled kindly at me among the tall glass buildings, reaching out a hand.

But that other vision with the two identical green-eyed strangers? One who held a sword to my neck, and the other stranger who'd spoken peace? Try as I might, I couldn't recall that frightening sight I'd had at the Warpath. I'd been looking through someone else's eyes. Impossible, yet somehow, I was sure of that fact. A chill crept over me, unsettling, like something sinister lurked in the blue shadows of the mountains.

I sighed and wiggled my bare toes. The only problem were the shoes. There was no way I was squeezing on Cora's fancy sandals, so barefoot it was, as always.

Something scuffled in the corner of the closet. Before I could investigate, Cora busted unceremoniously into the room, her black hair curled primly down her back, her face bright and dewy like some kind of impossible goddess. She was easily the prettiest girl in New Haven. She sauntered up behind me as I eyed her through the full-length mirror.

"Hey, Blue." Cora looked me over. "Thought you could use a little help. I brought your favorites for your hair. Just sit there. I'll do it."

She held thirty-seven beautiful blue daisies. Dad said they bloomed in the summer just to celebrate my birth. He changed their name from blue daisies to Blue's daisies—as if I were the master gardener of these flowers and orchestrated their blossoming to fit my own whimsy.

"And what are those for?" I asked.

Cora reeled. "Girl! Did I stutter? They're for your hair. Now sit down and shut up. This is not a night for your wild hair."

She rubbed a little walnut oil in her hands and smoothed down my frizz. The threads of hair combined as the facets of molasses, amber, and copper whirled together—each curl in its place. When she finished, she pinned the blue daisies in a crown around my head like a seamstress with a death wish.

"Ow!" I smacked at her hands.

Cora smiled and continued to stab the pins straight into my skull with no apologies. "Pain makes pretty, see?" She spun me around to face the mirror.

I took in her finished work, but all I could see was the end of my childhood and the slow, steady boredom of nothingness that was to come. Tears pricked at the corners of my eyes.

"Look, I know it's not easy to stand up there and announce your terrible future to the world, but"—she wrinkled her nose—"try to look on the bright side."

"The bright side of cow manure and Dingle-Berry Gerry?"

Cora bit her lip. "It'll be fine. It's better than being on sewage detail."

"I'm on *cow* sewage detail, Cora."

"Right. Well, I know how to make you feel better." One look at my face had Cora's eyes alight. "I'll make Kaleo ask you to dance, but not in an obvious—"

"No! I would actually die! I *never* want to see him. Ever again."

"What? I thought all you *wanted* to do was look at him."

"Never again. I hate him."

She had no idea the pain he'd put me through. Peach flushed my cheeks in splotches—humiliation, shame.

"Right." Cora rolled her eyes. "Well, there's no way you'll be able to go the whole night without seeing him, so, can't wait!" She smiled wickedly and swept out of the room.

My stomach twisted. If I caught just one glimpse of Kaleo, I'd pray for one of the mountain tops to fly off and smash me into oblivion, then lightning to strike my pile of crumbled bones.

My blue eyes seemed to flash in the reflection. I'd never be a beauty like Cora, but my eyes sparkled like minty icicles. Russet brown ringlets dripped over my shoulders and down my back. Bouncy and in check. No frizz, at least for now. I might even have grown into my button nose a bit. I was...kinda pretty.

A small smile formed on my lips—wait—are those greens stuck in my teeth? How long had those been in there?

That was another problem with my "gift." I marveled in the infinite beauty from the grand to the microscopic. But flaws? Those seemed to jump out to me in great detail—all the time. The spot where my bushy eyebrows weren't symmetrical or the faint scar on my cheek that stood out like a brand. Back when I was seven and I thought I was tough enough to wield Dad's sword, Elf Wrender. No one noticed the scar anymore, but I always did.

Whimsical flowers framed the tall mirror over my dresser. Dad painted them years ago. He made sure to add my blue daisies on my tenth birthday, to solidify their permanence in my garden.

In a blink, I watched as he painted the delicate flowers on the old wooden mirror those years ago.

The tiny paintbrush was at such odds with his massive fingers, and yet his hands moved deftly. With a few precise movements, a leaf appeared. He scattered several different flowers on the dresser as he worked. The strong perfume of the dogwood mingled with the roses in the slow breeze.

"You'll be surprised with how many people paint from their ideal. What they think something should look like. They don't stop and actually look at their subject," Dad explained as he worked. "Don't paint an object the way you think it looks. Or worse still, the way you wish it looked. Paint it as it is. Beauty and flaws. Life and decay. Nothing's perfect, Baby Blue. But it's beautiful all the same."

Art filled our home from every generation of Havens at Raleigh House. From Raleigh himself, who'd been an architect in his former life and rebuilt this old home, to my dad and siblings. Artistic talent ran in the family. I thrilled at the flowers and forest life covering our mirrors and walls. Great blue oceans, glittering cities, and snow-capped mountains told stories of where we'd been and where I'd never go.

Another scuffling sounded from the closet. It had to be another gross mouse.

"Tiger!" I called, "Dinner!"

Where was that cat when I needed him? I squealed and grabbed a nearby blanket to throw over the little critter. Better to catch it. This was Fox's arena. My little brother always had a stray or two he tried to tame. That's how we'd gotten our current rat-catcher, Tiger. From what we knew, Tiger was the last of his kind.

I crept slowly over to the closet door, careful not to swish my skirt on the ground and give myself away. A sniff sounded from behind the closed door. *Gross.* My heart leapt. I hadn't really liked rodents much since a feral possum bit my toe a year ago—except in stew.

My disgusted expression reflected back at me from the brass closet handle as I grasped it and pulled.

"Hah! Got you!" I hollered a mighty war cry and I threw the blanket of doom upon the poor creature. I jumped on top of the blanket—a jumbled commotion of tiny limbs and elbows flailed beneath me. The creature beneath me surged with a screech and wailed on me like a wild banshee.

I don't have a lot of experience with wild banshees, but I've had years of experience with furious little sisters, and well, within seconds I realized my mistake.

"Truce, Kyra! Please stop smacking my head!" I shrieked.

With a huff, the rowdy, squealing blanket gave up and fell on top of me in a sweaty heap. I struggled with the bundle of skinny, tangled limbs, careful not to mess up my hair that had been perfect, literally thirty seconds ago.

"Kyra! What're you doing? You scared the devil outta me."

One look in the mirror and my worst fears were realized. I was a hot mess of hair and flower petals. Why even try? I was about to light back into Kyra when I noticed she hadn't budged from where I tossed her. She laid out on our scratched wood floor covered in her patchwork blanket, cradling her head.

Anger fizzled out of me like steam from a teapot. This was Kyra. The unstoppable girl. She'd once been stung by no less than fifteen bees and didn't let out a single tear. She'd shaken her fist at those bees and dared them to come closer.

Kyra never showed signs of weakness. I got down next to her and attempted to comfort her.

"Stop! Mmmmmpfh!" she mumbled between sobs and pushed me away.

But I held her fast, stroking her through the blanket. Eventually she relaxed from a hard, stiff ball of a raging storm to a soft and steady calm.

We sat for a time in the quiet of our room. No sound but the gentle breeze tinkling the seashells hanging from the ceiling. A soft, buttery light streamed in from the window, the last light of day.

Kyra emerged from the blanket like a freshly birthed foal. A hot and sweaty mess of knots and rumpled clothes. At this point, Tiger found Kyra's lap and purred happily. She stroked him and sighed.

"What does it feel like to see so much?" Kyra whispered. "Do your eyes ever hurt?"

No one had ever asked me that before. No one.

I swallowed back my surprise. "In the beginning, when I was a very little kid, I felt like there was...sand in my eyes. They felt gritty, and it hurt when I opened them because I would see too much."

No one ever wanted to hear about my gift being hard. My siblings got mad if I ever mentioned the pain or intensity. Mama even said I sounded like "a cat complaining about too much cream."

"I liked the dark. The shadows and sunset. The bright sun and daytime were painful. Too many colors. It would stress me out to be somewhere with a lot of moving things. School was really hard for me, but I didn't want to stay home. What helped me most was when I learned to focus on one thing. Like the sky or a pencil or my fingerprints. Sometimes I get lost in the detail, but it's better to get lost in one small thing than in a hundred different shapes and textures and patterns competing all at once."

Kyra wrapped Tiger tighter in her arms.

"But, I struggled a lot until I told Mama Darla. She taught me to focus. That it wasn't a curse, but an amazing superpower. She gave me tons of comics, like Superman. He had x-ray vision so of course he was my favorite. I wanted to be just like him. Plus, I kinda had a crush on him from the covers of those old DVDs."

"Don't blame you," Kyra said.

I giggled. "Anyways, I started exercising my eyes—training them. I still get overwhelmed by color or intense patterns, but I know what to do now. I'll close my eyes and clear my head. It helps. It's not all bad. I bet you no one in the world is a better shot than me, probably ever in the history of the world. So, that's cool."

But Kyra continued to stare off, eyes red. Kyra never accepted help from anyone. But whatever this was? She'd have to let go of her stubbornness.

Might as well ask a tree to have a seat.

"What are you holding on to?" I prodded. "You sound like you're holding your breath."

She shook her head, her bottom lip protruding. Stubborn thing.

"You can trust me, 'Rae. I'm different. Strange. I've always been an outsider. But I'm okay with that now."

The truth of that statement resonated—struck me to my core. I *was* okay with being different. Maybe I'd started to grow into it.

Light filtered in through the windows highlighting Kyra's golden curls. They glowed like spun sugar. A fluffy, golden halo. Forty-seven freckles peppered her cheeks. She was so beautiful. A beautiful little mystery.

Kyra's golden eyes brimmed with tears as she whispered, "I can hear your heartbeat now. I always hear it. It changes when you're happy or sad, scared, or excited. I know yours from Cora's and Hawk's and Fox's and everyone else in this family. I can hear you from miles away."

"What?"

Tears dripped from her eyes. "Breathing, crying—hiccups are the worst!"

"Chewing at breakfast?" I asked.

"Ugh. Oatmeal's the worst and Dad makes the *grossest* sounds ever. I just wanna explode!" A laugh escaped through her tears.

I found my eyes stinging, too.

"You have enhanced hearing, Kyra?" I shook my head in disbelief. "How long?"

Her eyes dropped to Tiger and the room fell quiet. Seashells tinkled from the ceiling, and Tiger's purr filled the room. Mama and

Cora clanked pots and pans in the kitchen below, gathering food for the graduation tonight.

"I think...I've always been able to hear more than other people, since I was born, like you. Mama and Daddy said I was always quiet. I don't think I liked crying, even as a baby. It's too loud. I remember when I was two or three, I'd hear scratching outside all night long. I thought it was people building a house next to us. I'd ask Mama about when my best friend's house was gonna be finished. She never really understood. I'd hear them digging and tunneling at night, but never saw the work in the daytime. It wasn't until I was older that I realized it was a family of rabbits making that sound." Relief flowed out of her like a gushing waterfall. "And crickets—they are the *screechiest*! They sound like thunder crashing in my ears. They keep me awake till Tiger's purring finally drowns them out. They're constant. Dumb bugs."

That was my tough lil' Kyra, getting mad at crickets.

"Well, good news is, you're not going crazy. You're *gifted* like me. Don't you feel *special*? Isn't it just the best thing ever?" I joked. "But you're not alone. It's you and me."

Her face shifted to a tentative smile. Relief. I promised to take her to Mama Darla's and show her the Superman comics later. I told her all about what he had to do to adjust to earth after being born on a different planet, Krypton. Her eyes went wide at that.

"Is that where our powers come from? Are we from a different planet too?" she wondered aloud.

Laurel's words popped into my eyes. *"I still think aliens took over the bodies of the fallen. Ha ha."*

Not funny.

"I don't really know, but I can still see the day you were born like it was five seconds ago. Mama's tummy grew humongous. She screamed and hollered all night at Dad." I laughed. "You actually did kinda look like an alien with your smashed up head."

Kyra whacked my leg.

"I'll take you to Mama Darla's later, but right now, I gotta fix the mess you made of my hair."

"Hey, you jumped on *me!*"

The clock on the nightstand read just after five-thirty, and graduation was at seven. We crawled up to the mirror and sighed at our pitiful reflections. Twin disasters.

"Need some help getting ready?" I nudged her as a giggle escaped my lips. "Cora! We need you again!"

Kyra shot me a scowl.

"Oops, no yelling." I snatched her back up in the blanket and tossed her on the bed, lighter than I'd felt in days.

CHAPTER 10

Pledging Away My Happiness

BLUE

With a good hour to go until the ceremony, my twenty-seven classmates gathered around the few designated tables closest to the stage in the middle of the square, dressed in their lightest and brightest.

I took in every familiar face. We'd known each other our entire lives. I could tell you a good day's worth of stories about everyone. Most of us went as far back as the sunny evenings our mamas spent gossiping while breastfeeding us on our front porch rocking chairs. Our lives all planned out, we precious babies would mold this tough world we'd inherited into a better place. The next generation was always the answer to solving this generation's problems.

That was always the hope. And hope was what New Haven was built on, what was in its bones. Hope was buried beneath the white angels in the wood, cemented in the logs that built the first tiny homes and each building and creation since. Hope was in each seed planted.

We mingled by the wooden stage built into the side of a massive red oak tree, thick and gnarled with age. The branches stretched high above our heads, offering a beautiful canopy draped with hundreds of lanterns. Electric lights flickered within, reflecting from the white tablecloths to the excessive fruit pies.

I wanted to ride Pepper with a hot guy to the edge of the world with the wind in my hair.

I wanted to disappear into the woods, rip off this stupid dress, and float down the creek.

I wanted to kiss a boy; I didn't care who. Even Ferret-Face Frankie would do.

I wanted a massive whoopie pie all to myself—extra cream.

What I did not want was to commit to a lifetime of cow droppings.

And where the heck was Lily?

The band, Apocalypse Here, took the stage and kicked off their set. They knew every pre-war pop song in our collection. Hayden Bradshaw, an original Founder, was the hero to thank for that. Some say it took him fifteen years to compile our collection of music. When the world began to change, he'd known it was a matter of time before all of the computers and cell phones quit working, so he set to work gathering as many songs as he could. Sheet music, lyrics, instrumentals, vinyl...our town's collection was thousands strong.

The lead singer, Dallas—named after his ancestor from Texas—screamed out the words to "Free Fallin'" along with the drums, banjo, bass, harmonica, and electric guitar. His long, blond, sweaty hair flying. No shirt, no shoes. Just a pair of tight leather pants painted on his muscular thighs and a large gold earring gleaming on his upper ear.

Six-pack abs. Eighty-seven sweat droplets on his left pec. He got those muscles from his warrior training. He was a Falcon, on Kaleo's team.

I avoided his eyes, too. I imagined the two of them sharing a laugh over my fiasco with the burlap sack down by the outer wall.

Far on the other side of the festivities, Kyra kept an eye on a determined baby Shenandoah. She waddled closely behind partygoers carrying plates piled high with goodies, hoping for a small morsel to drop. Her plump fingers and cheeks were filthy with sticky frosting and dirt.

"Hellooooo Keeerrraaaah," I whispered, impossible to hear in this raucous crowd and live music. Lottie currently slayed the guitar solo in "November Rain" by Axel Rose.

Kyra's head snapped up. She stared at me from across the dessert table, her mouth quirked in a smile. My heart jumped.

She mouthed, "I can hear you. Stop being so annoying."

My eyes bulged. *No way.* "What the ham sandwich, Kyra? Are you messing with me?"

"Nope." She grinned. "And a ham sandwich sounds real nice right now, thanks."

"I ain't getting you no sandwich," I hissed. "You get me one. It's my graduation."

We both laughed, and I shook my head. What did this mean? What did it mean for *her*? For us? Were we the first of many, or had others been enhanced before?

Griff wandered past me through the dancing crowd, eyes searching wildly.

"I can't believe it's our night, Griff!" I grabbed his elbow and brought him to my table.

"Yeah, time and motion and cosmos spinning and whatnot—" Griff barely acknowledged my existence as he continued his search for Lily, obviously.

Where was she anyway?

After a jam of original songs, the band switched seamlessly to another favorite: "Lose Yourself" by Eminem. I welcomed the distraction and sang along to every word at the top of my lungs. The setting sun cast a brilliant orange halo over the evening. It was the magical time of night when you could imagine fairies and unicorns were real, and if they'd only just appear, they'd grant you a wish.

I swallowed hard, trying not to get lost in all of the movement, shapes, and lights around me. I *wanted* to lose myself like Eminem. I wanted to give in, to let the sweet static and pandemonium pull me under so I didn't have to do this tonight. It always took more determination to be focused. Centered.

I closed my eyes, willing the lights and shapes away. Willing away the hope and excitement. Willing away the vision of Kaleo's hate-filled face and the cutting words he'd spewed at me.

"You ain't nothing. Know nothing. Saw nothing. Got it?"

I prayed he was on border patrol or a secret mission to the moon or something. But as soon as I opened my eyes, they landed right on him.

Kaleo dismounted his horse by the back fence. I drank him up like a catfish in the desert, eager to take him in without his notice. The floating lights caressed his sharp features as he stood, a hand in his pocket, relaxed, eyes closed. He stood a head taller than everyone around him. His long, jet black hair lay down past his shoulders, still damp from a fresh shower. A blue bruise rimmed his left eye—a souvenir from me breaking his nose.

I smirked. *Good.*

His crisp, white collared shirt contrasted beautifully with his brown skin. Creamy linen pants hung loosely around his waist. I noticed with a thrill that he, too, was barefoot.

He seemed calm, relaxed, as he took in a long, slow breath. His eyes flicked open and locked on mine from across the square. Adrenaline rushed through my veins like a fire hose.

Stupid Kaleo. Go away.

"Hey, Blue." Griff handed me a napkin. "This is for your drool."

"Shut up." I bumped Griff with my elbow then slumped my head onto his shoulder, eager to distract myself. "So, you ready to work with the engineer geeks? Start building cars that launch into space?"

But he'd started scanning the crowd again, now oblivious to the fact I'd attempted to have a conversation.

"She's not here yet," I grumbled. "Griff, when are you just going to tell Lily how you feel? Just get it out there, y'know?"

"Who?" he asked absently, still scanning the crowd. He ran a hand through his hair. He was adorable. He'd really tried to look nice tonight.

Griffin's Dad, General Rose, silver hair sticking straight up on the sides in a buzz, neck about as thick as his muscular shoulders, strolled toward us. He'd just finished talking to my parents and my mom watched with feigned disinterest from behind the table as General Rose smacked me on the back.

Ow.

"Well, Lil' Haven," General Rose boomed over the music. "Your mother tells me you'll be over at Jim's. 'Sa pity we couldn't bring you onto the team, kid. Believe me, that brother of yours is a pushy one, too." Another smack on the back that landed like a brick.

Of course Hawk had tried to get me recruited. Maybe he wasn't such a punk after all.

"I wanted it too, sir," I said.

"I think I'd trade you for that Hawk any day, truth be told." Rose winked, then strolled off, hands clasped behind his back.

Griffin rolled his eyes, and guilt filled my heart. Not for the first time, I wished Griff's dad didn't treat me better than his own son.

"Nice to see my invisibility potion's working," Griffin said dryly.

"Seriously."

The first notes of a slow song began and someone tapped on my shoulder. I turned around and disappointment curled in my gut.

Ferret-Face Frankie stood before me, hat in hand.

Great. This night was just getting better and better.

"Wanna dance?" Frankie's bottom lip cracked almost as much as his voice.

"Got some of that potion for me?" I whispered to Griffin. I stood and smiled kindly at Frankie. "Sure."

He slid his bony hand into mine and led me to the dancefloor.

Where the crud was my wingman, Lily? Whatever a wingman was.

"You'll never believe what I got!" he began, but my eyes zeroed in on his skin and his words drifted far away.

Fifty-seven blackheads, ready to go.

Two extra-long black nose hairs curled up around the edge of his nostril—

"Blue? Did you hear me? It's a one-hundred-fifty-seven-year-old mint condition six-inch Luke Skywalker Black Echo edition," Frankie emphasized. "Did you know it was the rarest—"

"Excuse me." Kaleo's rumbling, deep voice sent a jolt of lightning down my back. "Mind if I cut in?"

My face burned as Ferret-Faced Frankie and I gawked up at Kaleo. His dark eyes locked on mine.

"You ain't nothing. Know nothing. Saw nothing. Got it?"

"Uhh...yeah, sure," Frankie squeaked and dropped his hands from my waist. "I...I'll tell you more about it later, Blue, I guess."

This was not happening. My stomach plummeted to my ankles— I couldn't move as Kaleo towered over me in the center of the dance floor. The cool grass beneath my feet turned to quicksand.

"Well, actually," I rallied, "I was gonna go get a drink." I spun away from Kaleo and stomped toward the refreshment table, my heart flying like a kite. I couldn't look at him. Couldn't touch him. He'd treated me worse than some dirty outsider.

Rage burned through the string and my heart kite crashed into the ground.

Kaleo grabbed my hand. "Aw, come on and dance with me, Freckles. Please?"

His smile could melt the Sahara Desert. Wait, was that a thing? I don't know. Couldn't think. Was this real life?

"You're the worst," I said.

Kaleo curled his arm around my waist and pulled me to him, then spun me slowly as the sun took its time setting behind the tops of the mountains in a golden, glowing haze.

The silence was almost too much, but I'd gladly go through hell and back before I'd talk first.

"Y'know," Kaleo started, "I've been wanting to talk to you for days, Blue. Ever since, y'know, when—"

"You tackled me to the ground? Yelled at me?" I stiffened. "Or was it all the other really jerk-move things you did? I have a list."

"Yes," he breathed, "when I did that." He scanned left and right, the rapid beat of his pulse speeding faster in his neck. He leaned in close—heat and the smell of fresh pine rolled off of him in waves. Dang, now my heart was racing too.

"I was doing my job," he whispered into my ear, sending chills down my spine. "I was...not myself. Look, I'm sorry. I just wanted to tell you...don't go back to that place down by the wall, okay? Things are...not safe."

A warning? Why? "What was in that burlap sack, Kaleo?"

He pulled me forward, grasping my shoulders as he searched my eyes. "It's dangerous. Even *talking* about certain things is dangerous. If the president were to catch you out in that part of the south wood, I wouldn't be able to protect you. Promise me. Just, promise me you'll never go back out there."

"Why? What is it?"

He huffed out a deep breath, sending the brown curls framing my face spinning. "Is it not enough to ask you to trust me?"

"Not really." I raised an eyebrow. "You've been acting like a fool."

He chuckled and shook his head, that same laugh I'd chased for years. The song should have been over minutes ago, but I could've sworn Dallas threw in a whole third verse and extra chorus. I looked over at the stage, and Dallas shook his sweaty hips suggestively. Did he just...*wink?* At *me?*

I frowned. "Is this song, like, extra-long, or what?" The image of Dallas's thrusting hips would be etched onto my eyes forever.

"Huh? I hadn't noticed." Kaleo's cheeks reddened. He ran a large hand through his silky black hair, sending a waft of clean air my way.

Was he acting...shy?

He took a deep breath. "You're right. Trust goes both ways."

I nodded, not sure what he had in mind. Kaleo grasped my hand, a question in his eyes. He gestured towards the weeping willow on the hilltop beside the square. "It's so loud down here, do you mind going somewhere quieter? Just for a minute?"

I wrinkled my nose.

"I'm not going to attack you again." He pointed to his black eye. "I already learned my lesson."

"Fine," I replied as my heart leapt.

Kaleo led me away from the square, up a small hill and under the swaying branches of the old willow. He dropped my hand, and we sat in the cool grass. We were far from the churning crowd below but the band's original downhome music floated up to us through the evening's warm breeze.

We sat beneath the willow for a time, watching the crowd spin in circles below us. My heart was doing more impressive gymnastics flips than my twelve-year-old self could ever imagine.

"So." Kaleo began, lip trembling slightly. "There was actually something I wanted to tell you. Tonight."

He huffed out a breath and turned his eyes up toward the stars, then seemed to find the grass more intriguing as he spun a dandelion. His hand went through his hair again.

"I wasn't even going to come tonight, but I just"—he shook his head—"felt really bad about how I acted, y'know, out in the woods. And I couldn't stand the thought of you..." Kaleo's throat bobbed as he swallowed. His large fingers continued to crush that poor dandelion into a squishy blob. "...I don't know...thinkin' badly of me, or that I meant you harm."

His eyes were everywhere except on me—but mine? I soaked him up in the faint silver moonlight, lost for words. Afraid to ruin this moment, but not knowing what this moment really meant.

Kaleo's chocolate eyes found mine under the willow tree and he whispered, "You're not the only one in New Haven with enhanced abilities."

CHAPTER 11

Three Dead Dandelions

BLUE

I sat rooted to the spot as my world tilted. What? How did Kaleo know about me? Did he know about Kyra? How would I keep her safe?

"I don't know what you're talking about," I chirped. "I don't know anyone who—"

Kaleo's half smile caught me off kilter. "C'mon, Blue. I've always known you were different. You've never been good at hiding your feelings, especially when everything is so...overwhelming."

I shook my head, ready to deny him again, yell at him, scream—

"How could you have followed me through the woods yesterday? I knew I'd lost you. No one could've tracked me out that far. But you?"

My face flushed with heat. "You're jumping to a lot of conclusions—"

"It was out by Raleigh's Sorrow," Kaleo continued as if I hadn't even spoken. "Remember that time, what was it? Eight years ago? That year you followed Hawk, Jax, and me out there?"

I was *not* having this conversation.

"Our stupid tradition where we go out and jump in the frozen lake after the first thaw. We told you to stay home, but you wouldn't have it." Kaleo chuckled. "Even at nine, you were a force to be reckoned with."

A laugh bubbled up my throat. "Y'all thought you were *so* brave. I had to prove that girls were better than boys."

"We pushed and shoved each other." Kaleo's eyes gleamed. "No one was willing to take the first plunge, and here you come, flying out of the woods like a screaming banshee, straight through the ice into that freezing water."

We chuckled. It was one of my prouder moments. I could almost feel the frozen shock of that water now.

Kaleo plucked up another dandelion and tore it to shreds. "There you sat, shivering on the banks, daring the rest of us to jump. The ice was so thick. Opaque. Impossible to see through."

I replayed that moment in my eyes. *Jax, a scrawny ten-year-old in his little shorts, shook next to Hawk and Kaleo on the banks of the lake. Puffs of hot breath, snowballs flying. Jax declared he was going to jump through the hole he'd made with a large rock and swim under the ice all the way to the hole I'd made when I jumped. None of us actually thought he would do it. But then he jumped...and disappeared.*

"He was gone," Kaleo continued, "stuck under that ice for forever. We couldn't see him, couldn't find him, until you..."

I nodded, but my stomach squirmed.

Jax struggled under that ice. A wild, trembling shadow. Pure terror in his eyes.

"You ran straight to where he was without a moment's hesitation and jumped," Kaleo said. "You saved his life."

Kaleo's eyes landed on mine for the first time in minutes. "That's when I knew—"

Worry spiked through me.

"—you were like me."

I met his gaze as my heart exploded from my chest. *Kaleo* was like me?

Kaleo's lip quirked. "Why'd you think I was up at your house all the time all those years? Hawk was always trying to get away, but me? I'd finally found a place where I belonged."

"You've always ignored me." I shook my head. "Treated me like an annoying baby."

"I was stupid. Hawk has always been so protective of you," he said. "I could never let on that I found you—"

A warm breeze ruffled my brown curls.

Kaleo's smile wavered, and he glanced back down to wretched dandelion number three. "Has anyone ever told you that you smell like hazelnuts?"

I released a breath and giggled. "What?"

He huffed out a tentative laugh, eyes peeking through a veil of ebony hair. "I could tell you every single dessert on that table back there, based on their scent alone."

He was confessing *his* gift to me. His gift of smell.

A smile touched my lips. "Hazelnuts?"

My stomach flipped as Kaleo smiled back, beautiful teeth glinting in the moonlight, real relief in his eyes. "Yeah, hazelnuts and poppies. It's nice, really nice."

Oh. My heart melted into a puddle of gooey-ness.

He ran a hand through his hair again. It fell in raven black ribbons around his shoulders.

"How does it work?" I asked gently. I knew what it meant for him to trust me with this. It was amazing. Eyes, ears, now smell? What other gifts were out there?

Kaleo closed his eyes and took in a long, slow breath. "Well," he said. "You must've had your blue daisies in your hair earlier today, but"—he reached a hand into my curls and plucked out a stray daisy, pressing it into his nose—"they must've gotten smashed or ruined. Your hair is covered in the smell of 'em, but now you have a beautiful crown of dogwood flowers."

I must've missed that daisy when I'd hastily fixed up my hair. He tucked the daisy into his shirt pocket, and my heart exploded.

I cleared my throat. "And that sack out by the wall?"

His smile fell. "I thought I'd smelled something out there. Something new. I was wrong." His mouth said the words, but his eyes seemed far away. "I'm just ashamed of making such a big deal out of nothing. I'm sorry. Truly. I never should've said those things to you."

"You ain't nothing. Know nothing. Saw nothing. Got it?"

I opened my mouth to speak when a glimmer of lavender flared miles away. A flash of blonde hair. My eyes focused unbidden on Lily riding down the mountain like the Shadow Elves were tearing after her soul.

Tears streamed down her face.

Dress covered in dust.

A scratch down her arm.

Fingernails caked in mud.

Lily's horse, Bruno, galloped full speed. She was chasing after someone.

Her pop, Joshua, stumbled up ahead toward town, red faced, his scraggly beard pasted to his cheeks. His eyes were wild, frantic. He waved his arms as if swatting at a swarm of angry mosquitoes, but nothing was there.

Kaleo followed where I looked and breathed deeply through his nose. "Fear. Joshua Potts is steeped in it."

He could smell *emotion* too?

I rose quickly. "No, he's just drunk again. Having another one of his episodes."

I hated that man.

"I don't smell any alcohol on him. Let me help—"

How could Kaleo smell alcohol from here? They were miles away.

"No. Lily doesn't want a scene. I'll go." I turned back to Kaleo, whose eyes flickered with worry. "Listen, thanks for talking to me and trusting me with your gift. I can't even wrap my mind around it. All this time I've felt so alone. Like I was bad somehow. *Weird.*"

Kaleo smiled. "Oh, you're plenty weird."

I smacked his shoulder with a giggle.

"You sure you don't want my help?" Kaleo's eyebrows knit together.

"Lils would be so embarrassed for anyone else to see her pop like that. I got this," I said. "But, I'll see you later tonight, okay?"

Kaleo nodded, smiling wider than I'd ever seen in my life. I focused in on his beautiful face as long as I could, memorizing every sharp plane and soft line. I might die happy right there beneath that tree.

But Lily needed me.

I kept my eyes trained on Lily as I ran toward my horse. Anger and worry ripped through me in equal force. She wore one of her best dresses, which wasn't much, patched up and sewn together more times than I could count. Well, I probably could. I could make out the threads from here, even miles away in the dim light of the evening.

Face, arms, hands, dirt, but no bruises. That was always my biggest fear, that Joshua would end up hurting her, but he'd never so much as raised a hand to her. It was the drinking, the swearing, the wildness in his eyes. Lily had been working since her mama died. She was always chasing after him, taking care of him, feeding him. No child should have that much weight on their shoulders.

I focused on Lily's mouth as I ran.

"Papa, nothing's there!" Lily shouted as she caught up to him in a field of wildflowers by the schoolhouse. "Calm down. It's okay."

"I see 'em. They're comin'!" he screamed, his eyes wide. "They're everywhere!" He sunk to the ground, the heels of his hands pressed into his eyes, dirty blond hair matted to his head.

I ran down the small hill, my dress flowing like a flag in a gale. The horses were kept in the hitching lot to the left of the square. I raised a quiet thanks to the heavens above that Pepper had been hitched up in front. I could avoid the horse poo gauntlet with my bare feet. *Thank you, angels of mercy!*

I untied Pepper's leather strap. "Let's go, Pepper! Lily needs us."

As soon as we reached open ground, we took off at a gallop. Lily radiated a low-burning lavender light. I'd never seen it as a sad color before, but as I guided Pepper toward Lily, her color exuded immense sorrow.

Bruno stood in a vast field of wildflowers, Lily still straddling the saddle on his back. Her light flared from the dull lavender into a startled brighter purple as Pepper and I approached. A path of smashed wildflowers indicated Lily's pop had tripped off toward home.

A hot tear trailed down my cheek as I faced my best friend. I slid off Pepper and raised my arms up to Lily. She was so thin and frail. So weak.

She fell into my arms and we collapsed onto the soft clovers.

Lily released the dam holding back her flood of tears and we both wept.

The sun set in a brilliant fuchsia behind the curve of the mountains, leaving the gentle stillness of twilight. Wind ruffled the tall grass as the lightning bugs danced in gentle orbits.

"Lily, I was looking everywhere for you." I stroked her shoulder as she lay curled up in the grass, her head in my lap.

"He's calmed down. He's gone home now," Lily whispered. "This was the worst I've ever seen."

I pulled the blonde hair from Lily's eyes. "Remember when we became besties? Right here in this very spot? You grabbed my hair and pulled as hard as you could 'cause you thought I was going to tell my daddy that you didn't have lunch again." I wiped a tear from my eye. "You've always been brave, always been willing to stand up for those you love."

"But you think I should stop believing in...him," Lily murmured. "He's never struck me once. Never hurt me. It's like I'm not even there. But he's sick. It's like he's seeing something else, Blue, and he's so scared. I can't leave him. He needs me."

Silence stretched on between us, then Lily cried, "But I'm just so tired!"

She whined like a wounded dog as her body shook. I'll never forget the sound as long as I live. I would never forgive him. Never, for putting my beautiful Lily through this. I felt a lurch as a small piece of my heart hardened to stone.

"He doesn't deserve your faith in him. Only God can heal him now. You've tried. For the last ten years you've tried. All it's done is tear you apart—" My voice broke on the last word.

She'd run to my house so many nights, I couldn't keep count. Most of the time she'd sneak into our house at two or three in the morning, shaking and crying. She'd slip into our crowded bed and slowly fall asleep.

I never understood why she'd always go back to him. My dad and I would take her back home the next day, but I never went inside. I'd watch from the rickety porch of that rundown mansion as my dad lifted Lily's pop off the ground. He'd clean Joshua up and fill their pantry with fresh food. The sight of Joshua, red in the face, scraggly beard, and drunk off his butt used to scare me.

Now the thought of Joshua Potts set me aflame.

This was it. No more. If he flew into another drunken rage or chased her around like a maniac again, I would end him. My father may have shown me how to be kind, but he also taught me how to fight.

"I love you, and you are coming home with me tonight. To stay. For always."

Lily sniffed. "Only for tonight, then maybe I could get a place in town or—"

"No. You are coming to my house, and you'll be my sister, just as we were always meant to be."

She inhaled, deeply. A single tear streaked down her cheek. Her pop was the only family she had left in the whole world. She looked up at me through her damp, blonde hair and nodded weakly. "Okay."

"Good." I smiled, helping her up. "Let's go to this dumb graduation and get it over with. This is the best night of my life."

"What do you mean? You've been dreading this night for months." Lil wiped at her face and fixed her dress. Her eyes glowed with a ghost of hope.

"I just got a new sister! And I got to choose her this time."

CHAPTER 12

Hazelnut and Poppy

KALEO

Poppy and hazelnut. Sweet and sharp. Pleasure and pain. Blue was all of those things. She'd filled me with such an overwhelming surge of emotion, that my mind went completely blank. Not like before down by the wall where that stench wormed and needled and I'd lost sense of who I was—no. Blue's scent soothed and excited. The emotions had not come from a place of fear.

A graveyard of smashed dandelions lay scattered about me. I chuckled. Something about her. I'd seen Blue every day for my entire childhood and had never felt so completely undone before. The sound of her laugh. The little dimple on her left cheek. The fire in those ice blue eyes. Her crazy brown curls. Why hadn't I noticed how beautiful she was before?

I hadn't been around her the past few months. Hadn't been around hardly anyone. Could someone change so much so quickly?

I should know. I had.

Next week marked the second anniversary of my mother's death. She'd been a victor over so many things. My father's abandonment, raising a son on her own, building a thriving business...but she couldn't survive the cancer that claimed her at last.

If I'd only been stronger, able to sense the *wrong* that multiplied within her sooner. I'd smelled the rot just a few measly weeks before she passed. But by the time I forced her to see Dr. Brighten, it'd been too late. I hadn't been able to save her. I'd been too weak. Emotion pricked at my eyes.

I pulled in another breath. Willow leaves and crushed dandelions. Dill pickles, black-eyed peas, deep fried catfish, black-bottomed pecan pie—my stomach growled.

The warm evening breeze brought a fresh gust of hazelnut and poppy, but this time, it was coated in fear, sorrow, worry. I shot off the ground. *Was she okay?* The emotions radiated from Blue as she rode out to her friend, filling my nose. But then—sickly sweet, metallic blood, rust—wrong. That smell hit me again. My constant companion these past two days.

I pushed the wrongness away and focused on Blue. Poppy mingled with Lily's lavender wildflower scent. She felt anger more than anything as she reached Lily in the field. I didn't know if I felt relief or worry. Her anger melted into sorrow, and I ached to run to her. Help her.

My heart thundered against my ribcage in response to the protective feelings welling within me. Completely unfamiliar, but I *did* ache. I *did* feel. I'd cut off my heart for so long. What did this mean? I'd already made it down the grassy hill and back into the crowd on auto-pilot.

But, Blue had been very clear. She could handle the situation with Lily and Joshua Potts. And I knew she could.

Jax danced with Willow Jones, wafting a contented smoky firewood scent. He'd finally worked up the courage. Good for him. I gestured for him to report in. He nodded, then whispered something in Willow's ear. Her cheeks flushed, and Jax flashed a rare, bright grin. Then, he strode over to me, head in the stars.

Jax's expression shifted when he caught my expression. He knew the pain that ate at me. Well, the previous pain. The reason I'd run out to the wall two days ago. He had no idea about this new strange aching with Blue. Dallas noticed the two of us and passed his microphone off to Lottie, one of the Talons at the bass guitar. He hopped off stage and jogged over. His scent, stinging salty sweat and fresh tobacco, reaching me before he did.

They'd been on high alert since that moment in the holler this afternoon. Once Dallas had tasted that water, I had to come clean. But, the guilt of betraying Zhao had melted almost immediately to relief. I was no longer alone in the knowledge. I was even more relieved when they'd both agreed with what Zhao had done.

Dallas hadn't been able to wash the taste out of his mouth since.

I signaled for them to follow as I jumped the fence by the horses.

"What's up, Sniffs?" Dallas's eyes glowed fiery orange after the rush of singing on stage. "Somethin' happen?"

"Maybe," I muttered, sniffing the air. But, Dallas's B.O. and the clotted blood in my nose continued to squash my ability. "Stand back, Dallas. You reek."

"What do you need?" Jax's usual response. He readjusted his ratty old baseball cap—the same one Hawk'd given him five years ago. I might have to toss that thing to my goats next.

"It might not be anything, but Joshua Potts was acting a bit wilder than usual," I said.

"Pssh. He's always going crazy." Dallas shook his head.

I gave Dallas a pointed look. "Dallas, you of all people should understand how it feels to be a little crazy." I raised my eyebrows. "And after what's been going on, I gotta check it out."

"Sure it don't have nothing to do with Lil' Blue Eyes who just ran off?" Dallas teased.

I shot him a glare that would've castrated a bull.

"Want back-up?" Jax asked.

"No," I said. "Stay here and keep an eye out. See if anyone else is acting strange. Put the Falcons on alert."

"How 'bout you check the mirror," Dallas said under his breath.

But Dallas was spooked. I never thought anything could rattle him, not until this afternoon. I hopped on Hekili and focused in on Joshua's unique scent. Usually unwashed, covered in alcohol, but tonight his underlying smell seemed to scream out in the void. An all-consuming terror radiated from him. I flew past where Blue and Lily lay out in the field of wildflowers, filling my nose with a pull of Blue along the way, like a junkie.

It wasn't hard to find Joshua as he tripped his way home. Fear surrounded him, but so did a sense of strength. He pushed down the fear with it now, hands balled up in fists at his sides. Head straight forward, eyes closed like a small child—as if by ignoring the fear, it'd go away.

"Joshua?" I asked lightly. I didn't want to spook him any further.

He continued to stomp along in the grass toward home, not even registering me in his vicinity.

I hopped from Hekili and tried again, louder. "Joshua Potts?"

With that, he whirled around, eyes wide. "Who's there?"

I could taste the alarm in the air. "Just me, sir. Kaleo Bannon, Captain of the Falcons."

People liked to hear my rank, it seemed to put them at ease when they were afraid. I was still getting used to the title.

"Cap. Kaleo Bannon, y'say?" Joshua's eyes trained on me in the moonlight. Hyper focused. Not an ounce of alcohol in his system. "Leave me alone, boy. I ain't done nothin' wrong."

"I know, sir," I said, keeping my voice light. "I just saw a disturbance and wanted to make sure you were—"

"Saw a disturbance?" Joshua mocked my tone. "Why don't you just have yer fun, then leave me be."

"I'm not making fun, sir, I just—"

"Seen enough?" Joshua's hands shot up in the air, eyes aflame. "Enough of the village crazy?"

"No, sir—"

"No, of course you ain't." Joshua laughed. "Y'all can't never have enough. Pointin' yer fangers, whisperin' under yer breath. Y'all done the same to my sweet girl, Lily Mae. She ain't done nothin' to deserve it." Joshua spit in the grass.

"You're all monsters!" Joshua no longer focused on me. His red eyes lit on the empty field around him, as if the rest of the village stood around us. "Y'hear me? Y'all are all monsters!"

He was sober, and yet—

"Can I help you home, sir?" It was the least I could do.

"You can't help me with nothin'!" Joshua growled. He turned toward his home miles up the mountain, but stilled. Joshua spoke over his shoulder in a chilling calm. "No one can help me. Help any of us. It's too late. Somethin' bad is headed this way. We're all gonna die."

CHAPTER 13

Moon–Shattering Handsomeness

BLUE

Breathless, we arrived at the party just in time to hear the president's booming voice in the microphone. Lil and I huffed and puffed, both wildly out of breath, cheeks flushed. Even Lily's usual straight blonde hair now lent her the look of a woman who'd been attacked by a feral rodent. She grimaced as I licked my thumb and wiped the smudges of dirt from her face. With just a few swipes, she was radiant.

She did the same once over on me, fixing my hair, face, and dress in a quick minute. We scrambled up the back of the stage and found our seats. "And we have blossomed into this beautiful community of New Haveners," President Zhao said. "Where, yes, we know heartache and pain, but we also know joy and gratitude. We know the feeling of pride that swells within us after a hard day's work."

The audience roared with applause.

"We are a chosen people, now one-thousand-five-hundred-fifty-five strong! Our ancestors were the strongest and smartest of their kind, brought together by fate to this blessed land in the Blue Ridge Mountains. They started the path we still walk today—"

My mouth watered as a wave of nausea hit me. *No. Not again.*

The electric lights buzzed overhead. My sight blurred into nothing.

I stood in darkness atop an old barn.

Wood creaked beneath my feet. The sliver of the moon my only light.

Desperation. A prayer in my heart. Aching. Longing.

Not my emotions. Not my eyes.

These eyes searched frantically, as if checking for an intruder. It was impossible to see anything but blackness. They were alone. They focused on the flint in their hands. It was hard to tell in the dark with these dim eyes, but these were large, capable hands. Crusted in dirt and scratches. The hands of a traveler. A fighter. My heart quickened.

"So, you finally grew a backbone, my old friend."

The words sounded from somewhere below. My heart hammered, causing my eyes to pulse. Fear coated my throat. Behind me, a man pounded his way up the ladder to the rooftop. The ancient wood creaked as though it might give way beneath his weight.

"Something must be done," I said, though it was not my voice. "You've gone too far. They must be warned. This is wrong and you know it—"

"I know that you will pay," the man from the ladder said as calm as death.

The man with the flint continued to strike it against the stone. A flash. A flame. His strong hands held the torch to the spark. The flame caught and sputtered.

He blew into the small fire and it flared to life. Hope flickered in my heart—no, in this man's heart. He turned and raised the torch high.

Green eyes flashed in the light of the flame.

A crooked smile. His handsome face shattered the moon above.

A challenge tugged at his lips.

He rushed toward me, slamming his body against mine and propelling me backwards off the roof—

The electric string lights flared back into view. My heart pounded wildly.

Who were those men? Where were they?

President Zhao continued her speech as if nothing had happened. As if my world hadn't just crashed down into a single, handsome, frightening smile.

Lily and Griff's eyes were up ahead on the president. I scanned the crowd. No one noticed me.

Fear tightened my chest.

I coughed, shaking as I gripped the edges of my wooden seat. Were they out there right now, planning an attack?

"We will not fail them," Zhao called. "We will not fail each other. We will grow, create, and we will thrive!"

Everyone saluted the president with their right fists pressed to their chests, their heads bowed. Zhao smiled and returned the salute. Zhao turned from the microphone, her eyes lingering on me as she took her seat in front of the stage.

"Thank you, Madam President!" Principal Allstair, our eccentric school principal took the microphone. "We ara' truly bless'd to live in this hallowed land and to have your astute leadership and guidance!" His backwoods accent was particularly strong tonight...usually a sign of the cup. His amazing eyebrows had a life of their own, as if a group of frothy gray caterpillars joined tiny hands and made a little home atop his brow. "Tonight is the night we look fo'wad to all year! The night we get to drank—"

Everyone cheered and raised a glass.

"We get to dance—"

More cheers.

"And we get to see our fine group of grad'iates take up their place in this fine communit-ay!"

With sweaty hands I wrenched my poor dress into clumps in my lap. The crowd shook before me. I pulled in a sharp breath. No, they weren't shaking, *I* was. My entire body trembled. I swallowed, my mouth dry. We were stupid, fat, comfortable hobbits—drinking and eating when who knew what evils stirred outside. My eyes found Kaleo's like a magnet. He stood by the back fence, a bit breathless, eyes on me.

He stiffened, his eyebrows knit in concentration.

Could he smell my terror? My confusion?

Farmer Jim, my future employer, sat at the table in front of Kaleo and noticed my gaze. He tipped his wide-brimmed hat to me. I managed a queasy smile.

"We'll sta't with our firs' student and the res' will follow." Principal Allstair hiccupped loudly into the microphone, then began calling names. As the graduates made their way to the stage, one at a time, to make their announcements, my fear didn't abate. Sweat dripped down my temples, ran a slimy finger down my spine.

Eliza would join her family in the veterinarian field.

Hank would work in the millinery, making clothes.

Charlotte would become the blacksmith apprentice of her dad.

Haven is pretty high up in alphabetical order, so when it was my turn, I walked on shaky legs to the microphone. I scanned the crowd, landing on my mama's encouraging face. My dad sat with Fox, holding a sleeping bundle of sweet Shenandoah wrapped up tight like a burrito. Kyra and Cora smiled conspiratorially together, their eyebrows wagging.

They had no idea what I was going through. What I'd seen.

"Hello," I blurted into the booming microphone. "I'm Blue Laurel Haven. I've learned a lot at our school and am grateful for my teachers through the years." Seemed like a good start. My palms dripped with sweat and my knee-caps bounced uncontrollably. I didn't even know they could do that. "Tonight, I pledge myself as..."

In the distance, thirty miles past the wall, a flame flickered to life. My mouth hung open on the words I had yet to say, my pulse racing.

I stared at the flame, afraid to lose the pinprick of yellow. It moved slightly, flickered, then was gone.

Someone behind me cleared their throat. A few giggles and murmurs floated about. I transported back into my head instantly. Back into this dress. Back to the front of the stage with my classmates —as though I'd awoken from a dream.

My heart dropped. Could Hawk or Pretty-Boy Joe have lit the flame? Lighting fires was strictly forbidden outside the walls, but if there was a true threat— Could it have been that dangerous gang of outsiders?

Our graduation meant absolutely nothing if we were about to be attacked.

"A light." I reached out with the tips of my fingers. No one heard me, but bubbles of uncomfortable conversation blanketed the audience.

Questions bloomed in my parents' eyes. A hand landed on my shoulder and jerked me forcibly to the back of the stage. I spun around and President Zhao pierced me with her tiger eyes.

I gulped down air like a goldfish on land. There wasn't enough. Couldn't breathe.

Principal Allstair called up the next graduate.

President Zhao grabbed me by the shoulders. "What did you say?"

"Nothing," I sputtered. All of these visions—I didn't want to be wrong. Didn't want to get into trouble.

"Tell me now, girl."

I swallowed back a lump in my throat. "I saw a light. I think."

"Shhh!" She motioned with her head to follow. "No need to incite a panic tonight."

We made our way down the back of the stage behind the great oak. She yanked me behind a building, surprisingly strong for her size. "Explain."

"There was a light. In the distance. Thirty miles outside the wall. It was small and moved slightly. Then it was gone." I deflated. Saying it out loud made it sound stupid. Impossible. I might as well add that aliens with puppies were falling from the sky.

Zhao's eyes searched mine. "Are you sure? No one else saw this light. None of us on stage saw it. Are you sure it wasn't a trick of the moonshine or the lanterns messing with your vision?"

My vision.

A silent roaring filled my head as I made the connection.

The light in the distance. The flash of fire on the barn rooftop. They were the same.

Zhao held my face in her hands and looked into my eyes, probably to see if I was drunk. Her eyes peeled through the layers of my story like lasers.

"Yes." I reviewed the pinprick of light in the distance quickly before my eyes. I prayed I was wrong, but I couldn't ignore this. "Yes. I am positive."

"What direction?" Zhao asked.

"South."

"Come with me," Zhao snapped as she turned toward the street. Her black hair whipped around her face.

Two massive shapes rounded the corner behind the stage. Kaleo sat astride his horse. He held the reins of his mare in one hand, the reins of President Zhao's stallion in the other. Zhao hopped up into her saddle without delay.

How in the Armageddon did he get here so fast?

"Come with me, Miss Haven. I have need of you." Zhao turned her horse and took off at a gallop.

Kaleo took me in. My slightly disheveled hair, my crumpled dress. I looked a little dingier than I had when we'd spoken up by the willow. I'd already ridden off into the sunset to save one friend tonight. Who knew I'd get the pleasure of riding off again?

Lucky me.

Well, wasn't riding off into the woods with a hot guy on my reckless "to do" list? I should've been more specific and taken out the life-threatening parts.

Kaleo's eyes danced with mirth as he grabbed my hand. "Oh, come on! It won't be too bad!" He hauled me up like a sack of grain.

As I landed in the saddle, Kaleo's warm body wrapped around me. His hot breath spiraled down my neck. I pushed down a crazed giggle that bubbled up, startled by my own body's ability to get distracted.

Kaleo leaned in to whisper in my ear and uncontrollable chills careened wildly down my body. "Don't worry, I'll lead. Wouldn't want you chasing off into the woods alone. That did *not* turn out well last time—"

Before I could protest, he spun Hekili around and we plummeted into the dark of night.

CHAPTER 14

Granny Panties

BLUE

K aleo said nothing as we tore a winding path after President Zhao, Hekili's hooves pounding beneath us. I leaned forward in the saddle, trying to keep a modicum of distance between the two of us, but it couldn't be helped. I fell against his strong chest and blushed, even as fresh waves of panic crashed over me.

I'd never really been afraid before. Not truly. Not like this. Everything had always been safe. Sure. Solid. But that light outside the wall threw a wrench into my ideal world, shattered my perfect little reality bubble.

The traveler's strong hands up on the creaking barn. The strikes of stone on flint.

If that vision was real, if that truly was the light I'd seen—then those outsiders were only thirty miles outside our wall. Hawk and Pretty-Boy Joe were in mortal danger.

We all were.

"Oye, caveman. I would be very careful whom you choose to ignore, my friend."

I was connected to these two outsiders somehow. The one who held the sword with a sneer, the other who asked for mercy. The man who smothered the beacon on the rooftop, the other who fought to light it. Identical on the outside, but inherently different at heart. One dark, the other light.

A green-eyed boy with a smile just for me. He stood in a sea of towering city buildings, a hand extended toward me.

Which one was he? The dark one or the light?

We stopped abruptly a few miles outside of the square, right by the southeast border wall at a broken-down shack. It looked as though it were about to sigh its last breath and collapse into a trash heap even the rats would scoff at.

Kaleo and Zhao dismounted from their horses as soon as we reached the ramshackle mess of wood. Kaleo offered me a hand, but I smiled and decided to show off. I'd been riding horses since before I could walk—I knew my way around. I threw my leg back around in an arch, dismounting in a swift move any country girl would envy.

My dress, on the other hand, had never dismounted a horse before, so it got caught up on the saddle. It took a long, slow, minute for my dress to rip completely up the side, all while my rear hung out for the whole world to see!

I squealed, grabbed my dress, and yanked it off the horse as quickly as possible. I prayed to the heavens above that Kaleo did not just see my underwear, because they were granny panties. Big ol' granny panties. My face glowed brighter than a freshly spanked newborn's butt! *Why?*

Thankfully, Kaleo turned away politely, allowing for me to smooth down my skirt. My poor dress, now with a massive tear down the side, had never looked so scandalous. Thank the heavens above Zhao hadn't witnessed the spectacle. She'd already stepped inside the shack.

Kaleo, still mercifully with his back to me, a bit red around his ears, cleared his throat.

"So, you all good back there?" He chortled. "All in one piece?"

"Shut up!" I smacked him on the shoulder. "I will *never* ride a horse again while wearing a stupid dress!"

He turned his head, his smile charming the woodland creatures for miles, and teased, "I don't know, it's quickly becoming one of my favorite things."

He cleared his throat, shook his head, then trudged toward the ramshackle hovel, shoulders back. Back to the straight, no-nonsense Soldier Boy we all knew and loved.

"Seriously?" I called after him, my face burning hotter.

I smoothed down my sorry dress and hurried through the front door of the shack. We entered a room cluttered with dusty boxes and locked cabinets. A solid wood table squatted in the center. Zhao unlocked a cabinet and rummaged through a stack of papers while Kaleo stomped toward an old phone to make calls.

Radio had always been a no-no, a tradition from the Shadow War days. It'd been too easy to intercept those radio waves. But wires— already antiques by the time the Shadow War began—buried along the entire town of New Haven became our saving grace.

This must be some sort of outpost for the warriors to keep tabs on each other. It didn't look like much, but neither did Mama Darla's cabin. Hidden in plain sight.

The ancient papers Zhao dug through were top secret. I knew this because, well, they all had TOP SECRET stamped across the tops along with the New Haven angel crest.

A quick glance at Kaleo and Zhao revealed their complete disregard for my presence. I used the time to study my surroundings. I could make out at least five pages deep of the thin paper. Reading between the pages from the sides proved more difficult and a lot more interesting.

My eyes caught on bank statements, land ownership deeds, then more excitingly—the Enforcer's Log. My pulse picked up. I scanned the entries in minutes, lingering on familiar names.

Raleigh Haven executed Malcolm Rice, aged 37, April 27th, two years after New Haven was founded, for turning S.E.
  Body dismembered, burned at outlook.

Piles and piles of old dusty folders containing suspicious reports littered the cabin.

Marlo heard Gwen whispering a mile away.

Gene stares at people, covers ears constantly, eats raw meats, bit my dog.

The log morphed from reports of suspicion to assaults, petty theft, land ownership, and law disputes.

Hugh Potts, aged 48, accused of assault and battery. Charged ten years hard labor.

Lily's Granddad. Names, dates, crimes, and punishments dealt for misdeeds covered page after page.

General Rose's name appeared quite a bit as a warrior leader in settling the occasional dispute.

The Enforcers had simply gotten less and less important to a shifting society focused on crops and land. They really did just disappear.

Kaleo's fingers moved over the rotary phone dialing up six-digit numbers. Forty-six fingerprints smudged on the plastic phone handle. "Falcon Team, code black. I repeat, code black. Meet at Rendezvous Point Bravo ASAP." He paused. "Yes, copy. Rendezvous Point Bravo ASAP. Send the Talons to reinforce perimeter—"

I wrung my hands, dust motes orbited in a wild frenzy in the lantern light.

A spider spun its thousandth strand. Its eight eyes shifted as it busied itself. I focused on the eight reflections of myself gazing back at me. My hair and heart were a wreck.

What was happening outside of that wall? How could we just stand around in this old shack? With every second that ticked by, I was growing more and more convinced that the light I saw was the one from my vision. It had to be. We could be overrun within the hour!

Zhao found the document she'd been looking for, and she shoved the other folders back into the locked cabinet. Her deep scar flashed in the light of the lantern as she beckoned for me to approach.

"Blue Haven, you claim you saw a light beyond our wall—out where many believe there are no survivors. Do you understand the magnitude of your declaration?" Zhao's voice was grave.

"Yes, ma'am. There was a light. I saw it. I know I did."

Still, I prayed my vision wasn't real. That this was all just a nightmare. That it had been a trick of the light.

Zhao laid an ancient map across the rickety table in the center of the shack. "Where was it? We need an exact location."

I wiped the sweat from my forehead and took in the map under the flickering lantern. I knew this map. Everyone in New Haven knew it. It was a map of our village; the buildings, hilltops, valleys, and mountains surrounding our home.

But this map was ancient. Bigger. The borders spread out farther than I'd ever seen. Reaching to the edge of the continent. I drank in the details to pour over later. Certain places were carefully shaded, as if someone were checking the surrounding area for something. An ocean lay only two-hundred miles away to the east. A large gaping stretch of land blackened with scratches and small skull drawings strewn about. The Great Gulf. What was that?

The square. Just hours ago, I stood on stage, about to pledge my life to farming. Now I stood in an ol' shanty outpost next to the president herself, preparing for a possible invasion.

I placed my finger on the map. "Here. This was where the light was coming from."

President Zhao and Kaleo's gaze pressed in on me, the importance of this moment etched in the set of their eyes.

Without warning, Zhao closed the distance between us. She grabbed my chin and whispered. "Can I trust these eyes?"

"Uh, yes, ma'am." My stomach lurched.

She focused on one of my eyes, then the other. "Show me," Zhao commanded. She gestured out the door. "We have approximately ten minutes before the Falcons arrive."

I jumped and caught Kaleo staring at me. He glanced away as if caught with his hand in the cookie jar.

I followed the president out the front door and into the black fields beyond. The horses nickered, ready for another ride, but we headed in the other direction. The tiny slice of a moon failed to emit more than a scratch of light. The same slight moon from my vision on the barn roof.

Cicadas and crickets sang a symphony with a cacophony of loud-mouth bullfrogs. Tall grass and wildflowers swayed in the balmy breeze.

In a blink, I picked up on some bits of hay, a ladybug, three arrowheads, and two feathers littering the ground.

Any other night, I'd be running along the grass and weeds, splashing my feet in the creek, or swinging in my hammock out back, a jar of sweet tea in hand. But tonight, I felt as if I stood teetering on the edge of a cliff. Kaleo appeared beside me within seconds. His towering presence didn't calm me.

"Let me speak plainly to you, Miss Haven," Zhao said. "I know that our town has...a history of treating those with abilities as a threat. But I am of the mind that those enhancements are a gift."

My heart hammered. Was this a trap? I looked to Kaleo for a sign.

He nodded. I could trust her.

"I am looking for the elite. We already have well trained, strong, capable fighters, but...new developments have me searching for those with strengths I do not yet possess. I understand it is a delicate matter, but the time for subtlety is over. My captain here"—she motioned toward Kaleo—"has reason to believe you might be such a person."

Anger flared. Kaleo set me up?

"Miss Haven, this will be your only test. If you pass, you will be a sworn-in warrior of New Haven with all of the glory and benefits the ranking has to offer. If you fail, you will return to your home and take up the job as, well, whatever other role you have secured for yourself. Either way, everything you have seen, heard, and experienced since you first claimed to lay eyes on that light remains strictly confidential. On pain of death as a traitor."

Zhao stated everything so efficiently that I had a hard time putting the harsh words and polite tone together in a way that made sense.

Kaleo widened his eyes at me.

What did *that* mean? I wrinkled my nose. *Stupid Soldier Boy.*

She continued, "Pray you do not disappoint me, for I can see in you a warrior's spirit. I hope I am not wrong."

My face flushed with heat. I glared at Kaleo but he looked away, his face dark and brooding, but no apology lurked there among the sharp lines of his jaw or curvy pillows of his mouth. *Stupid Mr. Perfect.*

"Tell me, Miss Haven, how many arrows made it to the bullseye in the three targets." Zhao motioned across the pitch field. "This is your test. You have five minutes."

She took a few steps back and folded her arms across her chest. I had a choice to make. I could pretend ignorance and make Kaleo look stupid, which was tempting, then go on to be a farmhand the rest of my life. Or I could take this chance and either be killed and burned or rewarded as a warrior.

The truth was, I'd already made my choice. In that moment back at the ceremony, when I told Zhao about that light, I was ready to be myself and damn the consequences.

Zhao was obviously aware of my sight abilities, but not my limitations. There was no light to speak of, except from the fingernail of a moon and insignificant stars. I almost opened my mouth to say just that when I envisioned my alternate future: my head down, a bunch of cows peeing and spraying methane gas all over me for the next fifty years.

Heck no. I had to do this.

I closed my mind off to the cows spraying poo, Kaleo's not-sorry mouth, and Zhao's threat of death, and instead focused on breathing —willing the stimuli to flee. I breathed in and out, nice and slow.

Warm air brushed my skin. Crickets chirped about me. Tall grass tickled the backs of my hands. I was grounded.

This was *my* home, *my* center, and I *would* do this.

Okay. Targets. First, I needed to locate them. If this was an archery range, then the targets were made from bales of hay.

Hay. Heat. Warmth. Comfort.

I opened my eyes.

The forms of the trees lining the field stretched into the shadows of night. I searched for the squat targets. I sought out the warmth of the hay. My vision picked up on tiny dots flying through the air. Small, warm insects flew about. Their blurry shapes dipped and dove about in the field.

Smaller shapes, squat and square, flickered into focus. Hay held the daytime heat long into the night, keeping the bales warmer than the surrounding nighttime air. Trace amount of yellow warmth emanated from the figures like a steady flame. It wasn't much, but it was there.

My heart pounded against my ribs.

Kaleo and Zhao's warm bodies flared brightly, emanating red and orange. Heat.

I saw heat. Temperature.

The tips of my own fingers glistened a bright orange-yellow as I held them up before my face. I turned and spun my hand through the cool purples and blues of the evening air. I gasped. A bright alien planet swirled before me like a neon galaxy. Yellow and emerald birds blurred past indigo tree branches. My heart soared through the galaxy on a warm breeze.

Three targets sat out on the field before me, spaced at varying distances. Fifteen, thirty, and sixty yards away.

Sweat beaded on my forehead. I rolled my neck and wiped my hands on the sides of my ragged dress.

I focused on the first bale.

Small plumes of warmth rose from the holes in the front of it.

"Four in the first," I announced.

No one confirmed or corrected me. *Okay.*

"The second target, the one at thirty yards, has three."

Onto the last, the one sixty yards away. It was easy to spot the tendrils of heat leaking from the arrow holes now. "One, no two. Right on top of each other. Whoever hit that is an amazing shot!"

Silence stretched on and doubt circled a cold fist around my heart.

"Thank you, Miss Haven. I pride myself on my skill with a bow." President Zhao stood still as death. "Heaven help us indeed." She strode over to where I stood. "Well, I'm afraid we don't have time for formalities, but you passed your trial. You are now an official warrior private. I expect your complete allegiance and obedience. You know the warrior's code?"

"I...honor, love—" I swallowed around the lump in my throat, stumbling over the words I dreamt of saying my entire life.

"Reverence, generosity, courage, and mercy forever," Kaleo finished for me. "We vow to fight to protect home and family above self. Protection. Safety. Life."

"Do you accept?" Zhao asked, clear by the strict line of her mouth there was no other choice.

My heart pounded in my chest. Of course, of course I did! "Yes. Yes, ma'am, I accept."

I raised my fist over my heart and bowed my head in salute. She nodded, saluted, then turned to Kaleo. "Your team should arrive within minutes. Prepare yourselves." Zhao strode toward the shack.

Bright colors of heat rose from my hands. The whole night was a colorful wonderland. Bouncing insects and gusts of heat rose from the ground. Wind sighed, cool and breezy. The crushing weight on my chest lifted. A sense of freedom filled me.

I did it. I was a warrior. And my mother couldn't say a *thing* about it!

Light orange heat pulled from Kaleo's body, slowly mixing with the greens and blues of the air. He let out a slow, steady breath. Orange and scarlet water particles flowed slowly from his lips and infused with the air around us, like hot breath in a chill winter. I reached my hand up to touch it, fascinated. He looked down at me, a slight quirk to his lips.

Whoops. In a blink, I slammed back into awareness, in my body and back on my feet. Thankfully he didn't have heat vision because I knew my face resembled the bright neon glow of a noonday sun about now.

"That. Was. Pretty wicked." Kaleo beamed.

"Thanks." I cleared my throat.

A bright orange figure burst out from the tree line on his red horse, covered in weapons. Male, long hair, broad, earrings, tall, thin but muscular. Massive eyebrows. Baseball cap.

"Kaleo!" I whispered and seized his mammoth arm. "Someone's riding out there. Look at the tree line."

I turned to run into the shack for protection and weapons.

Kaleo held onto me, my shoulder smashed into his ribs. "That's Jax. My team's arriving. I knew he'd be the first one here."

"Oh, right, Jax." I winced. Kaleo's right-hand-man. The one I'd saved from the freezing ice all those years ago. "But, how can you see who it is?"

It was as black as pitch out here and Kaleo didn't have my heat vision.

"You're not the only fancy pants 'round here, remember?" He pointed to his nose.

"Oh, right." My face heated. So many new things to get used to. I prayed my B.O. didn't reek to high heaven. Kaleo and I stood out in the music of the neon night. Horse hooves pounded from behind us as warriors approached the shack. Two, then three arrived.

"And I can trust the president with my sight? I mean, I can't believe I just did that. I was always told to keep my sight a secret—"

Kaleo nodded thoughtfully, lips pursed. "Your family was always good to me after my mama died. I ever tell you that?"

I smiled, surprised at the sudden turn of conversation. "Oh, thanks. Your mom taught me how to tie my shoes. Probably the only time I ever wore 'em."

Kaleo's eyes sparkled. "She was...the best."

I nodded.

"My dad was never around, y'know. And President Zhao, she'd grown up with my mom but lost touch after their lives went separate ways. Life and all that."

He side-eyed me in the moonlight and my heart flipped. "But Zhao, she felt bad for all the lost years, and she'd never had children of her own, so she took me under her wing. Helped me with the farm. Kept it running. She even lived with me for a while. She taught me a lot."

"So, you must be pretty close?"

He huffed. "She's not much for hugs and long meaningful conversations. But she taught me how to be strong, tough. She taught me how to *use* my senses to fight. How to hone my smell. Make it work for me instead of against me. She's a hard lady, but one you can trust with your ability. That I do know."

If he used his enhanced senses for his work, then maybe I could trust him with mine, too. My stomach squirmed. "About my sight, Kaleo. I've had these weird visions—"

"Captain?" President Zhao called from the shack.

Kaleo and I whipped around. My heart flew out of my chest, as if I were being caught with my fingers in the frosting.

"Your team is here. Time to prepare." Zhao's eyes shot daggers through me as we approached.

Okay, I'll let your precious Soldier Boy get to work. Sheesh.

We reached the ramshackle outpost by the border wall and a murmur of male voices vibrated from inside. Kaleo entered first, but I lingered by the door. I pulled back my hair, smoothed down my tattered blue dress, and cleared my throat, then I strode through the door with my head held high.

President Zhao and six massive male warriors crowded around that old splintered wooden table. Every head shot up at my entrance.

The lantern light bounced off of weapons, leather, hulking forearms, and fourteen inquisitive eyes. I shrunk into the floorboards.

One pair of eyes winked at me and I jumped. Dallas, lead singer of Apocalypse Here, smirked.

"Miss Haven, thank you for joining us." Kaleo broke through the intensity.

I nodded and strode forward. *Be confident.* My mom always said that fake confidence was better than none.

Yes. This was clearly where I was meant to be. All was going according to plan. Couldn't they tell by my pulled together appearance?

The amount of testosterone in this shack stifled my breath. Even Zhao, the only other female, exuded alarming amounts of the hormone.

All eyes fixed on me, like they'd never seen a girl before.

Brock nodded, easily the oldest of the Falcons at thirty. He'd been dancing with his wife and two little boys at the ceremony tonight. Now, all levity had disappeared from his handsome bearded face.

Jax, tall, broad as a bear, also bearded, with the manliest eyebrows on earth, tipped his baseball cap with a welcoming smile and pulled me in with a one-armed squeeze. As if I were one of them. He'd always been especially kind to me. Could have something to do with that whole "life-saving" thing in the ice all those years ago. He'd been to train at my house more times than I could count. Without thinking, his times at my house whirled before my eyes—326.

I sagged with relief and hugged him back, flashing him a sheepish grin. My eyes snagged on a stark red cut that ran a diagonal down his stubbled cheek.

In an instant, that strange tug pulled me under. No—

I stood in a field of grass and weeds. Below me, Jax lay in the dirt. His body twisted at an unnatural angle. Dead.

My head dropped. I blinked back into the shanty as if no time had passed at all. Jax tucked me into his side, holding me up. I clamped a hand over my mouth to stifle a scream.

"I've already explained the light and location," Kaleo's voice cut in. Did he smell the fear crashing through my veins?

Jax squeezed my shoulder gently while Kaleo continued to order his warriors with a stoic briskness. He told them where to go, in what formations, and whose mom made the best apple dumplings—I may have blanked out somewhere in the middle, coming to grips with what I'd just seen.

President Zhao stood back, eyes like a tiger's, reading everyone around her.

My ears perked up when Kaleo mentioned Hawk and Pretty-Boy Joe. They'd been across the wall for days with those outsiders. Urgency pulsed within me with every second that ticked by. I wrung my hands, studying the map closely. I memorized the trails Kaleo and his men would make across the terrain as they sought the threat.

"Blue," Kaleo commanded, "explain exactly what the light looked like and where you saw it. We need every detail you can remember."

I cleared my throat and pointed to the spot on the map. "It was here twenty minutes after sunset. It was a yellowish pinprick, almost like a candle flickering. It moved slightly, side to side, then jerked and sputtered out."

I stole a glance up at Jax, suddenly restless. The longer we stood here talking, the longer my brother was out there alone, maybe fighting for his life. And Jax? What if I was sending him out to his grave?

"Oye, caveman. I would be very careful whom you choose to ignore, my friend."

Kaleo finished his briefing within minutes. Every warrior saluted the president, then Kaleo.

"Protection. Safety. Life," they chanted in unison.

I stared at Jax longer than I should have, waiting for another vision to convince me I was all wrong. He tipped his baseball cap with a smile as he ducked out the door to the horrors beyond the wall. Maybe, if I replayed the vision, I could find a way to prevent it.

I played the scene of Jax laid out in the field in front of my eyes over and over. It was clear, bright, fluid, though it was dark outside. A chill snaked down my back. This vision had been through my own eyes. Still, it was a matter of milliseconds, images, feelings. No concrete clues to read into. I didn't want to get lost in his glassy eyes glaring sightlessly at the grass beneath him.

The grass pressed harshly against his unfeeling corneas.

The Falcons didn't waste another second as they grabbed their numerous weapons and raced out the front door into the night. Horse hooves pounded into the unknown across the wall.

Dallas brushed past me with a wicked grin, then leaned in, as if we were thick as thieves. "You like that extra-long slow dance with Pretty Boy Sniffles over there?" Dallas gestured toward Kaleo who was busy gathering his things. "He was throwin' out the vibes *so* hard, man. Had to do my bro a solid and play that song out nice and *long.*"

With a suggestive wink, Dallas wrapped his muscular arm around my shoulder and pulled me in, his blond ponytail tickling my neck. "Hey, your little blondie friend got a name?"

"Yeah." I flushed with the proximity of Dallas's face to mine. "It's I-Don't-like-A-Holes."

"Heh." Dallas smiled. "You think she'd go for a guy like me?"

I shot him a scowl that would've killed a possum. "Nope."

Dallas threw his head back in a laugh, then his heavy arm slipped from my shoulders, leaving me confused and blushing.

Once the Falcons cleared out, Kaleo stood before me. "Hey, I'll look out for Hawk. I won't let anything happen to him, Blue. I promise."

He nodded in farewell, then stomped out of the shack.

"Wait!" I called.

He paused in the doorframe, filling it completely.

I leaned in close and whispered, "Maybe—look for an old barn."

Kaleo's black eyebrows knit together. "An old barn? What d'you see, Blue?"

"I don't know." I shook my head. "Just a few strange images. I don't even know if they're real. But I saw about ten outsiders, Kaleo, confronting one of our warriors. I think. Hurting him. Then, tonight I saw a man on a barn lighting a beacon."

Kaleo's shoulders tensed. "Tell me everything."

I explained every last detail of those visions I could remember. I couldn't bring them back before my eyes as I could with the raven and this new one with Jax. They'd been hard to see. Dim and confusing. Not through my own eyes. I'd have to think on the whys of that later.

Kaleo's nostrils flared. Did he smell the truth on me, the fear, as I stood before him and described the green-eyed stranger with the sword—the man on the barn, striking flint with hope in his heart?

"I didn't think it was real until I saw that light with my *own eyes*. Right in front of my face. Now, I'm worried that I waited too long. That it's too late and if anything were to happen to Hawk or Joe or—"

"Hey," Kaleo cut in. "We train for this all day, all night. We're ready. And if we die protecting our people, our town, those we love"—his hands moved to my shoulders sending a cascade of warmth through me—"it's worth it. We know the risks."

"One more thing." Nausea rose into my throat as the image of Jax's sprawled out form dripped before my sight again. I blinked it away. "Just, be careful. Keep an eye out for...for Jax."

I grimaced, afraid I'd said too much.

Kaleo's eyes grew wide, but his mouth set in a straight line. He didn't want to know any more. I didn't want to tell him, either. Kaleo nodded, hopped on Hekili, and rode out into the black night.

I trudged back into the shanty, awaiting orders. That's what I was supposed to do, right? So, I just stood there in the outpost, watching the dust motes fly in and out of Zhao's nose, fear and worry flying about like wild sparrows in my body.

President Zhao stood, back straight, mapping out coordinates. The perfect soldier. I supposed I would learn that stance soon enough. I tried to mimic her now and fell a bit short. No one saw a soldier when they looked at me. All they saw tonight was a soft little flower of a girl. *Dresses.* They made it impossible to perform the normal occupations of daily life. Who invented them anyways?

President Zhao turned toward me. "It remains to be seen how valuable your information was tonight, Miss Haven. But, it's better to be safe than dead. Remember, you're a warrior now. A *trusted* warrior. Do not break that trust within the first hours of your appointment. You will find the consequences are not agreeable."

"Yes, ma'am," I promised, gut twisting.

"Go home and rest. The general will expect you at six tomorrow morning for your first day of training. I will send a rider for you. Have your horse ready. You are dismissed." She returned to the map.

The conversation was over. I took a step toward the door—

"Oh, and please wear something a little more suitable for your rank tomorrow," she bit out as an afterthought.

As if I had specifically hand-chosen this dress to frolic about the woods, jump around on horses, and pass my warrior trial. I staggered like a mindless ghost out the door.

I didn't register the long five mile walk home. Somehow, I set one foot in front of the other and ended up at my front door. The next thing I knew, my head was on the pillow, and I fell into a dreamless sleep.

CHAPTER 15

The Smell of Death

KALEO

Death beckoned to me through the dark of the night. My team followed behind on horseback, the slender moon our only light outside the wall, and that's how it had to remain. But, I was a tracker, leading by smell alone, able to hone in on the differentiating scents from miles away. Thank the angels in heaven I could phase out the odors of my men and their horses.

I picked up on the smoky woodfire scent of Jax, more aware of him than usual. He followed behind on high alert, crossbow nocked. If Blue was right, if she'd somehow seen something bad happen to him—

I shook my head. I'd do anything to stop that from happening. Anything.

Thunderheads rolled above us, converging on the dry fields of cotton and weeds we galloped through. The wind shifted, and I caught a whiff of Blue. Sweet hazelnut and poppy. I held my next breath with a snort. *Unbelievable.* Every time I thought I was doing okay, I'd find myself drifting off, trying to locate her flitting around town somewhere. It was sad, really, how good I was at finding her. She'd made it home now. Safe.

Despite my mounting dread, that knowledge helped me breathe a bit easier.

A storm brewed deep in the mountains. The thick breeze wound through the valley, carrying the cool promise of fresh rain mingling with the sour stench of—decaying flesh. The scent pulled me in like a dead lover.

I clicked my tongue and my team stopped on a dime. Whatever a dime was. I motioned Jax ahead. He hopped off his stallion toward the round blot decaying in the dry grass. Rot hung in the air like a festering cloud of carrion-eating houseflies.

I prayed my senses were wrong.

Lightning flashed, illuminating the sickly lump. Jax recoiled. Gasps filled the air. Blood mingled with red clay and putrid vomit. A blood drenched mohawk.

One of our warrior privates was dead, murdered out here on his warpath. His head had been left out here in the heat and elements for days.

My stomach roiled as I looked, for the first time, at a murdered human face.

Please don't be Hawk. Please don't be Hawk.

"It's Joe," Jax said as he knelt close enough to wipe off a smudge of mud from his face and blond hair. His face twisted in disgust.

Pretty-Boy Joe. Dead. Killed.

Just like Blue had seen.

Relief washed over me, followed quickly by deep shame. Yes, I was grateful it wasn't Hawk, but the death of another brother in arms filled me with a sick nausea. Who was capable of such reckless disregard for human life? Blue's vision of the outsiders had been real. She'd seen the future somehow.

Who were they? What kind of sick game were they playing?

Another question wormed into my mind—did these men have anything to do with the horrific package that'd been dropped over our wall two days ago?

I was convinced now more than ever that the thing had been brought to our village on purpose. I still had no clue why.

A sour smell stung the air, along with a film coating Joe's lips and chin. He'd used his cyanide pill, then the outsider had finished the job. The scents of my team spiked with alarm. Pure grief and pain.

Their sorrow was so overwhelming, I had to fight the tears that pricked the edges of my eyes.

I hopped off Hekili and closed my eyes as the smell of death grew, leading me to the rest of Joe's crumpled body. The aroma hung limp like a gray, cloying cloud, growing darker as it encompassed his hot corpse.

Sorrow in smell form.

Shallow breaths. I had to be strong for my team. I took in a pull of the coffee beans I wore around my neck and cleared my throat.

"Dallas, you and Brock find out what you can. Nothing goes unnoticed," I ordered. "We'll burn his body properly in the light of day tomorrow."

We hadn't made it to the point of interest yet. I didn't want to think about what horrors awaited us where Blue had seen that light. But this death was a bad omen. The first murder in a hundred years by outsiders. A raven nipped at the rotting flesh, and I kicked at it. *Disgusting beast.*

A burning hatred roared through me like a hurricane. It shut out every other thought but the steady beat of revenge. Revenge. Revenge. Revenge.

I sensed the shift in my men—the switch from fear to pure, unadulterated anger.

I didn't doubt for one second Blue saw something out here. I'd always felt that some evil had survived like a weed, growing through the cracks of the pavement. Here was the proof, lying at our feet.

"For now, we find out what we can. We're going to hunt these murderers down and kill 'em for what they did," I spoke into the darkness. "We've got a score to settle."

Lightning lit up the sky—flashed in the steel-set eyes of my men.

"Get what you can before the rain falls."

Blue's nervous warning to keep an eye on Jax took on new meaning. A very real threat waited out here. Outsiders. Hostile outsiders. She'd counted ten. Were there more? I knew better than to question Blue's instincts, and the devil knew she couldn't tell a lie to save her life.

The gathering thunderheads burst and rain fell from the heavens. The water did nothing to soothe the fire in my veins. The rest of my team followed on as the night closed in around us, ripe with a seething hatred and the scent of death.

CHAPTER 16

Screaming Sisters

BLUE

"Make it stop!" Kyra rolled around in our bed, a pillow smashed over her head. "Kill it!"

"Shut up!" Cora threw a pillow at her.

We all seethed with an angry annoyance this morning. After I came home completely exhausted last night, Kyra started into her obnoxious whining. She growled at us to be quiet at first, then she cried for us to just kill some stupid animal and get the wailing over with.

Even Lily's unending patience wore thin.

"Just go outside, Kyra! You're keeping all of us awake," I moaned.

"That *thing* is keeping me awake! It's screaming and crying and just won't stop! I can't take it for another second!" Kyra pounded the pillow on her head.

Tiger jumped off the bed, not keen on the possibility of getting squashed in the melee.

"How's that? Is *that* better?" Cora snarled, pelting Kyra over and over with her pillow. Dang, Cora really needed her beauty sleep.

I snapped out of my grouchy mood and remembered Kyra's ability. She must be hearing some creature wailing from miles away. She'd said the smallest sounds were amplified in the dead quiet of night.

"Hey, hey, hey," I hushed.

Cora and Lily flopped back down on the bed, rolled up in balls, and threw their pillows back over their heads.

"How about I sing you a song, okay, Kyra? Just focus on my voice," I whispered into the dark. She'd always loved it when I sang her to sleep when she was little. It'd been a while.

The sun had yet to rise behind the mountains. I listened outside —nothing but the slow pattering of the rain after a storm and our own animals stirring. The world lay hushed, dark, and still, but Kyra shook. I understood the pain of being overwhelmed. She'd trusted me. The least I could do was try to help—that and find this injured animal tomorrow and put it out of its misery.

Kyra remained a tight ball of fury as I curled up on the bed and softly sang one of our favorites. "You are my sunshine, my only sunshine—"

I drifted in and out of sleep, singing in a trance. I'm pretty sure Sirius Black and Yoda showed up in the lyrics somehow.

I woke with a start when my alarm chimed at 5:30 AM. I growled. Time to get ready for my first day as an official warrior. I ambled down the hallway like a zombie in a stupor.

As I passed by the boys' room I blinked, and *Hawk popped into view, hair a mess, feet blackened by filth and calluses hanging over the end of the bed. Sleeping like the dead.*

One more blink and he was gone. Just another vision memory of one week ago. Now the empty side of the bed hit me like a bad step into the ice melted waters of the creek. He had to be okay. He was strong and fast and no one had seen anything out there for a hundred years.

No one except me. Last night.

I slogged to the stables to saddle up Pepper. Mama tended to the goats in the back stall.

"Mornin', Ma." My voice ground out garbled and sticky after a sleepless night of singing.

Mama wiped her hands on either side of her jeans. Tiny drops of goat's milk soaked into the fabric. "Hey there, Blue. I wanted to catch you before you ran off this morning to the angels know where." She reached up to touch my cheek.

"Mom! You just milked the goats." I reeled. "Don't touch the face!"

"Alright, alright honey." She raised her hands. "But you need to tell me what's going on. You had a nice, easy job at Jim's, then you ran off with the president, and now you're a warrior?"

"How'd you know all that?" I asked. "I didn't tell you last night."

"Word gets around." Mama's eyes glistened. "Julian Rose called this morning to make sure we were aware."

My stomach fluttered. It was real. This was happening.

She looked up toward heaven. "Y'know, I was so relieved when you told us you were going into farming. So relieved. When your brother's gone, it's like a piece of my heart is over that wall with him." A tear drew a line down her rosy cheek. "Now you're going and taking another piece of me with you, and I don't know if I can bear it. Anything could happen, honey. Anything." She pulled me in for a hug, and her curly hair tickled my nose. "I told you I didn't want you getting mixed up with the warriors. What if they found out about your eyes?"

"But I can *use* my eyes, Mama. To protect us. General Rose'll look out for me."

Mama stiffened. "Honey, you need to be careful around some of those warriors—"

Dad strode into the stable. Blood coated the undersides of his fingernails from the raw meat we fed the possums.

"I'm going to be fine, Ma. Maybe I can be lookout, use my ability to really make a difference." Butterflies fluttered in my stomach.

My mom always worried. I couldn't wait to prove her wrong.

Dad laughed, deep and rumbling. "You've always been runnin' with your hair in the wind and toes in the water. Ever since you were a babe, my little woodland sprite. Off to wherever the wind'll take you. Just make sure the wind brings you home for dinner every now and then."

Dad got it; why was mom such a worrier? Dad reached down into his jeans pocket and handed me a small bundle wrapped up in a cotton cloth.

"What's this?" I asked.

"This is for you, Blue Laurel Haven, on your first day as a warrior. We thought it was time. This was my mama's, Mama Darla's, and their Mama Laurel's before. It was made by a Haven for the Havens. It made it through all the horrors of the Shadow War and now? It's said to contain magic." Dad wagged his thick eyebrows.

"Your mama and I have always known it would be yours, ever since you were a little one. I've worn it every day. Now it's your guardian angel to wear till you too can pass it down to your little ones." Dad's eyes misted over. He wrapped his large arm around Mama's shoulder.

I gingerly unfolded the soft cotton fabric to reveal the golden angel pendant the size of a long thimble on a chain. I'd seen it every day of my life, wrapped around my daddy's neck, but he'd had it polished. The angel was sturdy, heavy, yet intricate patterns had been carved into it—cutouts and symbols I didn't understand. Curiously made. I'd never seen anything else like it.

A lump formed in my throat as emotion choked back any words.

I placed the delicate gold chain around my neck. The golden angel settled right below my collar. Before I could say thank you, Dad and Mom pulled me in for a hug. Goats baaed and pigs shuffled about, but the moment stretched on. I lived in it—soaked it up.

As I turned to leave, Mama handed me a sack of vittles. Thank goodness for mothers. I saddled up Pepper, strapped up my knife, bow, and arrows and rode out to the front of the house.

Morning mist rose up from the cool grass. I glanced behind me one last time before the barn faded from sight. Mama flopped down on the bench, head in her hands, shoulders hunched up around her as the goats bleated for attention the next stall over, my dad's strong arms encircled about her.

CHAPTER 17

that Familiar Scent

KALEO

As the cool of the night gave way to the heat of the morning, our thirst for blood only intensified. I followed the lingering scent of the outsiders, but it had gone cold, washed out in the rainstorm.

Joe. Dead. His smell clung to the roof of my mouth. Try as I might, I couldn't rid myself of his death. Terror. Anger. Revenge. As if his soul cried out to me for vengeance and would not leave until I answered the call.

If Pretty-Boy Joe was dead, where was Hawk?

They'd been sent out on their warpaths, just like the rest of my team. To explore, learn about the land, and be alone for the first time in their lives. I drew back to my own path all the time to remind myself that I could survive out here on the land with just a hatchet and my horse. It had been one of the most frightening times of my life, but liberating and beautiful still.

Those privates weren't prepared for this. Our training had become so lax. And the defenses around our border? I shook my head. We weren't ready for any type of attack. New Haven had never been so vulnerable.

I cursed under my breath.

Laurel Haven must be rolling in her grave.

Since my trail ran cold, Dallas led us. He licked the mouth of a discarded metal canteen by Joe's dead body and set off, wet blond hair flying.

"The saliva on the lid was pretty diluted from the rainfall,"

Dallas explained as I caught up. "All I got was that he came from this direction. He's in his late teens, early twenties. He'd been eatin' a lot of rat meat."

I tried not to let my disgust show. I'd seen Dallas lick dried blood, boots, and even the occasional horse hoof to find a trail. His was an ability I didn't envy.

We rode out farther than we'd ever dared go on patrol before— uncharted territory. We were heading away from where Blue had seen the light, but we needed to find this murderous group first. It was priority number one. I had a feeling it was all connected somehow.

As we rounded a copse of trees, a new, yet all too familiar smell hit me square in the nose. It bled into my eyes and filled them with tears. That alien, metallic, wild smell. Alluring, good. It was the same scent I'd chased three days ago toward the gristmill and outer wall. But this scent was marred in decay and rot. Thankfully, it was still far enough away that I didn't retch right then and there.

"Kaleo, y'okay?" Jax pulled his horse up beside mine. He closed his fist, halting the team. "What is it?"

Jax held out his crossbow and nocked an arrow. He knew me too well.

My men followed on high alert.

"It's here," I whispered. "The same thing I found down by the wall. Dallas tasted it at the holler."

Jax blanched. "What? You mean *here*? This close?"

I nodded.

Jax swore forcefully, horror emanating from him. He cleared his throat. "What do we do, Cap?"

"They're here, aren't they?" Dallas pulled up beside us—eyes about bugged out from his head.

Brock and the rest of my team fanned out. It was time I told them what I'd done before it all went to hell. Maybe it already had gone to hell.

As I explained the happenings of this past week, nerves and

adrenaline spiked in all of my men, lifting off of them in waves like a reverse waterfall. But I couldn't focus on the fear, I needed to focus on the getting things done.

"I'll scout ahead first, then send a signal to follow," I said. "If you don't hear from me in five minutes, turn back around and ride for home like the devil's after you."

That might not be too far off.

"Hey, I'm right behind you." Jax nodded, face tight, agate eyes sharp. "You ain't gonna have all the fun."

Jax's smile didn't reach his eyes. I nodded. We dismounted leaving our horses with the rest of the men, and crept into the unknown. The metallic stench pulled at me, causing my nose and eyes to water. Calling to me, yet unbearable.

My sack of coffee beans was pointless in this onslaught. I needed something stronger. I reached into my pocket and pulled out a new addition. A fail-safe.

A blue silk pouch I'd folded up from the ripped fabric of a certain girl's scandalous dress, with her blue daisy crushed inside.

I took in a long, slow pull and closed my eyes—if only for a second.

Then walked straight into hell.

CHAPTER 18
Six-hundred-fifty-nine Glow Worms

BLUE

Pepper's hooves crunched the blue rock path leading from my house as I snatched a ripe peach from a hanging branch. Through the curtain of morning mist sat a murky silhouette of the rider I was to follow to my first day of training.

Juniper Jones was one of the only redheads in town and three-time arm wrestling champion at Wild Willy's. She graduated a few years ago, barely, but she was born a warrior. This girl grew up in one of the back-hills with thirteen brothers and sisters. It wasn't until her little brother, Ash, died from a farming accident that we found out their parents had been dead for years. Those kids had been hunting and fishing and living off the land like scavengers ever since. They were a tough bunch, all thirteen, well, twelve now.

Juniper was a legend. She got the hardest kill, an eagle, on her warpath, just like General Rose.

I pretty much geeked out every time I saw her.

She rolled her eyes as I made my way to her at the top of the hill. Juniper sat astride her painted horse, all relaxation and surety, as she sharpened her dagger like a total boss. A handkerchief wrapped around her head, wild red hair flaring around the sides and out of an old ponytail. She never put any time into her looks, but she drew you in like a magnet. Her clothes were always so strange, wrapped on like bandages.

Two-hundred-forty-seven freckles peppered her pale nose and cheeks.

"So." Juniper looked me over, unimpressed. "While everyone else goes out to kill the devils, I get stuck on babysitting duty. Great."

"Sounds good," I yawned, used to the razzing of a twin brother. "My baby sister, Shenandoah, is back there at the house. Just woke up. She'll need a good breast feeding."

"Psh."

"Hope you're lactating." I started to ride off like I knew where I was going. I wasn't quite sure since civilians weren't allowed near the base, but Hawk had hinted it was near the old train depot. I made it about fifty feet when Juniper pulled her horse up next to mine and rolled her eyes.

She huffed. "You're going the wrong way, Fuschia. Come on."

We rode off into the wood. At one point we headed in the same direction I'd taken as I followed Soldier Boy through the woods toward that strange burlap sack. But we didn't go all the way to the south wall.

"Promise me. Just promise me you won't go back there."

Kaleo swore it was just a burlap sack of flowers, that it had all been a mistake. But with his enhanced smell, how could he have been so wrong?

I needed to ask him what that was all about, but I was still confused. Which Kaleo would I get this time? The playful one or the dismissive jerk?

Kaleo's perfect face blinked before my sight, my favorite vision memory of him from a year ago. *I'd caught a glimpse of him as I rode by his farm—maybe a little on purpose. He was working the fields with his goats. They followed at his heels like love-struck puppies. He took a huge gulp of water, wetting his shirt in the process. He laughed to himself, then tipped the entire canteen over his head. It ran in rivers down his long hair, soaking his shirt thoroughly. Water clinging to his individual eyelashes. To his chest—*

Woah. I didn't know I could do slow motion like that.

I let the scene fall from my eyes.

I had to remember that he'd only been this amazing, dreamy guy in my little girl fantasies. Time to grow up and see reality. Who was he really? What was he protecting? I wanted to trust him, but I didn't know if it was my heart, head, or hormones talking.

Were the Falcons alright outside the wall? Were Hawk and Pretty-Boy? Or did they find something bad out in the wastelands?

Juniper motioned us forward. Excitement filled me with butterflies. I was here. This was happening. I finally got to lay my eyes on the warrior's base, and it was indeed at the old train station. Large brick walls surrounded the massive plot of land. Barbed wire spun through the top of the high bars, shutting it off from the rest of the town. Mechanics and scientists worked on the machinery, building new transports, ways to harvest faster, and contraptions to keep water clean. Griff worked here now.

Smoke evaporators had been invented here when this place was first founded. Back in the Shadow War days, fires were strictly forbidden. The smoke would alert unwanted attention to your presence from miles around. Bandits, marauders, elves. You know what they say, "Smoke brings death."

The Founders created a chimney system for each home that heated the water tank, then filtered out the chemicals from the smoke, leaving only invisible water vapor to escape through the chimney. Another way New Haven stayed hidden in plain sight and under the radar.

Juniper waved at the guard in the tower and the gate slid open. I tried to wipe the goofy grin off my face, but I felt like the little fat kid who finally got the whole cake to herself! If I could, I would squeal with excitement, but a warrior wouldn't do that, so I schooled my face into faux boredom.

Yeah, I'd seen a hybrid train/tank with large spikes of death on it. Run by corn fuel? Please. I'd seen more impressive things. I thought my eyes were going to explode with excessively exciting intake. My hands itched to touch everything in sight.

No one spared a second glance as Juniper and I rode through.

Mechanics covered in oil and grease laid under vehicles of all shapes and sizes, spitting sunflower seeds. Tools, wrenches, and loud electric saws spewed sparks in every direction.

Juniper whistled for me to keep up. I blinked and spotted our destination, an old mining elevator. Cool violet air leaked out from the shaft. *Of course it was in a cavern.* An attendant took our horses to the stables.

Gauging by Juni's wicked smile, this was going to be hell on shaky wheels.

"We're going down in *this* thing?" I asked as we stepped into the janky elevator of doom.

I expected it to be a fearful and shaky ride of death.

It was *worse.*

What were all of those scientists back there doing if they couldn't take a minute to add a few safety features? Did we enjoy ripping down a tunnel of unforgiving rock at a hundred miles an hour while rubble rained down on our heads as we contemplated our trip to God's celestial shore? This was more like an elevator into the Devil's Hell.

"Devil's holy hand-grenade!" I screamed.

Juniper threw her head back and crowed like Peter Pan all the way down.

We slammed into the bottom of the cavern. After I found my barely beating heart on the ground and put it back in my chest, I followed Juniper down a tight, damp hallway. Electric lights lined the earthy walkway, casting the limestone in a creamy green. The loamy dirt mixed with a stink of—yep, my B.O.

Hawk would be so proud.

Flecks of gold and burgundy shimmered in Juniper's hair as her breath echoed off the curves of the small tunnel. How many times had Kaleo or Hawk stooped through this cavern?

I'd envisioned this place so many times. I'd imagined the base in a wooden fort, like the ones our old founders built for protection in the early years. The large wooden beams were later fortified by layers of brick, mortar, and kudzu.

I'd imagined strong men and women fighting with spears and knives in rings, Gladiator style. Or hand to hand combat with black shrouded ninjas who soared through the air with deadly accuracy. Or maybe Yoda seated in a backpack teaching young warriors how to lift rocks with their minds—I needed to stop reading so many pre-war comics.

But all of those would be easily discoverable, which was why, when I stood at the opening of the actual warrior's base, my mouth popped open in awe. The tunnel opened up ahead to an enormous outcropping overlooking the biggest cavern I'd ever seen. It was massive, a whole village churning below.

My vision took over, flying around the cavern like a bat on crack. The warriors had been busy this past 111 years fortifying their base—making it a deadly, breathing masterpiece.

Stone beams fortified the cavern from floor to ceiling.

New Haven angel wings were etched onto every column—saw marks, burned in from their creation, stalactite dripping down the sides. Each crevice naturally carved by time, water, and air for millions of years, and then by the warriors in the past century to create spaces to train.

Two blacksmiths pounded steel weapons and armor. Bright flame and black shadows danced across the cavern walls. An armory lay behind the smiths, filled with every weapon imaginable. All emblazoned with our New Haven avenging angel wings.

Five warriors belonging to the Fangs sparred in the large training room below.

Juniper's brother, redheaded Rowan, smacked Scarlip Nigel on the backside with a wooden training sword. Nigel sneered. He always seemed to be sneering these days. Targets and weapons lined up against the wall like spectators.

Several monstrous chandeliers hung from the ceiling above the muscled fighters. The chandeliers looked like some sort of ancient medieval torture devices converted into delightful lighting appliances. How lovely.

The cavern rolled out endlessly. The enormity of the organization, the potential, staggered the imagination.

A map formed unbidden in my mind.

I finally tore my eyes away from the visual onslaught to see Juniper sizing me up.

Instead of mocking my dorkiness, she nodded. "I know, right? This place is...well, it's home."

The entire cavern was all curves and warmth. What wasn't rock or stone had been carved from natural wood. Cozy seating areas comprised of wooden tables, benches, and fireplaces dotted the space. Electric lights bounced off every surface. It wasn't a dank, old underground cavern, but a grand, open daytime palace of stone.

We made this. My people. It *did* feel like home.

Juniper clapped a hand on my shoulder. "Well, time to see the boss. You get to find out where they'll put ya."

"Wait. I won't be with you?" I asked, like a desperate child clinging to their mommy.

"I'll be briefed separately by my own superior. You'll have your own captain and team. I'm just another lowly warrior like you, but if you find you need a lil' help, I could give you some pointers."

Kindness from Juniper. *Try to be cool, Blue. Be cool.* "Thanks." *You're my hero!*

We strode down the halls and winding passages until we arrived at a large meeting room. A thick wooden table sat squat in the center of the cavern room where maps, figures, and books littered the walls and cabinets. A current map of New Haven lay across the table. This was an updated map from the ancient one I'd used in the outpost.

I glanced at it. Over half of the surrounding forty miles were marked with x's. But I couldn't help but notice how much of the area had *not* been marked off. I checked the map of the south wood, where Kaleo warned me against. Nothing there but a bunch of abandoned caverns marked *collapsed* or *condemned*, and the old gristmill.

"So, we wait here till your captain arrives to kick your butt."

Juniper leaned back in a chair and crossed her legs up on the table, bringing out her knife to sharpen again.

I shot her a look of displeasure, but didn't sit. I moved around the space, memorizing everything my eyes touched.

"Man, I'm surprised I just get to sit around and relax," I said to Juniper. "I thought I'd be scrubbing canteens for a week once I got here, or running about fifty laps with a large horse strapped to my back. This ain't too bad!"

"That could all be arranged," General Rose boomed behind me.

I almost jumped out of my britches.

Relief welled within me as I ran over and gave him a big ol' hug.

General Rose welcomed me with arms wide. "Blue! I knew you'd end up here, you precocious thing. Always got your toes in the trees and your nose in a fight."

"No, I do not!" I countered. *Why did everyone keep saying that?* In truth, General Rose had always felt like family, like an uncle. Besides my own Dad, I couldn't choose anyone else I'd rather have as my mentor.

The general was a stocky man, corded in muscle. His neck was the same size as his jawline and grew ever wider as it reached his massive shoulders. He had the same heavy-lidded eyes Griffin and his sister inherited. His salt and pepper hair stuck straight up in a tight flat-top. It was amazing, really, how it had always seemed to defy gravity. When I was a kid, I imagined he'd been struck by lightning. And now that his hair was mostly silver—it added to my lightning theory.

General Rose held me at arm's length, studying me. "Alright, Miss Haven. I have good news and bad news."

He released me and marched around the large conference room, hands clasped behind his back. "Miss Jones, you are dismissed."

"Thank you, sir." Juniper saluted and left the room without a backwards glance.

General Rose gestured for me to sit. "First of all, the president congratulates you on your appointment, but there are a few things you need to understand. Firstly, Zhao's the president and even though she takes a special interest in the protection of it, she's not the head of the army. I am. So, I will be your final word. That clear, young lady?" He lifted an eyebrow.

"Yes, sir." My stomach lurched. It went against my very nature, but there had to be a chain of command or else everything fell apart. I understood that.

"Also, I know we have a special connection, but I cannot be seen showing any special interest or esteem for you 'round the troops, y' understand?"

"Yes, of course. Sorry," I apologized.

He smiled. "Good news is, I'll be your overseeing officer until your permanent placement is solidified." He shifted to a more serious tone. "No doubt, you know of the special task force that was sent out to look into the occurrence of las' night. Heck, you practically sent 'em out to do it."

I nodded, but my insides squirmed.

"Once we get a few more of our warriors back, I'll find you your permanent team. You'd usually train with the other new recruits, but, as it is, they're out on their warpaths at the moment. Ever since that idiotic school stopped trainin' y'all kids, we've had a harder time findin' anyone who's got the right stuff. Folks don't seem to think protecting our borders is all that important anymore. Budgets and politics." He shook his head. "Ah well, we like to see who you mesh with. So, while the Falcons are out on duty and your fellow privates are out on their war paths, you'll train with a temporary team."

General Rose must have seen my worry because he added, "Hawk'll be home in two days. You'll be surprised how fast it goes. Don't you worry."

Why hadn't I ever worried for Hawk before the last few days? I never thought twice of him leaving on patrol or guard duty. How selfish and blind I'd been, lulled away in this safety bubble of New Haven, when all around us a world stirred with who knew what horrors.

That light was the first sign of life out there—a wake-up call.

"The bad news, well, your abilities, kid. They're known here and word of your powers are spreadin'," he leaned back on the table.

The world dropped under me. "But I thought only my family knew. H-how, how did you—"

"I've known you were gifted for a long time. Heaven's sake, been around your family for years. Practically saw you born. Lil' Hellion, if I ever saw one." He smiled. "Yep. There was no way 'round hiding it once word reached us that there was a light seen miles outside the wall. The president called in all hands-on deck and, well, after your little scene at the party last night—the warriors among the crowd put two and two together."

Silence. A kernel of fear lodged in my chest.

"And, I'm not sure how to tell you this, but you're not the only enhanced warrior we've got." He raised his silver eyebrows.

My heart kicked into a frenzy. Did he know about Kaleo?

"That's right, pup. You're not alone. The thing is, well, the kids who've been drawn into being warriors, the ones who have the best skills, have been *very* gifted. Just a few kids, mind you. I've been able to teach them how to use their growing powers, put their limits to the test without making much of a fuss. It's fascinatin' really." He grinned.

"Problem is, well, President caught wind of this recently. Now she's got it into her head to make a type of enhanced squad or somethin'. She wants an elite group of powered warriors. She wants you, Blue. Bad. So, all of them years your mama and pop tried to protect you and keep you from being used like a puppet"—he shook his head—"well, that may all be undone now, sweetie. But, you've got me here. I got your back, so does your brother. We always take care of our own." General Rose clapped me on the back. It didn't feel so much like a brick this time. "You're gonna be fine. It might be good for you to meet some other kids like you." He watched me closely. "Come out of the shadows, as it were."

"But, what about the Edict? T-the Enforcers?" My heart lodged in my throat.

"Aw, hells, nobody believes in that old mumbo jumbo anymore." He waved his hand dismissively. "I think we humans have been given a real gift. A real fightin' chance if them devils ever show up again. And they will, oh, we know they will. Everybody in this town's just too stupid or blind to see it."

I couldn't register what he said. All I could hear over the roaring in my head were the words *"you are not alone."* The same words I'd spoken to Kyra when she was broken. Were there others like me? Others who could see? Kyra, who could hear? Kaleo, who could smell? I was too excited to be worried about the whole president thing. Plus, Kaleo said I could trust Zhao. So what if I was part of some elite squad?

"So, there are others like me? Here?" I tried to hide the excitement in my voice, but he heard it. The excitement and, if I was being honest with myself, relief.

"Yes, lil' Hellion, you're not alone." He grinned. "Want to meet 'em?"

General Rose was not so kind as to let me go skipping off to make new friends. First, he gave me the Warrior's Code of Honor. As we read through that crusty old book written up by the Founders, I had to raise my hand and swear on every page.

The army was the first thing the Founders set up back in the day. I guess it would be important when the threat of imminent death hung over their heads every second. Things had gotten a bit more relaxed over the years, but was the same in spirit.

I was to stay clean, healthy, and strong mentally and physically at all times so help me God. Fight for our rights to life, liberty, and mercy. I swore to protect my family of New Haven with all I had been blessed with.

The chain of command was simple. The president was chief, then the general, and four captains—each with five to seven warriors.

Add in a few scientists and mechanics who created the weapons, and that was us.

"Of course everyone was a warrior, survivor, in the beginnin', but once they settled, started growing, the rule of thumb was one warrior per twenty citizens," General Rose explained. "That changed to a one in fifty about fifty years ago. Then we got stretched out to one warrior per seventy-five Haveners just this past decade. So, we've got 'round twenty to twenty-two warriors in all, depending."

I would report to my captain daily. There were the Falcons—Hawk's and Kaleo's team—Wings, the Talons, and the Fangs. I was just hoping not to be chosen by the Slytherins, I mean, Fangs. They were a team of slick-backed, greasy jerks. Where was my sorting hat?

"You'll be tested and pushed harder than you've ever been. Do it. Go for it. We don't truly grow as a people until we completely break down first and rebuild. Our own muscle grows that way. We have to break it, destroy it little by little in order to grow stronger," General Rose explained.

Sounded better than cleaning up after hundreds of dairy cows.

"And don't go lookin' to me for an easy ride," General Rose finished.

I knew that well enough from Griffin's life experience. His Dad was always so hard on him. No matter that Griff was the smartest kid in New Haven—he could never quite measure up. For some reason, though, the general treated me like the son he never had.

He grinned. "Alright, lil' Hellion. I've kept you long enough. Let's take you in to see a few of your fellow weirdos."

"Thanks a lot." I wrinkled my nose.

I followed General Rose through the dripping cavern toward a private training room. Echoes of metal clanging in combat flitted toward me. Rose moved aside, revealing three warriors sparring in the center of a small ring.

Six-hundred-fifty-nine glow worms lit up the ceiling among the stalactites.

A smile touched my lips, I knew these people. Juniper and a boy with tight blond curls were going at it. His name was Orin; I knew him from school.

My eyes widened as I took in Juniper's appearance. She was practically naked. She'd stripped down to a tight bra and tiny shorts. Juniper swerved deftly, kicking dust into the air as her wooden sparring swords collided with Orin's.

"Dang it, June!" Orin cried, as a thick layer of dirt coated his body, allowing Juniper to smack his exposed side with her wooden sword.

A tall man in his twenties wearing a cowboy hat, leaned up on the cavern wall. He studied the fighters, then took notice of us. He saluted the general, then the other two followed suit, sizing me up.

I was not alone. There were three other warriors with enhanced abilities, and Juniper was one of them. *Yes.* Of course I knew everyone, but now I'd been brought in. There was something special about meeting others like me. Other taboos.

"At ease, privates," General Rose commanded. "I'd like you to meet our new recruit, Blue Haven. She's gifted, like y'all, so show her the ropes."

Rose smacked me on the back then strolled out.

Orin, Juniper's sparring partner, walked up and shook my hand with a friendly grin. "Welcome to the Super Squad!"

"Stop callin' us that, Batboy," Juniper groaned.

"Well then, you come up with something better." Orin's ears flushed red.

He turned back to me and said, kindly. "Rose pulled us from our other teams just recently, and we haven't quite come up with a good name yet." He called back over to Juni, "And stop calling me Batboy."

"How 'bout the Stupid Squad?" Juni offered.

"That's not better." Orin deflated.

"You're not wrong there." I smiled.

"Super hearing," Orin explained as he pointed to his ear. "Can hear things miles away. Can be annoying, but helpful too."

Hearing like Kyra.

Orin was a few years older than I was in school but was always kind to me. There were days when we'd sit in companionable silence underneath the solar panels during lunch and watch the ants carry their bounties toward their anthills in triumph. Us, the weird, quiet kids who didn't like too much stimulation. Made sense.

"Hey, Purple." Juniper smirked as she spun her wooden sword with flair. "Excited to see what you can do with those pretty eyes."

My stomach squirmed. I wasn't used to anyone else knowing about my sight. This would take some getting used to.

Juniper's skin was so pale, almost translucent. She wore hardly any clothes at all, and what clothing she did have was wrapped on tight like bandages. She tugged on a pair of gloves. I'd never paid much attention before, but seeing as she was almost naked, her freckles stood out like polka dots on a ladybug. She was strong, tight, and lean, not curvy like me. I felt a bit uncomfortable as I tried not to stare at her bright, bare skin. My daddy would never let me go out of the house like that. Ever.

"Sensitive skin," Juniper said, acknowledging my attention. "Hate clothes. I'd go naked if I could."

Orin choked, his face beet red. The older man with the stoic beard and cowboy hat, smacked him on the back with a smirk. I bit my cheeks, stifling a laugh.

Skin sensitivity must be awful. How could that possibly help her as a warrior? I bet all I'd have to do was pinch her. How had she survived her crazy house full of brothers where being pinched must've been a daily occurrence?

"Pleased to meet ya." The older man tipped his hat. "Name's Zach, folks call me Hound."

"He can pick up on sugar in a snowstorm," Orin chimed in as he tapped his nose.

Hound was like Kaleo, super smell.

"Nice to meet you, too." I smiled.

Warmth spread through me. There were more people like me and they were...amazing!

"So, I still don't get Batboy. Is it 'cause bats have big ears?" I asked Orin. "Or is Juni saying you're crazy? I mean, for someone who has a nickname for everyone, this one seems a bit weak."

"You saying I have big ears?" Orin balked.

Oops. "No, I just—"

"Ha, just playing." Orin pursed his lips thoughtfully. "Actually, I just discovered something cool recently. You know bats are blind, right?"

"Blind as a bat." I shrugged.

"Well, we were training in the dark and—" Orin spoke as Hound secured a blindfold over his eyes.

My skin crawled. My worst nightmare—being blinded.

"Show her," Hound said.

"A'ight." Orin shrugged. "Toss something towards me."

Then he thought better of it and added, "Nothing sharp like last time, Junebug!"

Everyone backed up as Orin held his wooden training sword at the ready, blindfold over his eyes. Then, he did the strangest thing. He made a clicking sound with his mouth. My eyes went wide. Juni smirked with a wink.

The clicking continued as Hound beamed a small sack of corn at Orin's head. Orin spun and cut it down with his sword. My mouth popped open.

He couldn't *see* it. He *heard* it.

Hound threw sack after sack at Orin. Orin swatted and smacked the sacks down one after another like a Jedi, all the while clicking his tongue. He'd whistle too.

"Echolocation," Hound explained. "He hears the clicking sounds bouncing off the corn sacks."

"I *see* the sound!" Orin corrected, swatting down another sack. "In my mind."

"Like a bat," Juni added—hurling a sack at Orin's crotch with a little too much gusto.

"Hey!" Orin lifted up his blindfold.

Juni beamed another one at him.

Orin threw his sword on the dirt and rolled his eyes. He *saw* the sound. I wondered if Kyra could learn this trick.

Hound turned his deep-set eyes on me. "It might be your first day and all, but I find no reason to take it easy on you. Let's see whatch'er made of. Blue, you and Juniper are up next."

Oh no. Here we go.

He gestured toward the center of the dusty training room topped in a layer of glow worms. Juni and I walked toward the ring.

"This room is where we usually train," Hound explained. "We like to keep a low profile, keep our abilities off the radar. The general uses our special services when need be, with discretion. Alright now, Juni'll test you."

This should be interesting.

Hound tossed us both a long, wooden sparring sword. "Disarm!"

I whirled around, searching for Juniper. She'd been right next to me. As I spun and swung my wooden sword, Juni was on me like a pasty praying mantis.

Like a breeze, she flew, blazing auburn hair whipping my cheek.

I spun and she pirouetted. I jabbed and she jumped backward, almost before I made the moves. Before I even *thought* about them. *How in the...?* We danced in the cavern for a matter of minutes. Our swords flew in the air, so close, but never touching. I got the feeling Juniper was a cat playing with her food.

She smirked. "That all you got, darlin'?"

Aw, heck no.

I'd been leading offensive, now it was her turn. Her eyes flashed as I switched into a defensive position. Our breaths sputtered. Sweat dripped in rivers through the filth on her skin. Enough of this crap, time to use my greatest weapon. I pulled in a breath of air and swirling dirt and watched her closely. Her eyes narrowed as she raised up her arms in a defensive stance.

Not this time, honey. Your move.

We stayed that way for a few moments in a stand-off as I studied her ultra-sensitive skin. Tiny hairs on her arms, neck, and waist were raised like a cat's whiskers. She must use the air currents around her, feel the motions of her opponent.

I tried to focus, bring the air into sight, into color—so I could use it, too.

Juni winked, then rushed in for the kill, sword toward my chest. I blocked her just in time, but she knocked the sword right out of my hands. I was disarmed, but my fist landed square in her face before my sword even clattered to the ground.

"Holy devil!" Juni's squeal filled the cavern like a piglet with a papercut.

A broken nose was much worse than a pinch.

I was getting a little too good at breaking people's noses.

Orin sucked air in between his teeth with a look that said *"ooh, that's bad."*

Hound nodded in what I could only gather was approval.

But almost as soon as Juni screamed, she shut her mouth and wiped away the blood pooling under her nose. We locked eyes. Anger mixed with a dose of respect flashed. *Cool. Be cool, Blue.*

A replay of the match passed before my eyes, my fist landing straight into her nose. Her blood spraying three-point-four inches from her face.

If I didn't feel so bad, I'd be proud.

"Not bad for a newbie." June stood and brushed the dust from her sensitive skin. She took the bandana from her hair and held it to her face to staunch the blood.

Her arm hairs stuck straight out, searching to read the room. I wondered how the dirt particles felt on her skin.

Orin, Hound, Juniper, me. Hearing, Smell, Feel, and Sight. Not too bad for a Super Squad.

CHAPTER 19

The Killing Barn

KALEO

I signaled to my men. Jax and Dallas crept to the left, the others to the right. Their shadows flashed in the dancing lightning as they approached the barn. We had it surrounded, but I'd be the one who put my hatchet through the heart of that murderer.

The copper blood of most of those devil outsiders already coated our weapons and clothes. They fought savagely, like monsters, jumping from the trees in the dead of night as we tracked them. They'd laughed in our faces. Spit at us. If it hadn't been for my enhanced sense of smell, my men would all be dead.

But they'd never met anyone like us before.

I could still hear one of the men crying, "Dios! What are you?" as I'd put my hatchet through his chest. I'd never killed a man before.

I felt nothing but the rush of revenge—the drive to protect my people, as I said, "Your death." Their blood washed away in streams through the pouring rain, the metallic scent clinging to my nostrils.

Pungent, unwashed odors indicated two men remained in the barn ahead. Asleep. A fitful rest. The storm was close.

Lightning struck, and I counted to one, then kicked in the door as thunder crashed.

No light flickered within the barn. Musty hay and torched rat meat filled my nose. I sensed their adrenaline spike as the two men roused from sleep. They jumped to their feet. Confusion filled the air, mingling with a sting of desperation.

The two men, almost identical, took me in with sheer terror. Heaven knew what I looked like to them, soaking wet, hatchet and face covered in the blood of their comrades. Their fear fed a dark part of myself. *Good.*

They were different, yet both reeked of whatever sick place they'd hailed from.

"Fight with me one last time, brother," one of them said to the other.

I allowed them to arm themselves.

A flash of a knife as bonds were cut. Rope fell in the hay at their feet.

One of them had been tied up?

Lightning flashed, alighting their faces. The two men stood back-to-back, swords at the ready. They shared the same brown hair and green eyes.

The men from Blue's visions.

"The rest of your men are dead," I ground out between clenched teeth as my white knuckles gripped my hatchet. "They attacked us first without provocation."

I felt no regret for what I was about to do. An easy calm settled over me as I continued. "But we know one of you is responsible for the death of our man." I stretched my arm toward them; the hatchet flashed in another strike of lightning. "Which one of you soulless murderers did it?"

Fear soaked one of the men, anger filled the other. Calculation. I smelled the acidic scent of his mind working, twisting. Thunder clapped in the distance as rain pelted the tin roof. Blood dripped from the end of my hatchet.

"All clear," Dallas called from outside the barn walls.

The man on the right turned toward the other. He lowered his weapon a fraction. Brown hair stuck out in a wild mess. They'd been holed up here for who knew how long, killing their way across the country. Dead rats, hay, and sweat filled my nose. A week? Maybe two. The men looked at one another.

"Goodbye, brother," one said.

I didn't want to think about them as people. As brothers. They were murderers.

Now I was a murderer, too.

I gripped my hatchet in one hand, my sword in the other. One of the brothers raised his sword, ready to fight. The other lowered his. Adrenaline, fear, sorrow. It was time. I advanced, ready to end this, when the man to the right thrust his sword up. Not toward me, but toward his own brother. Straight through his heart.

My hatchet almost clattered to the ground, but I couldn't let shock overtake me. I had to kill the other man. *Now.*

"It was him!" the murderer cried, still holding the slumped body of his comrade.

Shock, betrayal, pain. The scents rolled from them.

The murderer's eyes refused to leave his brother's as he called to me. "He killed your man. I lit the beacon on the rooftop. I warned you. I was their prisoner. Y-you saved me!"

He stared into the eyes of his victim, transfixed, as the life left his body. A damning glare of betrayal looked back at him. Then, the killer's head fell onto his dead brother's chest. Blood seeped from the gaping wound, drenching the living man's hair.

Sorrow, guilt, anguish—it oozed from him, overwhelming me. Those emotions filled my heart as if I'd just killed my own brother. Tears pricked at my eyes. I shook my head, willing the pain away— but it washed over me all the same.

He lay, his back to me, completely exposed. Vulnerable. His life at my mercy.

No mercy for the merciless.

Raleigh himself would kill this man. None of these men had shown any restraint as they killed Joe then left his head for the ravens to devour. They may have done the same to Hawk.

These men did not deserve my mercy, yet— regret. Pain. Anguish —I tried to ignore the emotions as they surged from him, but I couldn't.

Cursing myself, I raised my sword and brought it down on his head, knocking him out cold.

CHAPTER 20

I Have to Stop My Sister from Committing Murder

BLUE

Barely standing on my tired feet, I hobbled through the warrior's base, heading toward home. I couldn't wait to fall into my little corner of night-night land and sleep.

I trudged my sore body through the base, visualizing where I was in relation to the above-ground world. The map I'd created spun before my eyes, and I chose the exit closest to Raleigh House. My legs and arms screamed to *please stop* as I climbed hand over hand up the sturdy wooden ladder. This thing was built for at least three warriors wide. If ever the need arose for a mass exit—these existed all over the cavern.

A very complicated locking mechanism was bolted to the door right above my head. Probably invented by a sadist. I learned how to unlock it earlier today. The code changed every few days. I turned the surprisingly silent latch and found myself peeking out of a well-hidden cave covered by a cascade of green kudzu vines.

Very, very clever. They'd been hiding in plain sight all along. This exit happened to be by the old creek in the middle of town. I felt a little giddy, like a secret spy from those dusty old novels. Faint sunlight filtered in through the vines with a pink glow—still late afternoon. But a storm was brewing. A flicker of lighting confirmed it. I almost threw my legs out of the tunnel to get home before the downpour, when I smacked my hand to my head.

"Pepper!" Through all of my training I'd forgotten my dang horse back at the stables in the old train depot. *Heaven help me.* I slumped back to the ground of the tunnel and leaned my head against the chill earth, hidden from the world and responsibilities of the day. The clouds burst and fat rain pelted outside my hideout. Purple thunderheads covered the sun, plunging my tunnel into a dark amethyst.

My arrows and bow dug into my back but I didn't care. I just needed a minute before I could rouse myself, turn back around, and get Pepper. Just a minute—

I AWAKENED to a bright crack of lightning. I threw my hands about myself quickly gauging where in the Sam Hill I was. My eyes adjusted to the inky black of the night in a blink. Cool musty rocks, dirt, and kudzu vines. A light rain sprinkled the woods outside. Another flash of lightning was answered by a rumble of thunder six seconds later. The storm was moving on.

I must have fallen asleep in the tunnel leading out of the base. I turned to crawl out when wet footsteps splashed beyond the safety of the vines. Instantly, I imagined a large wolf of death prowling right outside, ready to tear into me. Or maybe a zombie panda.

Time to be brave. I was a warrior now, dang it.

I pulled back the kudzu and traced the splashing footfalls to the silhouette of a skinny little girl stomping some distance off. She marched barefoot in her tiny little nightshift, her hair a fluffy halo in the moon's light. I knew that silhouette.

What time was it? The girl carried a large steel crowbar as she advanced with a fury and determination I only saw when justice was about to be dealt. I'd sure hate to be on the business end of that crowbar.

I scrambled out of the tunnel into the rain. But as soon as I moved, she bolted behind a tree as silent as a mouse. Water droplets twirled around her in a cloud, displaced by her breathing. She was pretty good at disappearing; I'd give her that.

"Kyra," I groaned. "What the devil are you doing out here all by yourself? I could have been a dang Shadow Elf bent on eating you for dessert."

She peeked her head out from behind the tree. The metal end of the crowbar reflected the light of the moon, and a sick thought entered my mind.

"You weren't just taking a little night stroll, were you? You were gonna kill that injured and helpless animal from last night!"

"I can't sleep!" Her bottom lip stuck out, but her eyes flashed with resolve. "If you could just hear that thing wailing. It cries all night! I'll be doing it a favor. It's in pain and so am I. It just needs to die."

"Kyra, Dad's gonna kill you! So's Mama! This is the stupidest thing you've ever done!"

Kyra couldn't care less that this upset me. She rolled her eyes and carried on walking. "I ain't alone anyways. Lily's been following me like some kinda creepo for miles. Thinks she's being all quiet-like, but her juicy chewing's about to drive me up a wall." Kyra growled. "I know you're there, Lily. This crowbar's for you next!"

A surprised yelp sounded from a few yards away. "What? You knew I was here this whole time?"

I rolled my eyes and followed after Kyra. Lily would have to catch up to us now that her cover was blown. The rain let up as we walked in silence, only the wind and trees keeping us company. Nights in the mountains were magical. The moon's silvery light glimmered on the water droplets gilding the clover underfoot.

A stillness settled the air. The bugs were all asleep in their little beds and the birds had turned in for the night. The woods transformed into a world of silvers, blacks, navy blues, and amethyst jewels.

"So, what were you planning on doing once you saw this poor little creature?" I asked. "You know you've never been able to kill any living thing. Not even a spider, which you hate."

"It's getting louder and louder. Do you hear it? It can't just be in my head." Kyra sped up like a fish on a line.

Lily caught up to us, huffing and puffing. Her footfalls sounded like a bucking bronco out here in the silence, but I heard nothing else. No crying or screaming. But who was I to question Kyra when I questioned my own sanity so often?

"Well, that was embarrassing!" Lily laughed. "How'd you know I was following you, Kyra? I thought I would keep a respectful distance, y'know? Be there if you needed me."

Warmth spread through me. Lily was so sweet to look after my sister. *Our* sister. Blonde, silky hair fell from Lily's ponytail into her face, and she rested her hands on her dirty knees. She wore Cora's old t-shirt and cut-off jeans. Not her usual dingy clothes.

"I've missed you today, Lil." I wrapped an arm around her. "How's my new sister? How're things at home? How's your new, but not new job?"

She smiled. "Oh, it's been *so* great! Your mama made the best sweet potato rolls, as always. So, so good!" She popped her belly out to show how much she ate, rubbing it in lazy circles.

My stomach growled angrily. "Got any of those rolls on you? I'm starving."

Lils fished around in her pocket.

"Do *not* eat around me right now," Kyra commanded. "I got a crowbar, and I ain't afraid to use it."

We jumped back from the menacing glint in Kyra's eyes. *Yikes.*

Lily cleared her throat. "Work's good. Spent the day at the farm training and breeding horses. Business as usual. But the Perkins' are giving me more responsibilities now, and I'll be getting paid for real instead of my pops using all my money for Amos's mash and—"

Was that guilt I detected in her voice?

"Lily. Your pop does not deserve your money or pity. He can take care of himself. That's all he's ever done anyways." I pulled her close as we followed Kyra deeper into the woods on our injured animal hunt. "But listen, you will *not* believe my crazy first day in the warrior's world of jedi training—"

My heart plummeted. Foreboding ran a cold finger down my back. In the faint light, I picked up on bright pops of dogwood pollen littering a recently worn path—the log I'd almost tripped over two days ago. I knew where we were. I'd been here before, chasing Kaleo from the warpath ceremony. We were just a few miles from the outer wall.

"If the president were to catch you out in that part of the south wood, I wouldn't be able to protect you. Promise me. Just, promise me you'll never go back there."

We shouldn't have come here—we might just find ourselves at the business end of something much more deadly than my sister's crowbar. "Kyra, listen. I've been here before. This place is dangerous."

Kyra marched on, drawn toward the sound. Oblivious to my words.

"Kyra! We need to stop," I whispered fervently.

She wouldn't stop. I scrambled to catch her as she stomped on a new trail of trampled weeds toward a large, twisting rock. Blue daisy petals lay scattered along the path. The same blue daisies that had been falling out of that burlap sack by the wall. Kaleo said it was just a stupid bag of flowers, now I wasn't so sure.

I grabbed Kyra around the waist and pried the crowbar out of her hand.

"No! No! No! Almost there. Don't touch me!" she screamed and bucked out.

I wrapped my legs around her middle and struggled to cover her mouth—an almost perfect reenactment of when Kaleo had jumped on to me.

Great. All I needed now was a broken nose.

"It's calling to me. *He's* calling to me. I can hear him!" Kyra cried.

Lily got a hand on Kyra's mouth and we lay out on the ground in a heavy-breathing mess of muddy limbs. I searched around us frantically, praying we were still alone.

"Okay, okay, Kyra, just *stop* and listen," I whispered.

Kyra's chest rose and fell as fast as a scared little chipmunk.

"I followed Kaleo out here to the south wood right after the warpath ceremony. He tackled me. Told me to never come back, that it was dangerous. He said President Zhao would punish us—severely." I loosened my grip. "I will tell you anything you want to know, but we have to get away from here in case someone comes around. Something feels *wrong*."

Very wrong—as if the woods themselves beckoned for us to come just a little bit closer while pressing a sharp knife into our backs. Lily's eyes widened, her hand still covering Kyra's mouth.

Kyra stilled. I scanned the woods again.

Three-hundred-twenty-seven trees.

Three straggler lightning bugs flashed in swirling orbits.

Lily lifted her hand tentatively from Kyra's mouth.

"I hear him, Blue. He's crying, screaming, calling out for help." Kyra's wide-eyes met mine. "We can't just leave him here. He's dying or hurt. They're gonna kill him. I know it."

I released Kyra and she scuttled an arms-length away. We studied one another. Tears welled up in her golden eyes.

"*You* were marching all the way out here to kill this thing! Now you want to save it?" I asked.

She nodded. "And I don't hear anyone else. There's us three and one more out there. That's it for a ways around. I know it."

"How far can you hear, Kyra? Because if the president or General Rose show up, we're dead. Just for standing around. And we have no clue what's out there. No clue if there's a place to hide or if that screaming thing isn't going to kill us. What does it sound like? I am not risking my neck and yours for some injured baby lamb," I stated. "We eat those."

"It sounds like a person speaking a different language." Kyra craned her neck. "He's crying, but it sounds really echoey and strange. It's hard to understand the words."

I reeled. "What?"

She paused and closed her eyes. "He's hitting on some metal bars. They're vibrating. He's got to be in some kind of prison or something. Sounds like he's underground."

"Underground?" Lily asked. "In some kinda jail cell?"

"A *person* is injured and screaming in some underground prison?" I asked in disbelief. "That's just so wrong on so many levels."

"I know, Blue. That's just what I'm saying. I can hear better now that we're close enough. He's right over there, under that rock." Kyra pointed to the strange rock twisting toward the star-flecked sky.

Caverns existed all over New Haven, most of them condemned. He must be in an old, unmarked cavern I'd never heard of before. I pulled the newer map I'd memorized in the warrior base's office today before my eyes. This area was completely unmarked.

"From far away it sounded like an animal crying. Now, it sounds like a person. I know it is! What if it was Fox or lil' Shenandoah down there, Blue?" Kyra pleaded.

I jerked back.

"And, well, I think he can hear us too," Kyra whispered in wonder.

What? Dread poured over my head and down my back.

"He stops screaming when we talk, then he cries out after we're quiet." Kyra shot me a challenge with her eyes. The world closed in on her. Fierce. Intense. Brave and determined. "And I'll never, never forget this sound as long as I live, Blue. *Never*. And I will *never* forgive you if you just leave him there! He needs us. Us! We are the only ones who knows he's here, and I'll be thrown down to the devil's hellfire before I let him die down there. Alone and crying out to me. Me! The only one around that can hear him."

Kyra finished her speech crisscrossed in the wet weeds, bottom lip out, with a fire flaring in her golden eyes. In that moment, I realized I'd follow this ten-year-old child into a horde of Shadow Elves and back—she just had to say the word.

Lily looked to me for the next move, as if I had authority on the matter, seeing as I was now a warrior as of twenty-four hours ago. I had a whole lot of one day under my belt. Yep. I was practically a veteran.

"If it's a dangerous outsider, we can't save him," I said. "You know that, right?"

Kyra nodded. "We gotta at least check. He's hurt and sad."

I couldn't believe what I was about to say.

"Okay, Kyra. What we are about to do is treason, death, and prison. Probably in that order. Y'understand? I will do this under two conditions. You stay above ground as a look-out—or an ear-out."

She nodded.

"Number two, if there's someone coming, you warn us, then you get the heck out. Got it? Lily and I can handle it from there." I spoke with an authority I did not feel.

In truth, adrenaline coursed through me. We *could* do this. With my sight, Kyra's hearing, and Lily's general scrappiness, we could at least check it out. My curiosity spun inside of me like a twister, picking up speed with anticipation. I couldn't help but admit I'd been wanting to come back to the south wood ever since Kaleo told me to avoid it. Maybe I was the sadist.

"Kyra, are you sure there's no one else around? Listen hard."

She closed her eyes for a few minutes, then nodded. Okay. I filled them in on my hasty plan, and we got ready for our ill-advised Operation: Secret Cavern Rescue.

It had to be at least three in the morning. The unholiest of hours. Thank the heavens I still had my bow, arrows, and dagger strapped on from my training earlier.

I found it very hard to trust in my ten-year-old sister's newly disclosed superpowers. Every shadow the moon cast on the tall grass was President Zhao jumping out to attack us. My heart barreled in my chest, my eyes pulsing along with it.

The large rock shot out eerily in the clearing, looming over us as we approached. We had to do this fast. So, I tried out my new trick. I focused on the cold air of a cavern, looking for an entrance. Slowly, naturally, the night transformed into a neon wonderland again, pinpointing the cool and warm. I smiled. This trick was getting easier to do.

Frigid purple air flowed around some sort of square metal imbedded in the grass. I crouched and searched with my hands. This had to be it. Some sort of well-hidden trapdoor. Thin tendrils of violet and blue curled around my fingers as I pulled the handle back. It looked disconcertingly similar to the doors surrounding the warrior's base. The rusted trap door cracked free, sending already loosened rust skittering down. It'd been used recently.

A jolt of panic bolted through me. Lily gave a *"well, here we go"* face.

I peered down into the cavern. A long, old metal ladder led down to a slippery brick surface over a hundred feet down. Electric lights strung between corroded wire sparsely illuminated the space. A large tunnel scrolled out below, dank and moist. The cavern hallway was empty, still I heard nothing. I signaled to Kyra.

Kyra started down the rusted ladder one rung at a time, shaking with nerves. She only needed to listen and point in the direction of the sound. Quiet. Fast. Efficient. Then crawl back up. She'd almost made it through the trapdoor when her hand slipped in the dewy grass above, sending a spray of loose rocks tumbling into the cavern below.

Lily and I grabbed at her arms as the rocks fell in an eternally loud clanking down the 153-foot ladder. The rocks plinked and banged down every single surface, echoing throughout the space below as we cringed, hearts in our throats.

Lily scanned for movement. At this point, all I could do was imagine Kyra's and my own funeral when Mama found out what kind of stupid we were up to.

To her credit, Kyra didn't scream. She held onto the ladder wide-eyed with shock. But she was fine. We were all fine. Just a few rocks. In and out. Fast. The only advantage we had was time.

"Kyra," I whispered. "Where is he? Hurry. We have to move."

My heart pounded a mile a minute. This was so idiotic.

"I hear him. He's over there. Down the hall. In the—wait. Let me try something." Then she did the unthinkable. She grabbed another couple pebbles and tossed them down.

I was about to toss Kyra in next.

Kyra held her ear down toward the bottom with her eyes closed, in a trance. "Yes, he's in the third room to the left." She pointed so I knew it was the actual left because she got her rights and lefts wrong most of the time.

Why was I trusting this child with my life again?

"Okay, okay, get up here, girl," I said. "You're making me nervous."

"This place is just one big cavern hallway with lots of rooms with bars. I think, like, twelve rooms," she said as she climbed out. She shook with excitement. "Blue! The rocks! The sounds—they were shining. I could see them."

Like Orin today with the corn sacks.

"Echolocation," I whispered, then shook my head. "Stop distracting me, Kyra. No time for your cool epiphanies." Vomit burned the back of my throat. "Let's go, Lil."

I shot a glare at Kyra that meant "*I will kill you if you get killed*" as Lily and I descended into the cavern of death. "You stand watch by that tree. Warn us about any intruders, then run like the devil's got your toe."

"He knows we're here," Kyra said excitedly.

"You're making this worse."

Only about three minutes had passed since we started this whole fool rescue, but my body shook with the stress of it all. One part of me rode high on adrenaline and curiosity. The other part cried out in a flurry of terror and defeat, wanting to curl up in a ball and suck my thumb in a dark corner somewhere.

Lil and I descended the rickety ladder to the bottom of the cavern. As I surveyed the wet, dark tunnel, Lily skipped off toward the third room to the left.

My bare feet scratched into the cold, damp dirt atop the bricks. I froze. Stunned. Like a piece of a puzzle I didn't realize I was putting together just fell into place. At the foot of the stairs lay a large burlap sack.

Old, dirty, and strangely crafted. Big enough to carry a substantial sack of potatoes. Blue daisy pollen covered the entire outside of the bag as the flowers spilled about in rough handfuls—smashed into the dirt. The same stupid bag of blue daisies that I'd seen down by the outer wall when Kaleo had tackled me and told me I was nobody. Nothing.

"It's just a bunch of stupid flowers."

"Uh, Blue." Lily's voice echoed through the darkness. "You need to see this."

My head spun. I broke out of my reverie, the blue pollen seared into my retinas, and ran toward her.

The brown and blues of the cavern bounced off the electric buzzing lights strung along the ceiling. This place hadn't been in use for decades, a relic of the ancient Shadow War days. A prison of sorts.

The first room flew into view as I took off toward Lily.

Thick metal bars, a dilapidated metal bed, a sink, a rusty corroded mirror.

This place smelled like old earth. Drips echoed ominously. A shiver went down my spine as I ran on. If the Warrior's Base was a palace of daylight, this cavern was a black pit of grisly nightmares.

Lily stood in front of the third room on the left. Stacks and stacks of crusty old mattresses were piled up to the ceiling before her. Like some twisted *Princess and the Pea* theatrical performance dreamed up from one of Edgar Allen Poe's nightmares. Except this was worse. A lot worse.

A muffled cry sounded from behind the macabre scene. Shakespeare's words flew before my sight.

"Hell is empty and all the devils are here."

A blueish electric light flickered over the stacks of ancient, stained mattresses. Many of them looked to have been home to rodents, cockroaches, or fat spiders. They were pre-war, covered in the blood of humans who'd been preyed upon by the unholy hordes of demons.

"I don't think we want to see what's behind door number three," I whispered.

Lily and I stood frozen in front of the stacks of filthy mattresses. Neither of us wanted to make the first move.

Who was this wall protecting? Us or him?

Scratches sounded on the other side and we jumped. Our hands smashed various parts of each other's arms as we squealed. My terror mounted with every muffled sound.

Dang Kyra and her stupid hearing.

Then I heard it. A soft, small voice. Muffled. As far away as a whisper on the wind. A melodic cry for help.

"Do you hear that, Lily?"

"Yeah," she breathed. "I think I do."

"Did the president leave someone down here to die?"

Or Kaleo? He'd brought whoever this was here in that burlap sack. I knew it. My face twisted in disgust. "We'll need to pull these mattresses back in stacks all together so anyone who came down after wouldn't know the prisoner was missing for a bit longer. It might buy us more time."

I sat on the ground, pushing with my legs while dust rained down on me as Lily worked on the ones above. I was grateful not to have Kaleo's gift right about now. I couldn't imagine the mildewy smell of old blood and filth. We worked quickly and quietly, sweat dripping down our backs.

As soon as the area was big enough for my body to fit, I crawled toward the metal bars. Lily peered in above me to get a good look in the dank cell. No sound came from the gloomy chamber. No movement. Silence hovered like a stale wind.

The smell hit me first. The prisoner had relieved itself in a corner of the chamber, filling the cell with a putrid sting. I tried to keep myself from gagging. The brick floor was covered in mildew and dirt. A steady *drip, drip, drip* sounded throughout the room. The bed was nothing more than a mess of metal bars. They'd used all of the mattresses to trap the sounds and smells in there.

Trace amounts of pitch blood spattered the brick floor and cavern walls. Seven blue daisy petals littered the floor.

"Oh, my goodness," Lily gasped.

A small huddled form shook beneath the bed, hiding under a tattered wool military issue blanket. Just a slight rounded shape, no larger than my two-year-old baby sister, shivering in the dark of the room. He must have run for cover after we moved the mattresses. Plates of half-eaten food and various fluids littered the floor.

My heart constricted. Tears pooled in my eyes. The shape was so small. Could it be a *child*? I stretched out my hand and gently called, "Hello, little one."

I tried to sound light, kind, and caring. The opposite of the monsters who put this small child in this awful dungeon. My heart hardened toward the president, toward Kaleo. I needed to protect this child, quickly.

"Come on, little one." I beckoned. "It's just me and my friend. We're here to save you. Get you out. Home. Safe." I spoke gently, but my neck prickled with a fear of being found out. We'd been down here for as long as I dared.

"Listen, buddy. We're here to help." Lily's bear-tight grip dug into my shoulder as she stood above me in the passage of mattresses.

Slowly, so slowly, the child crawled out from under the bed. One delicate hand flicked out, then the other. A very pale child. White as the moon here under the wavering fluorescent lights. His hair a lengthy silk and—so white. As white as his skin. Bright white. It covered his face in a delicate curtain as he crawled toward us, as soft as a dove's feathers. His fingernails were long, sharp, and dirty. He couldn't be more than two or three, judging by his size.

He looked up at us, and all of the air left the room.

His eyes. Black. Endless. Dark. Wild. Just like the ones from Raleigh's journal.

Lily and I gasped. We grabbed a hold of each other, shuddering. This child. It was not a human child at all. It was a Shadow Elf.

A Shadow Elf *child*.

CHAPTER 21

It's the End of the World as We Know It, For Real

BLUE

"Are you seeing this?" I trembled.

How was this even possible?

One, that the elves, the Shadow Elves of legend, still lived. Existed. Somehow survived the plague. Two, that they could actually reproduce offspring? This was a monstrosity. A scourge. A true hellion born on the earth. A demon-child made flesh.

My heart fought to leap from my chest as I took in the devil spawn crawling before me. White, flowing hair. Large, black, depthless eyes. Its long ears shot straight up into points, spattered in dried mud. Its blood shimmered a cold black, of course, dripping from the side of its mouth like the vampires I'd read about in dusty old books.

My skin grew cold as I recoiled. I loathed this creature. It was the reason my people all died. My kind. Humankind.

It wrapped itself back in the tattered wool blanket and shivered pitifully. It sat only a few feet from where Lily and I stood, cowering. Afraid of us? As if *we* might hurt *it*? Maybe it wasn't screeching for help at all, but to lure us in so it could eat us.

For now, at least, it seemed to just sit, silent and wondering. As if it, too, could not believe its eyes.

What was I thinking? Could it even *have* wonder? Thoughts? Feelings?

I couldn't help but study its face. It was a child's face. One that could have been human at a cursory glance, except for the unnatural whiteness. The largeness of the eyes. The long but delicate pointed ears protruding from the sides of its head. Its teeth must also be razor sharp in that small, pert mouth.

But with its calm appearance, it could pass for, well, not a horrific savage. That was about all I could say for now. And, it was a child, though a beastly one. Some instinct inside of me saddened to see it all alone with no mother to protect it—if these beasts *had* mothers. Or were they bred in the depths of hell?

Its cheeks were sunken in, lending it an alien appearance, almost beautiful in the fluorescent blue light of the murky cell. Other worldly, this little elfling.

How far away from home are you? How did you get here?

I stared into its eyes, and it glared unblinkingly back into mine. It, I mean *he*, didn't move. Kyra said he was male, though his features were very fine. Eyebrows almost invisible. White as a lamb. But faint gold stripes lined his neck, like a fawn. Just like the sketch from my ancestor's journal, and yet, not.

"Oh. My. Holy heavens above." Lily barely breathed.

I swallowed. Yeah. That.

With this one elfling, everything we'd ever known was—well, a lie. A fairy tale taught to us by well-meaning parents and ignorant grandmas. We were not alone. The Shadow Elves were not dead. And guess what else? They could reproduce. Spawn little devil-babies. And if that wasn't enough, another nugget of life-altering information pinged in my brain—maybe the worst truth of all. Our safe, protected town of New Haven was no longer secret from those demons of Hell anymore.

"Here you go lil' guy." Lily pulled out the crumbled sweet potato roll from her pocket and held it out toward the creature.

"What are you doing?" I hissed. The cavern echoed my incredulity.

The elfling flinched. His back curved inward, unnaturally. His feathery hair hung loose around the pointed tips of his downturned ears.

"Feeding the poor, starving thing. Look at him." Lily pouted. "He's all skin 'n bones. No one's fed him or even given him a proper bed. He doesn't even have his mama."

A chill snaked down my spine.

"Do they have mothers, Lily?" I asked. "I mean, look at it. Him. He's drawing you in. I think that's one of their powers. They have beauty so you feel bad for them, trust them. Then they lure you in and—*boom*. You're infected. Or you get eaten."

Laurel Haven's last words rolled before my eyes.

"Lovely things shouldn't draw you in and kill you. You almost want them to. They look like gods."

She was right. I almost wanted him to love me.

"Come on, Blue." Lily scoffed as she tossed the roll into his filthy cell. "Look at him. He's starving. Whoever did this, put this poor creature in here like this, they're the true monsters."

"Look," I said, "I get it, this is insane and sad. I feel bad for the elfling too, but what do you want to do? Take him home to Mama? Put him out in the shed with the goats? Maybe he can bunk with Fox while Hawk is out?" I shook my head, never once allowing my eyes to leave the creature. "We can't just release a *Shadow Elf* into our town, Lil. What if he bit you or me? Or Kyra? It'd kill us all."

Lily deflated. "But we can't just leave him here."

We watched in awe as the new creature shot out his bright white hand in a quick, animal-like gesture and pawed the sweet potato roll. He spun it in his hand, his large black eyes inspecting the morsel. Then, he flicked the roll into his mouth fast as lightning.

He sniffed the air, like a puppy, his eyes landing on Lily's pocket.

"Want more?" Lil smiled.

The elfing's eyes absorbed all of the surrounding light, yet—they seemed to swirl like stars in a galaxy. My stomach lurched as Lily tossed it another sweet potato roll.

"How many of those do you have, Lil? I'm hungry too," I teased, more out of habit than anything as we stared, mesmerized, at the elfling.

"So now what?" Lil's voice sounded high and airy.

My mind whirled with that unanswerable question when a thundering—"Blue! Lil! Someone on horseback! Coming! Get out now!"—sounded through the dungeon.

Kyra's harsh whisper carried throughout the contours of the cave and the word "now" echoed over and over ominously. We wasted no time springing into action.

"We can't take him. We don't know what he'll do—" I started.

"Agreed. We need time to think," Lil said.

Lil and I pushed the mattresses back into their original locations.

"I'll bring you some more food later, lil' Legolas, okay?" Lily motioned to the elfling.

"*Legolas*? From *Lord of the Rings*? Really?" I spat.

I stole one last glance at the elfling before completely shutting him off. Why did this feel so wrong? Sad? I memorized him, then placed my finger over my lips in a *shhh, be quiet* gesture, hoping he wouldn't start screeching again.

After we closed him back in, the survival part of my body sighed in relief. My raised hackles and adrenaline switched from fight to flight. But, guilt dropped like lead in my stomach. As if I'd just left a helpless kitten with its paw in a trap. Yes, he was a wild thing, but somehow not savage.

He'd looked into my eyes like he saw me.

I shook the thoughts from my head. He must have lured me in too. He got me to trust him with his unnatural beauty. Time to run.

Lily went hand over hand up the ladder. As I turned to follow, something at the end of the tunnel caught my eye. Stacks and stacks of untouched crates and among them—

"*Haven Family Genealogy*." Finger streaks brushed over the thick dust while papers stuck out from the top. The crate had been rifled through recently. Papers littered a desk and the floor.

Another piece of the puzzle.

"How far are they, Kyra?"

"Two miles. Hurry!" she called.

I could make it. I made a choice in a blink. I cursed my sight and made a run for it.

Heaven help me.

"Lily, you and Kyra—close up the trapdoor and run home now. I'm grabbing something real quick. I'll be right behind you. Do *not* wait for me. Swear it!" I called.

Nothing.

"Swear it, Lily! You take my sister home. I'll be right behind you. Don't wait for me!" I said frantically.

"I swear. But you better not be doing something stupid, Blue!" Lily whispered angrily as the trapdoor snapped shut.

My heart dropped as the sound of the door echoed throughout the cavern, sealing me in with that creature of darkness. The finality of that thud struck through me, but there was no time for second-guessing. I sprinted toward the makeshift office at the end of the dungeon. A prison cell no one bothered to lock up.

Each crate had the official seal of New Haven burned on the front. They were ancient. Mountains of dust and spider webs coated the office. But the papers strewn across the large, stately desk were clean. They'd been pulled out of the Haven Family crate just recently.

What kind of documents did they keep down here? I glanced around the room so I could soak in the details later. I grabbed some wrinkled papers and a small notebook labeled "Haven" from the desk and stuffed them into my bra. Time to make a run for it.

As I started across the tunnel, a loud mechanical screech deafened me. My ears! It had to be one of those old horrendous mine elevators. The sound roared from the opposite side of the cavern.

The elfling started into its ungodly scream again.

I'd never make it to the ladder in time. I sprinted out of the office, across the tunnel, and into the closest prison cell. I found the filthiest one. Its walls were completely slathered in mud and lichen. The moisture in this room made my hair 'fro up as if I'd been frolicking with static electricity. The earthy smell was strong but not terribly unpleasant, so I thought fast. Camouflage.

I slowly lowered myself into the mud. The caverns were chilly all year long, but this mud? I might as well throw myself in the freezer. It squished between my knees, toes, and fingers. I froze like an angel monument as the electric screech of the elevator landed with a resounding *boom*.

The elfling's cries died off into whimpering clicks.

No more playing around. I rolled in the mud, covered my face, and spread it through my hair. There was plenty of the stuff to go around, and to my disgust, I'd been wrong about the smell. So, so wrong. This had to be where my imaginary zombie-pandas had been pooping for the past hundred years. I tried not to gag as I breathed in and out slowly through my mouth. I crawled into the darkest and muddiest corner of the chamber and exuded invisibility. Maybe if I thought it, I would be it. At least the lights in this cell were permanently out of order.

Large boots pounded through the cavern. Each step rolled like thunder, growing louder and louder. I cringed with every footfall, praying that I remained far enough away from the interests of the intruder. I imagined a large green beast like the Incredible Hulk crashing through the cavern.

Boom, boom, boom. The footsteps grew ever closer, and I was ever closer to wetting myself. I was such a fool. What was I doing gathering these stupid papers? Who cared? I'd practically sentenced myself to death. All that was left now was for the Hulk to close the metal doors and lock me in.

The stomping continued and I swore I heard a man moaning. Was he hurt? Hulk stopped at the cell right next to mine. The one as far away from the elfling as possible, except for this uninhabitable one here. My heart shattered with trepidation. Another moan and a thud. Metal doors clanged shut and jangling keys locked up a cell.

A new prisoner? I prayed the Hulk would just drop off the moaning prisoner and leave. I had some poop on my tongue now. No gagging. This would be a terrible time to gag. Breathe. In and out. In and out.

The Hulk paused. His breath hitching, he sniffed the air like some sort of hound dog. Could it be Hound? or Kaleo? I didn't think either would take too kindly to me being here.

He walked toward my cell as I attempted to calm my racing heart. Calm my breathing. I shut my eyes so he wouldn't see the glowing white orbs of my eyeballs floating, so out of place in the dark mud. He walked, sniffing into the office across the hallway. I forced myself not to burst out of my mud pile and run for it.

He stalked closer toward my chamber. One step. Two. I could've sworn I felt the warmth of his body as the Hulk approached. Keeping my eyes—my greatest weapon— shut was the hardest thing I'd ever done.

"Hey!" the groaning prisoner called out next to us.

Hulk staggered back and stomped out of the cell. I let out a slow, quiet breath, thanking the poor soul in the prison cell next to mine. Thank you, Injured and Moaning Prisoner Number Two. You may have just saved my life.

"Hey! You just sss-aved me, right? We are on the same side. Those men held me prisoner. They were going to kill me! Y-you saw it." The prisoner's voice shook. "Please! I need medicine. I need bb-bandages. I will get an infection from my wounds."

His plea was met with silence.

"Or maybe, some water?" he asked, so pitifully. So sad and defeated. His voice carried a strange accent. "Just some water. I-I'll tell you anything you want to know. Please."

Drip. Drip. Drip of the cavern. Silence.

I'd almost forgotten we'd been waiting for an answer.

"You make me sick." I knew that voice. "You disgust me. I would rather see you rot than bring you anything. You are only alive because you have information. Where did you come from and why were your men outside our wa—"

"No! Not my mmm-men. No. No. My *enemies*!" he cried.

Literally. He may even be crawling on the ground by the sound of the scuffling noises—a grinding of dirt over brick. "They h-hurt me! I-I can tell you all I know. I *will* tell you. I was their prisoner."

I couldn't help but feel pity for this man beside me. He couldn't be much older than me. He begged for his life. And the immovable Hulk who'd been stomping and sniffing around all this time like a large beast? It was Kaleo. Had he no heart? No mercy? Give the man a little water for crying in the mud! Which, I guess I could be doing right now seeing as how I was covered in it.

"I can't stand to see another man beg. It turns my stomach." Kaleo spit on the ground. His voice echoed deeply through the cavern. "Shut up and think about your dead men. All of them. Dead. And my men are injured. One close to death. We did not seek that battle." Kaleo paused. "We show no mercy to those who have no mercy in their hearts. And I will *not* allow you to lead us into a trap."

"No! They were not my men- I- I would never—" the prisoner cried.

"*Enough!* Enough lies. I can see it in your eyes. Taste it in the air. You fool no one!" Kaleo was teetering between control and deranged.

Boots scratched on brick as Kaleo stomped away.

"I know where he is!" The prisoner yelled out desperately. "I know where they hold your man. The painted one with c-comb of a rooster. Please! You don't have much time to save him. H-he is in peril. And when no one comes for him in three days' time, they will kill him, and then they will come for me. They will have their blood."

Kaleo paused, if only for a second, and then he was gone. The elevator screeched back toward the surface. The dungeon echoed in silence as the prisoner beside me thumped onto his cot and groaned.

I didn't know how long I'd sat in the cell, covered completely in fecal mud, but my body shook uncontrollably. I tried to calm my breathing, but it was no use. My lower jaw trembled and my muscles jerked in fits.

I had to get out or I'd die of hypothermia. I didn't know who this prisoner was, but he was an outsider. He couldn't see me. All I had to do was sneak past his cell without detection and without making the elfling shriek. *No biggie.*

I wiped the filth from my face and slowly removed myself from the mud, rolling like a slug. Extra points for elegance as my shirt twisted up and poo sludge squirted out in a running trail down my abs.

Beautiful.

Slowly and steadily, I worked my way to the other side of the room where the walls oozed freshwater, filtering through the earth. *Nice room.* I ran my hands and feet in the pool of water to wash off as much mud as I could.

I reached the metal prison bars and listened for the moaner. He hadn't made a sound since Kaleo left. Not much more than a few growls of frustration, a jerky movement across the cell floor, and some banging on the cot.

My hands prickled as they went numb. My limbs shuddered. Not a great time for a nimble escape, but now was all I had. I'd never attempted so many daring escapes, rescues, and secret missions all in one day. My body grew weary of all of this adrenaline. My neck muscles flared and flexed like mad.

Note to self: freezing in mud plus adrenaline equaled uncontrollable limbs and almost certain discovery. At least I was learning a lot. If my jerky movements didn't get me found out, the horrific smell would.

I worked my way around the cell into the prison tunnel on my hands and knees, completely exposed. I chanced a peek into the cell next to mine, willing myself inch by inch. Just a little further.

A lump of a body lay curled up in the fetal position on the cot. The prisoner snored fitfully. As I made it to the end of the cell, I caught a glimpse of the prisoner's battered face. Even covered with blood, I knew him. The boy. The green-eyed mystery boy from my vision that day in the wood with the raven. The prisoner.

It was him.

I made it to the other side of his cell and sunk to the floor, stunned. With all of my other frightening visions, that strange moment in the woods had been forgotten. Now it scrolled before my eyes.

He smiled at me in that ancient city, holding out his hand and beckoning me to follow. Like I meant something to him.

Who was he? The cold man who'd held a sword to someone's throat? Or the one who'd restrained him? The one who'd lit the beacon on the rooftop? Or the one who'd blown it out? Try as I might, I couldn't recall those visions. I didn't know if he was the good man or the evil one.

Either way, he was an outsider.

I sat completely astonished on the cold brick. I'd seen two completely alien figures down here in the dungeons. One, a fearsome child demon, the other a handsome, injured stranger. Possibly an enemy, though I recalled his trusting smile from my raven vision.

Nothing new ever happened in New Haven. Ironic for the name, I know. So, I sat and reveled in his newness, if only for a moment.

Still shaking from cold, I got up and continued to sneak through the tunnel.

He was real. He actually existed.

Who was he? Where was he from? I found myself drawn toward him like a magnet. He had to be dangerous. All outsiders were. But in the cell sleeping off his injuries, he didn't look dangerous and didn't sound dangerous. Kaleo did.

There had to be a reason I'd seen this boy in a vision three days before. Why I'd seen him smile and reach out to me. His eyes were so genuine under the curtain of his brown curls. That glance, his hand out.

I made it to the ladder and through the trapdoor, barely registering where I was. My body trembled with cold, but my mind alighted with a million thoughts.

The elfling and the stranger, each capable on their own to rock the entire town of New Haven to its core. Each enough to make us question everything we'd been taught our entire lives. No wonder Zhao and Kaleo kept this from everyone.

We were not alone. There were others out there. And not just other humans, but the Shadow Elves we so desperately wanted to forget. They lived. And they reproduced. And they were right on our doorstep. How many more were out there in the undiscovered shadows of the world?

CHAPTER 22

Dark Angel

KALEO

S he floated through the wood at night. The moonlight was her lover, caressing her face and body. Making her glow as if she were an angel. A beautiful, dark angel in a trance, drifting through the trees and grass in a fog of seeing everything and nothing at all. Deep in thought and oblivious to my presence. I followed her with my eyes closed. She drew me in like wild honey dripping from a comb.

Honey, covered in the stink of cavern mud.

Why couldn't she leave well enough alone?

If I were being honest with myself, I'd known it was only a matter of time before she went back there. Now, Blue knew my great secret. Of course she did.

I searched my heart for relief but felt only fear tighten my chest. She knew I'd brought that elf child down there.

How would she ever look at me the same way again?

And now I'd added to the unmentionables down in that place. That filthy outsider. I shouldn't have hesitated to kill him.

I'd let that kernel of doubt blind me. The wave of emotion weaken me.

I ran through that moment in the barn over and over in my mind. What else could I have done? That outsider was the key to getting Hawk. But he was dangerous. I could taste it on the air around him— his calculating mind.

His weapons and clothing were so different from ours in New

Haven. Emblems with a fierce dragon devouring Shadow Elves with a gaping maw. Then, clenching screaming humans in its other clawed grasp. A dangerous village.

They were from another world, another kingdom—I'd heard them call out to their prince. Were there kings and queens, now?

I didn't care who they were. They'd murdered Joe then crawled out of the shadows to attack us without a word.

There was a war stirring outside the walls, and we'd been completely oblivious to it.

I wouldn't be complacent again. I couldn't be.

My thoughts drifted back to Blue as my nose pulled her in. My shoulders relaxed. My heartbeat slowed—this was wrong. What was I doing? Following this girl through the dark woods like some kind of wild man?

But, with everything I'd seen out there, I needed to make sure she got home safe. It's what I owed Hawk. That's what I told myself, anyway, as I slowly, achingly made my way along the path, making sure her way back home was clear, breathing in deeply.

My injuries could wait. My men had all survived out there. They were alive. It was nothing short of a miracle. I sent up a prayer of thanks as I made my way along the silent path. The pull of her scent my only guide.

I could still fix this. There was still time. There had to be.

CHAPTER 23

Neck - Deep in a Cover - Up

BLUE

I woke to a bright morning. My eyes ached. Chickens clucked outside as the golden sunlight streamed in through the windows at full strength. Clanking dishes and a low hum of conversation muffled up from downstairs in the kitchen. But, I lay alone in my bed. No sisters, no Lily. I straightened out my arms and legs in a loud, back arching stretch I felt all the way to my toes.

Ow ow ow ow. Every single inch of my body ached. My muscles, tendons—even my eyebrows—were sore from my first day of training. Thank the angels I had today off. A perk of Founder's Week.

As I made my way downstairs to get breakfast, my toes squished into something dark and cold. Mud covered the floor, and the scenes of last night flashed through my mind like a thunderstorm of my worst nightmares.

The elfling, the handsome prisoner, Kaleo in the dungeon, the fecal mud of death.

I remembered my hurried shower last night and the exhaustion that swept over me afterwards. I hadn't wasted time combing out and braiding my hair. I just flopped down in the bed, so my hair was in a state.

How could everything be so quiet and calm here when the world as we knew it crashed down all around us? I couldn't wrap my head around it all. I didn't try to. It was way too early.

This peaceful morning in my home felt like a dream. Any

moment now I'd wake up in that dark cell screaming, covered head to toe in mud. Or maybe that had all been a nightmare?

The muddy papers I'd stolen from the dungeon lay rolled up inside my shorts in the corner behind the door. Proof of last night. It'd all been real. I scratched my stomach as I entered the kitchen.

"Stupid lil'...!" I growled, as the hotcake I pulled from the oven burned my finger. Tangled hair covered my face as I balanced a plate piled high with hotcakes, a peach, and a jar of strawberry preserves. I turned and stopped dead. I was not alone in the kitchen.

Of course I wasn't.

And I hadn't even put on my bra yet.

Kaleo sat across from Mama and Dad at our massive oak table. My face flushed with heat as I considered throwing my food in the air to run upstairs. But, one look at their expressions told me my appearance was the least of our worries.

Mama patted the seat next to her, her eyes red and puffy. I walked around and sat down. Mama and Dad leaned away from each other, their hands clasped across the table.

My stomach dropped. It was as if someone threw a giant bucket of cold water over my head. Good morning! We have another surprise in store for you today. It'll be terrible!

"What's going on?" I asked.

I had to stop myself from staring at Kaleo. His face, usually immaculate, was a bit haggard. The beginnings of a beard covered his chin, and shadows lurked beneath his eyes. His breath hitched, as if he were in pain.

He was back. He was okay. I knew he'd returned last night, of course, but I hadn't gotten a good look at him. Relief flooded through me, followed quickly by anger. Did he know I snuck into his little psycho dungeon last night? Did he know I saw the secrets hidden there? I looked anywhere but at him, afraid I'd give it away.

Kaleo spoke first. "We expect the warrior privates home tomorrow, as usual, but if they're not back by the evening, we'll be sending out a search party." Kaleo turned to me. "I've asked your dad to head that up."

Dad's face was grim. I didn't dare see what was written on my mother's face. Fear sliced through me. What had Kaleo seen out there on his mission over the wall? What was he *not* saying?

"Is this the usual protocol?" Dad asked.

Kaleo cleared his throat. "President Zhao's just being a bit more cautious this year, that's all."

Lies.

Kaleo continued. "I know Hawk's just fine. He's strong and smart. So's Joe." Eyes darted to the left. *Lying.* "They'll be alright out there. It's not just about getting your first big game, but about finding peace. I'm sure he's just enjoying the quiet."

I was incredulous! After what I saw and heard last night? After I'd trusted Kaleo with my strange visions?

No, I couldn't let it show. I couldn't let Kaleo know where I was last night, what I'd overheard. But I kept track of it in my head. All of Kaleo's team had been injured over the wall, they'd killed a bunch of outsiders, and one of our own had been taken prisoner by them. Either my brother or Pretty-Boy Joe. Not to mention a hidden dungeon held one of those outsiders and a baby Shadow Elf. Two things that should not exist.

I shot Kaleo with a sour expression as my eyes read him. I took in his face, his pupils, and his pulse. I knew from a lifetime of watching my brothers lie to Mama about finishing their chores what a good liar was capable of. Hawk was an expert by now, but I knew his tells. Fox had become a star pupil to Hawk.

As my dad grilled Kaleo with questions about Hawk, I stared him down, watching for any hint of a lie.

Sweat beaded on his forehead, his pulse quickening. His blinking increased slightly, smile not reaching his eyes. His foot tapped on the ground, and he studied his hands at certain points.

Kaleo was not a good liar. I almost felt sorry for him.

Kaleo's kind expressions and handsome face made you want to

believe every pretty story he told. He was the kind of man that made you want to forget all the scary things of the world and run into his strong, capable arms. I'd always wanted to. It broke my heart to hear him lie straight to my daddy's face. To the face of the man who loved him like a son and who entrusted the life of his own son into his hands.

Kaleo respected my father, so why lie? If you could trust anyone, it'd be my dad, Bearon Haven. He'd take the shirt off his back for a stranger in need and strangle anyone else with it if you threatened his family. He hadn't lied a day in his life.

The more Kaleo skirted the questions from my parents, the angrier I got. The only thing stopping me from kicking his shins under the table was the complete worry in my mama's eyes.

Kaleo stole glances at my face, and I stared right back, my eyes narrowing. I would not act a fool, heaven help me. *I'm on to you.*

Dad stood up, his chair scraping loudly across the wood floor of the kitchen. I jumped. "Virginia and I have to get to work. I'll start gathering my weapons and prepping to get our son back if need be."

Mama nodded. Beneath the puffy redness, her eyes were flint.

Dad reached across the table to give me a kiss and whispered. "Go to the rock, see what you can. Send Kyra with news." A soft kiss on the forehead, then he and Ma walked out of the kitchen.

Before they were out the door Dad called, "We'll bring him home, Baby Blue. You take care of things here, alright?"

I nodded.

It wasn't hard to believe my dad when he looked like that. His back straight as a rod. His angular face tense and strong. Eyes like a stone. The embodiment of a true warrior. I wondered, not for the first time, why he'd never taken that path.

Dad mouthed, *"find out what you can,"* and his eyes shifted to Kaleo. Daddy was no fool.

The back door slammed shut with a bang. A quiet fell in the kitchen and lingered for a time. Kaleo and I sat at the table while dust motes flew about in wild orbits. Buttery morning light streamed in, casting ribbons of color across Kaleo's face. Warming his skin, softening his features.

Once the sound of the truck engine faded from ear-shot, I asked flatly. "So, what really happened out there, Kaleo?"

Again, silence fell like a hot blanket.

I dropped all pretense and studied him as he stared out the window behind me.

His pulse steady as a drum. His eyes unblinking.

Tall broad shoulders. Long black hair braided on one side and pulled into a ponytail straight down his back. Silky ebony strands glossed beautifully in the warm sunlight. Rugged stubble outlined his strong jawline, making him look even more manly. I found that I liked it. A lot. His eyes and eyelashes were dark, brooding now. Full of secrets, sorrow, anger, frustration, and beauty.

So much beauty here. As if he too were molded and formed to lure silly, naive girls into trusting him. To believe in his lies of safety and adoration. Then to devour their hearts, just as the Shadow Elves were made to devour their bodies.

Even as we sat in silence, I felt myself drawn into his power. Something about him. He smelled like wild pine trees and freshly cut grass. I knew he'd been keeping things from me, but who was I kidding? If he took me into his arms right now? I'd make out with him all morning.

My head filled with visions of jumping across the table and pressing my lips to his. I tried not to blush.

Kaleo's hand flew to his shoulder, smacking it, then he cleared his throat. "At first, there was nothing. We hadn't even made it to the point of interest yet, searching for the source of that light you saw, when I picked up on a scent."

Kaleo's voice rumbled through the kitchen. He spun his empty tea cup in front of him absently. Dark circles rimmed his eyes, and he slouched a little in his seat. "We'd never ventured that far out on patrol before. I followed the scent of death and decay before the storm washed it away, but it was a *strange* dead smell. Alien. After some time, we ended up near a stream. Near several wild hut-like things. Where *they* were dead."

I balked. Kaleo might be a warrior, but he'd lived in this peaceful little town his whole life, too. We didn't see a lot of death unless it was killing livestock for food. The ghost of what he'd seen flitted across his paler-than-normal face. Curiosity warred with worry, turning my stomach.

Kaleo stared out into nothingness.

"Eight dead in all. Slaughtered like pigs. But not *humans*, Blue." His chocolate eyes slid over to mine. "Not *people*. But, those demons. The Shadow Elves." He looked as if he were trying to convince me, convince himself. "I saw them. They'd been *killed*. Dead. But they'd been alive just days before."

"What?"

He scoffed. "Strange thing was, they weren't like I thought they'd be. I see 'em every time I close my eyes now." His eyes found mine. "Hawk wasn't anywhere near there. I know that. I didn't sense him at all. He wouldn't have ever gone so far in the outskirts anyway. None of us ever had before."

I nodded absently. My stomach dropped with every new revelation.

Kaleo's voice was barely a whisper. "But those elves had *built* those huts. Out of mud and animal skins, embedded with gemstones. And the elves themselves—they were clothed in skins, leathers, and had *bones* in their hair. What does that even *mean*?"

He looked at me as if I had the answers. Worry seized my chest. The elves had built huts? Dressed in fur like cavemen?

Kaleo sighed, the air from his lips rolled across the table and kissed my cheeks. It was tinged pink in the golden sunlight as a thought entered my mind.

"A new species," I said, more to myself.

He shook his head in both wonder and horror.

They weren't the mindless human-eaters we'd been led to

believe. At least not anymore. While we'd had our heads in the protective clouds of the mountains, they'd been evolving.

Kaleo focused his attention on the tea cup in front of him.

"But who killed them?" I asked. "Did you find the men from the barn roof? The one with the sword?"

His face twisted. "We followed a trail of carnage until it led us to that group of men you saw in your vision. Ten of them, like you said." The teacup spun as Kaleo's knuckles whitened. "They'd been holed up in some abandoned barn about thirty miles out. Traveling for months. Filthy. Smelly. Rotten. Looked like they'd been killing their way across the countryside." His shoulder turned in slightly. "We're lucky we found 'em when we did. They were in uncharted territory. They jumped out in the dead of night and set about attacking us. We had no choice but to kill them. All."

"You killed them? All of them?" I pushed. "Didn't you want to know where they were from? If more were coming?"

He flicked his golden-brown eyes up, and I lifted an eyebrow. *I see you.*

He pursed his lips. "Someone's been rolling around in the mud of a certain place in the south wood they were told *explicitly* not to go back to."

My heart leapt. He knew.

"So what if I was?" I countered. "I had good reason."

Kaleo huffed and leaned back in his chair. "So now what?"

"Now you tell me everything." I shrugged. "And I help you the best I can."

He dropped his head back in defeat, then sucked in a pained hiss and grabbed at his shoulder.

"Hey, you okay?" I found myself reaching my hand forward under the table. The rough edges of our fingers met. My whole body thrilled at his slow touch. The warmth, strength, and energy emanating from his hands filled my heart to bursting.

The whole house came alive with the electricity of us.

He cleared his throat, then dropped my hand as if it were a

firebrand. He grabbed onto his teacup again like it would save him from a fiery death. My face flushed.

"That wasn't the first time, y'know, that I smelled them." Kaleo started into a new story. "In the middle of Hawk's ceremony, a sweet, sickly metallic scent filled my head. Took every thought out of my mind. So, I ran."

My heart thundered beneath my ribcage.

Kaleo's eyes flew up to mine. "I followed that strange smell to the south wall and found that small elf child you saw last night. It'd been knocked out, wrapped up in a burlap sack, and thrown over our wall."

"Wha—?"

Kaleo shrugged. "Then you showed up and all I could think to do was... There was something about the smell. I couldn't think straight...after you left—"

After he yelled at me and ripped my heart to shreds.

"I hid the elf child best I could, then ran like a bat outta hell to Zhao. She was still up at the ceremony. She told me about the century old prison that'd been forgotten by time, the one you found last night."

I wasn't ready to tell him it had been Kyra who'd found it.

"So, we tossed it in there until we knew what to do with it." Kaleo shook his head. "But, its smell was so strong. We hauled in all of the mattresses from the surrounding prison cells to try and keep it from being detected. But even then, I could sense it from miles away. It has a particularly...strong, not terrible smell."

"Like what?" I couldn't help but be intrigued.

"Its smell is like nothing I've ever experienced. Like a wolf and a newborn baby. Earth, no, mud, and a stinging metallic scent that I can't quite place." Kaleo mused, "That moment you broke my nose? I think it saved me."

"You're welcome," I said.

Kaleo's eyes shot up to mine. A flash of ire. Silence filled the kitchen like a fat old guy—hot, sticky, and slightly uncomfortable.

"Who did it?" I asked. "If it was stuffed in a bag and knocked out, then who threw it over the wall? Why?"

"Your guess is as good as mine, but my bet's on that outsider in the prison. I plan to ask him all about it."

"And what about the elfling?" I asked. "He's so sad and hungry. You're treating him like a monster. It's filthy down there."

Kaleo ran a hand through his hair. "*Him? It* is a monster, Blue. Don't go getting attached to it. Don't forget what that thing is. It *wants* you to love it. Believe me, I felt that pull too."

My heart constricted. *Oops.*

Kaleo stared out the window behind me. "As soon as I found that elf child, everything changed. Zhao and I had spoken about gathering gifted New Haveners together for years. But this ramped everything up. We were working through how to go about it quietly, then you saw that light."

Kaleo's hands stilled on the teacup, and his eyes flicked up to mine. The kitchen melted away.

"Then what?" I breathed.

"Then we knew it was time. But, after seeing what I saw yesterday—" his eyes turned dark—"we may be too late."

Movement flickered in the window behind Kaleo. Two people hopped down the hill about a half mile away. Lily and Kyra carried a sack of books. Looked like they'd just taken a trip up Grandfather Rock to see Mama Darla. Kaleo took notice of my glance, then closed his eyes and breathed in deep.

"Lily and Kyra?" he asked without turning around.

"Yep."

Kaleo sat up, ready to leave.

"Wait." I grabbed Kaleo's warm hand. "One more thing. That prisoner down in the dungeon. He said we have three days to save one of ours outside the walls. One with a rooster comb. Do they have Hawk or Joe?"

"Those men, Blue, they're from a different world." Kaleo's lip curled. "They didn't hesitate to jump out and attack. They didn't try to talk to us, reason with us, come to some kind of agreement—nothin'. They came out with weapons trained and shooting to kill. I know for a fact that if I didn't have my ability, they would've killed us all."

Kaleo stood up so quickly he knocked back his wooden chair. The jarring crash broke the spell hovering over the still kitchen.

Kaleo cleared his throat. "That man down there is a murderer and a liar. He'd do anything to get free. Anything. I'll find out what he knows. So, please don't go back there. I'm gonna have to talk to Zhao about him. And Zhao *cannot* know you know about that place, seriously. Word *cannot* get out about that creature or prisoner. We just don't know what to do about all of this yet. There are things at stake that—I'm just going to pretend like we never had this conversation."

He started for the door as I said. "Well, y'all better come up with something good, 'cause it sounds like the outside world is stirring. You might need a few more people on your team. People you can trust, that's all."

He paused in the hallway, his back toward me, his large hand gripped the chipped white wall. "Yeah. That. I'm still trying to convince Zhao she can trust *me* half the time. She doesn't trust her own shadow."

"You know you're neck-deep in one heck of a cover-up?" I pointed out. "People will need to know. This is huge. I mean, they're out there. They're alive and *breeding*. Building huts. Wearing clothes? This changes everything."

"I don't even know what to think about it." Kaleo turned toward me. "And President Zhao is fanatic about keeping it tight until we know more. I've never seen her so—she's looking over her shoulder every second, certain someone's got it out for her. She thinks the whole thing is a trap. Our town's not ready."

"I don't think it's up to Zhao or you to decide who's ready," I said. "Ready or not, the outside has spoken—they want in."

"But what if they're all dead? They killed the elves, and we killed them and that's the end of it?" Kaleo posed the question more to himself. It hung in the air like a fluffy, wishful cloud. He filled up the hallway, searching my face, as if an answer lay there just beyond his reach.

"But what if this is just the beginning?" I said, sending a spike of foreboding with my own words. "Better to be afraid and prepared, than happy and dead. Ignorance is obliteration. You got the same lessons I did from my dad."

Kaleo nodded, understanding warring with denial in his eyes as he walked out the front door. I watched him through the kitchen window as he took his time untying and mounting Hekili, nursing his shoulder all the while. He was slow and methodical. Maybe he'd been more injured than he'd let on.

With a thrill of warmth, I smiled at Pepper, who I'd left at the warrior's base last night. But here he was. He was brushed down, watered, and tied up right next to Hekili. Kaleo brought my horse home safe. He met my gaze, grinned, then took off at a gallop.

CHAPTER 24

Fragrance and Memories

KALEO

I stepped outside of Raleigh House and let out a long, slow breath. I almost doubled over in sharp gasps, my sides in stitches. I couldn't keep this up. This house. This girl. She would be my complete undoing. Thank the angels in heaven for my injured shoulder. I kept smacking it every time my mind started to wander. Pain helped bring me back.

Then Blue touched my hand, and I'd almost jumped across that table and pressed those perfect hazelnut lips to mine. I wanted to feel her. Taste her. Her pheromones spiked higher than the water tower and the aroma about unbuttoned any decorum I'd gained over the years.

And I'd thought her usual scent was irresistible. She'd come down those stairs and—*bam!* Thank heavens her dad can't read minds because I'm pretty sure he would've pulled out his rifle right then and there and shot me dead.

I would've deserved it.

I chuckled darkly and shook my head.

Well, she wasn't too fond of me right now. That was pretty clear. She thought I was the bad guy, keeping that elf creature in such deplorable conditions. What was I supposed to do? Bring it home? Scrub it down in a hot bath and give it a rubber duckie?

I needed to trust my instincts, and my instincts burned within me. That elf child was dangerous. It was alluring, cute, beautiful, for a reason. Couldn't she see that?

A whiff of sweet corn breezed by, bringing a wealth of warmth. I'd learned sometime in my youth that smell was the closest connected sense to your memories. It had to be true because every breath I took pulled me back. I'd helped plant the rows of corn every year during my time here. Blue and Hawk would always end up fighting about the right way to do it. I chuckled.

Sitting at the musty wood table in the kitchen brought me back to the taste of the salty tears I cried over my mother's passing. Cornbread. Salted pork and cheesy grits. All of those dinners Virginia made for me, fed me like her own son for years. The laughter, the noise, the messes, the fights. A real family. So different from the silence that hovered like a stale wind at my house.

My own father was a rolling stone with a new family. He'd left Mama and I with a last name, a house, and heartache when I was only two. There were only a few traces of him left at my place, but I'd run into him and my step-siblings around town all the time. He'd nod and I'd nod and we'd carry on like we didn't share DNA.

But, Blue's father, Bearon? He'd taught me how to be a man. My shoulder rubbed against the branches of a heavy peach tree, sending a burst of sweetness into the air. I was immediately taken back to the rushed breakfasts after one of Bearon's wicked workouts. Hawk and I would huff and puff against the loamy front porch, sweat pouring out of our ears. Bearon always pushed me to my limits. He'd taught me to believe in myself when I'd been too afraid of my own abilities.

He'd never asked about my senses, but I bet he'd guessed. After seeing him with Blue, he had an idea about me too.

Bearon and his sons, Hawk and Fox, spent more mornings than I could count at my own measly farm, helping me muck out my stables, mend the fences, or weld a busted pipe.

And I'd just sat there at that man's kitchen table and lied to him about his own son.

Hawk was out there in the hands of a cruel enemy, or so a liar had said. Lies coated that outsider like a second skin.

I walked up to Hekili and took in another breath. Sweet corn and loamy earth. Raleigh House. Hazelnut and poppy. Blue. Funny, spunky, smart, sharp. Those crystal blue eyes that danced with mischief. I never knew if she was going to say something completely off the wall or crush my heart into a million pieces.

She didn't let me get away with anything.

Neither did Zhao.

Though, the thought of Zhao set my teeth on edge, I didn't want to fail either of them.

I hopped up on Hekili and spurred her on. "Let's go girl."

Blue's hazelnut and poppy filled my every breath, but faded with each thrum of my horse's hooves as we pulled away.

Time to get some real answers from that filthy outsider. I smiled darkly and rode out to greet his fate. I found I was rather excited about it.

CHAPTER 25

My Grammy is Hiding Stuff

BLUE

After Kaleo left, I rode Pepper up to Grandfather Rock while Lily cleaned the muddy pages I'd stolen from the underground prison. I stayed up on the rock for a good half hour on look out. Searching. Focusing in and out of the hollers, creeks, and clusters of green trees, desperate for any sign of Hawk. Every track had been washed away by the daily rain. A few squirrels, birds, even a cute little red fox emerged, but that was it—no news to bring to my father.

I knew where the answers were, in that underground prison with the poor starving elfling child and prisoner with the trusting green eyes. Or *murderous eyes*, I reminded myself. And a smile that killed the moon or whatever it was. Something tugged me toward the bunker those few miles behind me. Everything in me wanted to hop on my horse and ride down the mountain into the dingy unknown.

But Kaleo's warning rang out in my mind.

"That man down there is a murderer and a liar. He'd do anything to get free. Anything."

Instead of riding toward the bunker, I turned back home. Even as a thrill rushed through me. The thrill of our fingertips touching in the kitchen. The look in Kaleo's molten, brown eyes. What did it mean? It sent my heart flying through the woods on a phantom wind, as if I could soar.

Kaleo had no idea the effect he had on me. These senses—my sight. More often than not, I wondered if I would become a slave to my own abilities. The faces of Kaleo and the prisoner flashed before my eyes at night like a beautiful, dark fantasy—one after the other, making my pulse thunder, my face and body flush hot. Their eyes danced before me, drinking me in. Desiring me. Sending a fire burning through me.

By the time I got back home, I was a hot mess.

"Girl," Lily said, "you need a shower."

Lily and I stood side by side in my bedroom, staring at the crumpled papers I'd stolen from the dungeon. It was nice to have a distraction from all of these visions filling my eyes. *Hormones are real.*

"So, who wrote these pages again?" Lily fanned the almost-dry papers lined up on my window sill. She'd rinsed each leaf delicately with fresh water, then laid them out flat to dry.

"No clue," I answered.

The pages crinkled with age, and the writing was illegible. It was a handwritten language we'd never seen before. Curving lines and shapes formed delicate runes resembling something between Chinese characters and Ancient Aztec.

"Did Griff learn anything besides Korean?" I asked. "'Cause these don't look Korean."

"Hmm. Maybe." Lil looked thoughtful. "Maybe he knows Chinese or Japanese or Egyptian Hieroglyphics?"

I glanced at the inky characters. Each one as elegant as a work of art, but frightening in their newness. They dripped amethyst and purples in my eyes. Beautiful.

After a bit, we turned to the folded notebook I'd shoved down my bra—something we could at least understand.

The notebook was a recent endeavor. It contained my entire family tree written out in a careful hand. From Raleigh Haven all the way down to my baby sister, Shenandoah. A marking or circle highlighted each name. A sense of eerie dread settled in my chest. Like someone was watching me while I slept. But who? And why?

A red circle was sketched around Raleigh's name. Red circles and question marks were sprinkled throughout the pedigree leading up to my mom and dad. Neither of them were circled, but Darla Jane Haven, Mama Darla, was. Hawk and Cora had been crossed out, and the rest of my siblings' names remained unaltered—but a freshly inked red circle distinguished my name.

Not only did this notebook contain my family, it held all of Raleigh's progeny through every line. He'd been married twice. Once to Laurel and then to Nora years after Laurel's death. Their descendants through marriages and births were listed. On and on they went, page after page. I was a direct descendant through Raleigh and Laurel's oldest son, Kacey. A few other families were sprinkled in, but just as quickly scratched out.

"This is just creepy," Lily remarked as she stared at her own name on page ten with a question mark beside it. Apparently, she was Raleigh's descendent through Nora's daughter—a closely-guarded secret affair of her Mammaw Potts.

"I guess an affair isn't super surprising," she replied.

Lily's grandma was a piece of work.

Kaleo Bannon was also circled—a far distant relative, thank the angels in heaven. The Jones family was connected to us Havens. Juniper and her sibling, Redheaded Rowan, were circled in red. Rowan was one of the Fangs.

I had a pretty good idea what those circles meant. Someone was looking for enhanced people. But there were more names circled than I could've ever imagined.

There had to be over twenty pages of names and markings. Someone spent a lot of time searching through the genealogy of every family here in New Haven to pull all of this together. Some of the names were quick scratches while others had been carved into the pages, as if they'd been lingered over.

"Lil? What were you and Kyra doing earlier?" I asked as I flipped through the pages absentmindedly.

"We went up to Mama Darla's. She's got a pretty bad headache, but she gave Kyra a few books." Lily continued to fan the damp pages. "All these books about bats and some kinda fish in the ocean. A dolphin. Kyra kept going on and on about 'seeing' sound."

My mind flew back to Orin, blindfolded, wooden sparring sword in hand, swatting the corn sacks.

"I'm glad she told Mama Darla about her hearing." I smiled. Butterflies fluttered in my gut as I imagined the amazing things Kyra could be capable of.

The last time I'd been up to see Mama Darla was right after my Kaleo burlap sack disaster. Then I saw that light and—it all seemed so long ago. I'd shoved Mama Darla's journal under my mattress. Out of sight, out of mind.

"I give you a piece of me when I hand you this book and I'll be getting no rest till it's back in my wrinkled old hands."

"I forgot all about the book Mama Darla gave me, and she's circled in here," I mused as I pulled out the old worn journal from under the mattress.

Lily flopped on the bed beside me. I opened it up and started to read.

"June 21st

It's my birthday today! I just turned 10! My Poppy gave me this journal to write down all my portant thots. Pop says its the best way to help us memeber all the tymes we went throow. My favorite things are my brand new journal, piping hot hush puppies with cold butter, and —"

I DEVOURED THE JOURNAL. Mama Darla's voice popped out from the ink as I scanned each page. I could just see a scrawny ten-year-old Darla Haven laying on her bed, black spiky braids sticking up at every angle, feet up in the air, pen in hand.

"—Mama gave me nother scoldin today cause I saw something in my mind gain. I don't know how to stop it. I keep shutting my eyes and tryina stop it, but I keep seeing faces and things happening. She won't let me go to school with Cat and that makes me lonely. Sometimes I cry in my room. I ain't never been to town and never been nowhere but my own house and Papa Raleigh's. Sometimes he is shut up in his tower where its dark too. I thank maybe he is scared too now cause he is a little shaky. He gave me the prettiest necklace I ever had. It looks like it's made out of the golden sun. It's the shape of a angel. He says its magik and will protect me. Says it's my guardian. He says his wife that died used to hold it in her mouth when she was nervous, just like I do! He says I'm special too. Mama Nora makes me treats and always squeezes me too hard—"

"—Cat brought me a piece of licorice from town. She always brings me speshal things. She says if I try real hard to pretend I don't see any faces, then I can go to school with her. She asked Mama—"

"Things I hate: Collard greens, milking the goats, moskitos."

"Pop and mama are fiting again about me. Cat and I are under the covers and writing in our journals. Cat likes to draw piktures. She is like my opposite, but also exactly the same as me. We are going to always be together!!! But I get worried sometimes cause I look at Cat and I see her as a sad grown up lady. That's always the face I see in my head. I wish it was a happy face. She just wants to know if she grows up to be pretty or not. I don't ever tell her the truth. All I see is her when she's a screaming lady, sweting and stuff. Then I look at my pop and he always looks the same, just sleeping. My mama lies in the grass with my blanket in her hands and a bucket of soap water outside hanging up laundry to dry. I always see her taking a nap outside in my head. But her eyes don't close right. She doesn't like that story much."

MAMA DARLA HAD SPECIAL ABILITIES. She saw faces. Were they of the future? It was odd she'd mentioned her mother laying in the grass while putting her laundry on the line. Mama Darla's mother died of a brain aneurysm while hanging laundry.

If Mama Darla was gifted, then so was Raleigh, along with many of his descendants. The number of people with abilities grew exponentially the farther removed from Raleigh. As if time made us stronger? Stranger? Or maybe they'd been better at hiding their abilities than we were.

Genetics and abilities? This was way out of my wheelhouse.

"We need Griff," Lily huffed. "He could figure all this out in ten minutes. We're missing something."

"You're right. I think we've barely scratched the surface."

FOXHOLE. Lily found it when we were seven years old. She found most of our places, seeing as she'd always avoided home. It was just an old wine cellar under a half-burned pre-war house, but to us it was sacred. Above the door, carved into the threshold, was a sign reading "Fox Family established 2035." Thus, the name Foxhole was born.

The long-dead Fox family built this home with hopes and dreams in another world. Their family was established just a few years before everything completely unraveled.

Griff outfitted the whole cellar with a working solar-powered mini-fridge, hammocks, and old magazines. Though, lately our sacred space looked more like a mad scientist's lab, with his glass jars of chemicals and machinery littering every available surface. He'd added a few new meaningless equations to his chalkboard.

I slouched in my hammock as Griff hunched over a strange metal contraption. He pinched it carefully between tweezers. His tongue stuck out one side in concentration, black hair hanging in his eyes.

"So, what 'cha doing, Griff?" Lily asked.

Griffin muttered about internal combustion, thruster engines, and something completely unintelligible. Lily walked up and pressed her face right next to Griff's, staring deeply at whatever he held. Griffin's ears blazed bright red.

You could hear a spider bark.

In one swift and completely clumsy spasm—the wires, metal, and springs flew in every direction. Griffin stood up, swearing. He took off his magnifying goggles and wiped the grease from his hands on the front of his shirt. Smooth, buddy—like looking in a mirror.

Griffin recovered with a half grin, black smudged over his cheek. "And what news from the land above?"

Lily winced kindly, while I pushed aside his constant project—stacks of papers full of mathematical equations and ciphers his dad had him working on. He hadn't managed to solve many of them. It might as well be braille to me. I handed him his new project—the notebook and strange handwritten papers.

"We found these old papers up at Mama Darla's and were wondering what they meant," I said.

Lily and I decided to keep the elfling and underground bunker secret from Griffin for now, seeing as his dad was the general. The untold truths felt like lies gumming up my tongue. "It's all ancient characters and strange symbols, we can't make heads or tails of it. We thought you might take a crack at it. There's also this scary weird stalker notebook we found."

With a task in hand, Griffin's inquisitive expression shifted into all business. He took a hold of the papers and set to work.

It didn't take him long to find his name in the notebook. His whole family's. But his family didn't trace back to Raleigh. His line began at the founding of New Haven with a ten-year-old orphan, Lee Rose, of unknown parentage.

Griffin's father's name was crossed out and a large red x marked aggressively over Griff's and his sister Li's names. He didn't look surprised, but he rubbed his eyes in frustration.

We figured someone created the notebook to track people with abilities. It'd be easy to test the theory. We each had a list of names to scope out. If these people really were enhanced in some way, we'd find out.

Were these gifts genetic? Was this a notebook of some secret Enforcer? None of us really knew what happened to them. General Rose said they'd been absorbed into the warrior force. Mama said they were always around, always watching.

"Where d'you find these again?" Griff's eyes roved over the papers.

Lil and I shared a glance. Kaleo had put a lot of trust in me, I couldn't just blow it within the first hour.

"Hidden up at Mama Darla's in an old journal," I lied. My chest twisted with betrayal.

We decided to hide the papers in Foxhole and meet up later. Griff stayed behind to decipher the gibberish to see what he could make of the strange characters.

"This stays between us," I said.

Lily and Griff nodded, though the words didn't need to be said.

CHAPTER 26

Arrows and Explosions, You Know, the Usual

BLUE

Even on my day off, I rode Pepper toward the Warrior's Base. I blinked, reading the names on the list as we approached the old train depot:

Rowan, Dallas, Kaleo (smell), Brock, Juniper (touch)

I wrote them down so I could recall them in my eyes for reference. Kaleo's name shimmered a bright cobalt blue, bringing a smile to my lips. Since I was the resident warrior, it was left to me to discern what their enhanced abilities were. Plus, I was desperate for any news on Hawk.

The large gate to the train depot shrieked open to me as I nodded to the warrior on duty, a Talon. I wore my warrior garb—black t-shirt, green camo shorts, and a leather weapons belt slung across my shoulders and hips. It felt as natural as breathing.

"There you are, Orange!" Juniper called before Pepper had even passed through the threshold.

Gripping the saddle, I slid off. A group of scientists and mechanics stood huddled around a strange contraption in the center of the depot. They smacked each other on the back and whistled in admiration for the machine.

Before I knew it, Juniper slapped her arm around my shoulder and led me into the rowdy bunch. "Make room, make room!"

As she pulled me toward the group, nerves squeezed my gut. I'd been teased in school for my eyes and called an idiot or a freak for staring. But instead of the angry looks of fear I'd gotten from old people my whole life, the eyes that greeted me here were full of curiosity—and mischief.

"You can do better 'n 'at!" Juniper called out to me, scarlet hair glowing in the afternoon sun.

The growing crowd cheered and jeered.

My first shot had failed. The arrow buried entirely into the ground only fifty feet from me. I'd barely brushed the trigger with my finger.

"Hey! This trigger's a lil' antsy is all!" I yelled back.

Everyone laughed, and the teasing started up anew.

"Who made this janky thing anyways?"

The engineers and mechanics pointed fingers, elbowing one another.

"One gallon o' me paw's mash says she can't hit mor' n one!" someone called out.

Now they were placing bets. Perfect.

I stood by an old train engine holding a specialized bow that could supposedly shoot ten arrows up to 1,000 feet consecutively using pressurized air. A psycho machine-crossbow on steroids. Apparently one of the weapons specialists got to talking with the engineers over a pint at Wild Willy's about my sight abilities last night. They got a little over-excited, to say the least.

It was strange to think just a week ago I was afraid to stare for too long, afraid to give any signs away that I was gifted. Now, they praised me for my eyes. Maybe my sight wasn't this scary secret after all.

I held the ridiculous machine-crossbow prototype in my hands. It was heavy as sin, but packed some real power. They'd strapped it around my torso and shoulder for stability.

I was the only one who could actually see far enough to aim it. By the time I understood what was going on, most of the warriors had crawled out of the cavern to see the spectacle. It was Founder's Week, so everyone had a beverage in hand at all times. All the etiquette and rigor we kept throughout the year got thrown out with the elf vaccine, leaving us more mountain-folk than townie at the moment.

So, I squinted one eye past the massive expanse of the train depot, over the huge snaking cable cars, and through the tree line. Some giddy and most certainly drunk engineers rigged up a few approved explosives. They attached them to poles with some measly little bullseyes on them the size of a thimble. Well, to be accurate, they were *literally* thimbles. At least someone painted them a lovely shade of red. That was a nice touch.

"Welcome to Day Two. I ain't even supposed to be here," I grumbled to myself. Why'd I even get out of bed this morning?

Sweat dripped from my forehead, trailing down my chin. This was an impossible shot for anyone and who knew if this weapon was even accurate? Not that it mattered. My reputation would forever hinge on this moment, whether it was my fault or this dang machine's.

Stupid mechanics and their whiskey.

General Rose carried a large bag out by the train cars. Potassium nitrate. He nodded encouragingly at me and winked. From what Griffin told me, if the general wasn't training on how to kill the Shadow Elves, he was nose-deep in the old pre-war books, learning about how politics and societies ran in the old days. I didn't think he was taking up gardening with that bag.

I sucked in a deep breath. I focused on the wind caressing my skin, the shifting air currents. The breeze slowly transformed into ribbons of transparent color. Golden ochres and warm oranges whirled before me. I smiled.

"Let's go Blue Eyes! Show us whatchu got!"

Shooting automatic machine arrows 1,000 feet was not something I could've ever just wandered into an old train depot and expected to be able to do. Thank heavens for my dad's rigorous training schedule. I'd rely on my muscle memory, sight, and let the hours of training with my dad pay off. I'd thank him later.

I relaxed my face, shoulders, and arms. Loose but firm. I focused on my core. Strong. Immovable. I planted my feet and drew in a breath. The targets were arranged in a jagged line 900 feet away. I exhaled, adjusted for the wind, and focused on the first red thimble.

The crowd hushed to a complete silence.

BOOM! BOOM! BOOM! BOOM! BOOM! BOOM! BOOM! BOOM!

Eight small explosions echoed around us. So fast, yet automatic. I just aimed and shot, watching as the arrows pierced the colorful air. The ribbons of gold dissipated like smoke. I got lost in the faraway, my eyes steady on the targets, one arm straight, the other flying swiftly through the motions.

Eight targets, eight explosions. And one arrow left in the quiver. Not too bad.

Applause erupted all around me. The crowd whooped and hollered as tiny puffs of orange fire rolled up to the sky. You can educate and dress us up, but we'd always be wild mountain people at heart who love a good explosion. They clapped me on the back, carried me around, and screamed their admiration a little too close to my face.

I threw my head back and crowed.

I'd been offered and turned down more alcohol than could sink a ship, and within an hour, I was back on the hunt for the enhanced persons. Redheaded Rowan, Juni's older brother, nodded then jumped into the elevator of screaming death back to base. Before I could follow after, Juniper grabbed my arm and yanked me over to the smelting area of the train yard. The sting of fire and steel filled my nostrils.

It took me a minute to come down from my high. I grinned ear to ear until I saw the look on Juniper's face. My smile faded real quick.

"Hey, Fuschia."

"It's Blue."

"Same thing. Hey, we're meeting with our squad tonight. General's got some news. Says to come ready for action. Things might get a bit sticky, but we're the only warriors he can trust. Meeting at the old shed on Willow Lane at five o' clock. Don't be followed. Don't tell nobody. Got it, Magenta?"

"Yeah. Got it," I said.

Juni had already disappeared through the smoke.

"And it's *Blue!*"

My heart squeezed. I didn't understand anything going on. I scanned the dispersing crowd at the base, looking for any of the Falcons. No sign of a single one. If they'd been injured outside the wall, they'd be at the hospital or quarantine.

Kaleo was nowhere to be found. I'd even called his house, my heart fluttering wildly, but he wasn't there. I was almost grateful. I kept thinking about the stranger boy, the prisoner. I needed to know about Hawk.

"H-he is in peril! And when no one comes for him in three days' time, they will kill him and then they will come for me. They will have their blood!"

The deadline was only two days away. Kaleo promised he'd get answers.

Instead of heading down to the dungeon, Pepper and I raced up the mountain to see Mama Darla. I needed to ask her about her journal. She'd known more than she'd ever let on.

As I neared her cabin, I noticed a fresh set of hoof prints on the trail. Plenty of people went up to Mama Darla's to read from her library, so I continued on.

But, as I followed the trail, the prints diverged off the usual path.

Uneasiness clenched my stomach, warning me to turn and run. My dad taught me to listen to that feeling—that it was the difference between life and death. Because of the stupid gut-twisting, I tied Pepper up about a quarter mile from Mama Darla's. Off the trail. All was quiet and beautiful as I walked up to the perfectly normal cabin.

I let myself in back. *I must be getting paranoid with all of the craziness going on.* The grandfather clock chimed two 'o clock and I almost called out to Mama Darla when I heard raised voices.

"Where is it?"

I froze and caught the backdoor before it slammed shut.

"I swear, old woman, I have allowed for this place to exist free of policing all these years. You've been free to do as you will. Now, I am in need of a certain book, and you will produce it for the good of our village."

I stifled the squeal of shock and gingerly stuffed myself into Mama Darla's pantry.

"I know what you want, Madam President. You want Raleigh's last book," Mama Darla said. "I'm sorry, but it's not here."

She didn't sound sorry.

Mama Darla continued. "Someone's been stealing my books and journals left and right. Was it you, Madam President? Sneaking around my library at night, taking my books? Or have you been dispatching your wolves to do your dirty work? Lord knows what's in your heart."

A hush fell on the cabin.

President Zhao growled. "Pray I show you mercy, Darla, or you will find yourself turned martyr for this. That book is a matter of our land's security. *Humanity's* security. You know what it contains. If we do not secure *all* of them, we will not survive what follows. I expect to have it by the end of tomorrow or you'll find that you are on the wrong side of the law. You will be joining your dear sister at the mercy of the angels."

Silence. Zhao stomped toward the front door as Mama Darla called out the last word. "Keep an eye out for the one with the silver tongue. He'll be your undoing."

CHAPTER 27

Mama Darla Don't Care

BLUE

President Zhao stormed out of the cabin. My scared-stiff body dropped out of the kitchen pantry and onto the scratched wooden floor. I found Mama Darla staring into the fire, deep in thought. Even in the dead heat of summer she kept that fire blazing.

She spoke to me as if I'd always been there, her eyes on the flickering flame. "I was wondering when you'd get around to reading my journal."

"Yes, I read it, but we've got bigger problems—"

"I lived my whole life with faces in my head. Seeing those I love at their most pained and vulnerable," Mama Darla continued.

"But, the president just threatened—"

"I know, honey." Mama Darla grabbed my hand and pulled me down beside her. "You stop all that catterwalling and set yourself down. Now. This is your history. It's high time you hear it."

In Mama Darla's deep brown eyes, my worried expression reflected back to me. But she sat as calm as a Sunday breeze.

"So, like I said, I see faces, but it wasn't till my twin, your Grammy Catherine, died giving birth to your sweet daddy, that I realized I'd been seeing her last moments in my mind all those years. Her cries. Her anguish. Never to hold her precious baby boy in her arms. The baby she dreamt of her whole life."

A tear drew a trail down her round cheek. I knew the story, but had never really thought about Mama Darla's twin before. My real grandmother. So much sorrow and heartbreak.

Mama Darla continued, "When we were little girls, I'd see her last moments, crying out, and wonder why I couldn't make her smile. I wondered why she was always in pain. But all those years I'd seen her in her labor pains. I watched in horror as my vision came true that night."

Mama Darla closed her eyes. I wondered if she was recalling the vision again or if it was too painful. I swallowed back a lump in my throat.

"But your daddy and you children have been the most precious gift in my life." Mama Darla placed her soft hand on my cheek. "We Havens have always been gifted, honey. But sometimes I wish I could give mine away."

A sob burst from me. Hot tears slid down my cheeks in earnest as I hugged Mama Darla. I bawled until I had a headache, and her shoulder was soaked through with my tears. I cried for the grandmother I never knew. I cried for Mama Darla's terrible burden, seeing the last moments of someone's life.

A vision flickered in my eyes—*Jax's prone form splayed out in the dewy grass*—then vanished in a wisp of smoke. My heart sank. I'd seen death, too. Was this my curse now, too?

"Well, if it isn't Laurel's Guardian!" Mama Darla crooned as she lifted the golden angel pendant from inside my shirt. "This was Laurel Haven's, did your daddy tell you that?"

I nodded as I held onto the golden angel pendant.

"Yep. That necklace was your namesake's. She was born before the war. Fought like a savage, married Raleigh. No truer souls ever joined than them two, I reckon. They had two surviving children during the wandering years that made it to New Haven. My daddy, Kacey, their firstborn, was only ten when they arrived here and his mama died. He would tell me about his mama, but he never spoke about the time before. The time of wandering. Papa Raleigh was a broken man for many years. He put his heart and soul into this town. He wanted it to be all of the good things of the world, because they'd all seen such sorrow."

Mama Darla turned the delicate angel in her hand. "Laurel crafted that necklace herself from the scraps of gold she scavenged through the years. Was a survivor, that one. She said it was her guardian."

Mama Darla's eyes lit up. "Y'know, I used to blow in it like a whistle. Drove Papa's dog's crazy!"

I smiled down at the strange necklace, but we'd had enough story time. "How are you just sitting here? I heard the president asking about a missing book. She threatened to kill you! We need to get you out of—"

I stopped my frantic babbling as Mama Darla quirked her eyebrow and waited for me to shut up.

"Well?" I asked.

"Yes, darlin'," she answered. "Every single written account of any Founder—they're all gone. Someone's been sneaking through the caverns and taken them. The last one I'd been holding on to was stolen not four days ago. That one was the most important of 'em all. I don't rightly know who it is, but I can't produce what I don't have."

"Is that why you slept with your rifle?"

Mama Darla nodded. "Yes, darlin'. Didn't do me much good, though."

"So, what's the big deal? Who wants those dusty ol' things anyways?" I asked.

"Can you not think of any reason why they're important?"

"Um, they held information on the world before, what they did to survive?" I started.

Mama Darla's face fell. "Yes. What they did to survive."

Silence. She knit her eyebrows. "Honey, those books, one in particular, has the instructions to make a very dangerous weapon. In the wrong hands, it will destroy us."

"What?" My stomach dropped. "Why didn't you say anything? That weapon's been in the wrong hands for over a week now!"

"The only one I can trust is your daddy. He knows. You got enough to be going on with."

"Well, who has 'em?" I asked.

Mama Darla's eyes shifted toward her library. "I thought it was the president, but she just put that suspicion to rest. No, honey, like I said, there are very few people in this town who know about those journals, even fewer who know of the weapon, and none of them who can read it anyway. It's in code. Your great-great-grandfather knew how to keep us safe."

The words from Laurel's letter popped into view.

"They can be killed by the sword or rifle, but the smoke, that was the game changer. Raleigh knows. He'll write it down. And when he does, guard it with your life."

She smiled and patted my hand reassuringly, all the while my stomach fell through the floor.

The weapon was in *code?* I had a feeling I'd found those pages ripped out of the journal down in the dungeon, then gave Griff free reign to translate them. What if he actually figured it out? I should've covered those pages in poo-mud and left them at the bottom of the prison floor to rot.

"So, what does this weapon do?" I whispered, swallowing back the rising guilt.

"My daddy told me to keep it safe. He said, in the wrong hands, that weapon would destroy us from within." Mama Darla's eyes flashed. "Daddy said it was my solemn duty. He said, 'Keep that book in Haven hands, the hands of the angels.'"

Fear speared through me. Not only were outsiders a threat, but someone from within our walls fought to take us down.

"Don't you get that look on your face, honey. Don't forget who you're talking to." Mama Darla tapped her head. "I see things, remember?"

I blanched. "What do you mean? What things do you see?"

"Oh, lots of things, especially of people I'm connected to—and you, Miss Blue—" She laughed. "I am pretty close to *your* thoughts."

I rolled my eyes as my stomach squirmed.

"Met any strangers lately? Handsome, dark haired ones?" Mama

Darla offered playfully, but the accusation lashed out like a knife. She cackled. "Oh, yes, I know things, darlin'. I told you. You need to be extra careful of the handsome ones."

The world tilted around me as the stifling heat scorched me from the fireplace. Did Mama Darla know about the prisoner? The elfling? The notebook?

"All I can tell you is, if you find those books, which, I pray you do, keep 'em safe. I have this unsettling feeling in my heart that makes me afraid for us. Afraid for *you,* my dear. And all I see are faces. I don't know what they all mean. But for you"—her eyes searched mine —"It's all so jumbled. Almost like you have so many different destinies that my gift can't get it straight. I've never seen it before."

Mama Darla placed her soft hands on my shoulders. "Now listen to me. Don't worry about my fate. I know my life, and I know my death. I'm gonna meet Jesus and Cat and my mama and daddy with a big ol' smile when my time comes, Lord knows. But you, remember the journals, they belong to the angels. To the Havens. To the ones who will *protect the people.* That's what we do. Keep this place and the people in it safe."

RRRRRRIIIINNGGG!!!!! The jarring sound of Mama Darla's ancient phone cut through the house. We both jumped, eyes wild in alarm.

I answered the call on the second ring.

Griffin's voice on the other line sighed with relief. "I'm so glad I got you, Blue. Meet me and Lily at Foxhole ASAP."

CHAPTER 28

If Rats Could Talk

KALEO

My hand throbbed and my nose burned.

"Tell me." I shook hot, rusty blood from my fist.

The filthy outsider glared at me through his ratty hair and spit blood on the ground. "Not the best way to make friends."

"Neither is killing my people and leaving their heads for the ravens."

"That was not me. I fought for you. Warned your people—"

My nose, the stench of that elf child in the faraway cell, I only had another few minutes before I'd start to retch or go mad.

"Enough lies. Tell me where my man is"—a feral smile flashed on my lips—"and I might let you die quicker."

The rat smiled right back. "I do not think you were made for this." He nodded, assessing me. "You're big enough, that's for certain, but you don't have it in here." He signaled to his chest, exposed through his open shirt. It was marked with intricate tattoos. The tattoo over his heart was a dragon skull, a human heart crushed in its maw. Blood poured from its jagged dagger-like teeth.

"You know nothing," I said.

He smiled. He seemed to be enjoying his beating. "I've been beaten, tortured, pained my entire life, my friend. *This* is nothing."

CHAPTER 29

A Different Weapon

BLUE

"It has to be some sort of chemical reaction," Griffin explained. "Invisible ink. See, look—" He held three of the strange papers apart from the others. "These three pages are a code, some sort of key. You can tell by the way the characters have been spaced out. Room was left for the translation, some kind of invisible ink."

He handed the last page to me. It was written differently, almost in paragraph form. Like a message lay inked there, waiting to be translated.

"I've tried heat, lemon juice, vinegar, even my blood serum, nothin'." Griffin shook his head. "You can tell others have attempted and not succeeded."

Lil, Griff, and I sat in silence staring at the papers, willing the words to pop out. The wild, curving shapes seared into my memory, but didn't hold meaning. I held the papers up to the light and tried to uncover the hidden letters beneath, but it was no use. Another mystery left unsolved. *Good.* This had to be the coded weapon. I needed to get these pages back to the secret cavern at Mama Darla's.

Griffin sat, deep in thought, his hair stuck up at the ends where he'd been pulling at it. "But maybe," Griffin looked up at me, "maybe if I used someone else's blood? Just as a control?"

"You're really grasping at straws now, Griff," I replied.

I had a feeling we held the most dangerous papers in New Haven. I should burn these papers where we sat. But if I showed any sense of interest, Griff would read it from my expression or body language. I was terrible at this.

Lily laughed. "I ain't even sciency and I know that doesn't make any sense."

"I like to be thorough," Griff said. "Just to rule it out completely."

"What if you didn't need a human's blood?" I asked. I was going to put all of this to rest. "Like, what if you needed a Shadow Elf's blood?"

Lily cringed.

Griffin's head nodded slowly. "That's probably exactly what we need. Brilliant! That would keep it from being decoded for years, I mean—"

"Oh, well." I huffed, faking disappointment. I moved to gather the papers. "At least we tried."

"We have an elf," Lily offered, then slapped a hand over her mouth, eyes wide.

Wow, Lily. Just, wow.

Griffin laughed and shook his head. "Nice one. Keeping it in your shed out back with the coondogs, Lil?"

I schooled my face into an easy smile. "Yeah, Lil! Hilarious."

Griffin, who'd turned back to the papers, paused. The air thickened with tension as Griff's hooded eyes landed on mine. I smiled back at him, all the while my face flushed with heat, my insides squirming.

"What?" I squeaked. "Lily's just being stupid, you know how much she kids."

Griff's eyes tightened. Dang my stupid face. I pulled my mouth down.

"You're doing that thing with your mouth you do when you're lying." Griff's whole demeanor shifted. "What're you not telling me?"

Silence stretched on, pulling the tension in the air around like honey taffy. Griff's eyes narrowed as my resolve strengthened. Kaleo and Mama Darla trusted me with this. I would not fail them.

Lily, who couldn't stand any kind of fight, blurted, "We found a baby Shadow Elf in a secret underground prison yesterday—"

"Stop!" I cried.

"—and Blue didn't want to feed him, but I felt bad and tossed it a piece of Mrs. Haven's rolls, and he ate it and was kinda cute and I called him Lil' Legolas and—"

"Lily!" I growled. "What happened to '*we tell no one?*' not even Griffin?"

Lils pouted. "Come on, Blue. It's Griff!"

Griffin's face stretched with a sickly smile as his eyes bulged. But as he scanned Lily and me for the truth, amusement slid from his face. He raked his hand through his hair over and over again, his face twisted into a grimace.

"I'm gonna puke," Griff squeaked.

"The elfling is real." I deflated. "A childlike thing. And if you tell your dad we're all dead. 'Cause I'm pretty sure everything we're saying is treason and punishable by death." I threw an old Ironman comic at Lily and narrowed my eyes. "Remind me *never* to trust you with anything ever again, elf-brain!"

Griffin sat, mouth agape, like a trout out of water. "You found a *baby* Shadow Elf here? Like in our village?" Griff swallowed. "How did it get here? You sure my dad doesn't already know?"

So, I caught him up on the main points while Lily jumped in to clarify or be witty. She was all relaxed ease now that Griffin had been brought into the fold.

"Listen, this is just too much," I said as I gathered the papers. I needed to get them out of here, stat. I'd already done enough damage, no need to add "translated the weapon of death" to the list.

"Wait." Griff's eyes grew wide as he grabbed onto my arm. "Don't take these, I haven't figured 'em out, yet."

"Let's just do that some other day, alright?" I said. "I'm tired."

"Well." Griffin scratched at the crown of his head. "We don't want to use the elf monster's blood, but let's see if someone else's would work. Just one more shot. It'll clear up a theory I have. I need a placebo."

Mama Darla's words sounded in my mind. *"In the wrong hands, that weapon would destroy us from within."*

"Fine. Try mine." I shrugged. What harm could it do? "Then I'm going home and taking these with me."

Griff cleared his throat and rolled up his sleeves. The evil scientist within peeked through his wagging eyebrows. "Alright, Blue, give me your arm. This is going to be excruciatingly painful. You won't be able to use your arm for a month or so."

I flared my nostrils in annoyance. As Griff worked, Lily asked all kinds of encouraging questions, which made his ears blush pink as he fumbled through the process. Lily gasped and "wowed" while I rolled my eyes. Poor Griff was a goner. By the time he'd gotten my blood, let it sit for ten minutes, centrifuged and separated my serum, he was practically crowing. Lily had no clue what kind of effect she had on poor Griffy-poo. I needed to have a little talk with her.

Griff danced the clear serum-filled tube over to where Lil and I sat on our hammocks. "Drum roll please! Now, for the moment we've all been waiting for!"

Could this take any longer?

Griff grandstanded as he placed a dropper of the yellowish liquid onto the ancient page. "For science!"

It bubbled on top of the page for a second, then soaked into the fibers. We watched in awe as the curve of a line took shape inside the wet blot of my serum circle.

Gasps filled Foxhole.

"Woah," Lily breathed.

Yeah, that was an understatement. Curiosity won over heroism. The booklover in me had to understand such an ancient and beautiful cipher. Griff dropped blot after blot of my serum onto the page as words, phrases, and emotions in plain English blossomed.

My heart kicked up as I realized I was already translating the cipher. I'd been quick to learn, and the fastest reader ever, one of my gifts. Letters and numbers took on colors and meaning, allowing me to flow through a book or passage with ease.

This though, was like waking up from a strange dream. These characters dripping with a purple amethyst color were alien, but familiar. I couldn't help but remember how the same colors swirled in that elfling's black eyes.

I allowed my eyes to scan the cipher and work through the translation. Within seconds I knew it wasn't the weapon. Relief flushed through me as the excitement of discovery spurred me on.

As I worked, Griff and Lily sat in silence, all of our stomachs twisting in knots at the sheer momentousness of this, well, moment. Lil wrote out the words and phrases as I made my way through the last page written by my great-great-grandfather over 111 years ago:

Great (or large?) Secret. Me. Infect at start of sick(ness). Me bite by devil (demon?). My first wife death. Daughters death. Me Alive. Not death, but great change. Strong, Mighty. Survive. Human remain. Immune. No disease. No transform into Demon.

Second wife, Children, Immune. My children (presents ?) Gifts. Strong. Stronger than other human. Great Fear- forever life. Never Death like the Demon. Demons never age. I never age. I see Colors. I hear colors. Feel things, strong. Feel air. Taste memory. Haunted by devil. Had to create age. Have to create death. Too much. Feel too much.

-Raleigh Haven

A silence filled Foxhole. The kind of silence where you wanted to flail on the ground, scream and cry, then dig up the dead body of your great-great grandfather, throttle him, then ask him a thousand questions.

"Woah," Lily said.

Yeah, again. Lily always knew what to say.

"So, let's just talk this through." Griffin swallowed. "In the beginning of the plague, half the world just died. Then the others infected with Shadow Elf venom, they turned *into* the elves, right?"

"Right," I agreed. It was what we'd always been told. "But Raleigh didn't turn. He just, *changed?*"

"Does that mean," Griff's cheeks flushed pink, "that all of y'all Havens, descendants of Raleigh, have Shadow Elf blood? Or more precisely, their DNA? That's why your blood worked?"

My stomach squirmed. "Maybe?"

"And I'm one of 'em, too," Lily said. "Are we going to live forever?"

"Did Raleigh?" I asked. "Sounded like he had to make himself look old."

"Then, he killed himself?" Lily looked sick.

"He was infected in the very beginning with their venom," I said, in shock. "Before everything, but he didn't turn. It says here"—I held onto the paper like the Holy Bible—"he was *immune*. Is that even possible?"

"It has to be. And then he took on their enhanced characteristics." Griff nodded, piecing this puzzle together. "It's fascinating. Makes so much sense. That's why y'all have enhanced abilities. I mean, we don't know too much about the elves. Their abilities have been lost to legend, but we do know they had enhanced hearing, sight, smell, feeling. Because of Raleigh's immunity, he wasn't corrupted, he just maintained some of their enhanced qualities."

"Then passed them down to us," I said.

"Man," Lily grumbled. "Wish I had a cool ability like speed or flying or something."

"They couldn't fly, Lil." I shook my head. "But this knowledge—if someone had known back then, they would've killed him for it."

I thought back to Laurel's letter. During those times of wandering, it was a different world. Humans vs. elves. Any sign, any small enhancement, and you were dead. It was the first sign of turning. I thought of the red paint in the schoolhouse, The Edict. They didn't take chances.

How had Raleigh managed to keep his sensitivities secret? Is that how he'd survived for so long? They'd hunted us, my family. Many *had* turned into elves. Raleigh had good reason to keep this secret.

I let the thought sink in. I had Shadow Elf DNA. No one could ever know about this. Now it was *my* greatest secret.

I gathered up all of the documents, all the proof. This afternoon I was celebrated for my sight. They'd cheered as I'd fired off that machine crossbow. But if the safe people of New Haven knew I had the DNA of a Shadow Elf? If they had the knowledge of this notebook with the names of my family circled?

Fear would turn the peace of this small town into panic and suffering, just like that lady Mama always told me about, Scary Sally. Just like the names I'd read on the Enforcers' log.

"No one can know," I stated. "No one. They'd kill us."

CHAPTER 30

Coup Smells Like Poo

BLUE

I'd spent an hour theorizing with Lil and Griff about Raleigh's letter, but time was not on our side. Pepper carried me down the mountain toward Willow Lane for the secret meeting with the general Juniper told me about. I walked into the old shanty looking just like Hawk had before his Warpath Ritual. Weapons covered me from head to toe. I'd even shaved the right side of my head from my ear up to my side part in the style many of the warriors wore. It helped keep my hair out of the way when using the bow and arrow, plus it looked wicked. Red cardinal feathers, my first kill at ten, hung through my ear and fluttered at my shoulder.

I caught my reflection in the cracked glass as I walked through the front door. I had to admit, I looked formidable. Hot even. Literally, too, because, dang, it was like 101 degrees outside. I even had leather boots on. Figured it was time to dress like a grown-up.

My anxiety spiked with all I'd learned today. I searched for the traitor of New Haven in every face I passed through the square—for the one who'd stolen the journals and had the weapon that could destroy us all.

The main floor of the shanty on Willow Lane was empty, but I wasn't expecting anyone. I called out the birdsong I'd learned in my one measly day of training as I entered. Within seconds, the melody repeated from downstairs. I followed the sound through an old cellar door, my heart hammering all the way. *Juniper, if this is some kind of elaborate plan to intimidate me, torture me, or scare me, then—well, I'm not having it!*

My nerves frayed at the edges in more ways than one since I'd left Foxhole. The words of Raleigh were etched into my eyes. He'd been infected in the beginning, but was immune somehow. It was one of his greatest secrets. Now it was mine.

It made so much sense, but what did he mean about living forever? Or creating his own death? Were the Shadow Elves immortal? Did that mean we were too? Had he been the only immune person of his time or had there been others?

The old stairs creaked as I made my way down into the cellar. Several wooden boxes sat strewn about the dirt floor, circling around a small cracked table. A single light flickered above, highlighting the dust flying in the air like a whirlwind. The warriors certainly had a theme for their outposts. Fourteen people turned their attention to me as I made my way down the old wood steps.

General Rose stood in the center, two hands on the table—ready to get down to business. Juniper sat with her leg hanging lazily over a wooden crate, biting into an apple for crying out loud. *Did anything phase that girl?* Everyone else looked as tense as I felt, at least. Hound, the tracker, and Orin, Batboy, nodded to me. I joined them. The others in the room were either warriors from the Fangs or Talons, dressed in the yellow and brown camo respectively.

How did Juniper fare in this cramped underground bunker with dust particles sticking to her extra sensitive skin? I'd probably go crazy, but Juniper looked as chill as a winter breeze.

"Thanks for coming." General Rose broke the silence. "You're all here for a reason. Every one of you is from an elite squad. Handpicked. Though, some of y'all have more experience than others"—he winked at me—"you've all proven your worth and loyalty to me and our town."

He stood straight, hands clasped behind his back. "Now, I won't candy-coat this. I have troublin' news. Our town is in danger. I have recently learned of a plot by our own not-so-loyal president. She would keep us in ignorance of the menace that exists outside the walls, lulled into a false sense of security, so that we don't rise up against her."

The floor dissolved from beneath me.

"Just yesterday, one of my own—" General Rose nodded to Juniper—"uncovered a plot most foul. Most troublin'."

Expressions flickered between surprise, nausea, and dread, but not Juniper. *Of course not.* She continued to bite into her apple, betraying no emotion. My stomach plunged through the floor.

"Yes," the general continued. "I'm afraid our president has kept a terrible secret from us. Miss Jones, will you relay to the others what you told me, please?"

Juniper stood as quick as a whip and recited crisply, "I was on patrol and noticed the president ride off toward the abandoned area south of town. Eager for her safety, I followed her through the wood to a cavern deep in the mountains. There, I found a prisoner unlike anything I'd ever seen. All I could gather from my brief glimpse was that it was a little—Shadow Elf child-like thing."

Loud gasps filled the cellar. Orin's face turned green. Juni's brother, Red-headed Rowan's, eyes about bugged out of his face. I blinked, remembering to look just as shocked. I did my best to look nauseous. It wasn't hard.

I'd known it was only a matter of time before someone else found the elfling.

"A, a wha- now?" Orin guffawed, surely thinking this had to be a joke. His scraggly chin hairs tried their best to lend him the look of an adult as his half-smile withered.

Hound stood still as death, eyes tight. His face a stone.

"Thank you, Miss Jones," General Rose said. He then spoke of his growing distrust of the president over the last few years. Her complacency and lack of leadership. I stared, transfixed, at his silver lightning hair.

"We have become a lazier and lazier society. The elves, those hells damned creatures, are *reproducing* out there while we eat, drink, and go mud boggin'! We live out our lives in here like all's just fine and dandy. What does our Lord tell us about these last days?"

The general produced the well-worn New Testament from his back pocket and opened it. He always pounded the end of days passages, to the chagrin of his poor kids, Griffin and Li.

"And they did eat, they drank...they were given in marriage, until the day that Noah entered into the ark, and the flood came, and destroyed them all... I tell you, in that night...two *men* shall be in the field; the one shall be taken, and the other left. And they answered and said unto Him, Where, Lord? And He said unto them, Wheresoever the body *is*, thither will the *eagles* be gathered together."

A hush fell over the cellar.

"This!" The general smacked his Bible on the table with force. "This has already happened! The last days have been and gone! The Lord *took* His chosen ones up to heaven in that terrible plague. The righteous in the field, poof! Dead and gone up to Jesus. Leavin' the fool wicked here to burn. Now, through the last days of trial, Jesus has a *new* chosen blessed. *Us!* Wheat separated from the tares of the evil and wicked. We're all that's left. All that's right and just in this world. And them eagles, those demons of hell, those Shadow Elves, are circlin' us like their next big meal. Will we eat, drink, and do nothing? I can*not* be idle! I *will* not!"

I found myself nodding in agreement, though uneasiness squirmed in my gut. I'd just learned that a small part of me was Shadow Elf. Would the enhanced be the next target? My eyes jumped from a nervous Orin, to a hardened Hound, then to Juniper —who leaned back on an old crate. No sign of worry. No sign of doubt.

The general's eyes flashed zealously in the lone electric light buzzing from the ceiling.

Forty-three dead insects lay scattered inside the dusty glass forever.

"How long has she kept that lil' elf of hers secret down there? Tomorrow, at our sacred Naming Ceremony, we take back the integrity of this town. For righteousness. Then, we kill the elf!"

Dread ran in chills down my spine.

The efling's young, beautiful face flashed before me.

"Then, we put the president on trial. She *will* answer for her treason. It's high time we protect our way of life."

"Family! Safety! Life!" we chanted in unison. The words belonged to me now, but felt false on my tongue.

I HADN'T SLEPT a wink last night. General Rose charged his special squad with patrolling key areas of New Haven throughout the night. He'd organized everything down to the letter. I kept an eye on the outer fence of the warrior's base the entire night, searching for any sign of the president. No movement whatsoever.

I couldn't shake the sick feeling in my gut. A coup. Our president would stand trial for treason, then what? Death was the punishment for treason. It'd been over thirty years since New Haven's last capital punishment.

What did this mean for Kaleo? Would he be found guilty, too? He was just a captain, just following orders, but I knew his secret. He was the one who'd tossed the elfling down there. I needed to find him and warn him.

Dawn barely cracked on the horizon, and the roosters graced us with their cock-a-doodling. The sun rose a blood orange, sending a chill down my back despite the heat. This was it. The day New Haven changed hands. It didn't sound like it would be a violent transition, and the president *had* been lying. How could she keep such a secret from the rest of us?

This was exactly what I'd warned Kaleo about in the kitchen. The elfling's existence was not their secret to keep. Zhao and Kaleo knew we weren't the only enhanced people around. It was only a matter of time before Orin or Hound caught a whiff or peep from that thing. Come to think of it, how hadn't they sensed him sooner?

I met Juniper at the designated spot and we swapped posts. Neither of us had anything to report. I could barely focus. My brain sloshed along, half asleep in the quiet of a waking dawn after an all-nighter.

Pepper and I rode out to our new post—the dank prison under the twisted rock I'd pretended to need directions to. The dungeon that Juniper "found"—after the president, Kaleo, and Kyra.

So, I sat behind a tree to keep watch and report any movements in or out of the trapdoor below, mostly trying to talk myself out of sneaking down there.

The prisoner was dangerous. A killer. Kaleo said I couldn't trust him. But, my vision of him flashed before my eyes.

Trusting green eyes smiled as he held out a hand for me, a city bloomed up all around us.

I tried to re-see the other visions. The ones of the two strangers. The one with the sword and the angry scowl and the one who'd tried to stay his hand. But I couldn't.

That prisoner may be my only lead in finding Hawk. If Hawk didn't return by tonight, my dad would take a group of men out to search for him and Pretty-Boy Joe. What if they marched straight into a trap?

"When no one comes for him in three days' time, they will kill him and then they will come for me. They will have their blood."

I only had one shot to talk to this prisoner before everything went to hell in a handbasket. I must find out if those outsiders held Hawk or Joe—and find out how many others watched us from the shadows.

The trapdoor called to me. Pulled me in. It must be for a reason. Ever since I'd seen that prisoner's handsome green eyes in my vision those few days ago with the raven, I felt I was meant to meet him. Talk to him. There had to be a point to all of this, right?

I took one last surveillance. No one in sight for miles.

Then I did something stupid. I pulled up on the cold metal handle of the hidden trapdoor and made my way down into the dungeon.

CHAPTER 31

Curiosity Killed the Cats

BLUE

Only one person knew where my brother was—he just so happened to be a prisoner and enemy. But the coup was going down tonight. If the elfling was to be killed, so would this outsider, along with any knowledge he had.

I knew nothing about him, except that he and his group of outsiders fought against Kaleo's team of Falcons and lost. And that he had charming green eyes. He'd either held a sharp sword up to the neck of one of our men or a hand up to stop him. He'd either lit a beacon to warn us or moved to harm the one who did. It was all so confusing.

He'd screamed out to Kaleo, the night I sat covered in freezing mud, swearing he knew where his men kept our own man prisoner. He said they'd kill their hostage in three days, then come for him.

Curiosity killed the cats, I thought sarcastically, as I stealthily made my way down the ladder and into the prison below. Maybe that's what killed them all off, leaving Tiger the last of his kind.

I stepped as soft as a puppy's ear toward the cell of the prisoner, nice and slow. If I was careful, I could get a read on him before he noticed I was here—

"I know you are there," the stranger grunted from the cell. His voice was gravelly, like he hadn't used it in days. The strange cadence to his speech intrigued me—his foreign accent.

So much for stealth, but he was going to die tonight, anyway. It couldn't hurt to ask a few questions. I didn't have anywhere else to turn at this point.

I wrapped a handkerchief around my face and cursed myself for not having one large enough to cover my wild, noticeable hair. I peeked into the cell at the boy formerly known as Moaning Prisoner Number Two. He didn't look much better than the last time I'd seen him. He was still coated in blood, stubble, and his bruises had deepened in color, yet, his eyes sparked with a sharp intelligence.

Handsome. That same tooth with the chip I'd seen in my vision, green eyes, long eyelashes, filthy dark brown hair curling around his ears.

Deja vu swept over me, tingling down the back of my neck like a spider.

"Hello." The prisoner cleared his throat and flashed his straight white teeth. "Are you here to free me?"

What?

"No! I'm not going to free you." *What was he thinking?*

He flashed a devilish grin, and despite his filthy exterior, his eyes danced. "You can't blame me for trying, Ocean Eyes. With someone as beautiful as you in front of me, how could I not?"

My jaw hit the floor. He wasn't short on confidence, that much was clear.

"What does my beauty have to do with—? Y'know what, whatever, we're moving on." I scrambled for words. This was not how this interview was supposed to go. *I* was in control here. I was the one on the outside of the prison bars. "Anyway, Dirty Prison Boy, I need to ask you a few questions about our man across the wall. The soldier held prisoner."

Prison Boy's eyes lit up with mischief, as if we both shared a dangerous secret.

"Let's just say, Ocean Eyes, that the last person down here wasn't quite as friendly." The prisoner motioned to the splatters of blood littering the ground.

My stomach twisted—had *Kaleo* done that?

"Hah." The boy shook his head. "He asked me the same question about your soldier." The prisoner's expression shifted to derision, brown hair falling in waves. "I was not feeling inclined to answer him."

My heart dropped. Kaleo beat this man, then left him in filth to starve to death? Gathering up my strength, I smiled. Mama always said *"you'll catch more flies with sugar than vinegar."*

I waved my sack of supplies in the air. Nothing loosened a man's tongue like a full stomach. Mama had filled Pepper's saddlebags with vittles before I'd set off yesterday, bless her.

The prisoner's eyes followed the sack like a pup to a bone. I had him.

"But *you*, Ocean Eyes, I'll tell you anything you want to know."

I rolled my eyes, then reached in and tossed him some fresh bandages to dress his wounds. Then discovered the moonshine I'd won yesterday during my machine-crossbow explosion shoot-off. *That'll work.* I never thought I'd be using it as a bribe.

Understanding lit up his molten green eyes. He'd play my game for now.

"Your man who's missing? The painted one? I saw them take him," the boy said as he caught the supplies with a wink. He pulled the threadbare blanket tighter around his shoulders as he glanced sidelong at my bag full of provisions. "He was taken by part of my cadre, a traveling party, you could say. They'd already killed one of your men—"

My heart plummeted.

"—a blond boy with blue eyes, also painted in mud, but he took his own life before he revealed anything to the *prince*." A shadow crossed the prisoner's face. "A brave death."

He studied me as my breath caught in my throat. Pretty-Boy Joe. Joe was *dead*. His large family would be devastated. They were so proud of him. Pretty-Boy Joe, strong and brave 'till the end.

And I'd seen it happen.

"Oye caveman, be careful what you say, my friend."

If only I'd said something—warned him somehow.

Prison Boy continued, "The prince left his head out on your doorstep for the crows to devour."

I fell back against the limestone wall. I didn't want to hear any more. This boy was from a different world where life didn't hold value. He spoke of murder as if it were part of everyday life, cruelty a daily occurrence. And his prince? There were kingdoms out there? My world shrunk in around me.

"And"—my voice cracked—"the brown-haired warrior with the mohawk?" I motioned with my hands, modeling the appearance of my brother's hair.

The prisoner unwrapped himself from his blanket, revealing a tattered shirt and pants, tattoos, and a golden cross glinting through his shirt. Through the spatters of mud and blood, I noticed his clothes had been tailored by a talented craftsman to fit him well. Where had he come from?

He took a swig of the moonshine and coughed. With a smile of approval, he dressed his wounds.

"Yes, the rooster comb." He nodded. "He is held prisoner by a few members of the cadre in a secret location. They were to stay put until called upon by only the prince himself. A bargaining tool. They'll keep a closer eye on this one. He also attempted to take his own life."

A sorrow I could never have anticipated slammed into my soul. My throat and eyes burned. I turned my face away. *Oh, Hawk.*

"So, how do I get to him? Where do I find him?" I asked over the lump in my throat.

A wicked smile lit up his face. "You'll need the *prince* for that. The day before your soldiers came upon us and captured me, well, I'd finally taken a stand against him." He shook his head, soft hair falling into his eyes. "The prince had conjured a new, horrific plan to destroy your people, but I sent up a warning to your village in the night—"

I gasped. He was the one who'd lit the beacon on the barn.

"Your people saw it. It worked." A bitter expression crossed over his handsome face. "I've been a servant, hell, more like a *slave* for the prince most of my life. So, when I stood up to him?" A huff of a laugh. "He almost killed me right there on the spot. But it amused him more to— He settled for conquering your people and making me watch as you all suffered."

Silence fell for a moment. A smattering of drips sounded through the echoes of the cave.

Dirty Prison Boy poured some alcohol on his crusted wounds, sucked in a breath, and grunted. He ripped portions of the cloth with his teeth and wrapped it around his arm. Even with my worry and heartache over Hawk, I couldn't take my eyes off of him. His newness.

"So, you see, by the time your soldiers surrounded us, I had become a prisoner in my own company. I was to be killed in a most horrific way soon myself. The prince was just taking his time, dreaming up a death that would be fitting."

This prisoner sent up the beacon. He'd warned us. I searched his hands to see if they matched the hands I'd seen strike the flint, but it'd all happened so fast in my vision. But he *did* have the strong hands of a travel-hardened survivor.

"Sounds like his plan didn't really work out, then," I said.

The prisoner pulled off his filthy shirt in a hiss of pain. It stuck to him in places, scabs pulling free, causing fresh blood to run bright red. Again—

His clean, healthy smile, the dimples, the hand reaching out toward me. The towering, broken city—flashed before my eyes.

The vision was gone in a wisp of smoke.

His blood. Was it the *blood* that called up these images? At first, I thought the so-called spiritual raven was the vessel, but it must have been the blood on its claw that made the connection. But these sights must only work on certain people. Otherwise, I would've had a vision for every little scratch of blood I'd seen or animal I'd ever killed. And let's just say that would be a lot of visions.

"Where were you five days ago?" I asked as the prisoner continued to treat his wounds with alcohol and cloth. He didn't have the body of a boy, but of a man, with ribbons of immaculate tattoos etched upon his muscular shoulders and down his arms. As if he had sleeves made from the black shapes and swirls. It was unheard of to have such detailed tattoos at such a young age here.

The prisoner huffed. "We'd just arrived about fifty miles outside of hell. My prince was just getting started, Ocean Eyes."

I averted my eyes. "Stop calling me that."

Trying to get in my head with his charming smile and little pet name? *Please.*

"Then what shall I call you?" His eyes curiously searched mine. "I only meant to draw attention to your incredibly brilliant blue eyes, the color of the ocean. I meant no offense. I am only a humble servant."

He bowed to me, hand to his bare waist, revealing a whole other side of intricate images inked onto his back, scrolling across his shoulders. I scanned the art, catching images of elves, dragons, soldiers, kingdoms, and cryptic symbols. The designs were geometric in shape, the patterns beautiful and precise. But the imagery was frightening, as if dark spirits crawled out of his flesh.

Tattoos in New Haven looked nothing like his. Many people in the village chose to ink angel wings to their backs as a symbol of hope or tattoos of lost pets or loved ones.

Prison Boy caught me staring and smirked. I shut my eyes, heart pounding, and cleared my throat.

He covered his last wound, then pulled the crusty old t-shirt and blanket back on. He hissed as he slowly lowered himself back onto the cot. His brown hair hung off of the side of the mattress. Dried blood clung to the strands. He pulled his arms in tightly, as if he'd never be warm enough.

He studied me where I hid in the shadows of the flickering electric lights. "Your big, pretty soldier? I bet he didn't tell you too much about me, did he? I bet he didn't tell you that when his men surrounded us in that cursed barn, I fought on *his* side? *Your* side? *I* was the one who put my sword straight through the prince's cruel heart."

What? I schooled my face into my least accessible emotion —aloofness.

He snorted. "Of course he didn't. He wants me and all outsiders to be the *enemy*. It's easier that way. Cleaner." He nodded, his mouth turned down at the sides. "Yes, much cleaner. I'm sure he'd love to keep a prize like you all to himself. Wouldn't want you to go outside your little village and see there is so much more to this world."

Heat rushed through my stupid cheeks. *Prize?* He had it all wrong. The mere idea that Kaleo would want me to himself? *Please.* Kaleo was a god.

An awful wailing broke through the silence. The elfling. We slammed our hands over our ears as the unworldly sound echoed through the cavern. The prisoner jumped, his expression frenzied, as he ran toward the prison cell bars.

I jumped back into the shadows.

"The little shark? You hear it?" His eyes sparked like green emeralds. "It's a trap. *It was* the trap! A death sentence to this whole precious town of yours. If you love your family, you need to get them out. It's already too late for your people."

I'd been down here too long.

Clutching the sides of his head, Prison Boy begged, "Listen, if I tell you where that soldier is, will you get me out of here? I will tell you everything. The prince might be dead, but his men don't know that."

I narrowed my eyes. Pupils normal, pulse steady as a drum. *Liar.* He acted like this was some spur of the moment offer, and it may have worked on anyone else, because he was a good liar. A charming liar. I deflated.

Kaleo was right. This boy would do anything to get free, including flattering me.

"I can take you to them," Prison Boy continued. "I can dress like the prince, in his clothes, wear his ring, and from far away they would believe it. We looked like brothers. I took his place in the kingdom all the time when he was bored and wanted to cause trouble. Look, we can save the Rooster. I can help you. I'm the only one who knows where he is. You can trust me."

One after the other, his words smacked me in the face. It was true, I couldn't tell the two green-eyed strangers apart in my own visions through those murky eyes. They were like brothers. But I would never betray my whole world for the life of one stranger. Never. Even for my brother, who I loved more than anyone in the world. Hawk wouldn't want that.

"You must have no honor," I rasped, harsher than I meant to. "To suggest that I would sell out my people for some nameless prisoner? Who are you to me? I don't know you."

I lifted my head high, trying to look as if I meant every word, even as the boy's hope crumbled. "You are a stranger to me. How am I to know *you* ain't telling me some pretty little lies?" I quirked an eyebrow. "You think I'd just listen to your poor little sob story and fall right at your feet?"

But even as I said these things, a stone of hatefulness settled in my heart, growing more comfortable there. First with Lily's pop, and now this. My heart grew ever harder and crueler. I hated it, hated who I was becoming, but still, I held on to that stone in my heart like a lifeline. I would need it.

Prison Boy stepped back, his face an unreadable mask.

I continued through the elfling's shrieks, "I feel bad for you, I really do. It sounds like you've had a terrible life and that your kingdom...? Is that what you have? Yeah, your kingdom is a crap-fest. Your prince deserved to die. I'm glad you had your revenge. I wish I could help you, but there is no way I'd *ever* trust you and there's no way I'd *ever* betray my people. That's it. Bottom line. My brother"—oops—"would never want that either."

I tried to move on, hoping Prison Boy did not catch the last thing I just stupidly revealed. My *brother*! I mentally slapped my hand to my head. The elfling screamed off and on, and I prayed that was enough to distract him.

"Listen." I softened my voice. "You are going to die soon and there is nothing I can do for you."

Prison Boy's frenzy fizzled out. He knelt on the filthy floor of the cell. The light in his eyes dimmed. I knelt before him and pulled some extra food out of the sack. I needed more information, so I hesitantly tossed him a slice of my mama's pecan pie. He better appreciate the heck out of that gesture. I didn't give that up lightly.

He looked up at me, mouth agape, then dug into the food. He moaned and sighed with pleasure at the deliciousness. *He'd better.* He continued to wolf down the food, but flinched with every clicking screech of the elfling.

My voice rose. "You claim that you sent up that warning beacon. If you truly did, then please, tell me about the warrior outside of the wall. Any information you have can help me. I plan to go and find him. Alone. I'll risk my own life for this, but not the lives of everyone in my entire town. And if you help me, then at least you can die with your honor. That's more than most of us get."

The elfling's wailing stopped. The last notes of my voice and the elfling's faded away into haunting echoes.

My ears throbbed. I leaned up against the cold metal bars, my hands gripping them firmly as I peered at the boy curled up on the filthy floor. His body, long and lean. Too lean. Weeks of traveling. Months maybe.

That small ghost of hope had slipped from his face. His features were too delicate, too beautiful to be so broken. My heart tore, then knit itself tighter over that stone growing ever heavier.

The elfling's scream started up again, and I jumped. I covered my ears again, but then lowered my hands. This was not his usual deafening screech. He was—singing? An unearthly animal sound filled the cavern. The lilting voice of the small elfling boy unsettled my whole body, but made me want to weep for joy. He sang like a child, a high soprano, but with a measure of the untamed wild. Both the voice of a wolf pup and a little boy.

The elfling's song carried me away.

In a blink—

Pink meadows, purple and ruby mountains, caves, and streams flashed before me. Black, jewel-like eyes of an elf female looked at me with love. The eyes of a mother. White hair flowed like dreadlocked silk. Bright and luminous as dripping pearls. His mother. Pain and sorrow sliced through me. Heartache. Longing. She licked my cheek with warmth and affection. My sight flared crisper, sharper, brighter. Colors I never knew existed. But the space was dark, covered in weaving. It smelled of earth and felt like home. I was happy. I ran out into the light. I played in the water, picking blue flowers, catching frogs in a basket. I liked frogs. They tasted best when they were still hopping in my mouth. My stomach rumbled.

The elfling's song turned dark, switching to minor key.

Something scuttled nearby. I smelled them and my mouth watered. Something not like me. Something strange and dangerous. It grabbed at me and pulled me under water. I slashed out with my hands. Blood filled my nose. Fear. Pain. Hunger. A dark laugh. Pain, then, blackness.

The singing ended, and I found I was in my own body once more. I sat on the floor across from the cell of Prison Boy, as if no time had passed, and yet, I felt like I'd been in the elfling's home for a long, sweet afternoon. My cheeks were damp with fresh tears.

"Did you—" I asked the prisoner as I wiped at my cheeks.

He lay in a stiff ball, hands covering his ears in agony.

"It's over," I said. "The singing. It's over."

He lowered his hands slowly, peeking out through his dirty curtain of curls.

"Did you see that?" I flew high on the vision. I'd glanced into the pure, sweet mind of the elfling. It'd been magical. Bright. Beautiful— but it'd swiftly twisted into a frightening nightmare.

"See? You mean hear?" he said incredulously. "I've been hearing that filth for days. It needs to die. Listen, do what you want with me, but that elf thing is a trap. You need to kill it."

Where had I heard that before? Kyra had been hell-bent on killing the elfling before she knew what it was. Seeing him up close made me question everything I'd ever known about the beasts that were once human.

It must be because he was still a child. If he were an adult, I knew I wouldn't hesitate to kill him where he stood.

The evil eyes from Raleigh's drawing dripped back into sight. So blank, feral, and void of feeling—but beautiful.

So at odds with the mother's eyes I'd been shown, if the elfling had indeed revealed his thoughts somehow.

"Why? Why must it die?" I demanded.

Dirty Prison Boy's head shot straight up, and a flash of anger twisted his face before he schooled his expression. "Why? Why must you kill it?" His voice dripped with sarcasm. He was no longer flattering me. I felt more inclined to trust the annoyed Prison Boy than the charming liar. "Because it is a *killer*. It would love nothing more than to suck on your delicious bones right now, Ocean Eyes. Sure, it may seem sweet and innocent as a pup, but it will grow into an evil creature capable of more horrific cruelty than you can even imagine."

A chill snaked a claw down my back.

The prisoner's voice took on a storyteller's edge as he began, "I have seen these creatures in action. Understand that I was not always a lowly servant. I once lived in a small village, not unlike this one you have here. Filled with families, children running free, animals to eat and work the land. All was beautiful and peaceful. I lived with my brother and mother. We were happy."

I didn't want to hear any more.

The prisoner pressed on, his eyes far away. "Until the day we were raided by the Dragons, that evil King Armando with his son and heir. There are no words to describe that day. No words to express what I saw and felt. Well, at least none that I wish to speak of now.

After the screaming and crying, after the killings and the burnings, after they separated the children from their families to become servants and slaves—" He shook his head.

"King Armando delights in breaking his new subjects, you see. Once his soldiers have conquered a people, anyone who defies their new king—perhaps speaking ill of him or not fulfilling their workloads? King Armando makes a special example of them." A derisive snort. "Oh, he waits for it. He eats it up like a feast. Armando has his own *special* slaves he brings with him on his conquering tours. They are tied up and caged, not fed for days, sometimes weeks, so when the time comes for them to be useful—well, they do their work with bloodlust and fervor."

My stomach twisted.

The boy examined me, his eyes shining. "King Armando uses the Shadow Elves to rip apart any dissenters that cross him. Any that utter a single word against him are sent into The Tank with the sharks."

I swallowed hard. I could never imagine such viciousness. Never.

"And believe me, once you have seen that, you will *never* look at an elf the same way again. Pure savage." He spat onto the ground.

"I-I had no idea anyone could be so cruel."

"They are more than cruel, they are—"

"No." I cut in. "I meant the king. I had no idea anyone could be as cruel as the king. A true monster."

Laurel's words dripped before my sight.

"I almost wonder if humans are the worst of the evil in this world."

He fell silent. Water dripped throughout the cavern offering the only sound.

"Was, is, your family okay? Did they make it out?" I immediately regretted asking.

The prisoner's face swelled with a lifetime of sorrow and loss.

The elfling's song echoed through the cavern again, quieter.

My vision filled with darkness, metal bars of a filthy prison cell with piles and piles of mattresses. Bright as crystal. Light effervescent.

Yes, the elfling was definitely giving me these visions. *Incredible.*

"Please just kill it! I told you it is a trap. Every second we waste is a risk," the prisoner pleaded.

I was already gone. I ran to the other end of the dungeon toward the elfling and yanked back on the mattresses. As I did, the singing grew louder and lovelier. I pulled back the last stack of mattresses and glanced into the dank cell, almost in tears. One look at the elfling, and I fell to my knees.

He lay on the ground, wrapped in the sap green wool blanket, covered in scratches and bruises. His black as night blood peeked through his luminescent white skin, causing purple and blue bruises to bloom. He lifted his head slightly. When our eyes met, he whimpered like an injured pup.

He was *relieved* to see me?

I ran into a few surrounding prison cells and gathered their old blankets. I tossed them to him. And, having no idea what the elves ate, besides humans, and apparently live frogs, I gave him one of my mama's famous fried chicken legs.

He crawled toward me and took a few nibbles of the food. He coughed and shook, but within minutes, a small smile peeked at the corners of his strange mouth. Narrow, sharp teeth were visible in the thin curve of his lips. My stomach curled reflexively, but there was something alluring about him. Beautiful.

I tried not to stare at his body as he rearranged the blankets over himself, but curiosity won out.

His thin, frail, underfed, and bruised body looked as if it would break. I sucked in a breath as his strange legs were revealed beneath the blanket. Long and stretched, but muscular. Impossibly strong looking for any child I'd ever seen. His legs were covered in shining white hairs. His skin was pale and bright white all over, except for the places crusted with black blood or blooming with gray and purple bruises. His neck and back were covered in bright gold stripes, like a small duckling.

I guessed he was around two or three years old. Small enough to fit in my arms. But who knew how these creatures aged?

I could stare at him all day. He seemed to think the same, as he studied me with his large black eyes swirling with wonder. Strangely handsome and otherworldly.

I pulled the handkerchief from my face and said, "Blue."

Maybe I *was* under his sway. I repeated this a few times, then pointed to him with question in my eyes. I wondered if the elves had names or a spoken language. The elfling quirked his head side to side like a puppy, his large eyes blinking rapidly. Purple galaxies swirled beneath the thin tissues of his eyes.

A line from *The War of the Worlds* dripped before me.

"Few people realize the immensity of vacancy in which the dust of the material universe swims."

I was pushing my luck. Time to go.

I closed the elfling back in and walked past the other prisoner once more.

"Mason," he said. "My name is Mason."

Mason's head leaned against the metal bars—resigned to his fate. Even in the murky dungeon covered in bruises, his presence held a gravity of magnetism. "And if you are the last person I ever get to speak to, then I count myself lucky. I've lived almost my whole life as a servant to an evil prince, I-I had forgotten what kindness was."

He toed the empty pie tin on the ground.

"It has been beaten and twisted out of me all of these years." He turned to look down at me, eyes like stars. "I didn't know it could exist in this hateful world."

"You're welcome." A lump formed in my throat. I needed to leave before I felt sorry for this guy. Where was that stone in my heart again? I kept on walking.

"And if my story is known"—he called—"that I fought for what was right in the end. That I sent up a beacon and warned your people. That I defeated my prince. Then I know I can die with honor. Thank you for that gift, Blue."

I flushed. Of course he heard my name as I whispered to the elfling. *No big deal, right?* Mason would die, and if he spoke about me then—I'd have to cross that bridge when I got to it.

"And there's more, Blue. More I fear I must tell you before you leave this horrible prison." He took in a long breath.

How much more could there be? "I can't. I have to go—" I started for the ladder.

"The elves, they have superior senses," he explained. "Especially when it comes to their young."

I paused.

"We've learned through...research that they are able to hear each other from miles away. Younglings are extremely rare. I've only heard of them, never looked on one with my own eyes. But stories of the ferocious and feral new mothers are legend."

His eyes darkened. "A mother, she can hear and smell her young from distances not yet measured. And when her pups are in danger, she will tear through this world, ripping into everything in sight until her pup is safe."

Fear caught my breath.

"The prince, he knew this. He was sent out with an army of a hundred soldiers to claim a new village for his father's kingdom. We traveled for weeks from the south. Most of his men died through the horrors of the Great Gulf." He made a gesture across his chest and kissed his golden cross pendant. "The prince thought he would return home in shame. Then, his ranger scouted your village. You've hidden yourselves well, but it seems as if your people have gotten lazy."

Panic tore a ragged hole into me.

Mason continued, "Your village was too large to take on his own with his small party of survivors, but the horrible prince concocted a new, unheard of plan.

"Five days ago, we came upon a coven of wild elves. We slaughtered them all, except the mother. She was left incapacitated. We lost twelve of our own on that damned mission, but the prince only had eyes for your village. For his own *honor*. The prince *kidnapped* that baby shark and dropped it in your midst. Right under your sleeping noses."

I fell back into the cold limestone wall.

"Let the mother gather her forces, because they never act alone. She will call them to her, build up an army. Then she'll follow the scent of her spawn here, to your village. After you have been decimated, the prince would have taken the spoils for himself."

It all made sense now. The burlap sack was dropped off here on purpose as a little elfling bomb. Every single cry called his feral mother closer, bringing her army of Shadow Elves to our doorstep. They'd slaughter everyone in their path. Then New Haven, all of its riches and survivors, would be ripe for the picking. Whoever wasn't dead would be conquered in hours by that horrid King of Psycho Murderers. When Kaleo found that sack, he'd fallen right into the prince's hands.

"How long?" I growled. "How long do we have?"

Mason held my gaze. Maybe he was grateful someone else finally understood.

"It is already too late for this town. The mother is out there now, gathering her wild army of Shadow Elves as we speak." His eyes were full of pity. "Take your family, Blue. Save them, like I couldn't save mine, and run."

CHAPTER 32

Bats Out of Hellfire

BLUE

I left my post, jumped on Pepper, and we rode out like bats out of hellfire. We screamed across the grass and glade like an army of the undead were on our heels—and that wasn't too far off. Though, our particular brand of enemies were more of the alive variety, with large black eyes, razor sharp teeth, long and strong legs, fingers like knives and—I needed to focus. Pepper flew up the hills to Raleigh House.

I needed a plan.

I tied Pepper up to the back deck and ran into the kitchen. No one was home but Mama. It took me about three seconds to convince myself that I had to tell her everything.

"Mama!" I burst into the kitchen, trying to catch my breath. "Okay, this is all going to sound crazy, but you need to just stop cooking and listen to me. Everything, life as we know it, is over."

Mom turned from the countertop. She wasn't cooking but polishing a short sword in her hands. Elf-Wrender, Laurel's sword. My eyes grew wide. Its leather hilt gleamed, the shaft itself simple but bearing exquisite lettering engraved upon the metal. *Family is all. Protection. Safety. Life.*

"Just shining this up for your daddy. What is it, Blue?" Mama continued polishing.

"Everything is over. Everything. Hawk is being held prisoner outside the wall by some evil kingdom people. I know how to get to him. Well, I know someone who does, anyway. And there's a-a

Shadow Elf inside these walls, Mom!" My chin trembled. I didn't realize how much fear I held inside until I spoke the words. They came out in gushes as I sobbed like a child.

"What?"

"A real one! A *baby* one! And it was brought here as a trap and it's gonna lead its crazy mama elf here to kill us all! And—"

"Hawk? A Shadow Elf?" Mama's mouth dropped. "Honey, you're not making any sense—"

"Okay." I pulled in a staggering breath. "Listen—"

Mama smacked her hand over my mouth. Her eyes flew wide. "Quiet, honey. Now. You go on upstairs and hide. And no matter what you hear, don't come down here. Y'understand me? On my life. *Swear it.*"

I nodded as I choked on my tears, hiccupping uncontrollably. Shocked into soberness, I turned to walk up the stairs as Mama pressed the warm leather of Elf-Wrender into the palm of my hand. I looked back at her; a slice of terror flashed in her eyes.

"*Go on,*" she mouthed.

I padded up the stairs to Baby Shenandoah's nursery and sat by her door, trembling. She slept peacefully, curled up in a tiny ball. The whole house shook as the front door slammed open and boots stomped into the front hallway. I struggled to get my breathing under control.

The stomping continued into the kitchen where a booming voice crooned, "Ah, Virginia! Always so wonderful to see you, my beauty."

My stomach dropped. That was *not* my dad's voice.

"I knew I could expect to get you alone this morning, my dear. Finally—"

"Bearon isn't here right now."

"Oh, I think not." A husky laugh. "No. I've got ol' Bear preparin' to go on a little journey. He'll be a while."

Silence.

"Seems your usual planning ain't gonna work this time. But mine? Mine's working out just fine. Better than fine."

My mind cracked, unable to wrap around the idea of that man, downstairs, talking to my mama like he owned her—was General Rose.

"I think you need to leave." Mama's voice tinged with an edge.

"Yep, in a few hours' time, 'Ginia, you'll be looking at the *new* president." The general continued as if Mama hadn't said a word. "And with your loyal dog of a husband jumping across that wall to find your lost boy, well, it's a perilous world out there. Who knows what'll happen."

"You care for him, Julian. No matter what you keep telling yourself," Mama said. "I was there. I saw that fear in your eyes when you almost killed him. You regretted everything you did that night."

"I didn't do it for him, 'Ginia. It was for you. Everything I've *ever* done has been for you. For *us*. Can't you see? I've waited for you. Bided my time." General Rose's voice cut sharp as a blade. "Patient. I have been very *patient* with you."

I gripped Elf-Wrender tight in my fist as sweat beaded up on my forehead.

"I could have sent your daughter to the Enforcers years ago, but I didn't. She's *alive* because of *me*. I made the Enforcers go away, 'Ginia. Brought the gifted out of the shadows. I did all of that for *you, for us*. Why can't you see that?"

The Enforcers?

"Well, I am *done* being patient." General Rose was easily a foot taller than my mother and a trained killer. She didn't stand a chance. I didn't either. My gut twisted.

"Julian." Mama spoke softly. "I remember those days when we were in love, but we were just kids. That was eighteen years ago now. I thought Lanna—"

A scoff.

"–had helped you to move on? That you'd loved her."

"Lanna?" the general spat. "Lanna? She was a means to an end. I needed children, and she gave them to me. End of story. She wasn't strong enough to last through the birth of our second child. I can't abide that kind of weakness, 'Ginia, can't abide it. Made me sick. She made me sick and gave me *weak* children."

A chair scraped against the floor. Feet shuffled.

"It'll always be you, Virginia. It's destiny that's bringing us together now, finally. The wait is almost over, my darling. Don't worry, you'll be protected, as will your children, as long as you don't do nothin' stupid." He huffed. "That right?"

Silence.

"Y-you promise?" Mama asked like a child. Like a stupid, obedient little child. "To protect us?"

Anger flushed through me like a swarm of hornets. The sound of a kiss squeaked up the stairs. Nausea roiled in my stomach. I jumped up, ready to run down the stairs and fight the general, when a cry sounded from behind me. I jumped. Baby Shenandoah, bless her, was waking up from her nap.

"That's my baby. I need to go tend to her," Mama called.

I caught sight of her face as she came around the corner. Pure, unadulterated anger sparked in her eyes, then fear as she motioned for me to move out of sight. I scrambled from the door above the stairwell.

General Rose crowed up after her, "See you tonight, my darling. You know where to be and what to do—and of course what'll happen to your children if nobody shows."

The front door creaked open and slammed shut. "Only a few more hours my love!"

"I KNOW you think I'm weak, Blue." Mama paced frantically in Shenandoah's nursery upstairs. She patted Shenandoah's back for no reason, trying to soothe an already soothed baby—maybe soothe herself.

"I needed him to leave. The only way to do that was to look

complicit. He is a-a broken man, I think." Mama's frayed brown curls swung around her shoulders.

"Broken? He's crazy, Ma!" I shouted. "Like *insane*! How long has this been going on? Does Dad know?"

Mama marched in circles as Shenandoah cooed, grabbing at her lips. "Your father knows Jules-Julian, better than anyone. Julian was the baby of his family, so by the time he came along, his parents were busy running things in town. They sent Julian up to Mama Darla's during the day. So, your daddy and him, they grew up like brothers."

"I know all this, Ma," I said. Griffin's grandpa had been president of New Haven for five years, his grandma the secretary.

Mama's eyes dulled. "Your daddy was always brightness and goodness, where Julian was tough and sought justice. Together they wanted to build a better, safer place for us. They used to sneak over the wall as boys, bring back trophies, souvenirs. They had dreams, plans. They trained together, but of course their ideas were different. Julian spent hours in the caverns at Mama Darla's, pouring over old documents and books, trying to find the way to build a perfect society —and yes, he was also charming. All ease and charisma, and I was their friend. By the time we were sixteen, we were inseparable. I loved them both. But your daddy was shy and Julian...was persistent, so we dated."

"Ugh." I crinkled my face in disgust.

"He was *charming,* Blue. Kind, smart, and fair. So, as a young girl, I fell for him. It wasn't until later that he became overprotective. I thought it was sweet at first. But he was always so jealous of anything I did. Of anyone I ever spoke to that wasn't him. We withdrew from everyone slowly. I told myself it was easier, just the two of us. Easier than dealing with his anger. But I was stupid and naive. We never hung out with any of our friends, especially Bearon. He put Julian the most on edge. Afraid I'd fall in love with him at the slightest 'howd' you do?' Well, there was one night where it all reached a head." She swallowed.

I'd never imagined my Mama as a young girl before. Beautiful and desired, with secrets and worries of her own.

"Julian and I were going out to the creek. He wanted me all to himself. There happened to be some other kids at the holler that night. It was, truth be told, the night before Julian and your daddy were to leave on their warpaths. Emotions were high to say the least." She glanced up at me.

"What? Dad was going to be a warrior? I never knew that!" Nobody ever told me anything.

"That's because he never made it, honey." Mama's anxious hazel eyes, the same almond shape as mine, flashed in the streaming sunlight. "That night at the creek, I broke up with Julian. Let him get out his frustration over that wall with the elves and animals out there, y'know? Well, he wasn't happy. He yelled at me, loudly. He even —hit me."

I gasped.

"I fell into the creek, couldn't breathe. The others heard me struggling, heard Julian yelling at me, and came to help. Your daddy was one of 'em, thank the angels. He flew out of the woods, out of nowhere, and started wailing on Julian. The fight was bad. There was a lot of history and pent-up anger in that fight. I tried to stop 'em, but I about got knocked out in the process."

My stomach dropped.

"Well, Julian almost killed your father that night, honey. The only thing that stopped him, actually, was scrawny 'ol Joshua Potts. Lily's pop. Joshua came out of nowhere with a glass bottle of 'shine and whacked Julian on the back of the head. Knocked him clean out."

Lily's horrible father? Maybe that was why my daddy hadn't killed him yet.

"Somehow, Julian made it out to his warpath the next day. Your daddy, though, he was too roughed up to go anywhere. Joshua and I managed to get him home and care for him a few days while he healed up. He swore off warrior training and worked on construction after that. And, of course, we fell madly in love, had been for years, but never dared think it. Once Bearon and I got married, shortly after, well, your daddy tried to mend his relationship with Julian."

"Why would he do that after all he did?" I asked.

"Your daddy has a forgiving heart." It sounded like an apology. "But Julian does not. He believes I belonged to him before and always will. He thinks Bearon stole me away and poisoned my mind. But, honey, it's never been more than a word here or there. Not until you were twelve."

"Twelve?"

"Yeah, remember that time you spotted the *actual* needle in the haystack during Founder's Week?" Mama lifted her eyebrow.

I groaned.

"Yep. Ever since then he's been holding you and your abilities over my head. He began with little notes. Usually with a small word of his loyalty. Or how he is 'protecting' you from the Enforcers." Mama put Shenandoah down.

"I've always been able to handle him. He's never come to the house like this." Mama fanned her face. "I made sure your daddy is always with him when he comes by. I kept praying that your father's goodness would soothe his jealous heart."

"Sounds like being around Dad just makes it worse, Ma," I said.

"Well, now I guess you know why I didn't let you try out for the warriors. I didn't want you under Julian's possessive thumb."

My chin quivered. Mom tried to protect me from that abusive man. I never would've believed her if she told me General Rose was a possessive psycho before. I'd looked up to him. Respected him. I'd been a fool, too.

I bolstered myself. "Okay, listen. General Rose called me in yesterday because he's going to start a coup. He trusts me. I'm one of his stupid Super Team of Enhanced Idiots, apparently. He's going to declare martial law at the Naming Ceremony tonight and put the president and the daggum *baby elf* prisoner—*remember that*? To death! Also, we have an army of killer elves most likely coming this way to lay waste to our whole village. So, we ain't got time."

It was General Rose who'd stolen Mama Darla's journal. He was after the weapon—I just knew it. I stood up from the creaky floor, holding Elf-Wrender firmly in my hands, pulling in a steadying breath. *Give me strength.* "The way I see it is this, General Rose threatened my daddy, my brother, you, *and* me. Heck, the whole family. Now he's threatening to destroy our town. I don't care if you say he still has a good heart or eyebrows or whatever else, this ends tonight."

And that was how we hatched our whole tom-fool plan in twenty-seven minutes, including one quick potty break. Mama and Dad would take the family to a safehouse. I had my own mission to accomplish. If all went according to plan, we'd be able to get Hawk as the night fell.

I held Elf-Wrender out to Mama, but she shook her head.

"It stays with the Guardian." She eyed the golden guardian angel necklace I rolled around in my mouth. I'd started doing that when I was nervous, which seemed to be a lot more often these past few days. Together we stuffed several packs with supplies, mostly dried meats and fruits to last a small journey. I kissed my mama and baby sister goodbye and rode off into the complete unknown.

I had a terrible deed to perform. My heart was full, heavy to bursting.

CHAPTER 33

Exodus

BLUE

P epper was ready to go. He'd guzzled just enough water from our tank to tickle the algae-eating goldfish at the bottom with his long tongue. We were almost to the underground dungeon when I spied a rider, Lily. Then another, Griffin. They got here fast. I wished I had a bit more time to prepare myself.

We met under the shadow of a pine a ways off the twisted rock trapdoor.

"So." Griff huffed, out of breath from the ride. "What's this about, Blue?"

My heart constricted as I searched for an answer. Too soon to bring up his evil dad just yet, so I went for the most life-threatening first.

"There's an army of killer Shadow Elves on their way—ready to ravage this town. They're being called here by the cries of that elfling," I said.

Silence.

"What? How do you know?" Lily's hand flew to her heart.

"That prisoner down there, he told me," I admitted. "He also said he knows where Hawk is."

"You *talked* to him?" Griff asked.

"How're you gonna trust that guy?" Lily scolded.

"He's our enemy!" Griff cried.

"He'd say anything to get you to trust him!" Lily said.

"I know *I* would!"

"You can't be serious right now!"

"I still can't get over the fact that you actually *talked* to him!"

"Listen!" My voice cracked. "We ain't got time, okay? I don't want to do this but sacrifices have to be made. I'm not asking you to do it, I just—I need back-up. Are y'all with me or not?"

Silence. Pepper nudged my shoulder, comfortingly.

Lily's voice was barely a whisper. "But why does lil' Legolas have to die?"

Griffin shot her a reproachful look. "Tell me you're not serious?" Griff turned the full-force of his anger on me. "You tell us you're going to kill a *Shadow Elf* and she's worried about the elf? I'm more worried that the mother will still be able to smell its dead, rotting body, then come screaming for bloody revenge."

"Griffin!" Lily smacked his chest. "You don't mean it! It's a baby!" Lily covered her ears, beside herself with grief.

I sighed, resigned to the terrible deed. "I'm sorry, Lil, this is just, well, it's what we have to do. Mama said the best way, the old way, was to behead the elves, then burn their bodies in our fireplaces. The chimneys help siphon out their smell. I'll do it fast."

I hated the words, hated the thought of performing this act today.

"It's been here a whole week," Griffin countered. "If its mother's senses are so strong, who's to say its smell isn't on everything around town?"

"Got any other ideas?" I asked. "I'm all ears."

Silence.

"Then we burn him and bury his ashes deep underground. Hopefully that will be enough to cut off his scent. Enough to save us."

I STOOD face to face with the elfling. The only thing separating us was the thick bars of the cell. Lily stayed up by the trapdoor on watch. She was close to bawling her eyes out, she'd gotten so attached to him after just one visit.

Bright and beautiful lil' Legolas.

I found the key to his lock back in that dusty old office. Mason hadn't said a word as I'd trudged past his cell, but nodded in understanding. My face surely revealed my deep disgust. I didn't wanna! But someone had to do this before it was too late. Before the elfling's cries brought his feral mother ever closer. And if his screeching didn't, his scent or any other heightened senses these beasts possessed would.

I gripped Elf-Wrender behind my back. I felt like a dirty traitor as I stared into those large, black, wondering eyes. An entire world of colors swirled beneath the intricate layers of tissue. The elfling trusted me with the memories of his mother, and now I was going to kill him for it.

At least I could make it quick. One small death for the lives of everyone else. Seemed like a good trade.

How had I gotten so attached to this creature?

The elfling approached me at the bars, his eyes round with curiosity. His breathing rapid, like a hummingbird. My hand faltered. He was only a poor little child. A pawn in a game he didn't understand. He only called to his mother. Such a natural, beautiful thing—I'd done the same as a kid.

Drips echoed in the cavern as a rustling sounded behind me.

"Griff, tell me you didn't bring those old papers?" I asked with a shaky voice. Why in Armageddon? We'd already translated Raleigh's message. It seemed to be the key to the puzzle that put everything together.

"Look, Blue! It's just incredible. They, they have a written language." Griffin pointed to the cell walls behind the elfling.

I stepped back from my hyper-focused attention on the elfling and surveyed the prison cell before me. The harsh yet circular shapes stood out like a black brand in the fluorescent light of the cavern. The elfling used its own inky blood to mark runes and characters on the dingy wall. How had I missed those?

The elfling's head quirked to the side as he caught sight of the wrinkled papers in Griffin's hand. I slid Elf-Wrender silently into its sheath behind my back. These were indeed similar symbols. I tried to make sense of the lines and curves on the wall as my eyes ached and itched. I pressed my palms into my eye sockets and exhaled slowly.

"What does it say?" Griffin whispered.

I allowed my eyes to scan the cipher and work through the translation. I tossed the symbols from Raleigh's cipher up on the walls in my eyes and went to work.

Bright purple, amethyst, ruby red curves and circles.

I spoke the translation of the elfling's words aloud as Griffin stood stock still beside me.

"Take me to Mother. Humans Be Safe.

"Keep Me Here or Kill Me. Humans Death Fast and Pain More. Me Protect You."

"So, we save the elfling—actually *take* it to its freak-of-nature *mother* and it says it'll save the town?" Griff scoffed. "What's next? Fairy unicorns are going to slide down on a rainbow and offer me an ice-cold peach tea?"

"But just think about it. Maybe if we move his scent away from our town—off her radar?" I offered. "I can see far, but I wonder how long a scent can linger. I can ask Hound."

Or Kaleo. Where is he?

Lily kept watch above as Griffin and I whispered angrily, deciding the fate of the elfling.

"Bad idea, Ocean Eyes," Mason drawled from his cell through the echoing hallway, like a haunting ghost.

Griffin and I jumped. We forgot we had an audience.

"Shut up, you!" Griffin spat at Mason, then shook his head. "That *thing*, just being around it makes my stomach turn."

"I felt that way at first too, but then I saw in his mind. I saw his mother. I believe they have affection for each other." I sighed. "Look, it's almost like we have no choice. If I kill it, the mother *will* follow its scent and kill us all. But, if we can lead the elfling away from everyone with its scent and sounds, then *maybe* we give our town a chance."

"And who'll do it?" Griff challenged. "You? What do you think those elves will do to *you?* Give you a little kiss on the cheek and a thank you? This's suicide!"

I hadn't thought of that. My heart quickened with resolve. "It'd be worth it. I'd sacrifice myself for our people. For everyone else's lives, in a second."

I faked a smile, but my stomach dropped. If I was about to take this elfling out on a journey, I wouldn't have a chance to say goodbye to my mom, dad, sisters, and brother before—

"Again, bad idea," Mason called.

"Nobody asked you, outsider!" Griff snapped. He turned back to me, cheeks painted red. "This is not a joke, and it's a stupid idea. Don't you think we should talk to an actual *adult* about this? Maybe my dad will know what to do."

My heart dropped like a bad step off the docks. "Yeah, about that, Griff. I have something to tell you and Lil."

I called Lily down from watch duty at the trapdoor. The thud of her feet echoed from the ladder minutes later.

"What now?" Lily asked, out of breath. A tentative smile tugged on her lips when she found the elfling well and alive. That wouldn't last long.

So, I told them everything. I told them about General Rose and my mom, all the while eyeing Griff's face as it grew redder. Lily's expression shifted from worried to plain nauseous. Griff shot off the ground halfway through and paced back and forth in the damp hallway, seething with anger. Defensive. He punched the limestone a few times and swore. I wasn't sure if Griff was mad at me or his dad at this point, but we didn't have time to sort it all out.

"Listen, it's now or never. Saving this elfling is the best option," I said as the bright white creature studied me from his cell. "This is a new species, and let's be honest, we have no clue what's out there. We've been fed a steady diet of fairytales by adults our whole lives. Time to take matters into our own hands."

Griffin scoffed, his face a rare, unreadable mask.

"Y'all with me or not? I can't do this alone."

Lily looked back and forth between the two of us, cheeks flushed pink, then nodded to me. She hated it when Griff and I fought, but at least she was on my side.

I sighed. "Just help get me get the elfling outside the wall. I can take it from there."

Griffin stomped up the ladder to keep watch. In his defense, I had just told him his dad was a controlling psycho, still in love with my mother—fixing to take over the whole town. So, I could see how he had some thoughts to sort through. We just didn't have time to talk through the merits and politics of it all. This moment required action and we'd either be praised or damned based on how it all turned out.

I glanced toward Mason, remembering my vision. Was that vision of Mason in the city the future? Was I supposed to trust him—allow him to lead me outside of these walls so I could experience the moment when he looks at me with his kind eyes? Was that a sign I needed to make happen or would that happen no matter my choices?

The thought of being alone with the elfling in unfamiliar territory freaked me out. It might be nice to have a guide. But not one I couldn't trust.

What was Mason going to say before Griff shut him up?

I gnawed on my angel pendant.

We'd been down here too long.

Lily grabbed the burlap sack that started it all and tore it into strips. We needed to tie the elfling's hands together and cover his mouth somehow. I made eye contact with him, trying to convey a message with my hands. *You. Me. Go.* I didn't feel like writing it out in my blood.

The elfling just stood there shivering in his tattered blanket.

I motioned to the elfling, holding out my hands. "Come on Lil' Legolas, I need your hands."

This would be a lost cause if he couldn't pick up on my body language. He walked over, his movements quick, animalistic, as he mimicked my motion. At least he seemed to understand. His indigo bruises had healed quickly since I'd seen him last.

"Don't do this, Ocean Eyes," Mason whispered from down the dungeon hallway. "You need to kill it. It is drawing you in. You can feel it, can't you? The pull. The *desire*. The almost love you feel for it, no?"

"Shut up, outsider!" Lily had taken over Griffin's job of snapping at the prisoner.

I took in a deep breath, steeling myself for what I was about to do —free a Shadow Elf from its prison, take it out of town and across the wall to the angel knows where.

Heaven help us.

"No going back now." I placed the key in the lock and turned.

A muffled cry sounded overhead. The trapdoor shut with a crash. Mechanical screeching reverberated throughout the dungeon. Flashes of electrical sparks flew through the air. Lily and I stood frozen in the flashing strobed cavern.

The elevator landed with a resounding *boom*.

It was too late to hide. We'd been caught.

As the cloud of dust settled, General Rose strode out, followed closely by his warriors, Hound and Orin.

CHAPTER 34

Devil Breath

BLUE

"Well, well, well, lil' Hellion," the general crowed—his rugged face flashed in stark relief against the cold fluorescent lights of the cavern. It was like seeing him for the first time. "What, exactly, is goin' on here?"

Orin and Hound twisted Lily's and my arms painfully behind our backs.

I tried not to let the strain show in my face as I spoke. "I am trying to help us. Save us!" I sounded like a crazed zealot myself.

"Now, Hellion, what did I tell you?" the general said. It used to sound like a term of endearment, now he wielded it as an insult. "*I* tell you what to do. *I* command your every move! *Me!* Else there's chaos. We can't have you goin' off, takin' away my best specimen so you can play some supposed hero!"

Hound and Orin nodded, full of righteous conviction.

"The elfling! It spoke to me. It needs to go back to its mother or she'll bring a host of death down on us," I screamed desperately. "She can hear it! Smell it! We need to—"

Hound yanked up on my arms. Pain burst like stars in my eyes. A sting met my nostrils.

"Oh, you poor lil' thing." The general's eyes glinted with a feigned tenderness. "That devil's got you enthralled. It'd have you standin' on your head if it thought it could get him outta here. Don't you worry, darlin', I know exactly what's goin' on. Hound had this thing sniffed out as soon as it landed in this hole. I'm well aware."

"No, but we gotta—"

The general *tsked*. "So gifted. I'm so sorry you had to get mixed up in this sweetheart—"

Hound pressed a damp cloth to my nose—a metallic sting bled through my eyes. Black clouded my vision. General Rose's face swam in front of me. Couldn't. Breathe.

"—after what I promised your mother."

Darkness encircled me. Dirt scratched beneath my hands, cool and dusty. Rotted wood and mildew filled my nose. I leaned my head against a jagged pole as splinters dug into my skin. My hands tingled with numbness where they'd been tied behind my back.

Nausea roiled within me. I switched my sight to thermal. As easy as blinking, the pitch black dissolved into a colorful map of my surroundings. I sat in a small room, wood slats above my head, boxes in varying states of decay littered about the floor. I was in the basement of Willow Lane, where General Rose had told us all about his righteous plans to "protect" our town.

Of course he was the bad guy.

A bright, warm orange body slumped up against the opposite wall, wobbling back into consciousness. Mason. Now we were the same. Two prisoners. One an outsider and one a traitor to her own people—at least in General Rose's eyes.

He wouldn't give me a traitor's death for this, would he? He couldn't.

I thought about all the things he'd said to my mother.

"The wait is almost over, my darling."

I didn't think he'd be capable of those things either.

Footsteps above me creaked and moaned, sending a burst of dirt cascading through the wood slats. I shut my eyes, still dizzy from the drug I'd inhaled.

Through the slats above me I made out a single set of boots.

Size thirteens, black soles with chicken manure, pine wood shavings, horse hairs, 124 blades of smashed grass.

Hound. The scent tracker, not Orin, the super hearer. Hound's family owned a huge chicken farm. I wondered how he could stand the smell. He deserved all the chicken crap life had to offer as far as I was concerned.

I attempted to stand, wiggle my arms and hands loose from their bonds, but pain shot through my wrists. I couldn't get out of this alone. I needed help.

Mason stared at me from across the cellar, his curls falling into his eyes. Waiting for me to notice.

"You awake?" Mason asked.

I mumbled a garbled, "Yes."

Hound's boots pounded above us.

"You've been out for hours," Mason said.

Hours?

"What happened to my friends?" I whispered, knowing that if Batboy was around, he'd be able to hear us no matter how low I spoke.

"Your general brought us down here," Mason mouthed. "The blonde girl was sent somewhere else. Your general said her father is enough of a punishment."

Lily. Where was she?

In a blink, I stood inside Lily's bright bedroom. The door was covered in the locks she'd put up to protect herself from her pop's crazed episodes. But at the moment, she was the one who wailed and swore. I recognized her thin, pale fingers as she scratched at the door. The door must be locked from the outside.

"Pop!" she screamed, her voice hoarse. "If you'd ever, in your sorry excuse for a life, ever cared for me, then you better get up off your drunk ass and get me outta here!"

How did I see this? Through Lily's eyes?

A shuffling scratched up the stairwell. Adrenaline spiked through me—through Lily.

"Lil Mae?" Joshua Potts breathed behind the door. "That you? Er some cruel trick o' my damned min'?"

"It's me, Pop."

"You hadda lock yourself up in your room 'gain?" Joshua swallowed as a thump of his backside hit the floor on the other side of the door. His dark shadow cast a long black spear into her room.

"Jus' leave me, Lil." Joshua sounded defeated. "I can't fight these demons no more, and I can't tell what's real and what ain't. Jus' face it, I'm sick in the head." He huffed out a derisive laugh. "Devil's punishin' me for my misdeeds. Next time I see 'em, I'm jus' gonna let 'em drag me down to hell where I belong."

The vision vanished in a puff of smoke.

The sound of a throat-clear brought me back. Mason eyed me curiously.

"I'm still trying to wake up. I must have blacked out again." Heat crawled up my neck. I prayed I didn't look too crazy staring off into the distance just now.

"Did your eyes just glow?" he asked.

"Can you please stop," I huffed. Was he still trying to flatter me? "Where's my other friend? The boy?"

Mason's mouth twisted. "I didn't see him. So, either he escaped or he sold us out."

"He did not!" I hissed.

"Think about it. He stood watch, you don't hear from him, then you get captured without warning? Please."

"Shut up. My friends are loyal. Not traitors, like you. You killed your own prince," I spat, then guilt wormed its way in. He told me he'd turned against his own prince because he wanted to choose good over evil. He'd chosen to warn us, and here I was rubbing his face in it.

"Sorry." I wanted to move on. "Where's the elfling?"

Mason breathed in deep and looked straight at me. His green eyes swirled into pools I could swim through straight to his spirit. The colors spun in a mesmerizing web, a haunting story. In this moment, I only saw the boy in the city, arm outstretched. I saw the ghost of trust.

Anger burned in those eyes, but something else simmered beneath the surface. "The baby shark is to be put on display tonight. As are we. An example to your precious town of what happens when you break the rules."

Indeed.

My head fell back into the stiff pillar behind me. How were we going to get out of this one?

"You should have listened to me," Mason whispered harshly. "I told you to kill it. Now?" He shook his head with agitation.

"Hey, I found a better way, okay."

"Yes, of course." Mason's face lit with a feral smile. "This is a *much* better way. I'll be sure to allow you to make *all* of the decisions from now on!" His voice rose. "You are *obviously* much more adept at these things. I mean—look at us!"

"*You* allow *me*? Oh, and there *is* no *us*," I snapped. "The way I see it, you should be thanking me."

"Really, Ocean Eyes, how is this to be?" Mason scoffed.

"Well, this prison is a *big* step up from your last one," I teased. "Much nicer floors. Has less of that blood splattered everywhere, dark gothic feel."

Mason's eyes grew wide as he tried his best to keep his lips from turning up at the corners. A real smile.

A twin to the sweet smile he'd given me in my first vision of him.

That smile almost made this worth it. After everything he'd been through, the death of his mother and brother, forced into service to an evil prince, I couldn't imagine he'd done a lot of smiling in his life.

I held on to that almost-smile as the shadows and silence filled into the cracks of the cellar at Willow Lane. Worry wheedled its way into my heart. The shuffling of Hound's boots creaked above our heads, counting down until our time of judgement.

CHAPTER 35

Blue

KALEO

I knew exactly where she was. I could find her with my eyes closed in a hailstorm, but her scent had changed. She stung with fear. Worry. No longer the playful hazelnut and poppy. Now her pheromones let off a spike of adrenaline, almost overwhelming. Impossible to ignore.

But there were things set in motion that could not be undone. Zhao had been right about General Rose. He'd been after something for years, some kind of weapon buried in the old Founder's journals. By all accounts he'd gotten his hands on those and on Blue, too. She was in trouble, and I ached to run to her.

My men had their ears to the ground. Something was going down tonight, and I had my own choices to make. My own duties to perform.

Everything. This. It was all my fault. And tonight I'd have to pay for my folly with my own blood. But first I had to choose a side.

"So boy, you came to your senses, did ya?" General Rose stood before me with a cocky grin. "You got her?"

"Yes sir," I stated. I yanked the sack off my prisoner's head, her mouth gagged, her arms tied tightly behind her back. "I have the president."

Zhao's eyes shot daggers at General Rose. But when her eyes landed on me, they conveyed a deep pang of true hurt.

I pushed down the guilt. This was the only way. It had to end tonight.

CHAPTER 36

Dark Shadows of Justice

BLUE

Hound and Orin, the general's loyal dogs, kept guard over us for hours, keeping Mason and my conversations to a minimum. Thank heavens I had the small comfort of knowing my mom fled with the family tonight. Mama Darla, Dad, Cora, Kyra, Fox, and Shenandoah would all be safe.

At least they wouldn't witness my trial, execution, or whatever else the general had in store for me. I still couldn't imagine he would kill me. All of these years he'd treated me like the daughter he'd never had. Maybe he would show mercy.

In a desperate attempt, I called out to Kyra, just once. Dirt and dust rained down from above as Orin scrambled down the stairs, gag in hand. One look at Orin's flushed cheeks had me hoping I could persuade him to my side.

"No, Orin!" I cried. "You know this's wrong."

He winced. "Orders are orders, Blue. General's doing what's got to get done. Sometimes it ain't pretty, but Zhao lied to us all. Hid things, and I can't stand for that. Things gotta change around here."

"But what about the elfling?" I kept an eye on the bottom of Hound's shoes through the floorboards. "It's crying out to its mother. She's coming for us."

Hound called, "No consorting with the prisoners."

Orin stuffed the gag in my mouth with a wince and trudged up the stairs without a backwards glance. Great. Now I had a dry mouth and no hope of getting us out of here.

I'd spent a good hour staring at a particularly gross crack in the foundation where mildew built an intricate colony, when a few shadows flickered across the outside of the upper story.

Was it time for the Naming Ceremony and the general's power trip already?

The shadows moved silently along the back of the shack at Willow Lane. Two figures. One tall and dark, the other small and light. Hound and Orin stood at attention immediately.

The smaller shadow flitted to the front door with a quick knock.

"Hey, boys! Miss me?" Juniper's chirp muffled through the wood floor. "General sent me to give you the thirty-minute warning and check on the prisoners. They need to be ready for showtime."

"Sounds good, Juni." Relief coated Orin's voice.

"Who's here with you?" Hound asked. "I smell someone else."

"Is that any way to talk to a lady?" Juniper asked. "It's your upper lip."

"Yeah, I hear another heartbeat," Orin added reluctantly.

The dark shadow paused, still as death. I longed for my weapons. Elf-Wrender had been taken from me, along with all my other gear. Their absence hit me like the loss of a limb. I bet the general had my sword. I bet he'd been eyeing it since he was a boy, eager to get his sick, meaty hands on it.

"Well, Batboy, Big Hank and I are just supposed to check on the prisoners, make sure they're presentable. Lighten up." Juniper let herself into the shack. The black shadow followed like a storm cloud.

"Big Hank? That ain't Hank—wait that's—" Orin cried out as a fight erupted above.

The large black shadow swept in like rolling thunder, filling the room with clanging metal and screams of pain. Through the cracks of the wood, strong arms, dark hair, and weapons flashed. I couldn't believe my eyes. How could it be?

Juniper fought like a bird of prey in flight, landing on Orin's back and whacking him on the head with the leg of a chair she'd acquired. A messy, but brilliant fight.

The general's dogs were overpowered in minutes, gagged, bloody, and tied up like mummies in the corner.

This was a rescue mission.

The door to the cellar smashed open, and through the light of the doorway I saw my other rescuer fully. I never thought I'd see him strapped up like a warrior, saving my butt.

It was my daddy.

"Dmmmf?" My chin trembled. The gag kept me from all-out weeping like a little child.

"Hey, Baby Blue." Dad knelt down and kissed my forehead then removed the cloth from my mouth. "Sorry it took so long."

As he cut my bonds, I fought back the tears that stung my eyes. "You and Juni? How'd you find me?"

"How 'bout we focus on getting out of here, then we can talk through the details." Dad's love-filled eyes shifted to steel as they landed on Mason. "Who's this?"

"He's an outsider. Kaleo took him prisoner days ago. I don't know if we can trust him, but he's the only one who knows where Hawk is." At the shocked look on my dad's face, I added, "Hawk's being held prisoner by his people outside the walls. We need him."

Dad raised his hatchet and rounded on Mason. "But do we need his arms?"

Mason blanched a deathly white and looked to me for help. I shrugged.

Juniper called. "Havens! Reunion time's over. Time to move!"

Juniper, my dad, and I stood at the top of the water tower. Dad tied Mason to the pole behind us as we looked out over the evening through the kudzu vines concealing the tower from the world.

I watched from miles away as people milled about, found their seats, and tore into the crawdad boil. The Naming Ceremony was about to begin, though neither of the warriors had returned. My stomach clenched as I caught sight of Pretty-Boy Joe's mama and dad carrying in a melting strawberry shortcake. They buzzed with the excitement of seeing their boy return from across the wall. My heart ached with the sad truth. They had no clue he'd been killed by the prince of some foreign kingdom for heaven knows why.

No new names would be given for any of the warriors tonight, but I thought of a great one for the general—"Fights with Fist and Forked Tongue."

"Dad, I have to find that elfling." I tightened the string of my bow. "I have to get him out of here, away from everyone."

"One thing at a time, Baby Blue." Dad paced impatiently behind me on the water tower. "First we get Julian."

The steel in his voice was unlike anything I'd ever heard coming from him. A knife poised to strike.

"And Mama? Did she get the family to the safehouse?" I asked.

She'd given me the task of killing the elfling while she got the family out. Seemed she'd also found time to tell dad all about the general's "protection" too.

"See him yet?" Dad continued to sharpen his many blades. The hard line of his mouth twisted in the moon's light. This was a side of my dad I'd never seen.

"So, no forgiving and turning the other cheek tonight?" I asked as I eyed his tense shoulders.

He merely shook his head, eyes made of cold flint. "Honey, even Jesus said to forgive seventy times seven. I think I've reached, y'know, whatever the limit is by now."

I needed Kaleo. I needed him to sniff out that elfling. Neither Juni nor Dad knew where the elfling was, and they weren't willing to take an outsider's word for gospel. Their first priority was the coup. As far as they were concerned, the elfling could wait. But I felt the Mother Elf's approach like a ticking time bomb.

"So, Kaleo's down there with the Falcons?" I asked Juni. I scanned below, finding only townspeople getting their drinks and seats. All smiles and ease.

"Like I said, Turquoise, the Falcons and Wings are surrounding the square, taking out the warriors in Rose's pocket," Juni explained. "We don't even know if they understand who they're following or why. We need to be careful."

Her brother, Red-headed Rowan, was one of the warriors helping the general. Just following orders.

"I don't see Kaleo anywhere."

Juni glared at me. "He's there. He has a plan. He was the one who told us where to find you. Told me where you were and to get your dad as backup."

"How did he know?"

Juni lifted an eyebrow and tapped her nose, a smile spreading across her wicked face. My face flushed as I sniffed my armpit. Oh man, I wouldn't be hard to miss right now.

"So what?" I asked. "Now we just wait?"

"That's the plan, Sapphire, and we stick to the plan," Juniper answered for the twentieth time.

Where was lil' Legolas? I searched the square for clues, focusing in and out on footprints as I went.

Something was off. Something was wrong. The general's warriors hadn't budged. The Fangs and Talons stood stationed at every entrance and exit. Nothing was happening. I needed to get down there. Sitting up on this water tower watching the story play out below was not how I did things.

General Rose stood up on stage, arms outstretched. His shining moment playing out. I read his lips aloud. "—what we have, proud people of New Haven, is our very own leader, who we trusted with our lives, has been keeping *very* frightening secrets from us. Just recently, my life's research has been completed, with the help of my brave son—"

General Rose signaled to Griffin who trudged up on stage, his face white as a sheet. Sweat glistened on his forehead as he nodded, swallowing hard. Silence followed.

"What?" I whispered, not quite believing what I saw. It wasn't true. Griff? *My* Griff? He wasn't really helping his father all along, was he?

My heart fought to catch up to what my eyes took in. Griffin stood next to his father as General Rose placed a confident arm around his shoulder. Finally, a son he could be proud of.

"What's happening, Blue?" Dad asked. "You've gone quiet."

"It's...Griffin. He's up there standing next to his dad." His betrayal hit me like a hot brand to the heart. "I can't believe it. *Griff? He betrayed me?*"

I filled Dad and Juni in on what transpired below, as swear words spewed out of my mouth that I didn't even realize I knew. I'd gone from denial to sorrow to anger in about five minutes.

I was itching to get down there and punch Griffin in the throat.

General Rose continued, "And all of his tireless research has brought us a most treacherous discovery!"

The equations Griffin constantly worked on in class, in Foxhole, the ones I'd unwittingly committed to memory, came crashing before my eyes, but still made no sense.

"I know that in the past, we have feared certain abilities, enhancements in our own senses: sight, hearing, touch, taste, and smell. But these are not something to be feared, they are a *gift*. A genetic gift! And we *need* this gift for what is to come. For we are in terrible danger."

The townspeople stirred, setting their drinks down. The tone of the evening shifted. The general had the Haveners in his power, even the stone angels of the village seemed to still. In the quiet, I shot daggers through my eyes to Griffin. The liar. The traitor. His stupid mouth moved in a frenzy.

"*—trying to get to you. Using me as bait. Don't come here no matter what you see. He wants you. Run, Blue, run—*"

"Blue." Dad's voice boomed. "What's Julian saying now?"

I shook my head but the words *"Run, Blue, run"* ran through my eyes on repeat.

"Blue," Dad snapped. "What's happening?"

I focused in on General Rose.

"—sorry to be the bearer of bad news, but our beloved president, whom we *all* put our trust in—" The general gestured behind himself as President Zhao was pushed forward, her head held high, hands bound behind her, by Kaleo and Jax?

What? This had to be part of the plan, right? Kaleo's face was almost bored, but I focused in. His pulse raced in his neck, eyes searching, nostrils flaring.

"It is my unfortunate position to place her on trial for treason!" the general said.

An outcry erupted from the audience below.

General Rose held up a hand. "Now, now, our laws are what separate us from the beasts, and our president has been keeping a *horrifying* secret from us!"

The tension in the square was palpable, even from up here on the water tower. I searched every face on stage from Griff to Kaleo to Jax, the general, and the president.

Kaleo's eyes met mine, impossible at this distance. Maybe he picked up on my scent? He nodded his head once, barely, eyes shifting to the building across from him in a blink. I followed his gaze to the top floor of the bakery.

A whip of a blond ponytail, gold cuff earring, arrows—Dallas. A flash of a knife cutting rope, vapor, fumes floated in the air. Gun powder?

Dallas was about to blow up some stuff.

"Come on out, darlin', don't be shy now." The general plastered on a smile as he gestured behind himself, eyes spitting fire.

Pushed up on the stage, in front of the whole town, stood my trembling little sister, Kyra. Shaking with absolute terror, her eyes flew around frantically for someone, anyone. Smudges of dirt clung to her knees as if someone had tried to make her look presentable and failed.

Fear slammed into me like a gut punch I was powerless to stop. My knees crashed onto the metal walkway. The general's dogs,

Hound and Orin, stood a few paces behind her, smiles pressed into their faces. Their split smiles didn't reach their bruised, black eyes as their hands hovered near their weapons.

"It's a trap, Blue. Run," Griffin mouthed on repeat.

"Kyra! That devil has Kyra!" I yelled.

I didn't think. I jumped and raced down the water tower ladder.

"Blue!" Dad cried out.

"Let me fight!" Mason called as I went rung under rung down the rusted ladder. "Blue! Take me with you! Let me help you! Let me fight!"

Mason struggled and fought against his bonds long after I hit the ground and ran.

CHAPTER 37

Death Comes to New Haven

BLUE

I ran. The woods flew around me, an afterthought. Kyra. If General Rose had Kyra, then he held Mama and everyone else I cared about hostage. I had to get there, had to save her.

The wind whistled, screaming to me as I ran. *All my fault. This is all my fault.*

"Hey, Blue!" Juniper called from behind. "Hold up!"

Juni never used my name.

"Can't stop! Ain't gonna stop!" I cried through my tears. "Gonna kill 'im!"

Kyra's trembling chin, her skinny little frame, her eyes searching wildly for help.

"Stop! We have to come up with a plan. You can't just bust in there all screamin' demon," Juni yelled. "That's what he wants you to do."

"I don't care!"

Juniper grabbed my arm and spun me around. The next thing I knew, I slammed into a tree. Hard.

Somehow, I felt nothing.

Juni's face was inches from mine. "You *do* care and you *will* not play his game. Y'got it?"

Our breath caught and hitched as we stared each other down.

Juni's eyes guttered. "He—he fooled me, too."

Two-hundred-twenty auburn eyelashes fluttered over her left eye.

Juni wiped the spit from the side of her mouth. This was no time to be stubborn, and there was no time to waste.

"Y'know what? If he wants me, he's gonna *get* me," I growled. "You don't mess with my family and live. Family. Safety—*Death!*"

Juni shook her head, musing darkly, "Alright, Violet." A smile lit up her face, her eyes glowing with a menace. She'd hated being cooped up on that water tower as much as I had. "I'm up for a fight if you are. Let's *kill* that son of a devil."

JUNIPER and I crouched beside the bakery in the square. The stage glittered with beautiful twinkling lights as the sun fell behind the surrounding mountains. Oranges and reds ran through the violets of the sky.

The words of Legolas about the red sun rising in *The Lord of The Rings* scrolled bright gold before my eyes. I didn't have the energy to correct him that it was actually dusk, not dawn. I prayed it didn't mean blood would be spilled today. Either way, it was a creepy omen.

We hadn't seen a single soul since we'd crossed into town. Busy-body goats and dogs were our only companions. Everyone's eyes were glued to the spectacle on stage in the square. Juniper and I shared a look that said, *"this feels like a trap."* But as long as we knew it was a trap, then maybe we wouldn't fall for it, right?

The eerie sounds of the highjacked ceremony echoed through the square like an underwater ghost. Too many garbled microphone iterations to make sense of.

"Where's Falcon Team? Where's anybody?" I whispered as we made our way around to the back of the stage.

As if in answer to my question, a peal of explosions split open the sky. One after another, pops of gasoline and bursts of orange flame went off like a lightning storm in a hurricane. Juni and I ran into the melee while everyone else ran out wailing and shrieking. Complete chaos followed every turn. Fire billowed up from the rooftops of half the buildings in the square. Smoke blotted out the sky.

Juni and I pushed through the crowd of screaming New Haveners. They either tossed a child or two over a shoulder to escape the scorching flames or joined in the mounting efforts to fill buckets with water. Juni and I ran the gauntlet of overturned tables, chairs, and half-eaten food until we reached the center of the square.

If I hadn't been gifted with extraordinary sight, I would never believe what I saw beneath that giant oak tree. Griffin and Kaleo stood back-to-back, a weapon in each hand, fighting off the general's warriors. Kyra cowered beneath their protective legs. The general and President Zhao faced off in a duel for the ages, both with warriors on either side. Talon versus Wing, Fang versus Falcon. Weapons flashed, swear words flew, and hair. Lots of awesome hair whipped around among the muscled men and women.

A few warriors worked frantically to put out the fires still blooming on either side of us but others joined in the fight on stage.

"You said you wanted a distraction!" Dallas called out to Kaleo as he crashed into a warrior about to slash at Zhao's back.

"Way to overdo it, Dallas!" Kaleo yelled as he flung a knife at one of the general's men and got him in the thigh. "You sure know how to put on a show."

"More like put an *end* to a show," Griff sniped.

I was so happy to see Griff and Kaleo protecting my sister, I could kiss them both. I dashed up to the foot of the stage. Kyra held on to Kaleo's calf for dear life. It was the same size as she was.

"Cover me, Juni," I barked as I ran to my little sister. "Kyra!"

Kyra locked eyes with mine, pure terror in those golden orbs. I pushed a few tables over and grabbed onto her small frame. As soon as I had Kyra, Kaleo flew into full-on rage mode. With a glint in his eye, he grabbed his weapon of choice, his hatchet.

There was no stopping him as he punched, slashed, and chopped warriors' limbs, all the while his hair flew around him like a God of Thunder. It was a sight to behold. Anger, vengeance, and testosterone rolled off him in waves. But still, he held back. They all did. We'd all grown up together—we all valued life.

Griffin didn't look quite as competent. He dripped sweat as he shakily held his own up there with a short sword his father had given him long before the hope of his son being a warrior faded. Juni fired off arrows into legs and shoulders like a bandit, blood and yelps springing forth like fountains of justice.

We were going to be okay. I just needed to get Kyra out of the fire-blazing square. I held her like a small child in front of me, her lanky arms and legs squeezing my neck and ribs.

Kyra choked out my throat and cried, "He found us, Blue. The general, he knew where we were. Then, he- he took us and told us he was g-g-goin' to—"

"Shhh, it's okay Kyra. I got you." I comforted her as I ran away from the chaos. I had my own mission, and the Falcons, Wings, Juni, and Griff had this under control.

"He said he was gonna feed me to it!" Kyra banged on my back. "Right in front of Mama. And then Mama—she-she threw up! And we were all crying! Then he threw me in a room with him and shut the door!"

"What?!" I reeled, dropping Kyra on the ground in front of me.

Everything slowed. We stood in the center of the square among the tables. The smoke billowed around us, snaking to the sky. New Haveners ran around with buckets in slow motion. The fight continued on stage, but in this moment, Kyra's face was my only focus—every pore of her face visible.

"And then, Blue, then, he *talked* to me," Kyra said.

"The elfling? He *spoke* to you?" I grabbed her hand.

She nodded.

"Kyra, you gotta take me to the elfling, right now."

I spared one last glance behind me at the stage as the general, that imposter, swung Elf-Wrender at the president. Two warriors backed the general. The president had one backup. It was three on two as Kaleo fought his way to Zhao and Jax. The flash of steel and flesh.

General Rose's gritted teeth and silver hair blurred with Zhao's swift and sharp movements. But, she slowed. She was tiring. And she was injured. Her blood spattered the stage and soaked into the thirsty wood.

On instinct, I yanked Kyra behind me. Kaleo would never make it to Zhao in time. I raised my bow, nocked an arrow, and focused it on General Rose's throat, fifteen yards. I had a clear shot. I could make it, easy. He had my family. Justice called for his death. General Rose was going to kill Zhao.

Bloodlust burned in his eyes. Eyes he'd passed down to his son, Griffin. Eyes I'd known since I was born. Eyes of family. A brief flash of compassion for the man I used to know stayed my hand. I hesitated. That was all it took.

In that split second, General Rose thrust Elf-Wrender toward Zhao.

In a scream of fury, she went down.

"NOOO!" Kaleo's animalistic growl drowned out every other sound as he pushed his way to the president's side. Time stood still as inky blood seeped from her wound. The general stood over her prone form, a look of disgust smeared across his face.

The general's head snapped up, locking eyes with mine, his mouth downturned. A moment in time etched on my eyes forever. He whistled for his warriors to follow, eyes never leaving mine. He spit on the stage, wiped his mouth—blood mingled with sweat. Then he turned from the square, Elf-Wrender still wet from the blood of treachery.

CHAPTER 38

Hey Elves, Eat Here Free

BLUE

Chaos reigned as we circled the president's trembling, bleeding body. Kaleo tore his shirt and held it to Zhao's side. Panic flared in his eyes. Her breaths hitched, her chin shook as she tried to speak to Kaleo—tried to convey some sort of message to him. Her eyes pleaded, desperate.

Blood bloomed through Kaleo's shirt as it pressed into Zhao's wound. He called his men to him. Rallying. Rising up in the face of utter disaster. Zhao had cared for him after his mother died. Helped shape him into the man he was—and now her blood was on my hands.

I let this happen. This and everything General Rose did from this point on was on me. My fault. *I failed. I'm a failure.*

I always believed I was some kind of tough warrior, some brave soul—the fighter girl with the enhanced eyes. But I'd just stood there, arrow at the ready, and watched while General Rose had his coup. When it came down to it—I was a coward.

Kaleo barked orders for his men to carry Zhao to the hospital. No detail left untouched.

As the three Falcons ran off with the wounded president, Kaleo, Juniper, Griffin, Kyra, and the rest of the Falcons—Dallas, Jax, and Brock awaited orders.

"So, this is what a coup looks like," I grumbled. "Looks stupid."

I wanted to run screaming. I wanted to crawl under a mountain and never be seen again. I wanted to tear that man apart.

"Might as well put an 'Eat Here Free' sign up on our water tower for all the neighbors," Juni added, watching the smoke rise above us like an angry volcano.

Dallas gave her a withering look. "Hey, next time we need a distraction, we'll give you a call. I'd like to see you do better."

"I bet you would," Juni quipped.

"Listen," I interjected. "My family's in trouble, and the general's not done with us. We've got to get to that elfling before he does."

"What do you plan on doing with that thing?" Kaleo broke out of his glassy stare. His entire focus fell on me like a boulder.

Oh, don't get up in my face right now, Soldier Boy. I am not in the mood.

Lifting my chin, I answered, "His mother's out there. She's gathering a force of Shadow Elves to wreak havoc on our town. So, I had a plan to lead the elfling's scent and sounds away from New Haven—"

I dropped off as Kaleo frowned down at me.

"*What?* What's that look?" I challenged.

Kaleo's eyes gleamed. "What are you talking about? How would you know about this Mother Elf leading a force?"

"Well, since no one else will even *speak* to me! Y'all are too busy keeping your own elf-forsaken secrets, I had to crawl down into that stinkin' dungeon and talk to the prisoners my *own* self," I snapped. "So *that's* how I know."

Everyone pulled a face at that, as if I'd just said the most outrageous thing in the world. Heck, we'd all been keeping secrets.

"And you think you can trust that *filthy* outsider?" Kaleo growled. His eyes lit up with a new kind of anger.

"He fought on *our* side!" I yelled. "He killed the prince himself to help *y'all* win! He told me he'd sent up that beacon to warn us. So yeah. It's better than any of y'all have told me. That *light* I saw? Mason—"

"Is that *right?*" Kaleo's chest puffed up in my face. "That's what *Mason* said, huh?"

"Hey, you are not Mr. Perfect, okay. I'm doing the best I can. Feels like I'm the only one doing anything. I mean, are you *ever* gonna tell everyone how that elfling got here in the first place?" I interjected. "'Cause I know that story! I *know* who brought that elf-bomb *exactly* where those outsiders wanted it."

Kaleo deflated, hurt blooming in his eyes.

"So, don't try to act like you're some kind of moral authority right now," I growled.

Silence. One glance around me showed everyone's eyes were on their feet.

Guilt slammed into me. "Hey, we do the best we can with what we have in front of us. Sometimes it turns out to be the wrong thing."

The general stabbed Elf-Wrender into the president. Over and over. Blood sprayed from the wound.

I could've stopped him. I had the shot. I pulled Kyra in close to me, eager to feel her again. To remind myself that at least she was okay. But Baby Shenandoah, Mama, Cora, Fox, Mama Darla weren't.

"I hear him," Kyra whispered from my side. "The elfling—"

The hairs on my arms shot out. Chills spiraled down my back.

"—he says the bad man's coming."

WE HOPPED on the closest sugar-powered truck and ripped out of town. It happened to be my old teacher, Mr. Jackson's. He'd been an anal, buttoned-up strict man, so his truck was really, really clean. Like, immaculate. We made sure to fix that problem real quick. Within seconds, mud and ash caked into the wooden floorboards.

Dallas's axe hacked out the custom walnut dash as Griffin hotwired the truck. Griff, who'd been forced to hand over the cypher and journal. Griff, who'd been a means to lure me in.

"What? Wires and electricity are kind of my hobby," Griff replied when I'd gaped at his aptitude with thievery.

We tried not to take too much pleasure when my small dagger ripped a hole in the black leather seat. Even Kaleo smiled at that.

Juni drove as smooth as a cat on water while the rest of us eight tried not to smash our heads into the roof or fall out the back. Kyra told us where the general had taken my family, though his fresh tire tracks were hard to miss. Everyone knew where the haunted old mill was.

Dad took the family to the gristmill this morning to hide out until everything was safe, not realizing that the general had his own Hound sniffing them out all along. They could never be safe so long as the general had his superpowered warriors with him.

"I tried to warn you," Griffin said.

I eyed him warily.

"You know I had no choice," Griffin continued. "He had Kyra. Had your family. I had to play along."

"You really scared me."

"I'm sorry," Griff said. "My dad, I didn't realize, he's just—"

"The worst."

Griff looked away, his cheeks flushed pink. We jostled and bumped on our way up the hill. Jax kept a protective arm around Kyra.

"Kyra," I asked. "Why'd the general have you up on stage?"

"He was going to use me as a example. He was gonna say the president had been hiding people with powers, too."

"And to draw you out, Blue," Griff added from the front seat as we knocked along.

My shoulder bumped uncomfortably into Kaleo who still seethed with anger.

Griff continued, "He can't lose any of his precious *gifted*. Dad's been putting these equations in front of me for years. Making me hash out all of these figures, and I wasn't really sure what I was doing, because it was always coded. He has this whole system, a machine he uses.

"Well, just today, when his hound sniffed out Foxhole and he got a hold of that notebook—*his* notebook, I thought he was going to have a heart attack or something, he was so happy. He finally had the translation. *Your* translations." Griff's eyes met mine with a cringe. "He's been obsessed with people with powers for years, you know? Been looking into every family, every person who's ever lived in New Haven. Looked through every single Founder's journal and Enforcer's Log. He knew Mama Darla's caverns inside and out. I guess there were some pretty nasty things in those we don't learn in school. Anyways, he got the cipher from this last journal and now, with your blood, he finally has the key. And with my research, my math—"

The numbers, letters, and ciphers ran before my eyes. The chalkboard full of ever-changing equations. The stacks and stacks of papers in Foxhole—still meaningless.

"He was able to see a genetic link to the Shadow Elf blood. A genetic code. He thinks he's found a way to create—"

Griffin's face flushed, eyes darting. He pulled a deep breath in. Head down.

"To create what?" Kaleo's chest rumbled against my arm.

"What he was not able to create with my mother." Griffin's voice dropped. "The perfect human. Superhumans. A new generation of immune super soldiers capable of beating the Shadow Elves for good. And some old weapon to keep you all in check."

CHAPTER 39

Warriors Assemble!

BLUE

"They're in there. All of 'em." Kyra nodded toward the old gristmill.

It lay overrun with weeds, set against towering trees, a rushing creek, and rusted chain link fencing. Fresh muddy tire tracks ripped up the overgrown gravel drive. The sun's light had almost winked out in the brilliant orange sky, but flickering lanterns lit the jagged windows. A chill snaked down my spine.

This place always gave me the creeps. We called it the Shrieking Shack when we were kids, a nod to the creaky old shanty in Harry Potter. It was a spot you could imagine a toothy werewolf stalking out of the mist, ready to rip into your throat. Or a bright white Shadow Elf bent on feasting on your heart.

"How many?" I asked.

Kyra's mouth moved silently as she counted. "Eighteen heartbeats, including the elfling." She shut her eyes, willing all other stimuli away. "The elfling's still in the cellar, guarded by one warrior, two warriors on the roof, all heartbeats are elevated, so it's hard to tell the difference in the rest from here."

"That's a useful trick." Jax nodded to her as he loaded his rifle. His baseball cap was more rumpled than ever. He had kind dimples when he smiled and a rugged set to his features you wanted on your side in the heat of battle.

"Thanks." Kyra beamed.

Jax ruffled her fluffy hair and handed her one of his daggers. She smiled and sidled up closer to him. She'd taken a liking to the big lug of a warrior as we'd made our way up here.

We parked near a large willow, a half mile from the mill. The general had his loyal dogs with him, so he'd know we were well on our way. The most we could do was use our enhanced senses and skills. They had location, but we had the Falcons. The best of the best, though they nursed some fresh wounds.

Their injuries were pretty evident from their encounters outside the wall—the fight with the prince's men. I saw it in the moments Jax's voice hitched when his shoulder moved a certain way or Brock's knee didn't bend correctly. Kaleo favored his right side and shook out his left hand when he didn't think anyone was watching. Dallas mainly leaned against the truck, trying to sidle up to Juniper.

Everyone strapped up their weapons in the dark mist of the evening, but my stomach clenched with worry. I gestured for Kaleo to follow me across the gravel driveway to talk. We ducked under the large willow, the hanging branches obscuring us from view. The willow tree brought back visions of that dance an eternity ago—when he'd told me about his ability.

Smashed dandelions littered the cool grass. Kaleo ran a hand through his beautiful hair. A tentative smile.

"So, are y'all ready? You guys feeling...up for this?" I swallowed. My stomach twisted in knots and vomit burned in the back of my throat.

My family was in that crusty old wooden building with the most dangerous man in the village and a shadow elf and I had no idea what to expect next. *I'm not strong enough for this.*

"Hey." Kaleo wrapped his hands around my shoulders, sending heat and comfort through me. "We're going to get through this, okay? Just take a deep breath. You've been training for this your whole life. Heck, I don't know anyone who's more ready than you, right now, at this moment."

He looked down at me, the pinks of the sky dancing on his eyes through the quaking willow leaves. His hands heavy and reassuring on my arms. I let out a long breath, guilt and shame having a pain party in the pit of my stomach.

"Sorry for what I said earlier," I said. "About bringing in that elf."

Kaleo hung his head, his black hair cascading. "No, you're right. I feel as if everything that's happened since then has been my fault. As if I brought all this on. It's only right I try an' fix it."

My eyes pricked. He thought this was *his* fault? *I* was to blame for General Rose's every breath. "Listen, Kaleo, I'm not who you think I am."

Kaleo quirked his head to the side. "What're you saying?"

My thoughts scattered as a devilish grin lit up his face.

"You're saying you're not this crazy beautiful, hilarious book geek who's got *Lord of the Rings* memorized? The one who loves riding Pepper with your *mighty* scandalous dress flowing? Just so you can show off those amazing legs? Wait, that's *not* you?"

A huff of a laugh escaped my lips, my face heating. I punched him weakly on the arm.

Kaleo's eyes gleamed. "Those squirrels got *quite* a view."

His eyes softened, and I found myself falling.

"You're a Haven," his voice rumbled heavy and low. "Already an angel. Time to become what you were meant to be."

I looked up to him, questioning.

"An *avenging* angel," Kaleo finished as he lifted the angel pendant at the end of my necklace. The gold reflected in his warm eyes.

"I'm no angel, Kaleo. I-I hate him. How he threatened my mama all those years and then he tried to feed my sister to that elfling?" I shook my head. "But then I think about the kind things he's done. The days down at the creek with his family. He's Griff's dad. He's not all evil."

I couldn't tell him what I'd done or failed to do. The shot I didn't take. If Zhao died, he'd never forgive me.

"Listen, it's not up to you to decide if he lives or dies, it's the law.

And the law says usurpers die. What did Raleigh always say?" Kaleo asked.

"No mercy for the merciless."

He nodded. "They traveled this continent for twenty years happening upon communities of bad men and women. Men like the general who wanted control and power. I'm sure they hesitated in the beginning too." He breathed. "But sometimes justice has to come swiftly."

Kaleo's voice faded as the air in the woods shifted. The electricity. It buzzed. His eyes glistened like molten chocolate.

"I haven't been able to get you out of my senses, Blue." He reached up and gently wrapped one of my brown curls around his fingers, then brought it up to his mouth. He took a long, indulgent breath. His eyes landed on me. "Since the moment I breathed you in. I've been...entranced by you."

His lips were suddenly on mine. I reached up, wrapped my fingers into his soft, silky hair and pressed him into me. And I was kissing Kaleo under the willow tree by the old mill.

I closed my eyes and didn't see—I felt. I felt it all. Colors and light and galaxies and rivers and grass and planets. All I saw was him. Bright, pure, true, and so good.

My body melted into his as he pressed closer. We couldn't get close enough. His hands twisted in my hair, one hand ran down my side, sending a cascade of chills all the way to my toes. I smelled pine and crisp wind. I tasted dirt, honey, and sweat. His taste sent a thrill through me. My fingers ran down the curve of his back, feeling the strength there. He pulled me tighter as—

"Ahem." Juniper cleared her throat behind us.

"Ow!" Kaleo's hips smacked into mine as Jax swatted his butt with his rifle.

"Killer general on the loose?" Juni reminded us. "Family to save?"

"Alright, alright," Kaleo conceded as he rubbed his backside.

I stole a glance up at him, my cheeks burning. His face flushed, ears glowing red. He smiled, beautiful white teeth gleaming.

"Your orders, Cap," Jax nudged, massive eyebrows knit together. He held a protective arm around Kyra.

Kaleo cleared his throat.

I'd never seen him so...discombobulated. He shook his head, cleared his throat again, then shifted back into the Soldier Boy we all knew and loved, with a tiny alteration—a slight grin.

Kaleo reached for my hand and squeezed it, almost painfully. I closed my eyes, allowing his strength to fill me. The others gathered around the two of us. Griffin shot me a half-hearted wink, the rest of his face far from playful.

His father was in there. His father was the bad guy. *Poor Griff.*

"Alright," Kaleo whispered. Everyone gathered closer inside the protection of the branches where Kaleo had just kissed me. I smiled again, despite my fear. Adrenaline pumped through my veins. My kiss-addled brain struggled to keep up.

"We have our brute strength." Kaleo nodded to Jax and Brock. "Brains." A nod to Griffin. "Eyes." Kaleo nodded to me. "Ears." Kyra. "Touch." Nod to Juni. "Nose, me. And we have—" Kaleo's eyes shifted to Dallas.

Dallas crouched on the gravel path, arrows and ponytail peaking above his wide shoulders. His finger swiped an inky, wet blot, then brought it to his mouth. "General's bleeding. This is from" —he closed his eyes and moved his tongue in his mouth—"his left shoulder."

"Taste," Griffin breathed.

Nausea rose up my throat. I'd never heard of a gift like that.

Dallas groaned as he stood up, shaking his hips suggestively. A grin spread across his handsome face as he touched his tongue to another rock. "Yeah, that's the general's for sure."

Juni strolled over and swatted his hip.

Dallas continued, "Wow, this guy been piling on the garlic, or what? Aye, Griffin?"

He scanned the group, looking for a reaction. We glared back with daggers for eyes.

"Too soon?" Dallas shrugged.

We drew our plan hastily in the dirt under the willow tree. Time to go.

Kaleo pulled Griffin aside. "Hey, you gonna be alright in there?"

Griffin cleared his throat. "Yeah. I know it's my dad—"

"Listen," Kaleo said. "You have to decide whose side you're on *now*. You can't hesitate. He's made his choice and there's no going back. No saving him. When it comes down to your dad or Blue or any of us...who are you going to choose?"

Griffin swallowed, his face pasty.

"Because it's *got* to be us. Or else I don't want you within a mile of that mill, got it?" Kaleo commanded.

Kaleo and Griff assessed each other. They stood that way for a long moment. Kaleo was about to turn when Griff caught his good shoulder. "It'll be y'all. I'm on this side always. The right side of this."

Kaleo gripped Griff's shoulder and nodded. Then, Kaleo and Jax fell into this strange, seemingly well-rehearsed ritual of battle. Foreheads pressed together, massive arms on shoulders—some kind of manly pep talk. It lasted only a moment, but I averted my eyes. It was some sacred brotherly bond forged from a lifetime of friendship and training.

Then, they smacked each other, with shocking force, on their pre-existing injuries.

Sacred feeling gone.

I held Kyra's small hand, and we led the charge toward my family, safety, and life, flanked on both sides by our own super squad. We marched toward the Shrieking Shack and justice.

THE OLD GRISTMILL was a rickety two-story brick and wood building. There weren't too many places to hide. Most of us crouched on either side of the backdoor. A strange foreboding crept over me as a patch of grass waved in the breeze before me. The way the grass swayed in the twilight brought me back to my vision of Jax—dead.

Nerves clenched my heart. I tapped him on the shoulder. "I'll go first. You protect Kyra."

I pushed around him to the front. I must have had that vision for a reason. Maybe I could change his fate. Or maybe it wasn't his fate at all, just my creepy imagination acting up.

But I'd been right about the prince's sword to Pretty-Boy Joe's neck. I'd been right about the beacon on the rooftop.

Jax put Kyra behind him. She seemed to melt into the wood siding. The static roaring of the river below us ate at my bones—filled my ears until there was nothing but the river's mighty rush.

Then the grinding began.

And the screaming started.

Kyra, who'd been straining for any minute sounds, slammed her hands over her ears. The gristmill creaked and groaned as the water from the flume hit the watermill. Inside the building, the turnstile began to spin. The massive millstones started their grinding.

It was meant to grind corn and wheat to a fine meal for grits or cornbread.

Corn wasn't supposed to scream.

"Blood," Kaleo sniffed.

"Whose blood?" I asked. "Who's screaming?"

Kyra had only a moment to pull in a breath through her gritted teeth when the back door flew open.

Black, tarry smoke billowed from the open door in inky tentacles. But, we stood firm.

We had a plan.

Jax and I, bows at the ready, led the charge. Breathe in and out. Short and fast. My blood pumped—eyes searching wildly as shots were fired. The black smoke swallowed us whole. It filled my nose, my eyes. The gristmill oozed with the noxious smoke. Screams echoed from all around.

My eyes blurred as pain exploded through them. Tears ran down my cheeks. I faltered, momentarily blinded.

Jax yanked me back. "Blue! Watch—"

His body slammed backward into mine as an arrow thudded into his gut. Blood sprayed straight out in a spurt.

"Blue! Kyra! Run!" he garbled. "Kyra!"

I grabbed onto him, but his weight knocked me off the back stairs. He was so heavy. Time did not slow, like in books. No. It sped up. Another arrow hit Jax square in the chest. *Thud.* Sickening crunch on bone. He fell out of my arms and down. I couldn't hold him. I couldn't. He—

He lay in the grass, his unseeing eyes staring out into nothingness. Never to see again. His blood spattered in the dark blue grass like glittering rubies in the lantern light.

My vision, the one I'd seen in the old outpost the night I'd become a warrior, it flickered before my eyes and rested exactly over where Jax lay. Dead.

CHAPTER 40

Black Smoke

BLUE

Jax was dead.

He'd saved my life.

"NOOO!" Kaleo's cries echoed my own rage and sorrow. The sounds of a wounded wolf, ready for revenge. Pain cleaved into his soul.

Through the doorway, Orin stood with his bow at the ready and a black eye, a souvenir from my father's fist. His mouth hung open in shock. Even so, he had his crossbow trained on Kaleo's chest, directly over his heart.

Kaleo held his machete high in one hand, his other hand hovered above the hatchet at his waist. I trembled on the other side of the door.

"Drop it, tracker," Orin called out. His hands shook, lip quivering, eyes scanning. *Regret. Sorrow.*

"General doesn't want me to kill none of y'all gifted ones. But I can kill the rest, no problem." Orin lifted his bow to Brock's forehead. "So, you drop it now, tracker, or I swear—your boy, Brock, is the next to go. His wife and kids won't be thanking you. In three—"

Kaleo lowered the machete a fraction. The loss, the emptiness in Kaleo's eyes tore a gaping hole through me.

A warrior I didn't know well, Lottie, had her arrow trained on me from inside the shack, her eyes shifting from Orin to me. I trained my arrow right back. We knew the roof had two archers. Juniper and Dallas had gone after them.

"Two. Y'all are surrounded."

Hatred seethed through me as I growled, "You *killed* him, Orin. You *killed* Jax. Your friend. A good person. And for what? The *general*? You don't even know *why* you're doing this! My family's in there, Orin. My little brother and sister."

Kaleo's hand was at his hatchet, mouth twisted. Eyes hard. No surrender.

"You picked the wrong side," I stated flatly to my old friend.

Orin smiled at me kindly when we were kids at school, sitting at the picnic tables together watching the ants carry off morsels of food.

That Orin was gone now.

"One—" Orin's mouth trembled.

Kaleo's hatchet found Orin's chest. Blood bloomed onto his shirt. Orin's arrow grazed Kaleo's arm. I released my arrow and watched as it sliced into Lottie's throat. Shock split her face, her mouth in an "o." Blood poured in an arch down her chin like an inky rainbow.

A scene that would haunt me for the rest of my life.

"Juniper says we g-got 'em up here," Kyra relayed Juniper's message from the roof as she huddled behind the ancient wooden door. She shook, lips quivering, as she stared at the prone form of her newfound friend, Jax. Now dead. His baseball cap crumpled beside him.

The grinding dragged on, steady as a searing pain. The screaming continued, growing higher, louder. More urgent.

"Your father sure knows how to draw his victims in." Kaleo sneered at Griffin. Kaleo's eyes had gone dark.

Griffin gripped his sword tighter and flexed his jaw.

Four down. Eleven more to go. And only seven of *us* now. Juni and Dallas had the roof. They'd enter from above while our group hurried on.

I pressed Kyra behind me as Brock, Kaleo, Griff, and I entered the smoke-filled mill and skirted around the fallen bodies of Orin and Lottie.

"Don't look down," Kaleo whispered.

But I couldn't help my eyes as they took Lottie's face in. Her dead face. I did that. Took her life. A human kill. Different from all of the animals I'd killed for food and clothing. I wanted to scrub my hand, the one that'd pulled back that arrow and let it fly.

Lottie's face flew before me, hair crowned in dandelions. Laughing at the graduation, playing bass guitar, dancing with Hound. Love lighting up her eyes.

I'd seen her around town for years—the curse of knowing everyone's face. A whole lifetime of rights and wrongs make up a person. This was just her last choice. She chose to follow the orders of her general, and I'd killed her for it. My soul cleaved, forever broken.

If I wasn't careful, shock would overtake me, holding me back from moving on. I placed the crushing guilt into a box to open later. Adrenaline and hatred were my fuel, and I let them course through me. Kyra trembled behind me, reminding me that love, too, was a powerful fuel. My family was in there. They needed me.

The smoke hovered like a living, thrumming cloud, but dissipated the longer the door lay open. My hands shook as I took in the interior of the shack in a glance. The sounds of the mill ground on. *Focus.*

We huddled in an atrium, behind a wooden wall separating us from the main mill room. Rotten wood plank floors rotted with holes and mildew. Wood walls. There was one floor above us, but no feet visible through the cracks in floorboards. Chairs strewn about, cobwebs, metal gears, rusty old machinery, ovens, smoke.

Lots and lots of smoke.

A putrid, black cloud billowed out from the heart of the mill, blotting out the meager lantern lights. It stung my nostrils and eyes. Tears ran streams down my face. My vision blurred. We pushed in farther. The pounding of the gristmill grew louder, more rhythmic.

"Where are they?" Brock held his rifle at the ready. "Where's the screaming coming from?"

It sounded like Cora or Fox. My blood boiled.

"The smoke's making it hard to tell," Kaleo growled. "I think it's dulling our senses. Hard for me to make out the scents. Kyra can hardly take her hands out of her ears. Blue? Got anything?"

"My eyes are burning," I added as hot tears streamed in ribbons. Small needle-like pricks formed around my vision. I couldn't keep my eyes open, let alone see anything.

"Cora and Shenandoah are screaming." Kyra strained to hear over the gears.

I tried to peek through the door into the main room, but Hound and Scarlip Nigel, both in black gas masks, beat us to it. They spun around the wall, shotguns at the ready.

"Nice of y'all to join us!" the general called out through the fumes. "Please, come in."

As if he were inviting us in for some lemonade.

Hound forced Kaleo to his knees and disarmed him. Brock, Griff, and I lowered our weapons. Brock swore loudly. Scarlip Nigel spit on the ground and motioned with his rifle. They shoved us into the main room. Five other henchmen dotted about the space, all armed to the teeth.

In one swift movement, I aimed my arrow at Rose's throat.

"By all means, shoot me," General Rose sneered as he pressed Elf-Wrender to the throat of my little brother, Fox.

Hound and Nigel cocked their shotguns. I pulled in a breath. I couldn't fail again. Fox nodded, lips trembling as he tried to press them together in a firm line. But I dropped my bow. My eyes blackened. Thick, tarry smoke crushed me. The room blurred in an out of visibility.

As we were pushed farther into the suffocating room, I could just make out the figures of General Rose standing above Mama, Cora, Mama Darla, and Little Baby Shenandoah. They'd been tied up to a large millstone. The stone wasn't attached to the gears, from what I could tell, but if it had been, their bodies would grind down just as easily as corn or wheat. The thought sent a sickening flush through me.

Fox was tied up to a separate millstone attached to a contraption of gears and cables. The stone was in motion.

My family screamed again as my twelve-year-old brother's gear turned slowly. The general had rigged the gears—twisted them into a torture chamber. Fox trembled, his fist tied down beside him, his smashed fingers spilling blood in dribbles upon the wood floor. Red filled my sight, roared through my ears.

"What are you *doing?*" I yelled to the general. "Are you insane?"

Fox shook, his lower lip trembled. His eyes bulged out in agony.

"He's being punished," General Rose said. "He struck me with that hand."

"Turn it off!" I pleaded to the other warriors. I couldn't make out their faces in this smoke.

Scarlip Nigel chuckled darkly beside me, but no one moved.

"Release my family right now. Stop this madness. Please, I'll do anything—"

Kaleo's hand slipped into mine, sending warmth through me. I grabbed Kyra's hand, she took Griffin's. Brock stood by Kaleo, taking comfort in the steel of his own rifle.

"Oh, I know you will, Hellion. That's what I've been waitin' for." Lantern light blazed in the general's eyes. "You just keep runnin' off. Keep makin' everything so difficult. Just like your mother!"

He slammed his fist down on the millstone and Fox flinched. "Why can't y'all just stay put and do what I tell you to do? It ain't that hard. I just want everything to be perfect and y'all keep messin' it up!"

I blinked over and over, the pain in my eyes unbearable.

"You only have yourself to blame for any harm that comes upon your family, Hellion," the general continued. "Their fates are in your hands. So, think long and hard before you go and do anythin' stupid. Either way, what I want gets done."

"Dad?" Griffin called out. "What are you—"

"You just *shut up!*" Rose's face turned a dangerous shade of red.

"You are a *disgrace* to our family! To see you standing there as one of 'em. Ha." Rose spit on the floor and ground it in with the heel of his boot. "As if you were special, one of the *gifted*. You were a disgrace before you were ever *born*." Rose didn't even bother to look at his own son.

Silence ground on, a companion to the millstone still bloodying my little brother's hand.

"Y'know what?" Griffin clapped back. "*I* never wanted that. *You* did. You'd do anything to be 'gifted'. It's disgusting."

Rose strode toward his son and backhanded him. Blood shot from his nose. Griff fell beside me, his eyes rolling.

My heart flew out of my chest. "So, what is this great master plan? Huh? Let you be president? Then what? Watch you injure innocent children?"

Kaleo's nose flared as he tried to sense something, anything. Kyra strained to hear, but me? I couldn't see a thing. I was useless surrounded by this suffocating smoke. I choked on it. My eyes burned. Too much longer in this mill and my eyes would dry out of my skull. Tears ran rivers down my cheeks.

Through quick squints, I made out my mama mouthing, "run, save the little ones" and "I'm so sorry, Baby Blue, so sorry."

"The plan," General Rose bit out. "The plan is this, lil' Hellion—"

He paused, then his voice took on a patronizing tone. "Oh dear, lil' devil, is there something wrong with your precious eyes? Is this here smoke botherin' you?"

General Rose smiled, I think. I fought to keep my eyes open.

"Oh, yes. It should be really burning by now. Y'see, this isn't just your regular run o' the mill smoke. This was especially made by those ancients in the pre-war times to fight the Shadow Elves."

He nodded, taking his time, as he stalked closer and closer to my little brother Fox, who bit the insides of his cheeks. His last two fingers had been wrecked by that gristmill. His dirty cheeks were streaked with black soot.

"The Shadow Elves, whose blood you *share*. So, Hellion, what that *means* is that y'all precious Havens are the key."

This smoke was the weapon my ancestors had created to disarm the elves—and it was working on us.

"I can't have you tryin' to leave town just when all of my research is starting to make sense." General Rose smiled down at Fox.

"Don't touch him!" I yelled. My eyes cranked shut as if in a vise, twisting them tight and locking away the key. I'd never felt so much pain.

"Yes, our ancestors made this formula to debilitate the elves. Got the translations for the recipe just in time, thanks to you," the general crowed. "Y'see, their heightened senses made them the ultimate predator. They hunted their human prey, sensing their every breath. But their senses also made them vulnerable. Think of it like an exposed nerve—your eyes, the tracker's nose—your senses are always runnin' at an eleven. So, we just threw some gasoline on the fire, as it were."

My eyes were a lake of fire and pain and horror.

"Aw yes, Mama Darla," the general crooned. "I see now why you tried to hide those journals from me all these years. This's pretty tough to watch."

The wood floor shook as Kaleo fell beside me, groaning in agony. Kyra screamed out in pain. She rolled on the floor, helpless. A loud thud and Brock cried out.

"Kyra!" Mama squeaked. "Blue!"

"A weapon like this in the wrong hands could really do some damage," the general finished smugly.

"You were always smart, Julian," Mama Darla's voice strained. "But you'll never learn. Love ain't control. Love is letting go. It's trust."

Mama Darla coughed and wheezed. She was gifted too. She had to be in extreme pain.

"Well, *trust* is what I have bought myself, with this here formula," General Rose gloated. "This smoke is the weapon and with the blood of Raleigh Haven, I have the genetic key I need. The Shadow Elves are out there, Mama Darla. You never prepared us for this. And now the chickens are comin' home to roost and they're mighty angry. We need to rise up. We need an army that can withstand these creatures breeding out there on our very doorstep or mankind will be an extinct race. Gone up like a wisp of smoke."

"You're insane." Tears and ash caked my face. Fire. Burning in my eye sockets.

"Oh no, my dear. I'm a hero," the general purred. "I'm the only one who sees what's goin' on 'round here and has the guts to do anything 'bout it. Finally, we have a family, heck a whole town, of immune people and I'm just supposed to sit on my hands?"

I fell to the ground, shaking uncontrollably, my fingers pressed into my eyes. My eyelids quaked and burned as they tried in vain to protect me from the poisonous gases.

"Zhao, our beloved *president,* hid that elf filth under a bushel, pretending it didn't exist." General Rose laughed darkly. "My *own* Hound sniffed that creature out as soon as hers dropped it off in that hidden bunker. While they were busy whinin' about what's right and wrong, I got to *work.* Got the hard questions answered."

"What d'you do?" Griff wheezed.

General Rose rounded on him. "Son, if you haven't figured it out by now with that brain o' yours, you ain't as smart as you think you are."

Griff was trying to buy us time.

"Though, I must thank you, Captain Bannon, for bringing it home. That demon spawn proved to be the perfect test subject for the product y'all are now experiencing. It's important to be thorough."

"Go to hell," Kaleo ground out through clenched teeth.

Lil' Legolas *had* flinched away from Lily and me. He expected pain. The general must've been experimenting on him while he was down in that dungeon. A protective fierceness pounded through me, but before I could scream, Kyra roared up off the ground. She tore at the general like an angry dog.

General Rose yelped. "Someone tame this wild child! Really, Virginia, what are you teachin' your children? Tie her up with her family, Hound!"

Mama wailed, "You're a monster, Julian!"

Cora cried, "Don't you touch her!"

Kyra's kicking and screaming echoed in the gristmill, amplified over the constant grinding of the millstone and mechanical gears turning.

"Listen darlin'," Rose said to Cora. "It ain't gonna be all bad, now. We're just going to do a little reorganizing. This town needs to get its priorities straight, starting with a few new jobs, that's all. It's gonna be easy."

My skin crawled, despite the searing pain in my eyes.

"New jobs? What are you talking about?" Cora spat.

Don't say it, please don't say it.

"Well, darlin', we need as many gifted men and women as we can get, so, seein' as it runs in the family"—the words dripped like poisoned honey from the general's lips—"Matter-of-fact, y'all will be put on *family* duty full time, for the good of humankind. Matched with the best candidates for breeding optimal specialized humans."

A sick nausea rose up inside of me. *Breeding. Like an animal.*

"Though you, lil' Hellion. You've proven to be more trouble than you're worth. I guess you won't be needin' your eyes for your new role, anyway." General Rose's voice sounded from right in front of me. "Hound?"

A scuffling of feet in front of my face. Dirt kicked up my nose. I coughed.

I tried to throw out with my dagger, punch out a fist, or open my eyes, but it was useless. I shook uncontrollably. My eyes were lakes of flame. I lay wrapped up tight in a ball of agony on the ground.

"Leave her alone!" Fox screamed. "Don't you *touch* her!"

"Get up, Blue!" Cora warned. "Run!"

Kaleo grabbed at my arm and growled, "Blue!"

Someone wrenched me apart, pulled my hands from my face, and forced my eyes open.

"This is for Lottie," Hound ground out through his gas mask between clenched teeth. Hound held a shovel full of hot glowing ash above my head.

"No!" I screamed.

Burning ash flittered down from the shovel, into my eyes. A searing pain like I'd never known shot through me. Daggers stabbed, seared, burned as a blood curdling scream ripped through my throat.

My eyes. My eyes.

I would never see again.

I was blind.

CHAPTER 41

Blind

BLUE

My eyes. My throat. Burning. Wheezing. Coughing.
White hot agony shot through me with every breath. My eyes were hot coals of flame. But slowly, my lungs, my breath—the air began to clear. I drank in the air like a thirsty beggar. Gulping and slurping, tears streamed from my non-existent eyes. I was sure they'd been burned out of my skull.

"Tie 'em up," Rose commanded his evildoers.

I was falling, falling into a pit of pain and fire. The world was a black hole. Without my sight, I was nothing. I was an exposed nerve covered in hot coals.

It was hopeless. *I* was hopeless. We'd rushed into this devil-forsaken mill, pedal to the metal, and fell right at the mercy of the general. He was always two steps ahead.

Someone grabbed at my arm, pulling me up. Their hands were strong, but gentle. I grasped back, groping. Frantic.

"Are they? My eyes? Are they...gone?" I raised two trembling hands up to my face. I knew that I would press my fingers where my eyes used to be, so blue and bright, and feel two gaping sockets of open bloody skull facing back at me. Tears streamed down my cheeks and my body quaked uncontrollably.

"Come on now," a male voice whispered kindly. "I've got to tie—"

I shook off his hands. "Don't *touch me*! You've chosen to follow that evil man! Injuring and maiming innocent little children like my brother! He's got my two-year-old sister tied up. Look at what he's done to me!" I fell to the ground in a snotty heap. I didn't care who heard me. I didn't care who saw. I'd never see again. The general took that from me. I was nothing without my sight. Nothing.

I tried not to hyperventilate as I pressed my trembling hands along my eyelids, praying to feel the soft, round eyeballs beneath. Pain exploded through me again, but...my eyes still quivered there beneath the crusted round lids.

"Blue," Kaleo's strained voice called to me through my agony, but was cut short with a swift thud and groan.

I shook and burned as I curled back into a ball of white-hot pain. Someone dragged me over the wood floor. I couldn't fight them. They tied my arms behind my back and left me in a smoldering pile of blood and ash.

The brave girl with the sparkling blue eyes who could see for miles and fight like a warrior?

That wasn't me anymore.

Maybe it never was.

I couldn't see. I couldn't fight. I couldn't even move. My body ached like it'd been run through that grinding stone, leaving a shallow husk of a vessel laying in a useless heap on the cold wooden floor.

"—that elf is quite the specimen—" General Rose's voice cut in and out of my pained consciousness. "Hound, you and Rowan go and bring that thing on up. It brought out somethin' in the little girl, maybe it'll awaken something in the others."

Boots pounded by my head, down an echoing stairwell, and out of earshot. Rowan was one of Juniper's brothers. He was a good man. How could he just stand by and watch this happen?

My other senses were so shriveled and underused. They'd always taken a backseat to my sight. I tried to reach out with them now, praying for any kind of grounding. But I bobbed, disoriented, like a canoe afloat on a stormy lake with no oar or paddle.

Blackness filled my sight. Blackness filled my heart.

I could use a battalion of angels right about now. Laurel's words ran through my mind.

"*I promise with all the fierce love of a mother to guard it along with all of the hosts of heaven. But, as soon as you have to sell your soul to the devil and fight like hell—I'll be there holding the brandy and a rifle.*"

If ever I needed an angel holding a rifle, it'd be about now.

A gasp echoed through the mill room as boots shuffled past my head again. Hound and Rowan must be returning with the elfling in tow.

"Alright now, let's get a good look at this little shark, shall we?" General Rose crowed to his audience. "Looks like such a sweet, innocent little thing. Ha! That's what it wants you to think. This disgusting creature is what destroyed the world. And this's what'll build a whole new world, if we're not careful."

The dark pitch of my vision moved. Blurred. My heart stammered. I tried to open my eyes. Pain and fire stung and burned. I shut them quickly as tears streamed again. A light began to form, blurring through my tears, cutting through the dark.

General Rose's face twisted before me, as if I looked up at him with my own eyes, but these were not my eyes. The colors of the entire room flared effervescent and beautiful. Like looking through a crystal. General Rose sneered down at me, disgusted, but eyes drunk with power.

I caught my breath in wonder. The elfling lent me his eyes again, showing me what he saw.

"*You are one pathetic son-of-a devil, y'know that?*" General Rose snickered.

Don't cry, Blue. Be strong.

I held on to the elfling's sight like a selfish child. I took in the mill room surrounding me, where everyone was located. I didn't know how long this would last. The black smoke had dissipated through the open windows. I caught sight of myself, laid out on the ground in the dark corner. A broken, pathetic ragdoll lost and discarded. Forgotten.

I worked to spin my body into the elfling's line of sight. I needed to see my eyes, what Hound had done to me. Turning the wrong way at first, I quietly rolled the other way, confused and disoriented. It was like looking in a mirror backwards and upside down.

When I beheld my face, I had to bite down on my cheeks to stop a sob threatening to wreck me. It was worse than I'd imagined.

Cakes of mud, tears, and scabs of blood crusted over my eyelids. I tried to open them, but pain sliced through me. Whatever Hound had done to me, he'd done it bad. Kaleo, Brock, and Griffin lay tied up in a pile beside me, in a forgotten corner room behind a broken table. Completely unguarded. All eyes were fixed on the elfling. Kaleo had a giant goose egg on his head. His eyes roved feverishly beneath his eyelids.

The smoke was gone.

I looked back at the general's face as fear crept into my heart.

Was this the elfling's fear or my own?

"Now, what I want, demon, is to do some more experimentin'." General Rose's cruel smile grew. "You remember that now, don't you?"

I twisted my hands behind my back and almost yelped in surprise. The knot slipped free with a light tug. Whoever tied me up did a terrible job. I guess I'd been deemed a non-threat now that my eyes had been taken from me. I pulled the rope off slowly. Easily.

A flash of light and—

A cruel pair of large, black eyes flashed before me. These were not full of wonder, like I'd seen in the elfling's eyes—no, these eyes flared with bloodlust. His mother. White, filthy dreadlocked hair flew around her face and shoulders and down her back like a banner. Her teeth gleamed ivory, feral. She ran like the wind. Like nothing mattered but finding her child.

She ran like she was headed to slaughter us all. And she was not alone.

Mother Elf was on her way. Time was running out.

With General Rose distracted, we'd been forgotten. My sight went dark again, but I scooted over to where I knew my boys were. Through the blinding pain, I managed to nudge a limb of someone. I showed them my unbound hands, attempting to leave my face neutral. Within seconds, a back thumped against mine and I had a pair of hands to untie. I worked behind my back quickly, trying not to alert the general's men. I figured Griff or Brock would be on lookout, since my sight was in the dark again.

Sweating and struggling, the bonds fell to the ground. One free, two more to go. I waited for the next hands to bump against me as my heart pounded wildly. If only I could see. I tested my eyes. Pain exploded, and I bit my lip to keep from crying out. A river of hot tears streamed down my cheeks.

The elfling no longer gave me his eyes, so I thought back on this mill room. What I'd seen before I was blinded. Bright shapes dripped around me as the room flickered into view. Piecing together the elfling's multicolored vision and my dark, smoke-filled memory of this room, I knew where I was. Relief flooded me. All I saw were snippets of vision memories. Where people had been before. Not where they were now. But that was enough.

Another back pressed up against me then. Hot, fevered, sweaty. He swayed back and forth from that blow to his head. Silky hair fell around my shoulders. Kaleo. I found his hot hands and got to work untying his bonds, but Kaleo gripped mine with intensity. My heart thundered. His large hands dug into mine as his head pushed back into me, as if he couldn't get close enough. Red and gold flashed before my eyes, but I pulled free and worked to loosen Kaleo's bonds.

Was he punch drunk? *We ain't got time for cuddling!*

A demon mama was coming for us and an evil general held us in his clutches. Not the best time for nuzzling, but fire burned within me—almost stronger than the pain in my eyes.

Kaleo's face flashed before me, right before he'd kissed me under the willow tree.

The softness of his eyes, the urgency of his mouth.

I felt that now. As if I'd never feel him again. I pressed into him and squeezed his hands. He was free now, but would any of us ever truly be free again?

Using the memories of the room as a guide, I checked around myself for any kind of weapon. If my ancestor, Laurel Haven, had been a master of killing and death, then I would be too. I didn't care if it tore my soul apart.

Broken glass lay by the old window.

Perfect. I wrapped the discarded rope around my hand and scooted toward the window. Having no eyes was a terrible disadvantage. I imagined one of the general's warriors watching and laughing at my futile efforts, right in front of my face.

I picked up the memory of the cold glass shard, grateful it hadn't moved. It felt strange to lift it and realize it remained there in my vision on the floor, but was no longer there in reality. Everyone shifted and moved constantly, so my memories could only get me so far. I placed the shard into my rope-wrapped hand as relief flooded through me. I was armed.

A warm hand touched me carefully, afraid to startle me. I allowed the body to press up to my shoulder.

"We're arming," Kaleo whispered, barely audible over the noises of the general's crowing. "Can you see?"

How could he think that? "No. Going off of memory."

He paused. "General's getting out some kind of device, looks like another smoke bomb. We've gotta do something before he sets it off."

"Elf Mother's coming. I saw her. She's almost here," I whispered.

Kaleo swore under his breath. He placed a round, smooth thing into my hand. "Another weapon. Chair leg," was all Kaleo said.

I searched the tip and found a sharp, jagged edge. I had a glass sword in one hand and a wooden spear in the other. Not bad. The heat from Kaleo's shoulder pressed against me, and I almost saw red again. No, I *did* see red. He was red. The orange-red glowed faintly at first, then flared into existence. His eyes sparked bright yellow.

My heat vision. *Bless you, eyes. Bless you.*

The room blossomed into color all around me. Another world of hot fluorescent reds, oranges, yellows mixed with cold violets, blues, and greens. A world where I could see, even with my eyes closed.

Hound hadn't taken this from me.

I targeted the large, bright orange man who towered over the elfling.

"I have the general," I whispered to Kaleo. I was ready.

"But you can't see—"

"I've got him. He's mine."

"Alright." Kaleo shook his head. "On three."

His arms flexed as he moved to crouch. The room was mine to see, but I had eyes only for Rose. "Three! Two! One!"

Bloody scabs caked over my ruined eyes, but I walked into that room with my glass sword and wooden spear—a fire blazing in my eyes. Kaleo, Brock, and Griffin flew by. Rowan jumped out from his position to the left of me. I ducked under his fist, rolled and kicked out hard, knocking him to the floor. I whacked him on the head with my mighty wooden chair leg.

Griffin jumped on top of him, sending Rowan's cold blue sword and bow skittering. I moved for the bow, ripping the quiver of arrows from Rowan's back.

Within seconds I had an arrow nocked and that son of a demon, the general, in my sights. General Rose spun around, distracted by our uprising. His eyes narrowed on me. He gripped Elf-Wrender in his beefy hand, a challenge on his lips. No hesitations this time, only calm sureness as I took in a swift breath.

Through my heat vision a faint glow flitted about the general. Then another, in the form of... A person? Or spirits? Angels?

Confused for that crucial second, I cursed myself and let my arrow fly. General Rose swerved just enough that the arrow pierced the meat of his shoulder, right next to his thick neck. He flew back, eyes wide. Elf-Wrender, my father's sword—*my* sword—clanged to the floor. He scrambled to pick it up as I nocked another arrow and scanned the room.

More screams and yowls filled the mill. Kaleo and Hound, the scent trackers, fought viciously hand to hand, weapon to weapon. Griff took Rowan down, but Rowan wasn't putting up much of a fight. Within moments, Rowan and Griffin took Scarlip Nigel down together.

Brock fought two warriors at once, trading a wooden club for a metal sword. He then stood guard by the mill to protect my mother and siblings, his fatherly instincts kicking in.

I advanced on the general, arrow nocked. "You've done enough. It's over."

General Rose ducked behind the overturned table. "Aw, Hellion." He huffed, out of breath. "You have a knack for turnin' up at *exactly* the right time."

I stalked closer, arrow trained on him. Blood smeared across his teeth as he smiled. He licked it off and spat on the ground. Then he nodded in approval—as if *he* were responsible for my skills. *Please.*

"Y'see." General Rose reached his hand toward his pocket. "This ain't over yet. I happen to—"

"Nope." I let my arrow fly straight into his arm.

He yowled.

"We're going to get my family and leave. But thanks for trying to distract me with your *incredible* monologues. They're *really* special." I nocked another arrow and shot it into his muscular thigh peeking behind the table. "Too bad you're not."

General Rose's blood sprayed out bright red, the same shade as his face, as he roared out in pain. "You lil' Hellion! You—"

"No." I snatched Elf-Wrender from the blood-soaked floor. "*You* listen to *me*. You messed with the wrong Hellion and the wrong family."

I pressed the blade of Elf-Wrender into the general's neck. "No mercy for the merciless."

I wouldn't falter this time. I wouldn't fail.

The shack seemed to still as a vision flashed before my eyes.

I rode on an old horse. Bruno. Lily's pale hands held the reigns as they pounded through the dark blue wood. I was seeing through Lily's eyes again. She followed behind her pop. Both on horseback.

"How do you know where to go?" Lily asked.

Massive plumes of black smoke stretched up to the sky from the square below, but they rode on, farther from the smoke, through the mountains.

Lily's pop swatted and blinked at nothing in the dark of the night.

"Hey," he barked back, beard flying on the wind. "You're the one who told me to embrace these crazy demon thangs in my head. I'm just followin' where they lead, instead of fightin' 'em."

He blinked, trying to clear his eyes. "My eyes itch like the dickens."

"What do you see?" Lily asked.

Black trees flew by as they rode on.

A small smile tugged on his lips. "They're like these colorful smoke spirits."

Joshua Potts' face was younger somehow. Sober. Excited.

The flickering lights from the Shrieking Shack came into view as Lily neared the last outcropping of trees. Just then, my daddy, Bearon flew through the wood, followed closely by—Mason? He rode on like a soldier with a sword in one hand and a gleam in his eyes.

They were coming for us! My heart soared, then dropped like lead as I beheld the nightmare before Lily's eyes.

Horror, true and undiluted, filled her entire body and mine.

An army of ten bright, white, ethereal Shadow Elves surrounded the gristmill, led by a wild-eyed, feral female.

So fast. So beautiful. Unnaturally large black eyes the shape of almonds. If black was the absence of all light, then white was every color of the world blending together until it shone. That was them. Their skin shimmered bright in the darkness, as if crafted from light itself. Every color mixed and whirled inside of a gleaming white—it glowed from them.

They looked like they'd been cooked up in the devil's laboratory, created to lure and hunt down humans one by one. And that wild, dreadlocked female at the head? She was the elfling's mother, coming to claim her baby and kill every last one of us.

The images dripped away, leaving me standing with the tip of

Elf-Wrender digging into General Rose's neck, as if no time had passed at all. The neon colors of my heat vision took over the fog of Lily's eyes. The general eyed me with a mix of fear and hunger.

A small, melodic voice floated inside the old mill. A wolf pup and a whisper on a wind. A trickling meadow stream. The elfling.

A savage, clicking screech answered from outside.

"We're too late," Kyra called. "His mama's here. And she's mad."

CHAPTER 42

A Dangerously Gorgeous Death

BLUE

A scream—wild, guttural, and piercing—cut through the shack. We grasped at our ears, all of us but Kyra and the elfling. I hated this bright heated world. It was so alien. So foreign. I needed my eyes, my real eyes.

I turned my sword on General Rose. His hot red blood trailed out on the cold blue wood. "Where's the weapon? That smoke? We need it."

Before I could finish, Juni and Dallas burst into the room from the stairwell. "This whole place is rigged to blow! There's barrels of explosives lining the cellar!"

"Where have y'all been?" I growled.

Juni and Dallas caught site of me and their faces drained of heat.

"Oh, Blue, y-your beautiful eyes." Juniper's hand flew to her mouth.

"That the elf kid?" Dallas rounded on the elfling.

"Leave him alone," Kyra held her orange body as a shield for cold lavender lil' Legolas.

Kaleo pushed his way over to where I stood over General Rose. "Where's the detonator for the bombs, Rose?"

General Rose just sat there, mouth agape.

I stomped closer to him and smashed my foot into his leg. Hot, bright red blood seeped from his arrow wound.

He yowled, then pressed a fist to his mouth to suppress it. "Are you crazy? You're drawin' 'em in!"

"That's the idea. Where's the detonator?" I sneered. A plan was beginning to form, but my eyes never left General Rose's terrified face as I barked out orders. "Dallas, get ready to kick out that wood panel wall behind you. You're gonna throw my family out into that river below us. Griff! You cut everybody loose, *now!*"

"Everybody?" Griffin asked.

"We're getting out first," I said. "But that doesn't mean I want everyone else to get eaten by those damned elves either."

Even Hound, who'd ruined my eyes.

Juniper caught sight of her brother tied up to a metal pole. "Rowan!" She ran to him and smacked him on his redhead. "What're you doing workin' for that ol' fool?"

"He said it was a matter of our town's security," Rowan cried. "I was following orders! But I didn't tie Blue up too tight, I jus—"

"Shut up, Rowan." Juni smacked him again as she worked to untie him.

Griffin and Kaleo cut Hound and the other warriors who'd hurt my family loose.

"Go board up that door, now!" I commanded.

The general's men grabbed whatever furniture and machinery they could find to board it up. But Scarlip Nigel took one frantic look around and bolted out the front door as fast as his long legs could take him. His feet pounded down the front stairs.

"Shut that door, now!" Kaleo growled.

Hound and the general's other men ran to the old door and slammed it shut. They locked and shored it up with cold, blue, broken furniture. Shaking hands and hot sweat. Fear emanated from everyone's orange bodies, rising off of them in waves.

The elves were here. That measly door wouldn't hold for long.

Scarlip Nigel's blood-curdling scream ripped open the night. "Th-They're here! They're everywhere! Lemme back in!"

He scratched and pounded on the other side of the door as we stood stock still, none of us daring to make a sound. The general's men, bright orange, pressed against the cool purple door as it bucked. Their yellow eyes bulged.

"Please! Help me! It-It's got me—" Nigel's scream curdled.

We flinched as Nigel's howl was silenced with an eerie high-pitched clicking. My family huddled frozen in the corner, faces pumping red with adrenaline.

"Rose!" Kaleo demanded "The detonator. Now."

The tin roof of the second story cracked above us. The elves' talons scratched as they scrambled toward us. My family covered their mouths, their muffled screams escaping through their fingers. Mama held Baby Shenandoah, her tiny pigtail puffs in disarray, her eyes wide with a fear she was too young to understand. My pulse pounded through me. We stood as still as soldiers, but shook like rabbits about to meet the fox.

"There's ten of 'em," Kyra counted, eyes closed. "They've surrounded us."

"It's in my left pocket. I can't move my arms." General Rose's body shook in fits, hot orange blood oozing to the floor. "We gotta kill 'em! They'll take over the entire village. They'll kill us all! Someone, please—"

The elfling scurried toward the front door and freedom. The general's men pressed harder against the door, afraid of the small elf boy, but not willing to move aside. Hound gripped his short sword, ready to kill.

I held Elf-Wrender at the ready and whispered to Kyra, "Tell him to stay! We need him to protect us."

Kyra called out to him, then pointed to me. The elfling paused by the door, his cold, purple form turned. Black swirling eyes landed on me. His hands were bound and his mouth gagged with rope, but he'd been able to speak. I signaled for him to stay. I approached him in the center of the mill, slowly lowering my weapon. My heart smashed into my ribcage.

My faith, my life, my family, were in his small taloned hands—no larger than lil' Shenandoah's. He promised me back in his terrible prison cell that he could save us. I prayed it was true.

I knelt before him, completely vulnerable, his small venomous mouth one bite from my face. I placed a shaking hand gingerly on his chest. Fear coated the walls, whetting our tongues. Silence held its breath with a sense of awe. The gears of the mill had stopped turning minutes ago.

"Please," I pleaded.

The elfling's heart beat a mile a minute, his breaths coming in quick efficient pulls.

"Save us."

My hands were covered in General Rose's blood. It glowed orange on my fingers and dripped from the hilt of Elf-Wrender. I knelt before the elfling and wrote "save us" in the language of the elves. Then, I pointed to my family, my whole body shaking.

The elfling's eyes swirled before me; even with my heat vision they gleamed black, purple, and otherworldly. I stared into them, pleading. I lifted Elf-Wrender and signaled for his hands. His breaths quickened, a sweet metallic smell. Wild. Natural. Like a puppy's breath. I cut his bonds loose.

"What are you doing?" Hound demanded.

A window crashed in from the second story above, scrambling, scratching, the elves approached to kill. I cut the gag from lil' Legolas' mouth, my arm inches from his tiny, sharp ivory teeth. He stood still, thrumming with a wild energy.

I stepped back, my heart about to burst, as I gripped Elf-Wrender firmly and fell back toward my family. The elfling stood silently in the center of the mill, eyes on me.

The wooden door burst into splinters. The red-orange bodies of the general's men scattered to the floor. My warrior friends and I moved to cover my family as cool black, purple, and blue blurs burst in, faster than any creatures I'd ever seen. Screams and chaos echoed through the room.

The Shadow Elves were here.

Mother Elf sniffed sharply as her pitch-black eyes slid right to mine. Her thin nostrils twitched as she smelled her child's scent all over me. I soaked her in. Even with my heat vision, she was beautiful. Tall, strong, wild. Ferociously savage. A dangerously gorgeous death sculpted by the hand of the devil himself. I tried not to get lost in her stare. She was unbelievable. A truly beautiful creature from a fairytale.

The elves were like Raleigh's drawing, but he hadn't captured how much they shimmered. How much they entranced. A drawing could never capture their animated living quality. Raleigh's elves had been more primitive. They'd worn the rags of the people who'd died with the disease. These Shadow Elves wore the skins of animals wrapped about their lean, muscular bodies. Their hair grew long and bright white, some braided strangely, some matted and corded with bones. Some wore gemstones and bones wrapped around their necks as adornments. Mother Elf had two sharp amethyst crystals struck through the upmost point of her slender ear.

An irresistible pull tugged me toward her.

I wanted her to love me.

Kaleo buried his face in my hair, inhaling deeply. His hand gripped my shoulder protectively as his fingers dug into my skin. The pain of his grip jolted me from my trance. I blinked and shook the fuzz from my head. I'd almost forgotten where I was.

From the side, a bright red heat signature advanced in a happy stupor toward the mesmerizing blue group of ethereal elves. Hound.

He breathed. "You smell like—"

A male Shadow Elf with long hair bound in plaits and bones, turned his taloned hand on Hound. The elf slit Hound from his ear to his chest. Hound stood in shock as bright red blood bloomed onto his shirt. He stared at his ruined chest in disbelief, as the blood ran in ribbons down his legs.

Hound's mouth hardened. He gripped his sword to fight back. The male, a full head taller, grabbed Hound's shoulders in a blink and bit into his neck, feasting on his blood.

Hound's bellow shook the foundation of the gristmill.

The blood drained from my face and my throat closed up.

I hollered, "Kick out that wall *now*!"

Dallas smashed the wood paneling, and the sounds of the river roared below us like bubbling safety. A few elves peeled off, attacking the general's men in a blur of bright, cold blue.

The mother shifted her attention from me to General Rose with a predatory gaze.

General Rose held up a shaking, bloody hand, sheer terror in his eyes. His eyes strained to Griffin for a moment. "I'm so sorry, son. Please. Get the detonator. This place has to blow."

The general's other hand grappled desperately with his pant leg, unable to grasp the detonator because of his wounds. So close, yet impossible to reach as the mother elf approached.

"Mama, go!" I screamed desperately, not once letting the mother elf out of my sight.

Brock's beard bristled as he jumped to guard my mama. She clutched Kyra and Shenandoah closely, their faces bright orange. Brock sliced into an advancing Shadow Elf with his sword. Violet-blue blood sprayed onto his beard. The elf fell to his knees. Brock slashed again, mouth tight, and the elf was down.

Almost as soon as the elf hit the ground, a male rounded on Brock. Brock shot out with his sword to the elf's neck, but its talons shredded his arm, then chest.

Brock was dead before he hit the floor.

Mom screamed and pushed Cora and Fox through the jagged hole into the river, one after another, escaping the death before us. The horrific scenes of blood and screaming raged in neon. The warriors fought as blue and purple shadows blurred, red hot blood spraying.

The general was no more. Mother Elf had her revenge, her mouth clamped around his throat, gulping him down with a beastly clicking and gurgling. She then offered him to her elfling. I turned away as the elfling latched onto Rose's neck and drew in his blood.

"Dad!" Griffin choked, eyes desperate. No child should have to see their father die like this. My mama shoved Griffin out the broken wall and into the rushing river below.

"Come home, Blue!" Mama called to me as she jumped out with Baby Shenandoah and Kyra in her arms. Red-headed Rowan grabbed Mama Darla and took the plunge.

But I couldn't jump. The mother elf and elfling stood between me and safety. There was only one way out of this.

I'd have to blow this whole place to hell.

Almost everyone had jumped into the river below.

"Once it's done, you make sure nothing makes it out!" Kaleo bellowed to Dallas as he shoved him out the wall, leaving only himself and me behind.

We had to get to that detonator. This place had to blow. We couldn't let those elves get free. Was this my destiny? To die killing these elves to save my people?

Don't cry, Blue. I looked at Kaleo. He nodded, eyes sharp as flint and full of a deep sorrow.

The elfling stood between us and the eight feral elves. Rose's red-hot blood dripped from his small, sweet looking mouth. They stood thrumming with a wild energy as they looked to Mother Elf for their next orders.

This was our final stand.

For New Haven. For humankind.

CHAPTER 43

Laurel's Guardian

BLUE

The elfling stood between us and his cold, wild mother. Her eyes pierced through me as she sniffed the air, smelling her child all over me. Her nose flared as frenzy filled every elegant curve of her face. Her cold purple brightened a golden amethyst in my heat vision.

Mason had warned me. He said the mothers were feral. No amount of blood would satiate her need for vengeance. I cursed his dead prince for bringing the elfling here, for giving me this fate.

Now all Kaleo and I had to do was make it to that detonator in General Rose's blood-soaked pocket. No problem. There were only nine Shadow Elves between his body and us. The mother's head twitched animalistically side to side as she stalked forward, sizing up her prey. My heart kicked into overdrive as I gripped my sword.

Kaleo's eyes filled with true pain. "You distract, I go."

This was suicide; we both knew it. But our love story had barely begun. I'd just had my first real kiss. Kaleo's beautiful brown eyes melted through my heat vision, replaced by memories.

Kaleo's eyes burned daggers through me at the warpath ceremony.

Kaleo chased me through the woods, fury in his eyes. The moment I broke his nose.

Kaleo and I danced under the twinkling lights at the graduation ceremony, the night he told me about his abilities.

His brown eyes crinkled with a smile, teasing me about my dress.

Kaleo twisted my hair on his finger, the kiss under the willow.

It shouldn't end this way, but it must.

Tears streamed unbidden from my burned eyes—pain and nausea roiling through my core. But another vision flickered in my sight, one I had no control over.

The elfling showed me a memory, of—me. Through the bars of the filthy prison cell, I watched as I offered him food. My mama's famous fried chicken. In a flash, I stared into his eyes without a sneer, but with a smile of understanding. Another moment and I knelt before him in the mill, cutting off his bonds. Then the visions were gone.

The mother elf's eyes flashed at me. It was hard to read the black, but I wondered if the elfling showed her the same images. Her stance remained on the offensive, sizing us up. Her talons flared bright purple in the cold, dark room. The other elves stayed on high alert, but appeared to follow the orders of the female.

Then the elfling spoke. His savage, bright voice filled the mill. The female clicked back. Their communications were curious. Strange. Like beautiful, wild creatures living a simpler law. Kill or be killed. Hunt or be hunted.

There'd be no mistaking who the hunters and prey were in this scenario.

The elfling bent his head toward me as Mother Elf's eyes roved over my body. She didn't eye me greedily, desiring for my flesh. No, she looked me over as if I were a curiosity she hadn't puzzled out yet. The gristmill held its breath, as if it held just the two of us. Through my heat vision, only purple blackness swirled in her eyes, but she did not move to harm me. Even the warmth from the lanterns seemed to chill as it touched her flesh. She tilted her head, her eyes glowing with a young, instinctual intelligence as old as the world itself.

In a breath, she and all of the elves turned their brutal attention to Kaleo. A den of snakes, poised to strike. Fear thundered through me. The message was clear. The elfling protected me, but not Kaleo. Kaleo would be slaughtered.

The elfling lowered his head in submission.

Kaleo's eyes widened in true fear for a moment, then narrowed in resolve. He held his cold blue hatchet in one hand, machete in the other, ready to meet his fate.

Mother elf's gaze locked on o Kaleo, landing greedily on his neck.

"Kaleo!" My hand flew to my own throat automatically. She advanced on him, white dreadlocks flying, as I held Elf-Wrender out before me. But my other hand grasped at my golden angel necklace. Laurel's Guardian. Mama Darla's words rang through my mind.

"I used to blow in it like a whistle. Drove Papa's dogs crazy!"

"Kaleo!" I cried. "Run!"

Mother Elf raised her taloned hand, poised to swipe. Kaleo raised his hatchet. I lifted the gilded angel to my lips and blew. The effect was immediate. Mother Elf and all the others screeched a sound so high-pitched, the windows of the mill not already broken, shattered. Glass exploded in all directions. The elves dropped to the ground, covering their large, pointed ears.

I blew the whistle over and over again like a lifeguard in a hurricane, hearing no sound but the elves high-pitched shrieking.

"Go Kaleo!" I screamed.

He ran through the gauntlet of elves on the ground, making his way to the body of the general. General Rose lay surrounded by four or five elves, curled up in balls. But they lashed out viciously with their claws. I blew in my whistle relentlessly as Kaleo jumped over their quaking, hissing forms.

Kaleo would never make it to the general's prone form for that detonator. The elves were stunned, but rallied with every second that passed.

"Kaleo! Watch—"

A male elf with fangs as lovely as seashells stretched out with a taloned hand for Kaleo's ankle. I sent a dagger right into his strong back, sending him screeching. Kaleo spun, hair flying around his panicked face. A female gripped Kaleo's other leg. It was over.

I poised myself to run into the fray when—

Lily's Pop smiled. "The shadows are pullin' me in there. They're...

beautiful. Y'know? They look just like your mama and baby sister. Like an army of angels. Don't know how I missed it before."

He looked toward the old gristmill flickering with wild candlelight and shattered windows.

"Lily Mae, I ain't done right by you. But it's high time I did. This is my callin'. The angels. I see 'em now and they're callin' for me to follow."

"No, Papa! Come back! Don't—" Lily's voice cracked as she ran toward him.

A soaking wet Dallas grabbed onto Lily and held her fast.

"Stop! Papa! Please!"

A man with a tangled beard, sawed-off shotgun in hand, burst through the hunks of door and furniture littering the front atrium. His red face beamed like a lantern through his filthy beard, a strange look of clarity on his face. "I got this. I'm on the side of the angels!" Joshua Potts boomed with a manic laugh as he cocked his shotgun.

All of the elves turned their deadly attention on him. He let off one shot after another, firing into the elves at Kaleo's heels. Black blood, limbs, and organs sprayed through the air like grisly confetti.

A faint white glow surrounded Joshua Potts. One, two, three. More lights flitted about him.

The same I'd seen circling General Rose before I'd shot him with the arrows. Were they spirits?

The glowing forms rushed from Potts, creating a clear pathway to where the general's body lay. Pushing back on the elves.

Potts turned to me, eyes alight. "You see 'em too?" He cackled, his face bright with heat. "Maybe I ain't so crazy after all!"

"We need to set off the explosion," Kaleo called out to Joshua. "It's in his pocket. The detonator."

Potts ran to General Rose's body as an elf grabbed his leg and ripped into his meaty calf. Joshua howled and shot the elf's arm. Inky blood spattered on his face. He cocked his gun to fire again, but the deafening echo of an empty chamber filled the mill. He'd run out of rounds.

"It's in his left pocket!" Kaleo called to Joshua as he rushed to me.

Joshua ripped the detonator from General Rose's pocket. "You tell my Lil I love her, won't you, Blue?" Joshua's face set in steel as another elf snarled toward him. "You'll do that for me, won't you?"

Joshua turned the small detonator in his hand, staring in calm acceptance, as all of the elves turned on him, teeth and talons raised. Mother elf's blade-like fingers flexed. Without a thought, I grabbed the elfling and pressed him into the safety of my bosom. Kaleo rammed into me with his shoulder. The breath whooshed from my lungs. My back burst through the wooden paneling wall behind, and we fell.

Water enveloped us.

Everything exploded into flames.

CHAPTER 44

Swept Away

KALEO

W e plunged into the river. I had eyes only for Blue, but she swept away in the dark, wild current, along with the elf child she'd grabbed. I whipped my head around, searching. Fire, flames, smoke, and shattered wood flew through the air as the gristmill exploded above us. I fought against the tide, struggling to stay ahead of the mill crumbling around me. The entire building collapsed, much of it plummeting into the roaring waters below.

Water filled my nose and mouth as I gagged and spit. But that sweet metallic scent lingered—the scent of the elf child. The adults had a different smell than the child, more alluring. Stronger. Painfully bewitching. That's what took Hound in. If Blue hadn't been there, her hazelnut and poppy scent already filling my brain, driving me mad—I would've been lured to those beasts like a moth to a candle. Easy. Hound's death would've been my own.

I followed the light scent on the water and spotted the elf child tugging at something. I dove through the flaming wooden planks and smoke to see Blue. The elf child had her. It pulled at her in the darkness.

"Get your hands off her!" I yelled through the thundering waters.

I knew it heard me, but it continued to pull and pull on Blue. I dove in again, kicking through the broken shards of wood and glass littering the water. The kicking sent a wave of nausea and pain through my body. Red blood trailed behind me. My blood? I didn't remember getting cut, but it had all been a blur.

"You get your filthy hands off of her!" I hollered, my whole body shaking. I would end that creature. I'd seen what they could do. They were wild predators, capable of the worst kinds of atrocities. I wouldn't let that beast grow up to become one of them.

The pain in my leg intensified. I kicked toward Blue, toward the shore, toward the elf child. Through my bleary eyes, several dark shadows moved in my direction. I grabbed for my hatchet, machete, wooden table leg, anything—and came up empty. The shadows pulled Blue to shore. Bearon. Dallas. Griffin.

Kyra ran to the elf creature, holding out a hand.

"Don't touch it!" I cried, my legs giving out. My head fell under. Water shot up my nostrils.

My leg. A hot, searing pain radiated from my right leg. I grabbed it, wrapping my fingers around the stabbing burn. My fingers felt around the wound, the shape of a large, mangled circle. A bite? Had I been bitten?

No. It couldn't be.

Hands and arms grasped me, hauling me toward the sloping grass.

"You alright, Kaleo?" a voice asked. "Kaleo? You did it! You saved us all!"

"No." I shook my head, my every breath turning me toward Blue. I smelled her fear, her mind fighting to stay conscious where she lay in the cold grass, barely breathing. "Joshua did it. Blue and Joshua Potts, they saved us. Blue, is she? Where is she? They saved us—"

Pain seared up my leg and I fought a scream.

Griffin, I think, threw something over my leg, squeezing it. A cold fire exploded. I growled. Griffin jammed a stick in my mouth.

"Hey! Quiet, Kaleo," he urged me under his breath, ripping and twisting my leg. "I got you."

I pulled in a shaking lungful as a smell pummeled me from above where I laid out in the grass. That outsider? That son of a demon I caught skulking around that old barn. How could he be here?

Out of the corner of my eye, I saw him. The outsider I'd beaten in the prison—soaking wet from the waist down, a mop of brown hair, and a sword in hand. Who gave him a weapon? He reeked of both human and elf blood.

That outsider noticed my attention and smiled at me, a glint in his eye. His eyes flicked over to Blue, who lay in the grass near me. His disgusting eyes roved over her hungrily. His gaze shifted back to me, and he winked as he strolled off, sword dragging in the grass behind him.

Rage burst through me. Who let him out? Who gave him a sword?

Get him away from her—

From my Blue—

Someone—

Pain exploded from my leg as black clouded the edges of my vision and I knew no more.

CHAPTER 45

Tears that Scald and Scourge

BLUE

Mama held my head in her lap as the cool grass swayed in the breeze, tickling my arms and legs. I was alive. I was breathing. But my eyes? They saw only darkness.

I went to sit up and my head veered toward the ground. Cora, well versed in all things medical, called it "vertigo." I was too weak to bring the heat vision back. Too weak to try at any memories. So, I laid back and felt what it was to be alive.

Breathe in and breathe out. Pain and relief.

I'd crawled over to where Kaleo had called to me. He lay unconscious now. But I pressed myself as close to him as I could. I couldn't see, but the heat from his body grounded me. The steady rise and fall of his chest calmed me.

We made it. We were alive.

His heavy arm lay across my chest, hot and fevered. Comforting me.

My mama sang low as she cradled my head in her lap. "Take me home, country roads—"

Warriors barked out orders. Flames roared and echoed in the wood.

"—to the place I belong..."

Mama's gentle voice calmed my pounding heart.

The heat of roaring flames from the gristmill warmed me as I dug my fingers into the cool, blessed earth.

"If any of them elves crawl out of that fiery shack," I turned my head up to where I knew Mama would be looking down at me. "One of y'all will kill it, right?"

"Of course, Blue." A smile lined her voice. "I think you can have the rest of the day off. Your daddy and that foreigner are circling the mill now, watching for any survivors."

"Foreigner?" My heart kicked up. "You mean Mason? Who set him free?"

"Your daddy. He needed help and that young man's been killing those elves like he's been training his whole life, honey. He knows what he's doing."

"Of course he does," I said, more to myself. "Have Dallas keep an eye on him, Mama. He's from a dangerous place."

"Alright, honey," Mama combed her fingers through my wild brown curls, doing her best to avoid the tangles.

"How's...everyone else?" I asked.

"Baby Shenandoah and Kyra are okay. Still shaken up," Mama answered. "Griffin's tending to Kaleo right beside us."

Probably working to take his mind off of everything we just witnessed. Of his daddy getting killed in a most horrific way by a vengeful Shadow Elf.

Cora spoke from nearby. "Fox's hand will be a tough one. He's lost two and a half fingers, so he'll never be the same. Mama Darla is alright. Has a mighty bad migraine, but she's resting back in the shadows of the trees."

"Lily?" I asked. My chin trembled, remembering how Lily's Pop looked moments before his death. Like he'd just discovered a beautiful jewel as it slipped from his fingers. Regret. Sorrow. But also a frenzied joy of purpose. He'd saved our lives just like he'd saved my daddy's all those years ago.

As if in answer to my plea, Lil's soft voice broke in. "Hey, Blue." Her thin arms wrapped around me. She buried her head in my neck as tears ran down my cheek. "He's gone. H-he's—"

"I'm so sorry, Lil." And all of the pain and fear, the sadness, the sorrow for Jax, Orin, Lottie, Brock, General Rose, Nigel, Joshua Potts

—the loss of my eyes—it came welling up to the surface and crashed down. Hard.

More death than any of us ever had a right to know.

So, we cried, both of us laid out on Mama's lap, tears seeping through the scabs of my burned eyes. The tears both stung and soothed.

I WOKE UP WITH A PANIC—BREATHS choking in quick gasps. Blackness greeted me. I rolled my eyes around as pain spiked through me. My hands searched wildly, finding soft bedding, dry clothes, and bandages on my body. A large dressing wrapped around my head, covering my eyes.

Everything hurt. I was sore to the bone. "Ow."

"Shhhh, honey. It's okay, Baby Blue." Mama's gentle voice flitted in from beside me, her soft hand caressed my arm. "You're safe and sound in your own bed. Lil and Kyra are snug up right next to you. Dr. Brighten gave you all something to help you sleep. Everything's going to be alright. You blacked out, so Cora and I cleaned you up and dressed your wounds, honey."

"My eyes?" I had to ask. "Are they? Am I blind forever, Mama?"

My throat constricted. *Don't cry, Blue.*

She sighed. "We don't know. Doctor came by earlier and had a look. He says your corneas are a bit damaged, but they were tearing up so much, it was too hard for him to see. Your eyes were almost scarred shut. Looks like they are trying to heal on their own." Mama paused for a long time. "But he said he'd seen bigger miracles happen. There's hope, honey."

I let that small kernel of hope settle in my heart like a delicate seedling. Then a spear of dread shot through me.

"When was the doctor here?" I asked, "How long have I been out?"

Hawk. How long has it been?

"Just a few hours, honey. Calm down. It's almost midnight," Mama soothed. "You're all bruised up, have a major concussion, broke a finger, and have scratches all over your body—"

"Tomorrow." I sat up in bed. Pain lanced through me. Hawk's last day was tomorrow and then the prince's men were going to kill him. I turned to Mom. "Where's Mason? The outsider?"

"Your daddy's got him in the barn out back. Locked up. But, Blue!" Mama yelled as I shot out of bed.

My legs wobbled and gave out, but I steadied myself with a quick hand on the nightstand.

Strength! Where are you when I need you?

I willed the vision memories of my bedroom before my eyes, tossing them up on the black walls like a bucket of water. In seconds, my bedroom dripped into view in all shades and times of day and night. From every angle. I walked the space like a sighted person, finding my drawers easily. My clothes weren't exactly in the same places, but I felt for my cut-off jeans and t-shirt. I threw them on in minutes. All the while my body ached and screamed at me to lay back down. *Dang my broken finger.*

"Blue Laurel Haven!" Mama hissed, afraid to wake Lily and Kyra. "You better sit your lil' injured butt back in this bed right now or so help me—"

"Hawk's out there." I shoved my dagger into my back pocket. "He dies *tomorrow.* I'm going to bring him back."

"Hawk?" Mama reeled. "Your daddy told me all about what that outsider said, honey. It's a lie."

But she didn't know. I'd seen Mason, seen *us*, days ago in an old city. That was my fate.

"Take care of Lil." I nodded toward Lily, who I imagined slept fitfully. She was now truly alone in this world. Her pop had been haunted by his visions his whole life, taught to fear the beautiful gift he'd been given, and it'd driven him mad.

Lily's fate could've easily been mine. My whole family could've gone up in those hot flames along with those wicked elves. I gathered a few more weapons and placed a trembling hand on the door.

"Send word to Kaleo, Juniper, and Dallas. Tell 'em I've gone to get Hawk. They'll know how to find me," I said, about to leave.

"Blue." Mom's voice was low. "Your daddy is covering for the president while she either recovers or dies. I have to take care of the family. Just, stay. You've been through the worst of it, now you need time to heal. The others? Juniper? Dallas? Kaleo? They're *all* injured. Broken legs, sprains. They're all in quarantine. Cora's tending to 'em. We won't see her for a month until they're all clear."

"Kaleo was injured?"

"Yes, honey. He got hurt. Bad."

My heart dropped.

"No one's allowed to see them," Mama continued. "The only reason we're allowed in our own home is because we're far enough away from town. We can't leave the house for a month until we're cleared. I'm worried about your brother too, but he's been training for this. I know he'll make it home to us."

"No, he won't, Mom. Pretty-Boy Joe was murdered out there," I stated.

Mom choked on a surprised breath. "Your father didn't tell me."

"And they would've killed Hawk, too, except their leader wanted leverage. I know where he is, and I was meant to save him." As soon as I said the words, warmth spread through my chest. I *was* meant to do this.

Mason's handsome smile, his chipped tooth, brown hair curling around his ears, in the midst of a city. He held out a hand for me. The elfling's eyes flickered from behind him.

The vision I'd seen almost a week ago. I was always meant to go with him to save Hawk, dang it. That didn't mean I had to trust him.

My other visions came true. They'd happened just as they were meant to.

I tried to change fate and save Jax, but he died anyway. I didn't want to think that I'd actually caused his death by trying to stop it. I couldn't handle where that thought took me.

Maybe I couldn't escape my own destiny. My own visions were real, unchangeable, just like Mama Darla's. I needed Mason and I needed my eyes. The elfling could lend me his until mine healed. *If* they healed. The elfling wouldn't be safe here, anyway. Maybe I could find him a new home out in the wilds. He'd been in that vision too. The beautiful white elf I'd seen behind Mason.

"You tell 'em where I've gone, Mama." I strapped Elf-Wrender to my hip and grabbed my bow. "Tell 'em as soon as you can. They'll find a way out. I'm going to get Hawk."

I prayed Kaleo was okay.

In a blink, I switched to heat vision and watched as Mama held out a hand to me. Her face flushed with an orange warmth, her mouth set in a hard line. The red lumps of Lily and Kyra glowed, curled up in the bed. Tiger's tiny cat body smashed into Kyra's arms.

"Don't you leave, Blue Laurel," Mama rasped. "Don't you go off out there without your eyes. Without anyone on your side."

"I'll be back with Hawk," I promised.

"Stay, *please*. I can't lose both of you."

"Love you, Mama," I whispered.

Then, before I could stop myself, I shut the door to my bedroom, made my way down the stairs, out the door, and into the cold blue shadows of the night.

EPILOGUE

Fire Eyes

MASON

I woke to the sound of metal keys jangling in a lock. A sound I knew well.

"Get up, Dirty Prison Boy. You gotta take me to my brother." The voice of the village girl chirped. Sounded like sweet, sweet music to my ears.

"Blue?" I'd know her innocent little country voice from anywhere now. "What are you doing?"

"I'm getting your sorry butt outta here. Don't make me regret it." She swung open the barn door with a bang.

This barn was better than the last one I'd settled in, but it was still cold and filthy. I never wanted to be in another barn as long as I lived.

Salvation. I smiled.

By the time my eyes adjusted to the light of the moon, Blue stood before me—arrow aimed at my throat.

"Woah, woah! I am unarmed." My hands flew into the air along with my heart.

"Back up, Mason," Blue commanded me roughly. Dark scabs and burns coated her eye lids.

I tried not to smile. She'd been blinded. There was no way she could see me. I played nice and backed up into the barn as I studied the girl before me. What game was she playing? The moon gleamed, lighting on her tangled brown curls that cascaded around her shoulders, but her blue eyes were obscured by the shadows of night.

"So what? Are you going to free me or shoot me?" I said. "Make up your mind, Fire Eyes, because your brother doesn't have time for this."

With any luck, her brother would be dead.

She took a few steps closer to me, arrow inches from my throat. She trembled. It was charming, really.

"I need you to take me to him," Blue stared straight ahead. Up this close, I could really study her striking blue eyes. They were open. Still bright, crystal blue, but all around her eyes and eyelids were marred with fresh blisters. Burns. The whites of her eyes were as red and bloody as a corpse. I held my breath and slowly reached for the arrow aimed at my throat. Her eyes didn't move.

Her breaths came in quick gasps. She was afraid.

"Of course, Fire Eyes," I said gently. "I will do whatever you say."

I shook my head. This poor, adorable country girl. She was so far out of her league, but I didn't mind. Destiny had sent me a little gift to bring home to my father, the king. This girl was all the proof I needed that another untouched village existed. And there was something about this place. The people. They were bigger, stronger, smarter.

It wasn't the victory I'd imagined, but I could make it work to my advantage. I'd almost gotten my fingers on the shaft of the arrow as the side of her mouth lifted in a—smirk?

Fast as lightning, the ground kicked out from under me. My feet flew into the air as my back crashed into the wood floor. The wind knocked out of my chest. Before I could even scream, Blue's knees slammed on top of my chest, knocking whatever air I had left straight out of my lungs.

She pressed a sharp dagger to my throat and smiled down at me, a glint in her ruined eyes. I choked and struggled to breathe. *Air, need air.*

"Don't even *think* you can take me on, Prison Boy. Got it?" she growled.

I nodded over and over. *Air. Please. Air.* Black clouded my vision. *Air. Please.*

She growled once more, her face pressed up against mine. Dead crystal eyes bored into me.

Heat. Lights swirling. Blurred. Falling dark. Air— She hopped off of me and I rolled to my side, coughing. Choking. Breathing. Spit and snot flying.

I lay gasping in the hay for a few moments, recovering my breath and dignity. Minutes passed.

I sat up and leaned gingerly against the wall of the barn. A slight shadow from the moonlight cast over where I sat, gulping for breath, hay digging into my backside.

She'd knocked the world out from under me just like that. Had I gone soft?

"We're not going alone," she said.

She stood next to the elfling. Its hands were bound, but it glared at me with its massive black eyes filled with vehemence. A baby shark ready for revenge. My heart sank. It hadn't forgotten that I was the one who'd snatched it from its disgusting hut, knocked it unconscious, and tossed it over this village's wall in a burlap sack.

"I don't mean to sound ungrateful, but"—I eyed the little demon—"that's not such a great idea, Fire Eyes. You need to understand, that thing and I, well, we have history."

One she could never know about. To her, I was a sweet, kind-hearted servant boy. I seemed to be pulling off this act quite well. But there was no fooling that creature.

I'd have to find a way to kill it. Soon.

"It's not your call," Blue stated flatly as she packed her horse. She filled the saddle bags with sacks and weapons, preparing for a journey. "You in or do you want to stay here? Locked up?"

"No, no. I'm in, my princess." I bowed. Pain shot up my ribs. She'd bruised me; she may have even broken a rib, but I forced a smile across my lips. "Your wish is my command."

"Don't call me that," Blue turned her back to me and mounted her horse, pulling the elfling to sit up in front of her. I shivered. A speckled horse shook its mane beside her, waiting for me.

Freedom. Redemption. Salvation.

"Whatever you say, Princess."

ACKNOWLEDGMENTS

This book wouldn't have been possible without an almost-tragedy. Three years ago, my mom had a heart attack. My son and I flew out from California to my home state of Virginia. My parents lived nestled in the shadows of the Blue Ridge Mountains. As I grappled with living so far away from my mom while she recovered, I took hikes through the trails in the ancient woods. I reconnected with my childhood, nature, and with my soul. In those two weeks, the characters, setting, and story flowed through my mind like a healing breeze. I had no choice but to write it. The manuscript saw me through a terrible depression that followed—helped me escape into a world that only I could create.

I've had so much help along the way. My biggest fan and supporter of my dreams is my husband, Dave. He held down the fort, took care of the kids, dinners, activities—all the things I needed to get the work done. He never once questioned my sanity and always had advice (whether fantastic or ridiculous). He's read about seven chapters 100 times each, helping me work through the kinks. You are my light and my sunshine and I love you forever and ever, amen.

My son, Easton, who always asked "how's it going with your book?" He read through this book twice and talked with me endlessly about my characters, the story, and the ending. My daughter, Nora, who sent many a happy text about her love for Kaleo. My kids, Lily, Easton, Nora, and Rockwell have all supported me and are the inspiration for many crazy, unique qualities of my characters. You are my life.

My mom, Nancy Rainock, is my biggest cheerleader. She was the first to read through my fever-dream mess of a manuscript and encourage me to keep on going. Thank you for instilling in me a love of reading at a young age—and always having Star Trek and Masterpiece Theatre on. You also helped with the food inspiration, too. Whoopie pies for everyone!

Thanks to my dad, Norman Rainock, for helping me with my map and problem solving. He taught me to create, then to handle critique without getting my soul crushed. And that improvement of self is the key to unlocking greatness, but please—don't make a fuss about it. Thank you for filling my childhood home with art and music and laughter.

My beautiful sisters, Cora Oaks and Lorel Marshall, were incredible beta readers and helped guide the heart of this book. This book is, in many ways, a love letter to my sisters. Our bond is eternal and I love you both to the ends of the earth and forever after.

Thanks to my brothers—Gibbs, Orin, and Cordell Rainock—for answering endless random questions and being the inspiration for many of the brotherly shenanigans/attachments in this book. Love you all with my whole heart.

I have to thank my critique group—The Ravenquills—for working with me through countless google hangouts and weekly critiques to get my book ready for the world. Thanks especially to Cary Kreitzer, Amy Michelle Carpenter, Stephanie Barney, Cheree Myatt, Rebecca Yockey, Deanna Dietz, Quillen Johnson, Sara Peterson, and Jenni Curtis.

To my twitter and Instagram friends—the #llamasquadbooks. You were there for me during the crappy times in the query trenches. The salty convos, the tea, the memes. What a treat to be a part of such a supportive group of creatives! I'm excited to add every one of your books to my llama squad bookshelf!

Thank you to my muse, Chris Stapleton. Your bluesy, hard-hitting country was the soundtrack to Blue--through every writing phase and edit.

My mentor, Bonnie Swanson, helped shape my book. Thank you for your knowledge and understanding and working with me through all the ups and downs. Thanks to the Team Swann as well!

I had several fantastic beta readers who helped mold and shape the direction of the story. It was fun to talk through the book over fish 'n chips or a phone call. Thanks to Dave and Suzanne Morris, Jennica Galovan, McKenzie Gunderson, Markie Turner, Kim Barrus, Dana Coons, Everly Falke, Keith and Susan Stutznegger, and Jeff Stutznegger (who created my first treasured "fan art" of Blue and Hawk.)

I want to thank my editors, Jessa Russo and Holli Anderson, for believing in my vision and taking my writing to a new level.

I want to thank Immortal Works Publishing for your support and help along this journey.

I want to thank all of you, my readers!! You are what it's all about. I hope you loved my characters, hated some, and felt a few things while reading. I hope you were able to escape into a new world and have a little fun while you were there. If you enjoyed my book, then *please* leave a review and tell your friends! Join my newsletter on www.lenorestutz.com for more information and updates on Book II!

To all my friends and family, I say thank you. You have all buoyed me up and supported me in ways you'll never know. Thank you for the endless conversations, the questions, and the musings.

ABOUT THE AUTHOR

LENORE STUTZNEGGER

Lenore grew up running barefoot in the woods of Mechanicsville, Virginia with a dog at her side, five crazy siblings, and creative parents. She learned from a young age to hone her talents in art, trust in her voice, and compete for the most marshmallows in "Lucky Charms." She graduated from Brigham Young University in Art, married the love of her life, and lived in North Carolina for many years. She considers the South to be her happy place. She now resides in Northern California with her four spirited children, a pug, two cats, and backyard chickens in a new kind of crazy paradise. Lenore loves all things fantastical, from Marvel, Star Wars, and Harry Potter to shark, vampire, and alien movies. Supernatural and humor play equal parts in everything she writes.

This has been an
Immortal Production